AN UNEXPECTED KISS

"Don't worry," Cary said. "I promise I won't kiss you again. You have my word as a gentleman. Though I should like to point out that when I kissed you, you seemed to like it."

"What?" she cried, exasperated. "I thought you were a bat."

He glared at her fiercely. "You little beast! You did *not* think I was a bat."

"I certainly did! Don't you remember? I jumped out of the wardrobe—"

"Not that," he said impatiently. "Less said about *that* the better. I mean, this morning, outside. When I met you by the bridge," he pressed as she looked at him blankly.

"So you *did* kiss me!" Abigail exclaimed angrily. "I thought so!"

Cary's eyebrows shot up. "You *thought* so? What the devil do you mean?" he demanded. "Was there any doubt?"

"Well—"

She scarcely got the word out. He swung her around, pushed her against the wall, and drove his mouth hard against hers. He kissed her expertly, then left her mouth briefly and kissed her neck, his hands skimming boldly down to her waist. As she tried to speak, he claimed her mouth again. It was just as well; she had no idea what she would have said.

Cary stopped kissing her eventually. "What do you think of that?" he asked breathlessly, holding her steady.

Abigail was equally breathless. And trembling. And confused. But at least the feeling of desperate panic was subsiding and she now had a very clear notion of the sort of man she ought to marry . . .

Books by Tamara Lejeune

SIMPLY SCANDALOUS

SURRENDER TO SIN

Published by Zebra Books

Surrender
to Sin

TAMARA LEJEUNE

ZEBRA BOOKS
Kensington Publishing Corp.
www.kensingtonbooks.com

ZEBRA BOOKS are published by

Kensington Publishing Corp.
850 Third Avenue
New York, NY 10022

All Kensington titles, imprints, and distributed lines are available at special quantity discounts for bulk purchases for sales
promotion, premiums, fund-raising, educational, or institu-
tional use.

Special book excerpts or customized printings can also be created to fit specific needs. For details, write or phone the office
of the Kensington Special Sales Manager: Attn. Special Sales
Department. Kensington Publishing Corp., 850 Third Avenue,
New York, NY 10022. Phone: 1-800-221-2647.

Zebra and the Z logo Reg. U.S. Pat. & TM Off.

First Printing: January 2007
10 9 8 7 6 5 4 3 2 1

Printed in the United States of America

Chapter 1

Without so much as a pageboy to assist her, Abigail Ritchie inched her way through the crowds of fashionable shoppers in Piccadilly, her packages stacked so high that only her chin kept them from tumbling out of her arms. Any casual observer who saw her slim figure buffeted this way and that by the pressures of the crowd might have mistaken her for a lady's maid performing errands for her mistress. Indeed, the man who barreled into her, knocking her aside with his walking stick, had no way of knowing he had inconvenienced one of the richest young ladies in Britain. Had he been better informed, he might have been heartily sorry. As it was, he saw no reason to stop and offer either apologies or assistance to the solitary figure enveloped in a simple gray cloak. He simply pushed past her and continued on his way.

Abigail never saw him; her fur hood flopped forward into her eyes as she fell. Luckily, the Christmas presents tucked under her chin had not been dislodged in the collision, but she now had to regain her feet without the use of her hands. In the first attempt, she stumbled over her skirts as the heedless crowd surged past her. Her next attempt was forestalled by a pair of strong hands that picked her up and set her on her feet as if she had been a pawn on a chessboard.

"Ups-a-daisy!" said the owner of the hands. "On your feet, there's a good girl."

With her hood half-covering her eyes, Abigail could only see the lower half of her new acquaintance. He wore a long purple driving coat over buckskins and tall boots. In his gloved hands he carried a walking stick with a plain silver knob at the tip. A gentleman.

"Dulwich, as I live and breathe," he muttered angrily.

Abigail shook her head until her hood fell backwards out of her eyes, then quickly planted her chin atop her packages again. "Was it *Lord Dulwich* who bumped into me?" she inquired.

"Bumped into you, child? Pretty charitable," he said scornfully. "I'd have said he mowed you down like summer corn. I knew the man was a common drain, but I never thought him capable of knocking little girls down in the middle of a public street."

He turned suddenly to smile at her, and Abigail caught her breath. She could only stare. He was, quite simply, the most beautiful man she had ever seen outside of a painting. With his dark hair, pointed beard, and the tiny gold ring he wore in one ear, he looked like a gypsy prince. His skin was unusually brown for an Englishman's, which made his teeth look very white. She guessed his age at somewhere between twenty and thirty, but if he had claimed to be immortal, she would have believed him. He looked it.

"Beg pardon, ma'am!" he said gravely, though his gray eyes were laughing. "When viewed from the other side, you look precisely aged eleven and three quarters, or I should never have presumed to touch you. But I see from this side that you are quite grown up. Clearly, I ought to have pretended not to see you, like everyone else in this beastly mob."

Abigail's natural shyness rapidly transformed into terror. Handsome young men did not usually single her out for their gallantry. They certainly never teased her about her front or back sides. He made her so nervous that she almost wished he hadn't stopped to help her at all. Beautiful gypsy princes, she quickly decided, were best enjoyed from a safe distance.

"So thoughtless of me," he continued, evidently amused by her inability to speak. "As a gentleman, I ought to have made sure you were aged eleven and three quarters before I plucked you out of the dirt. Do please forgive my insufferable presumption. In future, I shall ask to see a baptismal certificate before I lend my assistance to any foundering thing in a petticoat."

Abigail knew she ought to thank him, but her tongue was tied, and her mind had gone blank. Her face was more expressive, though; it turned bright red, invigorating her freckles.

She would have been quite surprised to learn that, despite an undeniable overactivity of freckles, the gentleman had not excluded her from the ranks of beauty. Without being smitten by her in the least, he liked what he saw: curly apricot-gold hair; big, light brown eyes; a wide, pink mouth under a straight, short nose. She looked to him like a good English girl, a credit to her parents, and someone who deserved better than a shove in the back, followed by a trampling.

"Thank you, sir." Abigail finally forced the words out.

"That's better; I thought you were going into shock." With absolute false humility, he touched the brim of his hat. "Cary Wayborn, at your service, ma'am."

Abigail gasped, her shyness broken by surprise. "Did you say *Wayborn*?" she cried impulsively. "Sir, my mother was a Wayborn!" As she spoke, one of her parcels began to inch forward, endangering the delicate balance of the entire stack.

"You seem to have developed a strange bulge in the middle," he observed. "Since we are cousins, allow me to assist you." With his walking stick, he pushed the box back into place.

"Thank you, sir," she said breathlessly. "But are we really cousins, do you think?"

He studied her for a moment, seemingly oblivious to the bustling crowd surging past them. Abigail blushed again, knowing that he must be searching for some family resemblance. There was none, of course. *How could there be,* she thought hopelessly, *when he is like a painting by Caravaggio, and I'm an unsightly mass of freckles capped by frizzy hair?*

"You must be one of my Derbyshire cousins," he said, at the conclusion of his scrutiny.

His familiarity with her mother's family coaxed Abigail further out of her shyness. "Lord Wayborn is my uncle, sir. Though, to own the truth, I've never met him. It is generally thought that my mother married to disoblige her family."

Cary politely ignored this last, rather indiscreet revelation. "Then we are indeed cousins," he said. "And where were you going just now, before that feculent lout knocked you down?"

Abigail gasped in dismay. "You mustn't call his lordship insulting names, sir."

He snorted. "My dear cousin, I was at school with the feculent lout. Believe me, I do not insult. I merely describe. Now, where were you going? I'll carry your boxes."

"My father is to collect me at Mr. Hatchard's Bookshop, but there's really no need—"

"What a charming coincidence. I was on my way to

Hatchard's myself," he said, grinning. "Fortunately, I know a shortcut."

Abigail was not sure she believed a word he said, but before she could reflect on the propriety of accepting so much assistance from a stranger, he had exchanged her packages for his stick and was steering her boldly through the crowd. She was now doubly bound to follow him; he was carrying the servants' Christmas presents, and she had his walking stick.

"I don't often have business at Hatchard's," Cary said easily, glancing at her now and then as she struggled to keep up with him, "but I'm told a book makes a nice Christmas present."

He turned into an alley next to a tobacconist's shop, and Abigail stopped in her tracks. She had never been off the main streets of London before, and this rather noisome, narrow alley hardly inspired confidence. She could see no end to its darkness, and she imagined it to be filled with unsavory characters and stray animals carrying a variety of incurable diseases.

"Sir," she called to him nervously, "are you quite sure this is the way to Hatchard's?"

He had stopped to shift her pile of boxes. "If you could just take this little one under my left arm," he said, just as a small package popped out and hit the ground. "Not fragile, I hope?"

"It's gloves," said Abigail, stepping forward unthinkingly to pick it up. She was now standing in an alley for the first time in her life. To her relief, no desperate underworld character jumped out at her from the shadows. Indeed, the only people there besides herself and her "cousin" were a few honest deliverymen unloading a cart.

"I thought of getting her gloves," Cary murmured. "But my sister has got gloves enough for a dozen Hindoo deities."

To carry the little package more easily, Abigail slipped her finger through the twine binding it. "A book is a handsome gift, too," she said, holding her skirts up out of the frozen mud and horse manure dotting the cobbles. As she stepped around the manure-making end of the carthorse, she nearly collided with a broad-shouldered man carrying a large sack.

"Beg pardon, miss," he said gruffly, not looking at her as he tossed his burden onto a waiting pile. Clutching Cary's stick, Abigail scurried around him.

"My sister is engaged to be married," Cary went on, apparently not noticing her near mishap, "so I thought I'd get her one of those books you females can only read after marriage." He slipped past a large white sheet hung on a clothesline, and disappeared from sight. Abigail edged around the sheet, careful not to touch it, only to find that her guide was nowhere in sight.

"This way, cousin."

He had turned into another alley, this one so narrow they were forced to walk in single file. "What sort of books would you consider off limits to an unmarried woman?" she asked curiously. Somehow it was quite easy to talk to the back of his head.

"Oh, you know," he responded carelessly, "*Tom Jones*, *Moll Flanders*, that sort of thing."

"I've read them both, and I'm not married," said Abigail, inching forward in the darkness.

"And which did you prefer, cousin? The rake or the trollop?"

Abigail gave what she hoped was a sophisticated answer. "On the whole I found that *Tom* lifted the spirits while *Moll* rather depressed them. And you, sir?"

"Oh, I never read questionable material myself," he airily replied. "What would my cousin the Vicar say? I shall leave all such risky endeavors to Mrs. Wayborn. While I am out shooting pheasant for her supper, let her be tucked up in bed reading *Fanny Hill* for my . . . edification. So much more useful than embroidering my handkerchiefs, don't you agree?"

"I've never thought about it," said Abigail, wondering what Mrs. Wayborn would think if she knew her husband was in the habit of cutting through dark alleys with strange young women.

"Do you feel the wall growing hot?" he asked presently. "Shall we?"

Before Abigail could reply, he opened a door. A flickering crimson glow suddenly outlined his face. The hellish light, however, was accompanied by the comforting smell of freshly baked bread. Abigail entered the bakery first, a wall of heat slamming into her as she passed a row of huge brick ovens. The baker's apprentices gaped at them, making Abigail blush, but Cary was the picture of unruffled calm as he helped himself to a hot cross bun. "Cousin?"

Abigail mutely shook her head.

Cary led her swiftly through the front of the shop where customers lined up at the glass-front cases. Mainly servants from well-heeled Mayfair households, they parted respectfully to let Cary and Abigail through. In a few seconds, the cousins were out on the street again, and Hatchard's signboard was just ahead. Abigail felt as though she had been brought safely through a hostile foreign territory, but now was within sight of the British embassy. She drank in the cold, clean air and heard with pleasure the chatter of busy shoppers.

Her companion appeared unaffected by the adventure. Obviously, he was as comfortable in the back alleys of London as he would be in the court of St. James or a gypsy gathering. Abigail smiled at him shyly. "Thank you, sir. It was kind of you to help a complete stranger."

"But we are not *complete* strangers, cousin," he

pointed out. "We are *relative* strangers. Would you be good enough to open the door for me? My hands are a bit full."

"Oh, yes, of course," she said quickly.

Abigail felt safe inside Hatchard's Bookshop. The staff knew her there, and the senior clerk, Mr. Eldridge, came forward to greet her personally. Miss Ritchie was a voracious reader, and, better still, she always paid her bills, which was more than the gentleman with her could say. Mr. Eldridge frankly could not account for their having arrived together.

Cary gave Abigail's packages to an attendant, and she returned his stick, then extended her hand to him in farewell. "Sir, allow me to thank you again—" she began, breaking off as he gravely removed the package still dangling by a string from her little finger. Abigail decided that his departure would be a relief to her. If she was so incapable of behaving like a sensible woman in his presence, then the sooner he was gone, the better. "Goodbye," she said quickly.

As he bent over her gloved hand, she completed her disgrace by diving behind the sales counter, to the considerable surprise of the clerk. Cary was perhaps even more astonished by the maneuver. "What *are* you doing?" he demanded, leaning across the counter to look down at her.

Abigail frantically gestured for him to be silent. "Lord Dulwich," she whispered, her eyes round with terror. "He's here! Please, sir, don't give me away!"

"Wayborn," said the Viscount of Dulwich, tapping Cary on the shoulder. As Cary slowly turned around to face him, his lordship went on, "I thought we'd seen the last of your purple coats. Heard you were rusticating in Hertfordshire amongst the haystacks. On a pig farm, or some such thing. What's the place called? Tattywood? Tinklewood?"

Cary leaned against the counter. "I'd tell you, but then you might visit me."

His lordship sniffed, then turned to the clerk. "You there! I'm looking for some idiotic rubbish called *Kubla Khan*. The assistant is too stupid to help me, and I'm rather in a hurry."

The clerk answered as smoothly as he could with Abigail crouched at his feet. "I regret to inform your lordship that Mr. Coleridge has not yet published his famous fragment. It will be out in the next few months, I believe."

The Viscount was infuriated. "But I am Lord Dulwich, man. I want it now."

"The man can't pluck a book out of thin air," Cary Wayborn pointed out reasonably.

"This is no concern of yours, Wayborn," his lordship snapped. "But that's you all over, butting in where you don't belong. Have you no conduct?"

"That's rich, coming from you," Cary said. "When I just saw you knock a girl to her knees in Piccadilly without so much as a 'Pardon me.' If that's your idea of conduct—"

"What girl?" said Dulwich, with a sneer marring his aristocratic features. "A pet of yours, perhaps? I daresay she's been knocked to her knees before and will be again."

Abigail stifled a gasp. Never in her life had she heard such rudeness.

"As a matter of fact, the young lady is my cousin," Cary said coldly.

"I beg your pardon," said Lord Dulwich, without so much as a hint of regret. Indeed, he sounded rather proud that his insult had pricked its mark. "You should tell your cousin to watch where she's going. The stupid chit stepped right into my path. It was her fault entirely."

"No, it wasn't," Cary said hotly. "I saw the entire

disgraceful incident. You shoved her in the back, and, let me tell you, when I bring the matter up at White's—"

"You wouldn't tell the Club!" said his lordship, a whine entering his haughty voice.

"You sniveling toad," was the only reply his lordship received.

"What do you want, Wayborn?"

"I want an apology, Pudding-face," said Cary. "My cousin don't wish to see you, of course, so it will have to be in writing."

Mr. Eldridge was very prompt in providing writing materials for his lordship at no charge. To Abigail's astonishment, Lord Dulwich offered no protest.

"What's her name, this cousin of yours?" he inquired testily, dipping the pen in the well.

"I'm not telling you her name, Pudding-face," Cary said scornfully. "Write this: 'The odious Lord Dulwich humbly extends his profoundest and most sniveling—!'"

"Look here!"

Cary ignored him. "'*Most sniveling* apologies to the young lady whom he so savagely assaulted in Piccadilly this afternoon. By his failure to offer any apology or assistance to her on that occasion, he has forfeited his right to call himself an English gentleman. Furthermore, his lordship does hereby attest and affirm that he is in fact the most feculent lout ever to disgrace the British empire. Yours in utter moral failure, et cetera, et cetera.'"

"Look here!" Dulwich protested. "Can't I give her ten pounds instead? Twenty?"

"In my family, we don't exchange currency for insults," said Cary. "I need hardly tell you how the members of my Club will react if I tell them what you did. Besides, where would *you* get twenty pounds? Your father's cut off your allowance, or so you said when you asked me to hold onto a certain I.O.U. just a little longer."

"For God's sake, lower your voice!" Dulwich snarled.

"Now sign and date it, if you please." Cary took the scrap of paper from the Viscount, inspected it briefly, then seemed to forget all about the matter. "I'm looking for *Tom Jones*, my good fellow," he pleasantly told the clerk. "Would you be so kind as to direct me to it?"

"I was here first," Dulwich objected. "I want *Kubla Khan*, and I want it now." He rapped on the counter with his stick, and the unhappy Mr. Eldridge offered to put his lordship's name on the waiting list. "List?" the Viscount demanded. "What list? Who's on it?"

"Quite a number of our best customers, my lord," Mr. Eldridge replied. "Indeed, the demand has been so high that the publisher has already called for a second printing."

"Very well. Put me on your beastly list," said Dulwich impatiently.

"I'd no idea you were such a devotee of Mr. Coleridge," Cary remarked.

"I'm not," his lordship growled. "I despise all poetry, and all poets too. But, unfortunately, my betrothed is rather excitable on the subject."

Cary laughed shortly. "Don't tell me you're engaged. Who is the poor creature? I should like to send her my condolences on black-edged paper."

"The lady is well aware of her good fortune," his lordship coldly replied. "Look here, you fool! If the book arrives before January the Fourteenth, I shall buy it. If not, never mind."

"And what, pray, is the significance of January the Fourteenth?" Cary asked.

"That is my wedding day," Dulwich replied, "not that it's any business of yours. I've no intention of wasting money buying my own damn wife a silly book."

"Very sensible of you," said Cary. "And you say the lady is aware of her good fortune? Capital. Allow me to wish you joy. I don't think I've ever seen a man so deeply in love. Why, you're positively radiant."

Dulwich's face turned nearly black with fury. "I am *not* in love with her, you ass," he hissed. "I want her father's money, and she, I suppose, wants to be a viscountess. When we marry, I shall be able to settle all my debts, including that little bet of ours. Look here, Wayborn, if you start spreading it around that I'm marrying for *love*, I shall have to call you out."

"Steady on," said Cary, stifling a laugh. "I shan't tell a soul you're after her money. After all, if you don't get *her* money, I may never get *mine*."

"What are you doing there, you damn fool?" his lordship suddenly snarled.

Abigail nearly jumped out of her skin. But Dulwich had not discovered her hiding place; he was addressing Mr. Eldridge. "Imbecile! You're putting my name at the *bottom* of the list. Who is entitled to come before my Lord Dulwich? The Misses Brandon? I think not."

As Mr. Eldridge watched in dismay, his lordship seized the book and proceeded to cross out the Misses Brandon in order to insert his own name at the top of the page. "I shall make all my friends aware of the staff's impertinence," said Dulwich, jerking on his gloves, "and I predict that Hatchard's will be out of business in a month's time!"

He paused, as though waiting for Mr. Eldridge to seek to detain him, and then Abigail heard the doorbell ring as his lordship left the shop. A moment or two passed before she felt safe enough to lift her head. Mr. Wayborn was leaning across the counter looking down at her. "You can come out now, monkey," he said lightly. "The nasty man has gone away."

Abigail climbed to her feet. "I daresay you think me rather childish," she stammered, "but I simply can't bear scenes. It would have been so very embarrassing to see him."

Cary took her hand and led her around the counter. "I think you did exactly right," he said. "I only wish I had the courage to run and hide whenever I see the old Pudding-face."

"I wasn't hiding," she said defensively. "I–I dropped my gloves."

"My dear infant, you're wearing them."

"No, not these—the gloves I just bought." She had the little box wrapped in brown paper to back up her story. "And then, of course, I thought it might look a little odd if I were to suddenly appear from behind the sales counter . . . so I rather thought I'd better stay where I was."

"I see," he said, not believing a word of it. Gravely, he held Lord Dulwich's written apology out to her. "His lordship wanted you to have this."

Abigail shyly plucked it from between his gloved fingers. "Did he actually write all those things you told him to?" she exclaimed. "How could he be sure I wouldn't expose him?"

He laughed. "Because you're my cousin, that's why. You're a Wayborn."

He looked at her very warmly. To cover her embarrassment, she quickly turned to the clerk. "You *will* put the Misses Brandon back on the list for *Kubla Khan,* won't you?"

"Of course, madam," the clerk assured her. "It was remiss of me not to tell his lordship that this is the sixth page of a very long list. I shall place the Misses Brandon at the bottom of page five." As he wrote, he smiled politely at her. "Might I help you find something, madam?"

"Please attend the gentleman first," said Abigail. "I'm just waiting for my father."

"In that case, let me bring you something to look at while you wait," said the clerk. "I won't be a moment. I'll have my assistant find your book for you, sir," he told Cary. "I believe you were interested in Mr. Fielding's *History of a Foundling*, popularly known as *Tom Jones*?"

"Who is this Kubla Khan?" Cary asked Abigail when the clerk had gone. "There must be two hundred names on that list."

"Do you not know the story, sir?" Abigail asked excitedly. "The poem first came to Mr. Coleridge in a dream. When he woke up, it just sort of *poured* out of him onto the page, as if the poet were merely a conduit between this world and the next."

Cary struggled to keep a straight face. "Fascinating technique," he remarked.

"Unfortunately, as he was putting it down on the page, he was interrupted by a man from Porlock, who *would* talk business, and when poor Mr. Coleridge sat down to write again, the rest of the poem had passed away like the images on the surface of the stream into which a stone has been cast. Why are you smirking?" she demanded.

He was thinking that she was quite a pretty girl when she forgot to be shy.

"Was I smirking? I beg your pardon. But it should be rather obvious to anyone that Mr. Coleridge is simply too lazy to finish his work. He's invented a rather feeble excuse, a fairy story, to help him sell a fragment. Is that not some excuse for smirking, if indeed I smirked?"

"What right have you to accuse Mr. Coleridge of making up a fairy story?" Abigail demanded huffily.

"You're quite right," he murmured, though he still appeared amused rather than contrite. "I withdraw my cynical remarks. I withdraw my smirk."

"I should think so indeed," said Abigail crisply, as Mr. Eldridge returned with a book.

"Good God," said Cary. "Blake's *Songs of Innocence,* unless I miss my guess."

Mr. Eldridge looked at the gentleman with approval. "*Songs of Innocence and of Experience*, sir. A combined volume, very rare. Mr. Blake prints them all himself, you know."

Abigail shook her head regretfully. "I'm afraid I don't quite understand Mr. Blake," she said. "I read part of *Heaven and Hell* last winter, but it was so strange that I had to set it aside for my own peace of mind. And, you know, people say he's not a patriot."

"Not a patriot?" said Cary, frowning. "What do you mean?"

Abigail dropped her voice almost to a whisper. "During the war, he was suspected of printing seditious material, and when the soldiers came to his door and said, 'Open in the name of the King!' Mr. Blake answered, from behind the door, 'Bugger the King!' Which, I daresay, is not a very nice thing to say about one's sovereign," she quickly added.

"Or anyone else's sovereign," Cary agreed, just managing to keep a straight face. "But the war is over now, cousin, and we are once again free to insult our betters as much as we please, without fear of reprisal. In my opinion—if you happen to be interested in my opinion?"

"Yes, of course," Abigail said civilly.

"In my opinion, Mr. Blake is a visionary poet without the aid—or excuse—of opium, which is more than your Mr. Coleridge can say. But if Blake is too strong for you, cousin, there's bound to be a little Wordsworth lying about the place."

Abigail was indignant. "I rather like Mr. Wordsworth!"

His smile widened. "I suspected as much. He's so perfectly harmless."

"It really is a very fine volume, madam," interjected Mr. Eldridge, still hoping for a sale. "Nothing frightening in it at all. If nothing else, Mr. Blake is a master of the copperplate."

"If the tiger is good, you should buy it, cousin," said Cary decisively, reaching for the book. "There," he said drawing her attention to a poem entitled, "The Tyger." At the bottom of the page was a cartoon of a muscular beast with amber eyes as big as saucers. Its fiery orange body bore irregular umber stripes, but in no other way did it resemble a tiger.

"It appears to be smirking," said Abigail critically. "And the poem . . . It's like a nursery rhyme, isn't it? 'Tyger Tyger, burning bright, in the forests of the night . . .'"

"Remind me never to visit your nursery!" Cary said, laughing.

Mr. Eldridge looked inquiringly at Abigail. "Madam?"

She shook her head. "Perhaps the gentleman wants it."

"Excellent tiger," said Cary. "Wish I could afford it, but I'm rather as poor as Adam at the moment. My man of affairs has ordered me to retrench. You wouldn't happen to know of anyone looking for a house in the country, would you, cousin? I've got one to let, and I could certainly use the rent. It's an old dower house, a cottage really. Only six bedrooms."

"Have you tried advertising?" she asked politely.

"Good Lord, no," he answered. "I couldn't possibly advertise. Advertisements always draw the very worst sort of people: people who read advertisements. If you should hear of anyone interested in a place, do please send him my way," he said, feeling about his waistcoat for a card. Finding none, he took Dulwich's apology from her, turned it over, and scrawled rapidly on the back: "Cary Wayborn, Tanglewood Manor, Herts." "A recommendation from my fair cousin would be enough for me," he added with a wide smile.

Flattered, Abigail tucked it into her reticule just as the assistant appeared with *Tom Jones*.

Mr. Eldridge took a ledger from beneath the counter. "Oh, dear," he said, clucking his tongue. "There appears to be an outstanding balance on your account, sir. Nearly ten pounds."

"Is there?" Cary replied, unconcerned. "Remind me about that sometime, will you?"

"I think he's trying to remind you of it now," Abigail pointed out.

"Is he?" Cary said sharply. "Are you trying to remind me of it now, Eldridge?"

"No, indeed, sir," the clerk said meekly. "Would you like this wrapped? We've some very special Christmas paper printed with holly wreaths. It was the young lady's idea."

Cary glanced at Abigail. "What, this young lady?"

"It's been a very popular service this season. Only a penny more, sir."

"By all means." When Mr. Eldridge presented him with the package tied up with a red ribbon, Cary seemed pleased. "I daresay my sister will think I did it myself. And now I must bid you adieu, cousin," he said, turning to Abigail.

"Must you go?" Abigail blurted without thinking as he took her hand. "I'd like to present you to my father," she quickly added. "He'll want to thank you for your kindness to me."

"I should very much like to meet your father, cousin, but my aunt expects me in Park Lane. I was meant to be there three quarters of an hour ago, and I am never late."

Abigail reddened. "It's my fault you're late now. I'm so sorry."

He smiled. "You've provided me with an excellent excuse for my tardiness, at any rate."

Though she in no way wanted him to go, Abigail was relieved when he did. Having one's wits scrambled by a good-looking stranger was decidedly unpleasant. Much better to be left in peace with a cup of tea and a quiet volume of Wordsworth.

Mr. Eldridge was more than happy to provide her with these comforts. He showed Abigail to the private sitting room and brought her a pot of tea and *The White Doe of Rhylston*. "I suppose my cousin, Mr. Wayborn, buys a lot of books for his wife," Abigail remarked, idly opening the little green book to its title page.

"Did Mr. Wayborn marry?" Mr. Eldridge replied, pouring her tea into a Worcester cup. "Oh, dear. I failed to wish him joy. Shall I put *The White Doe* on your account, madam?"

"No," Abigail said, arriving at a sudden decision. Closing the book, she held it out to him. "No, I think I'll take the Blake after all, Mr. Eldridge."

"Very good, madam," said Mr. Eldridge, pleased.

When Mr. Ritchie arrived to collect his only child some thirty minutes later, he found her deep in thought over a book, staring at a picture of a smirking tiger. "Abby! You will never guess who I saw in Bond Street just now," he said, in his thick Glaswegian accent. "My Lord Dulwich, that's who. Someone's getting sparklers for Christmas, I shouldn't wonder!"

Abigail smiled fondly at her father. The sole proprietor of Ritchie's Fine Spirits, est. 1782, was not a gentleman, but he was still the best man she had ever known. He was also one of the richest men in the kingdom. "He certainly knows how to make an impression," she tactfully agreed with him. "Would you be terribly disappointed if I didn't marry him after all?"

Chapter 2

Heedless of her long black skirts, Juliet Wayborn ran down the stairs of her aunt's town house to greet her brother with spaniel-like enthusiasm. The mourning dress and jet ornaments she wore in honor of the sixth Duke of Auckland became her quite as well as the white satin wedding gown she had ordered for her forthcoming marriage to the seventh Duke of Auckland.

"Careful, monkey," Cary said, laughing as she flung herself headlong into his arms. "You wouldn't want to break your nose this close to your wedding day. Speaking of which, I saw the man's grays being walked up and down the street. I take it he's here?"

She nodded. "Just back now—he's been called to Auckland twice this month, poor lamb. I see you still have that horrid little muskrat growing on your chin," she added severely. "And the earrings! You're not going to wear earrings at my wedding. You look like a pirate!"

"I've missed you, Julie," said Cary, surprised how true it was. His rustic existence in Hertfordshire was a lonely one. In London, he had been something of a local celebrity, a man of fashion whose perfectly matched chestnuts had proved unbeatable in countless races, but in Hertfordshire he had few friends. Most evenings he sat alone at his fireside, his only company being Angel, a mongrel pup he had recently purchased from a gypsy for tuppence. "Anyway, it's only one earring."

"Oh, that's much nicer," she snorted. "And don't even *think* of wearing one of your shabby old purple coats, either! I want all the men in pearl gray. Go to Mr. Weston tomorrow."

"I shall have to come as I am," he said, brushing what proved to be baker's flour from his purple sleeve. "Mr. Weston won't give me any more coats until I pay my bill."

"If you need money—"

"Don't," he said.

She didn't.

"You're horribly late as usual," she chided him as they walked arm in arm up the stairs to the salon where their aunt Lady Elkins received visitors when she was not enjoying a spell of ill health. "Ginger has eaten all the muffins, but I shall make him give you his all next week."

"I'm afraid I won't be with you next week, Julie."

"What?" she cried in disbelief. "But it's Christmas week, Cary. We're all going to Surrey, same as always."

"Not this year, I'm afraid," said Cary, wistful, but resigned.

"No, you must," she protested, digging her fingers into his arm. "Next year I shall have to be at Auckland, you know, and every year after that. It's my last Christmas in our father's house, Cary. We're just making our final plans now, and you're in them."

"Sounds ominous," said her brother.

"Ginger!" she cried, flinging open the salon doors. "Ginger, Cary says he won't go to Surrey with us for Christmas. What are you going to do about it?"

Geoffrey Ambler, the seventh Duke of Auckland, climbed to his feet. Juliet had not quite tamed the enormous redhead, but he now accepted being called Ginger by his future duchess without so much as a grimace of displeasure. The death of his father had hit him hard, postponing his marriage to Juliet, and plunging him, for the first time, into a world of tedious responsibility. Like Juliet, he was dressed in deepest mourning, and the ravages of new pressures and cares showed in the lines and shadows of his craggy face. Nonetheless, he gave Cary a quick, boyish smile that went a long way towards explaining Juliet's adoration of the fierce-looking redhead. He said, with a lot of northern England in his accent, "I shall need a mallet and a very large sack, but I think I can manage to change his mind, my love."

Cary offered his hand. "Hullo, Auckland."

His future brother-in-law winced as he shook hands. His father had only been dead for eleven months and his new title was still a fresh source of pain to him. "Please don't call me that. Auckland was my father. When I hear the name, I find myself looking behind me to see if he's there. Geoffrey will do. We're practically brothers, after all."

"I was just telling Cary about our plans for Christmas," said Juliet brightly.

"Which explains his refusal to go into Surrey," the Duke said, his green eyes twinkling.

"Nonsense! Everyone loves a good private theatrical, and Cary's no different."

Cary snorted rather violently.

"*Twelfth Night*," Juliet went on bravely, undeterred by her brother's lack of enthusiasm. "I'm to be Viola, of course, and Ginger will be my beloved Duke Orsino."

"You're joking me," said Cary. "Sir, is it even possible that this is true?"

"If music be the food of love, play on," the Duke said sheepishly.

"You see?" Juliet said proudly. "He's coming along very nicely, I think."

"Honestly, why do you put up with her?" Cary wanted to know.

"Because he adores me, that's why," said Juliet. "And Serena has agreed to take the part of the Countess Olivia."

Cary started in surprise. Lady Serena Calverstock was seated behind him and he had not been aware of her presence until Juliet made it known. Given that she was wearing one of the new high-brimmed poke bonnets, it seemed a strange oversight. He could remember a time not very long ago when he had possessed an almost supernatural sense that made the hairs on the back of his neck stand up whenever Serena was near. Now, nothing, despite the fact that, if anything, she was even more beautiful than he remembered. He bowed to her impassively. "Madam. You're looking well, but then you always do. Look well, that is."

The dark-haired beauty felt the coldness behind the compliment and colored slightly. "Mr. Wayborn," she said. "We have all missed you in Town this last year."

"I have been in Hertfordshire, overseeing my estate. It's in absolute disarray, I'm afraid."

"If it is, it's your own fault," said Juliet, rather disloyally, Cary thought. "You've neglected it shamefully for years."

"And it will take me years to set it right. But I find I don't miss London as much as I thought I would," he said, now lying through his teeth. "I find country life very peaceful. The people are simple and kind. The young ladies of Hertfordshire are not so artful and designing as the London variety."

"You can't be talking about the Mickleby girls," Juliet

scoffed. "They're practically cannibals when it comes to you."

"I find them charmingly transparent," Cary replied. "It's the London opacity I can't tolerate. Miss Mickleby and her sisters harbor no secrets. They would all very much like to marry me, if they can't get anyone better."

Serena could not remain insensible to the hostility of her former admirer. "I beg your pardon, Juliet, but I fear I've stayed too long," she said, pulling on the sky-blue gloves that exactly matched the immense plumes nodding on her bonnet. "I do have appointments. Would you be so kind as to ring for my maid?"

"Allow me, my lady," said Cary, all but leaping across the room to pull the bell rope.

"Wait, Serena," Juliet pleaded. "I haven't told Cary the best part yet. Cary, you're going to be Sebastian, Viola's brother. It's a very small part, hardly fifty lines. Say you will," she quickly begged him. "Who better to play the part of my brother than my actual brother, after all? And, don't forget, in the end, Sebastian and Olivia fall in love. You can play that part, surely, if Serena plays hers."

Cary looked at Serena with hard gray eyes. "I believe we have already played those parts, Juliet, and I, for one, don't care to repeat the performance."

"Please do excuse me," Serena breathed, jumping to her feet. Her ivory pallor had been replaced by a scarlet blush that decidedly did not match her blue ensemble.

Juliet ran after her friend. Supremely unconcerned, Cary closed the door behind the two women and flung himself down into the nearest chair. The Duke of Auckland sat down too, but did not speak, for which Cary was deeply grateful.

"Look here, old man," Cary said after a moment. "Might I ask a favor of you?"

Geoffrey Ambler looked a little hunted. Over the past

few months, a great many favors had been asked of the
new Duke of Auckland. Then he reminded himself that
Cary was Juliet's brother; he, at least, had some right
to ask. "Of course," he said, with some of his old generosity of spirit. "Up to half my kingdom, or, rather my
dukedom. Ask away."

Cary spoke carefully. "I should like to stress that I've
not yet come to the point where it's necessary, but I want
to ask you to buy the chestnuts, if it comes to it. I know
you have your grays, but Julie ought to have a good
driving team of her own. I couldn't possibly sell them to
anyone else, and you know what they're worth."

The Duke sat up straight. "Sell your chestnuts? You
can't possibly be serious. Why, Cary Wayborn without
his chestnuts is rather like . . . like . . ." His grace tried
to find a suitable simile for this unprecedented occurrence, but he was no Shakespeare.

Neither was Cary. "Rather like Cary Wayborn without his testicles, I should imagine. Look, I'm hoping it
won't come to it, but if it does, may I depend on you to
buy them?"

"If you need money, old man—"

"Do please refrain from finishing that sentence,"
Cary interrupted. "No, it's kind of you to offer, but I
couldn't possibly accept. The estate is on the dunghill
because of my neglect, and who should suffer for it but
myself? Anyway, I don't think it will come to it. I'm
sure it won't. But may I depend on you if it does?"

"Yes," said the Duke seriously. "Yes, of course."

"Juliet is not to know I've asked you," Cary warned.
"She'd only start throwing humpbacked heiresses in my
way. I've no intention of marrying a bank account."

Having concluded this embarrassing business, Cary
went upstairs to pay his respects to his aunt Lady
Elkins. When he returned to the salon after a game of

piquet with the old lady, he found his sister pouring out the tea. Her mood was that of an avenging angel.

"How could you be so beastly cruel to Serena?" she demanded. "I can remember a time when you wanted to marry her."

Cary reddened. "And I can remember a time when you counseled me against it! Now you seem to live in her pocket. I would not have come to my aunt's house had I known she was here. I didn't see her carriage in the street."

"No, she walked here with her maid," Juliet explained. "I wish you would forgive her, Cary. If you only knew what Horatio had put her through, you'd pity her. Seven years of a secret engagement, and then he spurned her! I call that infamous."

"Whatever he put her through, it wasn't enough," Cary replied. "She knew I was utterly infatuated with her beauty, and she let me go on like a fool, dangling after her, when all the while she was engaged to my cousin. I have no pity for her."

"But Horatio is more at fault," Juliet argued. "He drove Serena mad with his coldness and his contempt, until she had no choice but to relieve him of his obligation to her. Only yesterday, he was walking towards her in Bond Street, and, when he saw her, he crossed to the other side and pretended not to see her. You would not punish her like that, surely."

"No," Cary admitted.

"Horatio is an ass," said the Duke, with the air of one giving the last word. "Just because the Prince Regent gave him that ruddy snuffbox doesn't mean everyone in London has got to see it three times a day. Somebody ought to take it away from him and throw it in the Thames."

"Ginger's right," said Juliet. "That snuffbox is the only thing in the world he really loves. Horatio without his snuffbox . . . Why, that's rather like Cary without his chestnuts."

"What do you mean?" cried the Duke, startled by her clairvoyance. "Why should you say such a damn fool thing? Cary without his chestnuts! I never heard such nonsense!"

"You can't blame Horatio for everything," Cary said quickly. "Pompous ass he may be, but he didn't force her ladyship to flirt with me while she was secretly engaged to another. When I think of how she led me on, I could throw *her* in the Thames. Why don't you ask Cousin Horatio to play Sebastian to her Olivia?"

"Horatio does not deserve her," Juliet protested.

"Well, monkey, at the risk of sounding conceited, Serena don't deserve *me*."

"You men!" she said scathingly. "You love as no man has ever loved before—that is, until the first real test of your devotion, and then it all goes out the window with the bathwater."

"'Love is not love which alters when it alteration finds,'" said the Duke of Auckland, unexpectedly entering the argument, "'or bends with the remover to remove . . .'"

Juliet took her lord's hand and recited the sonnet with him, "'Oh, no! It is an ever fixed mark that looks on tempests and is never shaken. It is the star to every wandering bark . . .'"

"Woof, woof," said Cary, irritated by his sister's treacly tone.

The Duke looked at him seriously. "No, no, it's not that sort of bark, old man. Julie explained it to me. In this case, 'bark' means 'ship.' As in 'disembark,' you know."

"Ginger's really been studying his Shakespeare," Juliet chimed, glowing with pride and temporarily forgetting that she was very cross with her brother.

"Self-defense," the Duke explained. "She's forever quoting him at me."

"And now you're graduating to private theatricals," Cary remarked.

"All the world's a stage," the Duke replied.

"Wrong play, Ginger. Guess who's going to be Malvolio," said Juliet, turning to her brother, her gray eyes gleaming. "When you find out who I've got for Malvolio, you will *want* to come home for Christmas."

Cary stared at her in absolute horror. "You haven't dragged our brother into this crackbrained scheme of yours, have you?"

"No," she admitted. "Benedict is too stuffy. He wouldn't even let us use the library at Wayborn Hall for a theater. We've had to take Silvercombe. No, it's not Benedict. You'll never guess who it is, not in a hundred years."

Cary smiled. "In that case, monkey, you had better tell me."

"Mr. Rourke!" she said, unable to contain her triumph any longer. "Lord Ravenshaw wanted him for *his* private theatrical, but who wants to spend Christmas in Cornwall?"

Cary looked at her blankly.

"The actor! Mr. David Rourke, Cary. You remember him. He was Shylock last year."

"Oh, yes. I thought you hated him. Didn't he run off with your maid?"

Juliet frowned impatiently. "That is all forgiven. He's returned Fifi to me, and my hair has never looked better, not that you men take any notice."

"He's costing me a fortune," the Duke put in. "Rooms at the Albany. Private hairdresser. Open-ended accounts with Mr. Weston *and* Mr. Hoby. Pretty well for an Irishman!"

"I see," said Cary, whose own accounts with the famed tailor and bootmaker were firmly closed, at least until he got his estate back in the black. "But I'm afraid that not even Mr. Rourke can entice me to Surrey this Christmas. I shall be at Tanglewood."

"But you always come home for Christmas," said his sister, "except that one year when you ran mad and enlisted in the Army. We were so very annoyed with you."

"My tenants and neighbors are expecting me to give them a Christmas Ball," said Cary, "and a New Year's Day Ball, too, I shouldn't wonder. Not to mention a St. Stephen's Day treat."

"You never bothered with all that before," she said suspiciously. "What's really keeping you in Herts? Don't tell me the *artless* Rhoda Mickleby has captured your heart!"

Cary glared at her. "Juliet, as you have pointed out to me over and again, I've neglected Tanglewood for years. I'm trying to correct that now. As for Miss Rhoda, I'm quite safe from her. Some old aunt of hers has promised her a Season in London, and, as you know, catching husbands in the country cannot possibly compare to chasing them around Town."

"You can start afresh at Tanglewood in January," said his sister, refusing to give up her scheme. "There's no point in turning over a new leaf this late in the year."

"The trouble with January," Cary told her, "is that it has two faces. One looking into the past and the other to the future. No, I'm sorry, monkey, but it will be a great scandal if I don't keep my word. I won't see you at Christmas. I shall miss you nearly as much as you miss me, but it can't be helped."

Juliet reacted to this disappointment with a petulance unbecoming to a duchess in training. "You needn't play Sebastian, you know, if you don't wish to," she said waspishly. "You can be Olivia's uncle, Sir Toby Belch. Or Sir Andrew Aguecheek—no, no, he courts

Olivia as well. I know! You could play the part of
Feste, Olivia's Fool."

Juliet was a fine-looking girl with a cloud of dark
hair, wide gray eyes, and a slim athletic figure. Pique
only served to enhance her natural beauty, but, as her
brother, Cary was immune to both her tantrums and her
charms. He still remembered her as the disgusting
object that, at the age of three, had broken his favorite
toy horse.

"I shall take my leave of you now, you little beast," he
said. "Kiss me goodbye."

"I want you to come to Surrey!" said Juliet, in case he
had not understood her. "I hate to think of you all alone
in that drafty old pile at Christmas when you ought to
be with your family. But I suppose you have a mistress
there," she went on spitefully, "and a half-dozen brats,
too!"

Cary laughed bitterly. "As a matter of fact, I'm up to
my ears in involuntary celibacy."

It was no more than the miserable truth. There was
not even one obliging widow in his neighborhood. His
cousin the Vicar kept a very tight rein on the private
lives of his parishioners. Wherever Dr. Wilfred Cary
saw even a hint of impropriety, he took ruthless action
to eliminate the threat. As for the artless young ladies
Cary had boasted of knowing, he could not say two
words to any of *them* without raising expectations he
had no intention of fulfilling. Worst of all, he lacked the
disposable income one needed to secure temporary love
in London.

"You have in me a kindred soul," the Duke said
sympathetically.

Juliet flashed him a warning look. "What keeps you
in the country, if not a woman?" she demanded of her
brother.

"Duty, monkey," he told her resolutely. "Duty. I owe

it to my tenants. I owe it to my neighbors. I owe it to dear old Grandmother Cary, who left me the drafty old pile. I owe it to her memory not to let the place fall to ruin."

"If you could just forgive Serena," said Juliet, over-riding his protests. "She has money, Cary. She could help you with the place."

"No, Juliet," he told her curtly. "I will make that estate turn a profit by main strength if I have to, and I don't want to hear another word about it from you."

Juliet remembered that commanding voice from childhood. It was her father's voice, and both her brothers seemed able to summon it at will. It always made her tremble and want to cry. "All right," she sulked. "You needn't shout at me."

Cary had always been fond of Juliet, even when, at the age of eight, she had found his battered copy of *Fanny Hill* and showed it gleefully to their eldest brother, Sir Benedict Wayborn, who had proceeded without delay to burn it. "Cheer up, monkey," he said gently. "I'll be with you in spirit. And I got you a nice present." He handed her the gaily wrapped package from Hatchard's. "Everyone else is getting a dead pheasant, I'm afraid."

"What a pretty package," said Juliet, her suspicions renewed. "A woman must have done it for you. Who is she, Cary? Some opera dancer, I suppose."

"Cheeky madam! The clerk at Hatchard's did it for me, if you must know. It's a new service they're offering. I actually met the young lady who thought it up."

Juliet grinned. "I knew there had to be a girl. What exactly did she think up?"

"Christmas wrap."

"Nobody invented Christmas wrap," Juliet scoffed. "Christmas wrap has always been."

The Duke suddenly laughed. "You mean like the stars and the mountains?"

"If you don't mind, sir, I'm interrogating my brother," said Juliet, refusing to be thrown off the scent of a promising new trail. "Was she *very* pretty, Cary?"

"Actually, she's one of our Derbyshire cousins," said Cary, avoiding the question. He knew from experience that telling his sister he had met a pretty girl was the surest way to turn her into a Cupid's helper. "Lord Wayborn's her uncle. You must know her. You know everyone."

"I do know everyone," Juliet said smugly, "but his lordship must have two dozen nieces, if not more. He had a dozen brothers and sisters. What's her name?"

"Don't know," said Cary. "I didn't think to ask."

Juliet stared. "Didn't think to—! And, of course, a lady couldn't volunteer the information," she said, exasperated. "Who was with her?"

"No one."

"No one?" said Juliet, in disbelief. "She must have been with someone. Her mother? A chaperone? A maid?"

"No one," said Cary. "Unless one counts Lord Dulwich."

The Duke sat up in his chair, demonstrating that he had actually been following the conversation between brother and sister. "One don't, as a matter of fact."

"No, indeed," said Cary. "An absolute negative quantity. One subtracts him, rather."

"I don't understand," said Juliet. "Was this girl of yours *with* Lord Dulwich?"

"No, she was quite alone when the filthy beast knocked her down," said Cary, remembering the incident with renewed anger. "He shoved her out of the way in Piccadilly, and she fell, poor mite."

"Somebody ought to shove *him* into the bloody river," snarled the Duke, "except there'd be no grave for me to dance on. Look here, Cary, if you want to call him out,

I'll second you. He can't go about the place shoving girls in the back. Not in *my* England."

"I hadn't thought of taking it quite so far," said Cary, modestly. "I just helped the girl to her feet and showed her the shortcut to Hatchard's. You know, through the bakery?"

"Oh, yes," said the Duke, who knew London almost as well as the other gentleman. "There's nothing quite like a bun straight from the oven."

"What did she look like, this cousin of ours?" Juliet inquired, not in the least interested in shortcuts or buns or even Lord Dulwich's grave. As the sister of two eligible bachelors, she prided herself on knowing all the marriageable young ladies on the market, and for Cary to have met one whom she could not immediately identify irritated her. "Was she pretty?"

"She was noticeably human in appearance," Cary equivocated.

"What does that mean?" Juliet demanded.

"I didn't want to kiss her," he explained, "but neither did I feel compelled to run away."

Juliet sighed. "That doesn't much narrow things down, I'm afraid. I've met three or four of our Derbyshire cousins, and they're all presentable but rather plain. The word for that is 'tolerable,' by the way. You might use it instead of 'noticeably human.' What color is her hair?"

Cary knew better than to reveal that the girl had hair the color of hot buttered scotch.

"Brown, of course," Juliet answered her own question. "The Wayborns are all brunettes."

"She's not a Wayborn herself," said Cary. "Her mother was one of the earl's sisters."

"The man had seven sisters," Juliet complained. "Your mystery girl could be anyone."

"Not anyone, surely," said Cary, amused by Juliet's

frustration. He was himself only slightly interested in the identity of a girl he probably would never see again in his life, but Juliet was like a dog with a marrowbone she couldn't crack.

"It could be the Vaughn girl," she said hopefully. "There's a scandal in there somewhere, but no one's talking . . . *yet*. I'll find it out though. See if I don't."

Cary chuckled. "Sorry, Julie. This girl's about as scandalous as a pot of tea."

Juliet wrinkled her nose. "Too bad. How was she dressed?"

"I expect her maid was responsible."

The Duke appreciated the joke, at least until Juliet indicated with a look that she did not.

"What? No, you fathead. I mean, what sort of clothes had she on?"

"Oh, you mean what sort of clothes had she on," said Cary. "I thought you were asking me how her clothes got on her body, which, of course, is a question no gentleman ought to answer, even if he is in full possession of the facts. Warm cloakish thing, gray, with fox fur at the ends, entirely unremarkable. Hood, no bonnet."

"Marry her," said the Duke. "I can't bear these foolish new bonnets. I turned to the left in church the other day, during a hymn, and some woman's feathers got on my tongue."

"I daresay I *will* marry her," said Cary, stifling a yawn, "if my sister can ever suss out who she is. Really, Juliet, I thought you knew everyone. I thought I could depend on you."

Juliet bristled. "Well, is there anything *useful* you can tell me about her?"

"She likes the poetry of Wordsworth, but isn't quite sure about Blake, even though she quoted what must be his most immortal words: 'Bugger the King.'"

Juliet was shocked. "She *said* that?"

"Mr. Blake said it first, and I daresay *he* enjoyed the advantage of knowing what it means," Cary said, laughing. "Our poor cousin merely repeated it. What else? She prefers *Tom Jones* to *Moll Flanders*, both of which she has read, even though she is *not* married. And, like everyone else in London, she's waiting with baited breath for the publication of *Kubla Khan*."

"She seems bookish," was the Duke's deduction.

Cary admitted that appearances were against the lady, but offered an alternative explanation. "We were talking in a bookshop. Had we fallen down an abandoned well together, our conversation might not have been the same."

"What had she to say about Lord Byron?" Juliet demanded.

"Not a word. She spoke only of Wordsworth, Coleridge, Blake, and Fielding."

"Why, she sounds perfectly vile," said Juliet, a little relieved. After all, she was under no obligation to know young ladies who admitted to liking Wordsworth. "Could her father be a military man? Did she say anything at all?"

Cary laughed. "Like what? 'Forward march'? 'Present arms'? She *did* say that her mother is generally thought to have married to disoblige her family."

"It *is* Miss Vaughn," said Juliet in triumph. "Cosima Vaughn. Her mother was Lady Agatha Wayborn, who married Major Vaughn, the rudest man in Dublin—something of an accomplishment, there being prodigious competition for the title! But I can't think why they've come to London if the girl's merely tolerable. She has nothing but a thousand pounds in the three per cents, and that's certainly not enough. She would have married better at home."

She bit her lip almost savagely. "More to the point, how could she afford *fox*? *I* never had any decent fur until after my engagement. Cary, are you quite sure her cloak was trimmed in fox? It must have been squirrel. Trust *you* not to know the difference."

The Duke laughed suddenly. "Major Vaughn—good God, I know him. Once the Lady-Lieutenant—my aunt's cousin by marriage, you know—asked him why he'd named his daughter Cosima, and the Irish rogue answered, 'Cosima bastard, that's why!'"

He roared with laughter, which not even a look from Miss Wayborn could quell. In a moment, Juliet was laughing, too. It had been quite some time since they had laughed together, and perhaps they laughed a bit harder than they otherwise would have done.

"And to think," said Cary, brushing tears of hilarity from his eyes, "I might have met the man himself if I hadn't been late for my appointment in Park Lane."

Chapter 3

When Abigail returned her engagement ring to Lord Dulwich, she expected a certain amount of private re-crimination from the jilted man. To her surprise, he merely disappeared from her life. Abigail, who dreaded all unpleasant scenes, was immensely relieved.

The public uproar that followed, however, was worse than anything she could have imagined. The fact that her mother had been Lady Anne Wayborn was entirely forgotten, while it was discovered anew that her father, Mr. William "Red" Ritchie, was not a gentleman, but rather the reverse: a Glaswegian and a purveyor of Scotch whisky. For a woman of such imperfect descent to break her engagement to an English lord was tanta-mount to a peasant's revolt, and, in the view of the Pa-tronesses of Almack's, deserving of punishment. This created some difficulty, for, as Lady Jersey dryly pointed out to Mrs. Burrell, Miss Ritchie could scarcely be cast out of all good society when she had never been permitted into it.

Lord Dulwich, meanwhile, was not immune to the scorn and ridicule of his peers, who openly despised him for having offered his ancient name to the Scotch heiress in the first place. His lordship retaliated by accusing Miss Ritchie of replacing the Rose de Mai, the carnation-pink diamond in her engagement ring, with a piece of worthless glass. In response to the accusation, Red Ritchie took the unusual step of purchasing twenty thousand pounds' worth of loose diamonds from Mr. Grey in Bond Street, merely to demonstrate that Miss Ritchie could buy and sell a hundred Rose de Mai diamonds in an afternoon spree.

No one was surprised when legal briefs were filed in Doctor's Commons. His lordship alleged that Miss Ritchie had stolen his diamond, and Red Ritchie filed suit for slander.

Abigail could scarcely venture out of doors without being pointed at and whispered over. People who would never have condescended to know her now went out of their way to give her the Cut Direct. Her uncle, Earl Wayborn himself, who had never communicated with Abigail in her life, not even upon the death of her mother, his elder sister, now petitioned to have the spelling of his family name legally changed from Wayborn to Weybourne in an effort to distance himself from the scandal.

Abigail went out less and less, and when Mr. Eldridge of Hatchard's kindly began sending her the latest books, allowing her to choose what she wanted and send back the rest, she stopped going out completely. And yet, despite being a virtual exile in Kensington, she was dismayed when her father announced his intention of sending her into the country until the Dulwich affair was settled to his satisfaction.

The announcement came at dinner. Abigail set down her knife and fork with a clatter. "No, Papa," she said, her quiet, genteel voice at odds with his Glaswegian brogue. "I've done nothing wrong. I refuse to be driven out of my home. I won't leave you."

Red's mind was made up, however. "I've spoken already to Mr. Leighton. He agrees with me. It's settled."

Mr. Leighton was her father's personal solicitor and would never have considered disagreeing with his most affluent client. Abigail was no more argumentative than Mr. Leighton; she knew argument would be futile. As long as she never asked for anything that did not coincide with his own wishes, Red Ritchie was an indulgent parent, but on the occasions when father and daughter disagreed, he gainsaid her ruthlessly.

"Please don't send me to Aunt Elspeth in Glasgow," she begged.

Fortunately, the tyrant had no idea of sending his only child farther afield than St. Albans or Tunbridge Wells. "You're not going into exile," he assured her. "I've asked Mr. Leighton to look for a suitable situation within easy distance to Town. Hertfordshire or Kent, I'm thinking."

"Hertfordshire!" Abigail instantly thought of the handsome "cousin" who had come to her aid on the fateful day Lord Dulwich had so rudely bumped into her. She could now think of him without the crippling terror she had experienced at the actual time of their meeting. She had even begun to believe she could see him again without losing the power to think or speak intelligently. *He* had a house for rent in Hertfordshire. She would much rather stay in a cousin's house than a stranger's, and, of course, she would be absolutely delighted to meet his wife.

"We know no one in Hertfordshire," Red Ritchie explained. "You'll be called Miss Smith, and absolutely no one is to suspect that you're my daughter, not even your chaperone."

Abigail had some objections to the scheme. In particular, she doubted the efficacy of calling herself Miss

Smith, but, having secured Hertfordshire as her haven, she was loathe to awaken the tyrant in her father by questioning his judgment. "And who is to be my chaperone?" she inquired pleasantly.

"Some auld woman of Leighton's," was the only answer forthcoming until Mr. Leighton himself arrived the next day with a portfolio of houses he deemed suitable for Abigail's needs.

The proposed chaperone was revealed to be the mother of his first wife. A middle-aged widow, Mrs. Spurgeon was entirely dependent on Mr. Leighton, who was only ten years her junior. She had lived with the solicitor throughout his first marriage, and, after the death of her daughter, the arrangement had continued for reasons of simple economy. However, the introduction of a second Mrs. Leighton into the household had made necessary certain changes that had little to do with money. Mrs. Spurgeon and the second Mrs. Leighton cordially despised each other.

Abigail liked her father's private solicitor enough to take his former mother-in-law from him without question, but, to her dismay, the portfolio he presented did not include a dower house attached to Tanglewood Manor. She brought the oversight to his attention.

"Tanglewood Manor," he repeated thoughtfully. "An old college chum of mine is the Vicar at Tanglewood Green in Hertfordshire, Miss Abigail. There is nothing advertised, but I'll make a private inquiry. Many of the best families prefer not to advertise, you know."

Red Ritchie had left the choice of house entirely to his daughter, and so the matter was settled within a week. Red had but one demand, and, as long as Abigail promised to safeguard her health by drinking a *quaich* of Ritchie's Gold Label every day she was away, she was free to do as she pleased in Hertfordshire, and Mr. Leighton was authorized to keep her in funds.

She could now look forward to making Mrs. Spurgeon's acquaintance. On the way from Red's Kensington mansion to his own modest town house in Baker Street, Mr. Leighton explained that his mother-in-law would be traveling with her latest nurse-companion. "Mrs. Nashe comes to us very highly recommended," he assured Abigail. "The Countess of Inchmery was her most recent employer."

"Is Mrs. Spurgeon ill?" Abigail inquired. "If so, Mr. Leighton, I wonder if it is advisable for us to remove her from London at this time of year."

"She is not ill," replied Mr. Leighton, his mouth tightening. "She has been examined by every doctor in London. She *was* ill, Miss Abigail . . . but it was quite four years ago. At that time, she so enjoyed the attentions of the young person I hired to wait on her that I believe she is determined never to be well again!

"She is a difficult woman," he went on, "but, rest assured, *you* will not be expected to wait on her, Miss Abigail. I've made it clear that Miss Smith is the daughter of one of my clients, and most definitely not her servant. Her nurse and her maid will see to all her needs. Do not feel you must spend one instant in her company if you do not wish to."

"I'm sure she's not as bad as that, Mr. Leighton," said Abigail mildly. "I would not mind in the least being useful to Mrs. Spurgeon."

Mr. Leighton did not attempt to dissuade her from this view. Rather, he trusted that his mother-in-law would soon convince Abigail that he was speaking the gospel truth.

As they drove into Baker Street they found a scene of disarray. Mrs. Spurgeon herself was standing in the street directing the placement of what appeared to be the trousseau of a royal princess onto the baggage coach. Abigail's chaperone was a massively built lady swathed in a billowing garment of the deepest black, but the overall impression she gave was of brute strength, not bereavement. Her face was a hard slab supported by more than one chin, and she had the cruel, dark eyes of a rapacious Mongol chieftain. If she had ever been pretty or young there was no sign of it now, except for a mass of bright yellow hair dressed in a style far too girlish for a stout woman of her years.

A woman of strict propriety, Mrs. Spurgeon refused to get into the private chaise as long as Abigail's maid was in possession of it.

"If you are accustomed to traveling in the company of a servant, Miss Smith," she bellowed in a voice a master of hounds might have coveted, "I am not. I suggest you put her in the second coach with the rest of the baggage. *My* standards will not be compromised simply because *you* do not know what is right."

Abigail explained that Paggles had been her nurse when she was an infant, after having performed the same service to her mother before her. "Besides which, she is elderly and infirm," she added, hoping to gain Mrs. Spurgeon's sympathy.

While claiming to suffer from a variety of illnesses herself, Mrs. Spurgeon had no sympathy for fellow subscribers. "If she is too weak to travel with the baggage, then you had better turn her off. When my last maid wore herself out after only ten years, we sent her to the poorhouse. There she makes baskets out of reeds. A basket is a very useful thing, Miss Smith."

Abigail was horrified. "Paggles will *never* be sent to the poorhouse, Mrs. Spurgeon!"

The lady stared at her. "I hope you don't mean to pension her off, Miss Smith," she said severely. "It is very bad for servants to be pensioned off. Is there anything worse than calling upon a new neighbor only to discover that it is, in fact, the pensioned-off dogsbody of a Cabinet

Minister? I vow, it is getting to the point where they expect—nay, demand—to be granted a pension. The *look* Smithers gave me when I turned her off without a character, when it was the doddering old fool who dropped the tray—! Why should *I*, a poor widow, pay an annuity to someone who is of no further use to me?"

Paggles had grown frail in her old age; Mrs. Spurgeon's clarion voice was enough to reduce her to tears. Though it was not in Abigail's nature to court strife, she dearly wanted to rebuke Mrs. Spurgeon when Paggles clutched her arm in terror, wailing, "Please don't let her send me to the poorhouse, Miss Abby! I'll sit in the other carriage, if that's what she wants."

Abigail decided it would be cruel to force Paggles to remain in the chaise merely to satisfy her own urge to triumph over Mrs. Spurgeon. "No one is sending you to the poorhouse, darling," she assured Paggles, as she helped her into the baggage coach. She gave Evans, Mrs. Spurgeon's maid, a handful of shillings to look after the old woman.

Mrs. Spurgeon now assumed the chaise, and called for her birdcage. Abigail would not have objected to a collection of lovebirds, finches, or canaries, but when a servant brought forth a large brass cage containing a scarlet macaw with evil-looking claws and a monstrous beak, she became alarmed. Most parrots, in her experience, were well-behaved, but some sixth sense told her this one was trouble. "Oh, no," involuntarily escaped from her lips, a reaction that seemed to please Mrs. Spurgeon.

"You must treat Cato exactly as you would an intelligent child, and say nothing before him you would not wish to have repeated, Miss Smith," said she. "Some people find it disconcerting. But I believe that one should always guard one's tongue."

After no further delay, other than Mrs. Spurgeon's

being sure that Evans had forgotten the medicine chest, and Evans having to convince her that she had *not* forgotten the medicine chest, the chaise proceeded up Baker Street at a sedate pace, followed by the baggage coach.

With her considerable bulk and her parrot cage, Mrs. Spurgeon took up one side of the carriage, leaving Abigail to share the other seat with her nurse-companion. Mrs. Nashe proved to be an attractive young widow with the soft manners and speech of a true gentlewoman. Mrs. Spurgeon remained indifferent to any conversation between Miss Smith and Mrs. Nashe until the former complimented the latter's clothes. Mrs. Spurgeon then felt obliged to inform Miss Smith that Mrs. Nashe's smart clothes were all cast-offs from Lady Inchmery, a former employer. Needless to say, Mrs. Spurgeon did not approve of the practice of giving one's clothing to one's servants. In her opinion, it was nearly as bad as granting them pensions.

As they turned onto the Great North Road, Abigail proposed opening the curtains. There had been snow, and the countryside was bound to look like a winter wonderland in the morning sun. Mrs. Spurgeon, who certainly knew how to dampen youthful enthusiasm, curtly informed Miss Smith that views of rollicking countryside invariably caused her to vomit. Ditto the flickering of lamps. Therefore, the three ladies were obliged to sit in the carriage with the curtains closed and the lamps doused; Mrs. Spurgeon's threat, though not quite believable to Abigail, was too horrible to be ignored.

Contented with the arrangements, Mrs. Spurgeon went to sleep, and her snoring was quite as stentorian as her speaking voice. "How do you bear it, Mrs. Nashe?" Abigail whispered.

"My husband was only a poor lieutenant," the nurse-companion replied, pausing to squint in the darkness at her employer. A loud snore reassured her. "When he died of wounds he sustained at Ciudad Rodrigo, I was left destitute, to make my way as best I could. Mr. Leighton pays me very well, you see, and I have an elderly mother who depends on me for an income." As she spoke, she caressed the simple gold band she wore on her left hand, and the expression of longing in her dark eyes would have melted the hardest of hearts.

"All the same, I could not do it," said Abigail.

"She's lonely and unhappy, Miss Smith," Mrs. Nashe said gently. "I know what that's like, you see. And, compared to my last situation, this is ideal."

"Oh? Was her ladyship a harsh mistress?"

"The Countess was merely indolent, but her son, Lord Dulwich—!" Mrs. Nashe shuddered delicately. "When I left Cliffden, I felt I'd made a narrow escape."

"Lord Dulwich!" cried Abigail. "He told me his mother was dead."

Mrs. Nashe's eyes widened. "Do you know his lordship, Miss Smith?"

Abigail blushed. "A little," she said.

"I assure you both his parents are living. *They* are fine people, but the son is no credit to them. He'd take the most shocking liberties, then tell me if I ever complained to his mamma, she'd only turn me out of the house . . . which, of course, is exactly what happened. Her ladyship had some vestige of a conscience, however; she gave me a few clothes, and a very good letter which enabled me to find a place with Mr. Leighton. I'm happy to be where I am, Miss Smith. At least there are no men to molest me."

"I'm very sorry for you, Mrs. Nashe."

"Please do call me Vera—I can scarcely bear to be called Nashe. It reminds me of all that I have lost," she said, dabbing her eyes with her handkerchief.

The reassuring snores abruptly ended, and the lonely and unhappy Mrs. Spurgeon banged on the roof with her stick until the coachman opened the panel. "Stop at the first inn you see," she barked. "And do slow down, you fool! Your reckless driving is making me quite nauseous."

"Slow down, you fool!" screeched her macaw, making Abigail jump.

The panel slid shut, and Mrs. Spurgeon suddenly confided to Abigail that her bladder was no bigger than a button. "We shall be obliged to stop at every half mile. Inconvenient, I know, but it can't be helped."

"Inconvenient" proved to be rather an optimistic view of things. At their fourth stop, Abigail looked longingly at the baggage coach as it went on ahead of them. Refreshed after a nap and a pot of tea, Mrs. Spurgeon proposed letting Cato loose in the carriage for the rest of the journey. Abigail objected in the most strenuous terms.

"You would not keep a child in a cage for two hours together, Miss Smith," cried Mrs. Spurgeon, quite shocked by the young woman's cruelty.

"I might," said Abigail, rather tartly, "if the child had claws and a beak."

"Claws and a beak! Beaks and claws!" screamed the macaw.

"There's really nothing to be afraid of," Mrs. Spurgeon said smugly, opening Cato's cage and allowing the large bird to climb on her shoulder.

Abigail shuddered in revulsion. Cato had more in common with a small dragon than with the sweet little tame goldfinches she herself kept at home.

"Don't worry," Vera Nashe assured her. "I'll give him a cuttlebone to chew."

"Do please keep him on your side," Abigail urged Mrs. Spurgeon, just as the scarlet macaw, sensing her fear, beat his wings and crossed the distance between them. His long gray talons closed on Abigail's shoulder and his beak fastened on her ear. One icy blue eye peered into hers. "Claws and a beak!" he croaked.

Abigail screamed in terror, and Mrs. Nashe was obliged to rescue her.

Mrs. Spurgeon said repressively, "It's really only a tiny amount of blood, Vera," as Mrs. Nashe pressed her handkerchief to Abigail's torn earlobe and Cato returned to his mistress.

Fortunately, Mrs. Spurgeon had not exaggerated the extreme smallness of her bladder. When the chaise stopped at the next inn on the Great North Road, Abigail quickly escaped. She was relieved to see the baggage coach standing in the yard. Without bidding her chaperone adieu, she sought refuge in it, unceremoniously knocking a bandbox from the seat next to Paggles, who opened her shawl and wrapped her young lady up in it. The scent of lavender, which had comforted Abigail since she was a child, soon lulled her to sleep in the swaying coach.

Evans woke her as they drew near the inn at Tanglewood Green. Paggles's white head was resting on Abigail's shoulder, and the young woman gently moved it aside to look out the window. Snow was falling thickly, and the sky was quite gray, but, despite this, the Tudor Rose was doing a roaring trade, judging by the amount of traffic.

"The river's frozen ten feet thick," the hostler explained to Abigail, who had not yet judged it safe to leave the carriage, "and all the young people do be skating on it." The coach had driven across a broad stone bridge less than half a mile back, and Abigail guessed that the inn's back garden went down to the banks of the same river. The Tudor Rose was a charming half-timbered building, and, had it not been so crowded, Abigail would have been glad to go in.

"Would you be wanting a hot cup of cider, love?" The hostler winked at her slyly, and Abigail realized the man must have mistaken her for a servant, not surprising as she was traveling with the baggage.

"No, thank you! Is Mr. Wayborn here to meet us?" she inquired from the window. "I am one of the new tenants for the Dower House."

"The young squire's been called away, miss," he said more respectfully. "He waited for you all the morning. He left word for you to be looked after here. I can send a boy after him."

A few young men were jostling about in the yard and one of them looked at her saucily. "It's far too crowded for us to stay here," Abigail said decisively. "I believe we must go on."

"The young squire—" the hostler began.

"Mr. Wayborn would not expect you to argue with me," said Abigail, feeling Paggles shivering. "It is out of the question for us to wait here in this noisy place, and if we do not leave now, the snow will keep us here overnight. Kindly tell the coachman the way to the Dower House. And we shall require another hot brick, if you please."

When the boy brought the brick, Abigail herself tucked it under Paggles's feet. Mrs. Spurgeon's maid seemed amused that the young lady should lavish so much attention on her servant, but Abigail did not care if she appeared ridiculous. Paggles had been the only servant to stay with Lady Anne after her marriage to Red Ritchie, and she had always been more like a grandmother to Abigail than a lady's maid.

The Dower House was not more than three quarters of a mile from the inn. As the coach rounded a bend of tall, ice-laden elms, Abigail looked out of the window. Her mouth fell open. The coach rolled to a stop.

"Good heavens!" Abigail cried in disbelief.

The house at the end of the drive was a handsome square cottage of rosy stone, half covered in ivy, exactly as it should be but for one thing. A very large elm tree had fallen on it recently, crushing the roof and upper attics of the left-hand side, and spraying shattered glass from the upper windows across the snow. A few men in frieze coats were standing about, shaking their heads over the mess, their breath freezing in the air.

"What is it, Miss Smith?" Evans wanted to know.

Without answering, Abigail flung open the carriage door and jumped out, forgetting in her haste to let down the step. She put her foot down, expecting to encounter something solid, then ended up falling nearly four feet down, landing in a heap in the snow.

"I believe it is customary for the lady to allow the gentleman to open the door for her," said Cary Wayborn, helping her to her feet.

Abigail leaped at the sound of his voice, which she immediately recognized, and completely forgot about the elm that had fallen on the Dower House. She had been quite wrong in thinking she could see him again and remain rational. The sight of him and the nearness of him instantly shut down the best part of her brain. Her throat went dry and she could only stare at him helplessly. If she had been able to move, she would have run away from him, but her legs were rooted on the spot, and, besides, he was holding her hand. She was acutely aware that, despite the cold, he wasn't wearing gloves, and his hand was quite as brown as his face. This was not how she had envisioned their second meeting.

Cary's faith in his sister's knowledge of London's debutantes was so strong he did not doubt for a moment that he was looking at his Irish cousin, Miss Cosima Vaughn. While vain enough to believe she'd come to Hertfordshire in pursuit of him, the extreme boldness of the move puzzled him; he had judged her to be a young woman nearly crippled by shyness. Yet here she was, staring at him like a pole-axed doe with those oddly appealing light brown eyes.

"Good Lord," he murmured aloud. "It *is* you, isn't it? I'm not imagining things? You *are* my cousin from Piccadilly? Aged eleven and three quarters from the back, aged twenty-one from the front?" He began to smile at her, his eyes growing warm as the initial surprise of seeing her wore off. He was starved for female companionship in Hertfordshire, and he thought she might fill the void very nicely indeed. He might even succeed in discovering the scandal that had thus far eluded his inquisitive sister Juliet. Making her blush had already given him more pleasure than he'd had in a month. Better still, she was his cousin, and, as a blood relation, he could tease her and flirt with her as much as he liked, without arousing ugly gossip.

Abigail guessed he was the sort of man that made every woman he met feel special, and she tried to resist his smile. Sternly, she reminded herself that this was a married man.

"What brings you to Hertfordshire?" he asked politely, taking her hand.

Abigail began to stammer.

"Take your time," he encouraged her. "I don't mind the snow falling on me."

She took a deep breath and expelled the words all at once. "You did say if I knew of anyone's wanting a house."

"But, surely you're not Mrs. Spurgeon?" he said, startled.

"I'm traveling with Mrs. Spurgeon," Abigail explained. She watched, fascinated, as a drop of blood trickled from Cary's nose. It was rather like watching an archangel bleed.

Unaware he had sprung a leak, Cary looked into the coach and saw Paggles sleeping amongst the boxes. "Is that her?" he inquired in a low voice. "Why, she's positively ancient."

"She is my old nurse," Abigail said, searching in her fox muff for a handkerchief. "Your nose is bleeding, sir."

"I'm not a bit surprised," he answered, taking out his own handkerchief to wipe his nose. "A carriage door banged into it quite recently."

"Oh, no!" Abigail cried, unaware just how recently this mishap had occurred. "People ought to be more careful."

"You're quite right," he agreed, holding his head back while applying pressure to his nose. "It was very careless of me to stand so close to the door."

"Oh, I didn't mean *you*, sir!" Abigail said, mortified that he should have misunderstood her. "It's entirely the fault of the person in the carriage. He ought to have looked out first, before he flung open the door."

"*She*, cousin."

She fell silent, and when he brought his head down again, he noticed a telltale sheepishness in her eyes. "Does it hurt very much?" she asked, wincing in sympathy. "Really, I'm so dreadfully sorry. It's just that I looked out the window and—and I saw the tree . . ."

"What tree?" he inquired politely, putting away his handkerchief. "I've a good few trees hanging about, in case you haven't noticed. Was there one in particular that intrigued you?"

Abigail blinked at him in disbelief. "That tree, sir," she said, pointing. "The elm."

"Oh, that tree," he said, indulging in what she thought a very odd sense of humor. "I was hoping you wouldn't notice it was an elm. I'm quite bored with elms at the moment. I've been hearing stories about them all day. People who wouldn't know an elm if one fell on their houses have suddenly become quite garrulous on the subject."

"But it *has* fallen on your house, sir," she stammered. "And it is an elm."

"Yes, of course, it's fallen on my house. Did you expect it to remain rooted in one spot forever and ever? We had an ice storm overnight, and the tree—pardon me, *the Elm*—lost its balance. Fortunately, my house was there to break its fall. The prevailing opinion is that it's my fault entirely."

Abigail frowned. "How can it be your fault if it was an ice storm?"

"Thank you for taking my part," he said. "Apparently, the Elm was dead, and ought to have been cut down a year ago. Anyone could see it was going to fall over at the first gust of wind. By 'anyone' I mean, of course, everyone except me."

"What on earth are you going to do?" Abigail asked.

"I say we ignore it," he said, tenderly feeling the end of his nose. "Perhaps it will get tired and go away if we pay it no attention. I've a great many trees on the estate, and the vast majority of them are immensely well-behaved. Let us pay attention to them instead."

"But where are we to go?" asked Abigail.

He raised his eyebrows. "Go? Don't you like Hertfordshire?"

"We can't possibly stay in the house now," said Abigail, unnerved by his apparent unconcern. Her father was the only man she had ever really known, and, while neither quiet nor morose, verbal capers were not in Red's line. Cary was so different that he baffled her.

"Don't you like trees?" he teased. "They are generally thought to be pleasant things. Not that tree, of course. *That* is a very bad tree. But you mustn't let it ruin all the good trees for you. Think of the shade they offer in the summer, the little birds who nest in their sheltering

branches . . ." Reluctantly, Cary relented in the face of
her utter bewilderment. Miss Vaughn evidently had no
brothers; she was quite unaccustomed to being teased,
which, naturally, made her irresistible to him. "Not to
worry, cousin," he said cheerfully. "I've a team of crack
woodcutters on the case. You'll be tucked in bed by
nightfall."

"What?" cried Abigail. "Even if they were able to
clear it all away by tonight—which I doubt—we could
not possibly sleep here. Why, half the roof is gone!"

"I'm only joking you, cousin," he said, chuckling.
"Of course you'll have to stay at the Manor, provided
the elms have not yet attacked it. It's only half a mile
across the field, nearly two miles by way of the road. I
have my horse. I'll take the shortcut and meet your
coach at the house. I'll tell your driver. Let's get you
back in the carriage before you freeze."

"But, sir, we could not possibly—I mean, we could
not stay in your house—"

"I don't see why not," he answered. "You were going
to stay in *that* house and it's mine. Or do you suppose
it belongs to the tree now?"

"But the manor house," Abigail persisted. "Is that not
where *you* live, sir? I couldn't possibly ask you to leave
your home."

"My dear girl, you couldn't possibly ask me to share
it," he pointed out. "The Vicar in these parts happens
to be my cousin, and he's beastly strict."

"Where will you go, sir?" Abigail asked.

He chuckled. "You needn't look so forlorn. I shall
only be as far away as the gatehouse. I'll be honest with
you, cousin," he went on cheerfully. "I can't give the
rent back because I've spent it already. The desperate
pity of it is, I spent quite a bit on the Dower House!
Cleaning it, painting it, patching over the rat holes.
Those chimneys hadn't been swept since God was in

short coats? You'd not believe the detritus that came down the flue in my lady's bedchamber. Owls' nests, and bats' bones."

"Bats!" breathed Abigail, searching the cold gray sky in dismay.

"Damned expensive, sweeps. The truth is, my dear cousin," he added, taking her hand in his, "if you can't convince Mrs. Spurgeon to take the Manor instead, I shall be ruined."

"But you can't ask your wife to remove to the gate-house," Abigail pointed out.

To her surprise, he laughed. "No, I don't suppose I can."

"I daresay the gatehouse would be adequate for our needs, sir," said Abigail, rather doubtfully. "We are only three—Mrs. Spurgeon, Mrs. Spurgeon's nurse, and myself."

"Nurse? That settles it. Mrs. Spurgeon's health will not permit her to be consigned to the inconveniences of the gatehouse. I shall take it, and leave you ladies to the comforts of Tanglewood Manor. No, I insist. I give you my word that my wife won't object to the scheme. I expect Mrs. Wayborn to remain quite mute on the sub-ject, as indeed, she is on every subject."

Abigail stared at him. "Do you mean that your wife is a mute, sir?" she asked, shocked that he would joke about such a serious matter.

"She might be," he carelessly answered. "I really don't know."

"How can you not know?" Abigail cried. "I don't under-stand you, sir."

"No," he sadly agreed. "You're not very good at rid-dles, are you? I'm not married, you see. But I daresay my wife *is* wandering about the earth in search of me as we speak, poor girl. She could be mute. She could be Irish, for all I know. I'm fairly certain she hasn't got a hunchback or a mustache, but, then again, I'm such a spiritual fellow that her beautiful soul might be quite enough for me. She mightn't even be born yet, though I must say, I find the thought of marrying a girl nearly thirty years my junior a bit daunting."

"But of course you're married," Abigail argued. "I distinctly recall that you mentioned your wife to me. You said Mrs. Wayborn did all your reading for you."

He raised his dark brows. "Did I? I seem to recall something along those lines. What I meant was that, when I do marry, she will have the job. Unless she should happen to be blind. I couldn't ask it of a blind woman."

"Then there is no Mrs. Wayborn to object to your living arrangements."

"Not at present," he qualified. "But if I know anything about my future wife—and I think I do—she wouldn't object to staying with me in the gatehouse. As long as we two are together, her happiness will be complete. In any case, you must take the Manor."

"Yes, of course," Abigail agreed faintly as he let down the steps for her and helped her climb back into the coach. She felt utterly and completely stupid.

Chapter 4

One of the Manor's wrought iron gates had come loose from its post and was propped against the wall of what Abigail supposed to be the gatehouse—a dingy stone box that looked more like an abandoned rookery than a human domicile. The manor house did not disappoint, however. With its large, mullioned windows and its chimneys rising like decorative spires from the roof, Tanglewood was as fine an example of a Tudor country house as she had ever seen. The red brick facade was clad with ivy, and outside the entrance was a small timber portico, with room enough inside for two rustic benches and a boot scraper.

As the coach rolled up the drive, Abigail saw Cary Wayborn step out from the portico, a barking dog at his heels. The animal had the fox-like head, short legs, and deep, bow-front chest typical of a Welsh corgi. By concentrating on the dog instead of the master as he helped her from the coach, she found she could breathe quite normally.

"The house is much too big for us, Mr. Wayborn," she said worriedly, turning to help Paggles, only to find that the efficient Evans had the situation in hand. "The rent we paid for the Dower House can't possibly be enough."

The corgi launched itself at Abigail, demanding its fair share in the conversation. Its stump of a tail was wagging so hard its entire rear end was in motion. "Quiet, Angel," Cary snapped, to no avail. The dog jumped energetically at Abigail's skirts. Abigail solved the problem by scooping the small animal up in her arms.

"Worst dog ever," Cary remarked lightly.

"No, indeed," said Abigail, which Angel mistook for an invitation to lick her face.

"There's no question of asking Mr. Leighton for more rent," Cary added. "It's not his fault my tree forgot its manners, after all."

It had not occurred to Abigail before that Cary would think Mr. Leighton responsible for the rent. Of course, he had no way of knowing the truth. She was no longer Miss Ritchie, the Scotch heiress who had jilted Lord Dulwich; she was now the anonymous Miss Smith, ward of Mrs. Spurgeon.

They hurried inside out of the blowing snow. The entrance hall was lit by a huge fire blazing in the massive stone hearth. Abigail set Angel on the floor and looked around, idly brushing at the short red hairs the dog had left on her cloak.

Angel ran straight to the fire where two well-worn tapestry chairs had been arranged with a large footstool littered with newspapers set between them. A few crewel-work cushions had been placed on the deep wooden sills beneath the tall windows, but the room offered no other seating. Only one or two carpets had been put down on the floor, which was stone in some places and in others composed of odds and ends of timbers laid out in a hound's tooth pattern. The walls were of beautiful linenfold paneling, darkened by smoke and age, and the coffered ceiling, which was rather low, featured the double rose of the Tudors.

Abigail, who had always lived in the most modern, convenient London houses, instantly fell in love with it, musty smell, smoking chimney, and all. She could imagine the place filled with sixteenth-century ladies and gentlemen, the ladies in rich brocade skirts and ruffs of starched white lace, the men in velvet doublets and hose. She imagined how Cary Wayborn might look in doublet and hose, and decided he would do very well. He already had the pointed goatee and golden earring favored by the young men of Queen Elizabeth's court.

"Mrs. Grimstock is making us tea," said Cary, clearing away the newspapers. Abigail hurried to help Paggles into one of the chairs, while Evans went to find the housekeeper.

Cary watched curiously as she removed her cloak and placed it over the old woman like a blanket. Though rather too sensible in its design to be fashionable, Abigail's dark blue dress was of good quality. It fit her slim body very well, and the deep, rich color made her short, curly hair look more than ever like butterscotch. Even from behind, there could be no mistaking her for a child. Cary felt his blood grow warm. It had been far too long since he had enjoyed a woman, and judging by this one's reaction to him, it was not going to be a very long conquest. Though she was obviously a virgin, he was experienced enough to know the many ways they could enjoy themselves without spoiling the girl completely. All he needed was to get her alone.

Cary disposed of his newspapers and returned as Abigail was pulling off her gloves. "He eats gloves," he warned her, removing what proved to be a walnut from the dog's mouth. "Shoes too—sometimes with the people still in them."

To Abigail's enormous relief, she found that, when

her handsome, unmarried cousin was at one end of the room, and she was at the other, her bashfulness remained under control. It was only when he got within arm's reach that she turned into a stammering fool.

"He's still a puppy. I daresay he'll grow out of it," she said intelligibly, just as the housekeeper arrived with the tea tray. The folding table was in its collapsed state at one side of the fireplace, and, as Abigail was closer to it than anyone else, she set it up without thinking.

"Mrs. Grimstock," Cary said sharply. "This is my cousin, Miss Vaughn, from Dublin. She hasn't come all this way to set up tables for us."

Mrs. Grimstock did not look like a Grimstock at all, but was rather a plump, middle-aged woman with a pleasing scent of candied ginger. "I beg your pardon, Miss Vaughn," she cried.

"Smith," said Abigail, confused to suddenly have *two* names that were not her own. "I'm perfectly capable of setting up a tea table, Mr. Wayborn. But my name is Smith."

Cary frowned slightly, but accepted the correction gracefully. "Yes, of course," he said smoothly. "My cousin, Miss Vaughn-Smith. Or is it Smith-Vaughn? I quite forgot you were hyphenated."

"I am not in the least hyphenated," said Abigail, staring at him. "I am simply Miss Smith. And I'm not from Dublin. Whatever made you think so? I'm from London."

"Yes, of course," he agreed, beginning to laugh. "I must be drunk! Mrs. Grimstock, *this*, of course, is my cousin, Miss *Smith*, from *London*. She is *not* my cousin Miss Vaughn from Dublin, after all. I hope that's clear. Will you do me the honor, cousin?" he added, as Mrs. Grimstock withdrew.

"Do you the honor, sir?" For a moment Abigail

stared, confused. "Oh, the tea! Yes, of course," she said quickly. "How do you take yours, Mr. Wayborn?"

He grinned at her audaciously. "With a spot of whisky, generally," he said, waiting for her gasp of ladylike dismay.

"There doesn't seem to be any," she said, dismayed, to be sure, but not gasping. "Shall I ring for the servant?"

"Here," he said, pulling out his flask, wondering how far she would take the joke.

To his astonishment, she quietly took the whisky and poured it with a liberal hand into both cups. "Sugar?"

"Two, please," said Cary. As he came forward to take his laced cup, he could scarcely keep a straight face. He fully expected her to choke on her own tea-and-whisky, but to his astonishment, it seemed to slip quietly down her throat, as if by long-established custom.

"One doesn't often get such quality here," Abigail remarked, unaware she had done anything controversial. "The Irish like to keep the best for themselves."

"My groom's an Irishman," Cary explained. "He can get me anything."

"I do like a little Irish in my tea. Though it's not good for you at all. Not like scotch."

Cary choked.

"Have I put too much in your cup?" she asked, concerned. "It does take getting used to."

"I'm all right," Cary said with dignity. "Is . . . Is scotch good for you, do you think?"

"Oh, yes," Abigail said seriously. "A *quaich* a day is absolutely essential for the blood."

"What in God's name is a quake?" Cary wanted to know.

"About this much." With her thumb and index finger, Abigail measured two inches.

"I wouldn't know what a *quake* does for the blood," said Cary, laughing. "But I can tell you from experience that a *bottle* is very bad for the head. I brought a case of scotch up here when I first moved in, drank it out of sheer boredom, and it nearly killed me."

Abigail smiled to herself. Her Glaswegian father had always told her that Englishmen could not hold their liquor, so she did not think any less of her cousin for his admission. "This is a beautiful house," she said presently.

"Is it?" he replied, shrugging. "If you like drafty old piles. It started out as a cow byre."

She seemed deeply interested, so he went on, "As the Cary family prospered, they started adding on rooms. Things really got going for them when Henry VIII granted them a few thousand acres belonging to some stubborn Catholic neighbors, and by the time Elizabeth came to the throne, they were pretty well-established. In honor of the Virgin Queen, they built the house in the shape of an E." He set his cup on the mantel. "Shall I give you the tour?"

Abigail glanced at her old nurse, but Cary said quickly, "Let her rest. The servants will look after her."

"But Mrs. Spurgeon and Mrs. Nashe must be at the inn by now."

"It's very likely they will have to stay the night," he told her. "It's been snowing all afternoon. I don't know that a carriage could get through. You don't mind being trapped here with me, do you?" He held out his hand to her, and smiled.

"But you will be at the gatehouse, surely," she objected nervously.

"Yes, of course," he said, pulling her to her feet. "Though I really think you ought to ask me to stay for dinner. I hate dining alone. Then, after dinner, you should play cards with me."

He delighted in the way her eyes grew big with alarm at the prospect of spending an evening alone with him. "Come now, Miss . . . er . . . Smith, we're cousins.

Surely there can be nothing improper in dining with one's own cousin. You would not send me to the gate-house with no supper and no company—apart from my misshapen dog, that is."

"What's the matter with your dog?" she asked, puzzled.

"What's the matter with him?" he said, drawing her along with him towards the next room. "My dear girl, you must have noticed the manufactory forgot to give him legs and a tail."

"He's a corgi, Mr. Wayborn," Abigail chided him. "He's absolutely perfect just as he is."

In complete agreement with her, Angel got up on his hind legs and licked her hand.

"You mean you've seen his kind before?" Cary asked curiously.

She nodded. "Yes, in Wales. The farmers use them to drive their cows down the road."

Cary chuckled. He now realized that she was teasing him, probably getting him back for leading her to believe he had a mute wife tucked away somewhere. There was no possible way a little dog like Angel could be used to herd anybody's cows. "I generally use mine to chew on the furniture," he said cheerfully. "If you like old family portraits, come have a look at these."

"Oh, yes," said Abigail, almost tripping over the excited corgi. Angel had not expected her to move so quickly and immediately tried to herd her back to her chair. Failing that, he decided to nip at her heels to make her go faster. Cary pushed him aside with his foot and closed the door in his face, after letting Abigail through. The dog could be heard barking hysterically.

The fire had not been lit in the next room and it was noticeably colder, though the rows of mullioned windows admitted enough light for Abigail to see the paintings hung on the wall. At a glance she recognized the work of Bettes, Gower, Van Dyck, and Lely. Clearly Mr.

Wayborn's ancestors had spared no expense in immortalizing themselves. She was surprised by how many of the people were fair-haired; the Wayborns were usually dark.

"These are my mother's people," Cary explained. "The Carys must have had some Viking blood, I think. But here's a fine young Wayborn you know." He stopped before a portrait of a fair woman with three children, painted by George Romney. The children were as dark as the woman was fair. "My mother," said Cary. "This handsome fellow is me, of course."

Abigail smiled at the little boy in short coats teasing a tabby cat with a ball of yarn.

"And that loathsome creature polluting my angelic mother's lap is my sister Juliet."

"She was a lovely baby," said Abigail severely.

"A blot," he insisted. "Take my word for it. Sucked her thumb until she was nine."

"Who is that?" Abigail asked, pointing out the older child standing behind Cary's mother.

"My elder brother, Benedict. My half-brother, I should say. His mother was my father's first wife, but Father insisted on all his children being in the portrait. Poor old Ben! He doesn't seem to want to be there, does he?" He moved away quickly and stopped at another painting. "Here's a lady that looks a bit like you, cousin. The infamous Lettice Cary."

The painting, most definitely by Anthony Van Dyck, showed a green-eyed young woman with hair the color of a fox's pelt peeping from beneath a jeweled cap. Her delicate face was nearly white, but the artist had modeled it carefully in his palest colors, giving it life. Lettice's golden brows and lashes had been painted hair by hair with the artist's finest brush, and the cheeks and small mouth were stained the faintest imaginable pink. She was dressed in Jacobean finery, her white dress studded with pearls and emeralds, her upstanding white lace collar like an intricate spider's web against the dark wood paneling behind her. Seated on what looked like a throne hung with heavy scarlet and white curtains, she seemed to be leaning backwards slightly. Abigail saw no resemblance to herself whatsoever.

"Do you really think I look like her?" she asked curiously.

"Only a little," he replied. He looked at her, then at the painting. "You both have saucy eyes. Aren't you going to ask me why she's infamous?"

"Why?" asked Abigail, turning beet-red. No one had ever described her light-brown eyes as "saucy" before. She decided he was merely teasing her again.

"When she was quite forty, she ran away with her lover, an Italian musician twenty years her junior. How is that for a spot of scandal? This portrait was painted when she was a young bride, of course, but she already looks pretty restless, wouldn't you agree?" He placed his hand on Abigail's shoulder as he spoke.

Abigail could neither agree nor disagree; her tongue was tied, and all she could feel was his hand burning through her clothes like a hot iron.

"The ring on her finger is still in the family," he added, as Abigail moved away without replying. "The Cary emerald. I'd show it to you, but it's kept in our vault in London."

"I daresay these portraits are worth more than your emerald, sir," Abigail murmured.

"Perhaps. But no one wants to buy the men, and I can't bear to part with the ladies."

Abigail caught sight of a set of miniatures arranged inside a curio table beneath a window. "These are very fine, sir. You have Henry the Eighth, four of his wives, and his daughter Elizabeth, all set in gold. You even have Anne Boleyn," she added, tapping the glass. "Most people would have thrown out her portrait when she was beheaded."

Cary pretended to be interested for the pleasure of moving closer to her. She was so engrossed in the miniature portraits that she forgot to shy away from him. "I daresay she was restored to the case when her daughter Elizabeth became Queen," he theorized.

"You're missing two Catherines," Abigail pointed out. "Catherine of Aragon, and Catherine Howard. One divorced, the other beheaded. If your collection were complete, it would be worth a small fortune."

Cary's interest became genuine. "How small, do you think?"

"Easily a thousand pounds," Abigail said promptly. "Quite possibly more."

He stared at her. "You're mad. A *thousand* pounds?"

She nodded earnestly. "If you could find the two Catherines, in good condition."

"There are some other miniatures in my study," he said, leading her quickly through a door down a long, dark hallway into a small, untidy chamber with low casement windows. Unlike the formal rooms she had already seen, this one had not been paneled, and the original plaster and beams were exposed. Cary went to a large cabinet and, after rummaging in a few drawers, brought her a large box in which a half dozen miniature portraits had been casually jumbled together. He began taking them out and arranging them on his desk, after clearing a stack of unopened correspondence out of the way.

Abigail picked up one. "Why, this is Henry's daughter, Mary," she exclaimed. "How extraordinary. I've *never* seen a miniature of Bloody Mary, sir. She was so hated in her lifetime, there wasn't much demand for her portrait, large or small."

He shrugged. "Worth much?"

Abigail shook her head in regret. "As I said, she wasn't very popular."

Cary held up another, this one depicting a slim girl with carroty hair and demurely folded hands. "Could this be a young Elizabeth?"

Abigail smiled at him. "That, Mr. Wayborn, is Catherine Howard. And this boy here is Edward VI, son of Henry and his third wife, Jane Seymour."

There were several more miniatures in the box that Abigail could not identify, but no Catherine of Aragon. "If you could find *her*, Mr. Wayborn, you would have an enviable collection; King Henry, all six of his wives, and all three of his children. I might value that as high as three thousand pounds."

"I'd sell it in an instant."

"Shall we put Catherine, Mary, and Edward in the table with all the rest?" Abigail moved towards a door, but found that it was locked.

"That door leads out to the gardens," Cary said, leading her to the correct door. "I'd take you, but the grounds aren't much to look at in winter, unless you like brambles and snow. We do have a traditional knot garden that stays green, if you'd like to see that." He smiled to himself, thinking it would be great fun chasing his skittish cousin through the maze.

Abigail demurred because of the snow, which was still falling.

"I suppose eventually I shall put in some modern French windows," he said on the way back to the portrait room with the miniatures. "At Wayborn Hall, where I actually grew up, we have French windows leading out to all the terraces."

"On no account," cried Abigail, quite forcefully, "are you to put in French windows, Mr. Wayborn! You mustn't do anything to compromise the historical integrity of the house."

Cary raised his eyebrows. "It's my house, cousin," he reminded her, laughing.

"But you can't!" cried Abigail. "It would spoil the whole house if you did."

Cary grinned. When provoked, she quite forgot to be shy, as she had when he'd questioned Mr. Coleridge's integrity in Hatchard's Bookshop. "I suppose you think my ancestors were wrong to put in chimneys and staircases when they had perfectly good fire pits and ladders."

"No, of course not," said Abigail. She held strong views on the subject, he could tell, but she struggled to present them effectively, while he, without caring half as much, could talk circles around her. "A chimney is one thing. But to put French windows in a beautiful old Tudor house—! I think that would be a crime, Mr. Wayborn. You ought to be restoring Tanglewood to its original state, not disfiguring it with French windows."

Cary couldn't help laughing. "I told you what it was originally—a cow byre! Do you really want me to restore it to its original state with a bunch of moilies and milkmaids?"

Abigail pressed her lips together. She could not compete with him in open debate, but, in her view, the only way to truly win an argument was to be right, and he was definitely wrong.

Cary couldn't resist teasing her throughout the rest of the first floor rooms, threatening to replace every arched doorway with a French window. Abigail did not once laugh.

"Don't sulk," he finally told her as they came to the main staircase. "I couldn't possibly afford to have French windows put in. The historical integrity, as you call it, is perfectly safe."

Abigail was delighted to see the exposed timbers at intervals in the plaster walls upstairs. In the hall, the plaster had been painted a green that had darkened with age, but clear, lighter areas showed where paintings must have hung until quite recently. She guessed, correctly, that Cary Wayborn was selling off the treasures of the house little by little.

"These are the two best rooms," he said, coming to two doors at the end of the hall. "Since you're my cousin, I think you should have one of them. Mrs. Spurgeon, I suppose, may have the other."

He opened the first door.

It was not a very large room, but Abigail thought it was perfect. The casement window allowed in plenty of light. The paneled walls were painted a creamy white, and the coffered ceiling was decorated with the red and white double rose of the Tudors, symbolizing the union of the Lancasters and the Yorks. The feather bed was set on a huge, intricately carved box of walnut. From its four posts hung red and white crewel-work curtains. The only other furnishings were a large wardrobe against one wall, a small washstand with a mirror, a little chair near the window, and a stone fireplace that, at present, was cold and dark.

"I know this room!" Abigail exclaimed.

"Seen it in a dream, have you?" he teased her. "In novels, the heroine always comes to a room she has seen before in a dream. She usually faints in the arms of the nearest man."

"I recognize it from the painting downstairs," she told him sensibly. "This must be where Lettice Cary sat for her portrait." She pointed at the red and white bed hangings. "She must have sat there, on the bed." It occurred to her all at once that she was alone in a bedroom with a man, and she became rather flustered, to his immense enjoyment.

"I daresay only Lettice and her husband would have known she was sitting on her marriage bed. Apart from the artist, of course." He grinned. "I always thought she looked as though she might fall over backwards at any moment. Now I know why."

"*This* is not original to the room," she said, moving quickly to the wardrobe.

"No," he agreed, "but there's a secret to it I think you'll like."

"What sort of secret?"

"I'll show you," said Cary, opening the heavy carved doors. "There's a secret door in here. If you press it in a certain place, the panel slides back."

"A door to a secret room?" Abigail asked eagerly.

"Not a secret room, more's the pity. Just an ordinary, everyday secret passage between two ordinary, everyday bedrooms." He gave her his wickedest smile.

"But why would anyone want that?" she asked, puzzled. "Why not simply go out into the hall and use the door there? Why go crawling around through somebody's wardrobe? It makes no sense."

"It's all very strange and mysterious to me, too," said Cary, his gray eyes laughing at her innocence. "But I must correct you on one point. One does not go crawling through the wardrobe. It's really quite as comfortable as walking through a doorway." He demonstrated this by stepping inside the wardrobe. "See? I needn't even crouch down."

"But there aren't any clothes hanging in it now," Abigail pointed out. "I imagine it's rather annoying to have to go through a lot of dresses and coats to get through to the other side."

He ignored this unworthy statement. He was busy feeling along the back paneling of the wardrobe for the secret spring. "It's stuck," he said, annoyed. "Warped from the damp, I shouldn't wonder. This never happens in books—the secret panel always slides back at the merest touch of the hero's finger, with a sibilant hiss, I might add." He stopped trying to force the panel open and looked at Abigail. "Give me a hand, will you?"

"Of course," she said, without thinking. Cary doubted the girl had ever refused a direct request for help in her whole life. She was, in fact, such a nice girl in every way that, if he hadn't been so sure that she was going to enjoy what he planned to do, he might not have done it. As soon as she was in the wardrobe with him, he pulled the door tightly closed, sealing them together in the darkness, pulled her close to him with both hands, while at the same time kissing her mouth. Even in the dark, his aim was true.

Abigail felt something warm and furry brushing against her mouth and went berserk. She burst out of the wardrobe, brushing away from her body wholly imaginary vermin. "Mr. Wayborn!" she gasped. "There is a *bat*—or a *rat*—in that wardrobe!"

Once or twice in Cary's life, he had come across a female who, inexplicably enough, did not want to be kissed by him, but none of them had ever resorted to inventing small rodents.

"A rat or a bat," he repeated sourly. "In the wardrobe, you say?"

Abigail jumped onto the bed, frantic for a place of safety. "I felt it touching my face, and then—oh, God! It *moved*."

"There isn't any bat," he said sharply, now quite annoyed.

"There is too a bat," she insisted, treading on the featherbed to keep from falling over. "It's in that wardrobe, and I am *not* coming down from this bed until you find it and kill it!"

Cary began to believe she was serious, which did not improve his temper. No one had ever mistaken his kiss for the attentions of a small flying mammal, and his vanity was wounded. Grimly he climbed out of the wardrobe. "Stand still," he told her angrily. "Close your eyes."

Abigail obeyed. "Oh, God! Is it . . . Is it on me? Is it in my hair?" she whispered weakly.

"Quiet!" He climbed up on the bed next to her. For once she didn't shy away from him. Very gently he took her by the shoulders and tried again, pressing his mouth to her clenched lips.

Abigail's eyes popped open.

"It was not a bat, you silly girl," he told her. "It was me. I was kissing you."

"That's it exactly. That horrid, furry feeling—" Abigail broke off, mortified. "I beg your pardon, sir!" she breathed. "I didn't know it was you. You—you were talking about bats earlier at the Dower House. I'm absolutely terrified of bats, you see."

He sniffed. "I had noticed a slight aversion."

"I thought my heart was going to burst, it was beating so fast," she said, climbing down from the bed. "I do hate them so."

"What? Kisses or bats? I'm not often mistaken for a bat, cousin," he said sharply. "I think you owe me an apology."

"It—it must have been your beard I felt," she explained, growing red in the face. "I'm so sorry, Mr. Wayborn. It's just that it was dark, and I wasn't expecting—" She broke off in confusion. It seemed to her, though perhaps she was wrong, that *he* was the one who ought to be apologizing. After all, she hadn't given him leave to kiss her. She had never given anyone leave to kiss her in her whole life.

"You weren't expecting it," he scoffed. "Isn't this what you came for?"

Abigail stared at him. "What?" she asked in a small voice.

"Why did you come to Hertfordshire? To see me again, that's why. Admit it."

Abigail gasped at the man's unabashed conceit.

"I know when a woman is attracted to me," he said. "You've been staring at me all afternoon. You stammer like an idiot whenever I get within two feet of you, and if your face got any redder, it would be a tomato."

At this moment, Abigail liked Cary about as much as she liked Mrs. Spurgeon's macaw. Indeed, Cato and Mr. Wayborn had a great deal in common. They were both physically beautiful and unforgivably rude. "I did *not* come here to see you again, you conceited ape," she snapped. "You had a house to let. You obviously need the money. I was trying to help you. I had no idea of— of anything else. I thought you were safely married! I came here expecting to meet your wife. I did not expect to be mauled in a wardrobe."

Cary shrugged. "It was only a kiss," he said coolly. "A bit of fun. Most girls enjoy it."

"I am not most girls!"

"Clearly."

Absurdly, Abigail felt rejected. She turned away from him to look out the window. Her chin was going wobbly, and she knew she was about to cry.

"Who in the deuce let that dog up the stairs?" Cary muttered, just as Abigail became aware of a commotion in the hall. In the next moment, the corgi knocked the door open and bounded into the room, barking excitedly, followed closely by a servant girl carrying a jug.

"That wretched cur is not allowed upstairs, Polly," Cary said severely. "He eats the plaster off the walls and hides marrow bones under all the pillows."

"Yes, sir," the girl said. "I've just come to build the fires, sir, and to tell you that the other carriage is stuck halfway up the drive in the snow. The lady says she can't walk, sir. She wants to be carried up to the house in a chair. A *sedan* chair."

Muttering under his breath, Cary left the room.

"I'm Polly, Miss," said the servant, a sturdily built, blue-eyed lass with red cheeks. "I've brought you some hot water." She set the steaming jug on the washstand and closed the doors of the empty wardrobe. "Whatever you do, Miss," she said, giggling, "don't let the master get you in the old press. He got me in there once and the next thing I knew, my skirts was over my head! Of course, he was only eleven at the time and hadn't a clue what to do with me once he got me. I expect it'd be a different story now," she added wistfully.

Abigail washed her face and hands, tuning out Polly's chatter. She could not flatter herself into thinking Cary Wayborn had kissed her because of some powerful attraction; clearly, molesting young women was simply a matter of course with him. She wished she had never come here. Her hero, the gypsy prince who had rescued her in Piccadilly, was no hero at all.

Was there even a secret door, she wondered, leading through the wardrobe to the next room, or had that merely been a ploy to get her inside? When Polly was gone, she went into the wardrobe and felt along the back panel. When she pressed it at the top, it sprang back instantly.

With a sibilant hiss.

Chapter 5

"This takes me back," Mrs. Spurgeon screeched in Cary's ear. "To be in the arms of a handsome young man again—at my age, too! On my wedding night, my dear husband carried me across the threshold. Of course, I was a mere slip of a girl then. I was light as a feather."

"You're still light as a feather, Mrs. Spurgeon," Cary muttered, grunting from the exertion of carrying the stout lady through the portico into the house. He would much rather have been carrying Mrs. Nashe, who was a good three stone lighter and extremely attractive. He tried to set his burden on her feet just inside the door, but the woman clung to him, crying, "Oh! Don't drop me, sir! I break like the finest porcelain when I'm dropped."

As he struggled towards the fireplace, his knees buckling under the lady's weight, he saw Miss Smith enter the room. She looked as though she'd been crying, and he felt a stab of guilt.

He'd behaved very badly. Abigail was the first likely female to come his way in months, and he had pounced on her like a cad. Living alone in the country had left him more desperate than he cared to admit. Indeed, his housekeeper would have been shocked to know the young master had eyed her broad rear end more than once. He was definitely not a monk by nature, and Miss Smith had some right to consider herself ill-used.

All the same, he told himself, it was only a kiss. There was no need for the girl to carry on as if he were the villain of a horrid mystery. It was not as though he had made any serious attempt on her virtue. Frankly, she was behaving like a ninny, and he had no patience for ninnies. He could only hope that Mrs. Nashe would prove more congenial.

"There you are, Miss Smith," Mrs. Spurgeon boomed, catching sight of her ward. "Take my muff. It fell in the snow. It's quite wet. Where's Evans?"

"No, don't!" cried Abigail, darting forward as Cary nearly dumped Mrs. Spurgeon in the chair still occupied by Paggles. He managed to shift to the other chair in time, but lost his balance and fell on top of Mrs. Spurgeon as she landed. His nose lodged briefly in her bosom, and he doubted he would ever get the smell of sweat and talcum out of his nostrils.

"Oh, this *does* remind me of my wedding night," she giggled.

Cary removed her arms from his neck and leaped to his feet, bowling into Miss Smith, who was standing behind him. Fortunately, the footstool broke her fall.

"Pardon me," he said, offering her his hand. She gave him a look of such intense dislike that he flushed, and, withdrawing his hand, he went to help Mrs. Nashe instead. The pretty widow was struggling to carry a very large birdcage nearly filled by a scarlet macaw.

"What a gorgeous bird," he said lightly, looking at the woman, not the bird, as he relieved her of the cage. She looked up at him through her dark lashes, which he took for encouragement. "Is it a canary or a canard?" he asked.

Mrs. Nashe laughed softly. Cary was enchanted by the flirtatious sound.

"Go and find his perch, Evans," Mrs. Spurgeon commanded, and a thin gray woman seemed to materialize at her bidding. Cato caught sight of the lady's maid and shrieked in a fair imitation of his mistress's voice, "Evans! Where's my yellow wig?"

Cary and Mrs. Nashe smiled in shared amusement. The young widow had charming dimples, he noticed, and smooth skin. *She* was not adverse to a little flirtation at any rate.

Abigail was not distracted by the bird's indiscretion. "You are not thinking of letting that *thing* out of its cage!" she cried, jumping up from the footstool.

Cato turned his icy blue gaze upon her. Shuddering, Abigail moved closer to Paggles.

"The cage is too small for him to live in," Mrs. Spurgeon replied. "He's not a lovebird, Miss Smith. He hates being in a cage, don't you, Cato?"

"Lovebird!" cried Cato in a mocking screech that made Abigail's flesh crawl.

"He's quite a talker," Cary said approvingly, noticing with some amusement that the closer he brought the birdcage, the farther away Miss Smith moved. "Friend of mine had a macaw for a while. But it never spoke a word of English—just screamed all day long."

"Cato is a remarkably intelligent bird," said Mrs. Spurgeon proudly. Abigail's was the only voice of dissent, and Mrs. Spurgeon waved her off like a duchess swatting a fly. "Piffle! Cato did not attack you, Miss Smith. He was only being friendly. He's perfectly tame."

"He *bit* me on the ear," Abigail reminded her.

"Mr. Wayborn, do look at Miss Smith's ear and tell me do you see a mark."

Abigail hastily covered both her ears. "Mrs. Spurgeon, I absolutely forbid you to let that bird out of its cage."

In no time at all, Cato was in possession of his freedom and his tall perch. Angelically, he preened his red and blue feathers. Abigail rather huffily took Paggles out of the room, keeping a close eye on the bird as she backed out. Cary and Mrs. Nashe were so enjoying their silent courtship that only Mrs. Spurgeon seemed to notice Miss Smith's departure.

"Silly girl," she said, gazing complacently at her handsome young host, who hastily turned from the younger widow to the elder. "Why Mr. Leighton thought she would suit me I can't think. I was quite relieved when she took herself off to the baggage coach. And that stupid old nurse of hers! I've had quite enough of Miss Smith. I've half a mind to send her packing."

She smiled coquettishly at Cary, but the effect was spoiled entirely when Cato lifted his head and said, quite clearly, "Not my wooden teeth, you fool!"

Cary struggled to keep a straight face. "Here's Mrs. Grimstock," he said, relieved to see the housekeeper. "She'll show you upstairs to your rooms."

"Upstairs?" Mrs. Spurgeon pressed her hand to her breast as though he had suggested she take up residence in Cato's cage. "I'm afraid my legs are far too weak to negotiate stairs, Mr. Wayborn. Unless of course, you would like to carry me up to bed every night," she tittered.

"We do have a few rooms downstairs," Cary said with what he hoped was unruffled calm. "My man's moved most of my things to the gatehouse by now."

"*Your* room, sir?" Mrs. Spurgeon sprang to her feet like a young gazelle. "Do let's see how the man lives, Vera," she cried, forgetting how weak her legs were. "There's nothing I like better than poking about the chambers of a bachelor—one learns the most shocking secrets."

"I assure you, I have no secrets, madam," Cary said stiffly.

"Everyone has secrets, Mr. Wayborn," said she, following him down the hall.

"Oh, yes, indeed!" she cried when she was standing in Cary's room. "This looks to be a comfortable bed! It will do very nicely. What do you have there, sir?" she demanded, as Cary began removing a few things from his desk. "French letters?"

"English bills, mostly," Cary replied, trying to preserve an air of politeness with this impossible woman. He was afraid her coarse, inquisitive comments were going to ruin his budding affair with the attractive nurse, but to his relief, Mrs. Nashe gave him a sympathetic smile. Evidently, it took more than French letters to shock her. But then, he remembered, Vera Nashe was a widow, not a silly virgin who would go into histrionics over a little kiss.

Mrs. Spurgeon went over the room thoroughly, looking into the privy closet and the dressing room with its copper tub. "Evans can sleep in here. I like to have her close by."

"Poor Evans," Cary murmured for Mrs. Nashe's ears alone.

"Is there a room hereabouts for Vera?"

"Poor Vera," Cary murmured, and Mrs. Nashe looked at him with dark glowing eyes, an unmistakably intimate invitation. He felt himself becoming quite excited at the thought of stealing into his own house later that night, creeping through the halls like a burglar, then slipping into bed with a willing woman. With any luck, Vera would be as randy as himself.

"I think I might have something suitable for Mrs. Nashe right down the hall," he said pleasantly, offering Vera his arm, "if not closer at hand."

Alas, Mrs. Spurgeon insisted on seeing the small guest room first. "It's much bigger than your room in London, my dear," she said, "but then, this is a gentleman's country estate. Dower house, indeed! Mr. Leighton would not be so cruel as to put me in a vile little dower house."

"I will leave you to settle in," said Cary, bowing politely. "If you should need anything, you've only to ask. My servants, and, indeed, myself, are at your disposal."

Mrs. Spurgeon held out her large hand. Her bejeweled rings did nothing to soften the masculine effect of hairy knuckles and thick, flat nails. Suppressing his revulsion, Cary kissed it.

Mrs. Spurgeon fluttered her eyes at him and showed him her good ivory dentures. "You *will* come and dine with us tonight, Mr. Wayborn, won't you? I insist! I could not in good conscience send you away to the gatehouse without your supper, after all. If you're afraid to be alone with me, sir, Vera will be there to act as chaperone."

Tonight, he told himself, he would be in full possession of the ravishing Mrs. Nashe. Surely he could endure a few hours in Mrs. Spurgeon's company, when such rewards were promised him afterwards? With a speaking glance to Vera, Cary accepted the invitation.

"And after dinner, whist, of course," said Mrs. Spurgeon, "though it means Miss Smith will have to partner you, Vera. You might as well stay with us, Mr. Wayborn, until it's our bedtime. No sense in your spending a lonely night at the gatehouse like a monk."

"None indeed. You're very kind. I confess I *have* been a monk all this long winter."

"Tonight I insist you break your vows," she cried. "But not yet. Run along now, there's a good boy. Unless, of course, you want to help me change into my evening clothes!"

As Cary went out, he spied Miss Smith carrying a heavy tray upstairs. She exasperated him; as Mrs. Spurgeon's paid companion, she had no business performing the tasks of a menial. "One of the servants will do that for you," he called up to her.

Abigail looked down at him scornfully. "I'm bringing a little soup to my old nurse. I can manage very well, thank you, Mr. Wayborn," she said, continuing on upstairs.

Cary flushed; her last remark seemed to rebuke him for not helping her himself. He was heartily glad she had not responded to his kisses, the priggish little miss. If she had, it would have made things quite awkward between himself and the fascinating Mrs. Nashe.

Almost more irritated with Miss Smith than he was pleased with Mrs. Nashe, he walked down the snowy drive to the gatehouse. A primitive place, it boasted a single room with a ladder leading up to a small loft with a sagging iron bed. The gardener evidently had been using the place as a depository for broken pots and other doubtful rubbish. The fireplace smoked so badly that his tea tasted of soot. There was no convenience, only an earthenware chamberpot, which he sincerely hoped was not cracked like the old brown teapot.

Dressing for dinner was a challenge. The only looking glass in the place was so badly in need of re-silvering that he was compelled to set his dressing case on the mantel and use the tiny mirror set inside the lid to tie his neck cloth.

When he returned for his supper at the appointed time, he found Mrs. Spurgeon awaiting him arrayed in a splendid scarlet gown that ill-advisedly left one brawny shoulder bare. In a shocking upset, her yellow wig had been replaced by a green and gold head-wrap adorned with peacock feathers. Mrs. Nashe was with her, quietly reading. Cary was charmed by Vera's more discreet appearance; she had changed into a simple low-cut gown. It was black, but draped with a sheer silvery muslin that softened the effect of mourning, and her twist of dark hair was held in place with a silver filigree ornament. Her skin looked very white, and would look even whiter when pressed against his own naked flesh.

Miss Smith was not present, but Mrs. Spurgeon, after complimenting her host effusively on his formal evening attire, suggested they go in to dine without her. She took Cary's arm possessively, and Vera followed with Cato, who was soon set up on his perch in the dining room.

When Abigail finally arrived, twenty minutes late, the others were halfway through their soup. Getting Paggles settled in the room next to hers had taken longer than Abigail had expected, and several items that she remembered packing seemed to be missing from her baggage, including all of her silk stockings. She'd been forced to wear heavy woollens under her dinner dress, and stout walking shoes instead of her pretty satin slippers. They made an embarrassing noise on the wooden floor.

She edged into the small dining room cautiously, keeping her eyes fixed on Cato, who was acrobatically hanging upside down from his perch. She was so concerned with the macaw's movements that she scarcely noticed Cary rising from the table to mark her entrance. She had changed into a white dress, and hung a gold locket on a black velvet ribbon around her neck. In the candlelight her curly hair looked a deep golden-orange color and her freckles could hardly be seen. She had done her best, he supposed, but her appearance gave him no cause for regret.

As Abigail slipped into her seat, Cato slowly righted himself on his mahogany perch, looking at the newcomer first with one eye and then the other. He squawked, apparently outraged, as she drew her napkin into her lap. Cary watched, amused, as Miss Smith silently debated whether or not it was worth risking Cato's displeasure to pick up her spoon.

"Your soup is cold, Miss Smith," Mrs. Spurgeon informed her. "We waited for you half an hour, but you really can't expect us to eat cold soup for your sake."

"The turban, you fool!" Cato shrieked at her.

"Take the soup back to Cook; have it warmed," Cary murmured to the nearest servant.

"No, indeed," said Mrs. Spurgeon. "It's quite her own fault for being late. Quite your own fault for being late," she loudly repeated for Abigail's benefit.

"I don't care for any soup, thank you."

Cato heard Abigail's voice and called out to her sweetly, "Beaks and claws!"

Cary had remained standing. "Would you like a glass of Madeira, Miss Smith?"

"Yes, please," she answered without interrupting her surveillance of Cato, but, as he began mixing the wine with water, she looked at him. "What are you doing? Is that *water*?"

"Of course it's water," said Mrs. Spurgeon severely. "A lady does not drink wine straight from the bottle, Miss Smith."

"I must say, I've never been offered wine, then given pink water," said Abigail.

"Then you are not a lady," Mrs. Spurgeon explained solicitously.

Cary was embarrassed for Miss Smith; Mrs. Nashe concealed her smile behind a napkin.

"It seems to me," said Abigail, "that our Portuguese friends have gone to a great deal of trouble to make the wine. I see no reason to spoil it with water."

"Portuguese friends!" cried Mrs. Spurgeon, as though the two things were incompatible. "Do you have *Portuguese* friends, Miss Smith? I certainly don't. All my friends are *English*."

"Portugal was our ally in the war, Mrs. Spurgeon," Abigail said angrily.

Mrs. Spurgeon remained indefatigably insular. "And I don't know what your nasty foreign friends have to do with Mr. Wayborn's lovely Madeira."

"Madeira is a Portuguese wine," Abigail coldly explained.

"Swine?" Cato echoed uncertainly.

"Mr. Wayborn, is this true?" cried Mrs. Spurgeon, aghast. "I couldn't possibly drink a *foreign* wine, sir. I must have *English* wine—by my doctor's order. Haven't you got any claret, or a nice Beaujolais?"

"The only thing the English have ever managed to bottle is gin," said Abigail, "and I hardly call *that* fit to drink."

"Perfectly dreadful in tea," Cary agreed easily, winking at Vera.

"But Portuguese wine," said Mrs. Spurgeon, unhappily.

"I think it's very patriotic of Mr. Wayborn to serve Madeira," said Mrs. Nashe. "I, for one, will never drink French wine again."

"French swine?" Cato inquired politely.

"Her husband was killed by the French at Ciudad Rodrigo," Mrs. Spurgeon called down the length of the table. "It's given her a loathing of all things *francaise.*"

"Good God," said Cary, looking at Vera. "I was at Ciudad Rodrigo."

Abigail sniffed. "*You* were at Ciudad Rodrigo? The *battle*?"

Cary frowned at her. "Indeed, Miss Smith. I saw it from the infantry. The ranks."

Mrs. Spurgeon goggled at him. "The ranks? You mean, you were not an *officer*?"

"No, ma'am. My elder brother wouldn't buy me my colors, but I wanted to do my part for England, so I left Oxford and enlisted in the ranks as Mr. John Smith."

"Smith!" said Abigail.

He looked back at her. "Naturally, Smith. When I want a false name, I always go with Smith. I reach for it again and again. So you see, we really *are* cousins."

"Some people *are* called Smith, you know," said Abigail, her cheeks red.

"A great many, or so I understand," he agreed. "That is chiefly what makes it such a useful *nom de guerre*. When one calls oneself Silas Tomkyn Comberbache, one finds oneself subjected to uncomfortable amounts of scrutiny."

"Good heavens," Mrs. Spurgeon murmured as the soup was withdrawn and the entree brought in. "I hope this is not mutton, Mr. Wayborn. I have a very small, sensitive stomach. It cannot digest mutton. If this be mutton, sir, I shall be quite ill. I shall vomit!"

"It's veal, Mrs. Spurgeon," Cary hastily assured her, "which, as I'm sure you must know, allows one to enjoy the taste and appearance of mutton, without risking the old indijaggers."

He was, Abigail noted, an exceptionally charming liar.

"And what did you study at Oxford, sir?" Mrs. Nashe asked presently in her quiet voice.

Cary smiled at her. "Promise you won't laugh? My brother thought I was suited for a career in the Church. He was mistaken, of course."

"I don't know about that," said Mrs. Spurgeon. "Where's it written that a good-looking man can't be a fine clergyman? I'd rather be damned by a man like you, Mr. Wayborn, than consecrated by that grinning disfigurement, the Archbishop of Canterbury."

"Thank you, Mrs. Spurgeon," he replied. "But I could never bring myself to excommunicate a woman. It was one of the things that made me so unsuitable for the Church."

Abigail snorted.

Cary turned to Mrs. Nashe. "What was your husband's regiment? Perhaps I knew him."

"He was with the cavalry, sir. Lieutenant Arthur Nashe."

Cary frowned. "That's odd. I don't remember having cavalry at Ciudad Rodrigo."

Mrs. Nashe hastily covered her eyes with her napkin. Her shoulders shook with grief.

"You were in the ranks, sir," Abigail angrily pointed out. "You had no way of knowing what the cavalry were doing! I daresay Wellington made his plans without consulting you."

Cary was dismayed, to say the least. "My dear Mrs. Nashe," he said quietly, "do forgive me if I've offended you in any way. I never meant—I must have been thinking of Badajoz."

Mrs. Nashe turned her head to one side and sobbed outright. Cary grimaced as if in pain. As much as he disliked tears and hysterics, he felt guilty for having induced them with such a blunder. In his London days, he had charmed women with ease, but in rustic exile, his skills seemed to have rusted over. In the space of an afternoon, he had met two attractive females, driven one to scorn, and the other to tears.

Mrs. Nashe smiled at him through her tears, which somehow made it worse. "It's just that I can't bear talking about it, you see," she bravely explained. "*Dear* Arthur! How he suffered!"

"One might think *you* were Portuguese, Vera," Mrs. Spurgeon observed, "the way you carry on. Eat your veal. If he were here, your husband would not approve of these hysterics."

"I beg you will excuse me, Mrs. Spurgeon," gasped Vera, her face red.

Perhaps it was selfish of him, but, as the pretty widow fled the room, all Cary could think was that he would definitely not be welcome in her bed that night. If only things hadn't gone so wrong with Miss Smith. She did look rather fetching in her white dress.

Perhaps he could get back into her good graces . . . ?

"Well done, sir!" Abigail snapped, throwing down her napkin and running after Vera.

"Come and sit by me, Mr. Wayborn," Mrs. Spurgeon cooed, her good ivory teeth glinting in the candlelight. "The fire's so warm, I scarcely need my shawl," she added, flinging off that article to expose the immense powdered shoulder of a sibyl. "So it's to be piquet after dinner, instead of whist. Oh, well. I think you'll find me a worthy opponent, if the stakes are high enough. What shall we play for, hmm?"

Cary stifled a groan. I'm cursed, he thought, as Mrs. Spurgeon heaved her bosom at him.

Abigail quietly knocked on Mrs. Nashe's door. "I was wondering if you might like some tea, Vera," she called. "You didn't eat very much. Would you like a tray?"

Vera surprised her by opening the door. "I'm really quite all right," she said, smiling bravely. "You mustn't fuss over me, dear. I'm just being silly."

"I don't think you're being silly," Abigail said quietly.

"Of course I am. If Arthur were here, he'd say the same. Stiff upper lip. Life goes on."

"It was unforgivably rude of Mr. Wayborn to say he didn't remember there being cavalry at Ciudad Rodrigo! Of course there were cavalry. Our host is not a very nice person, I'm afraid. I'm heartily sorry I brought us all here."

"*You* brought us here, Miss Smith?" Vera's dark eyes widened in surprise.

"Yes," Abigail said, wringing her hands guiltily. "It is all my doing, but, you see, when I met him in

London, I thought he was . . . Well, I thought him quite perfect, actually."

"But he isn't?" Vera smiled gently. "Most men aren't, you know."

"He was so kind and helpful. I thought I'd met a Knight of the Round Table, right there in Piccadilly. But I was mistaken. He led me to believe he was married, when in fact, he isn't."

Vera blinked at her in confusion. "You mean he led you to believe he was *not* married when, in fact, he *is*. That *is* dreadful."

"No, no," said Abigail. "He's not married at all, but he made me think he was."

"Indefensible," said Vera, hiding a smile.

"Indeed. If I'd known he was a bachelor, I should never have trusted him! I should never have come here. Forgive me, but I must warn you, Mrs. Nashe. He's already tried kissing me, and you're quite five times as pretty as I am. You mustn't let him get you alone."

Mrs. Nashe laughed softly. "He reminds me so much of Arthur. Sinfully handsome, but perhaps just a little . . . impulsive. I never loved him any less for that. Tell me, Miss Smith, do you think I might get away with hiding in my room the rest of the evening? I absolutely loathe playing cards with that old witch."

"Leave it to me," Abigail assured her. "Are you certain I can't do anything for you?"

"Quite certain. But perhaps there is something I can do for *you*." Vera looked rather pointedly at Abigail's heavy walking shoes. "I've a pair of evening slippers I could lend you."

Abigail laughed. "You're very kind, but I seem to have forgotten to pack any stockings. All I have are my woollies. No, please!" she said, as Mrs. Nashe went to the trunk that sat open on the bureau in her room. "I'll be able to buy stockings in the village tomorrow."

Mrs. Nashe pressed the white silk stockings on her. "We're bound to be snowed in, by the looks of it," she said. "We can't have you tramping through the house in those clunky boots like a bailiff! I wonder," she said, as though experiencing a sudden thought. "We stopped at any number of inns today. Do you think someone could have gone through your belongings?"

"And taken my stockings?" Abigail laughed aloud. "Heavens, no. There's a much simpler explanation. My nurse Paggles is quite absent-minded, I'm afraid. When I was packing, I caught her several times taking things out and putting them away. When she saw the trunks out at home, she got it in her head that we'd only just arrived, and I couldn't convince her we were actually going away." She glanced down at the stockings Mrs. Nashe had given her. "Just my sort, too. From Daughtry's in Jermyn Street?"

"Where else?"

"You're so kind. I'll tell the others that you're lying down with a sick headache and you're not to be disturbed."

"Good night, Miss Smith."

Abigail ran upstairs to put the borrowed stockings away, then checked on Paggles in the next room, using the door in the hall, not the secret panel in the wardrobe; Paggles would likely die of fright if someone suddenly jumped out of her wardrobe. She found the old woman snoring contentedly in the four-poster bed, with Mr. Wayborn's corgi nestled at her feet. She built up the fire, pulled the blankets up to Paggles's chin, then went back down to the dining room.

Mrs. Spurgeon had moved as close as she could to Cary, who was seated at the head of the table, with Cato's perch beside him. "Beaks and claws," Cato greeted Abigail coyly.

"So you have come back, Miss Smith," Mrs. Spurgeon observed without pleasure.

"Only because I'm hungry," Abigail retorted, slipping into her seat.

"And thirsty, too, no doubt." Disentangling Mrs. Spurgeon from his arm, Cary poured Madeira into a crystal goblet. "Take this to Miss Smith," he told the servant.

As Abigail took her wine from the servant's tray, Cato suddenly swooped from his perch and flew down the length of the table towards her. For a moment, Abigail could only stare in horror, then, hastily and ignominiously, she sought refuge under the table, overturning her chair in the process, and pouring half the Madeira down the front of her dress. The clatter of her falling chair was completely lost in the chaos that followed.

Where Angel had been hiding she had no idea; she had thought the corgi was upstairs in Paggles's room. Evidently he had slipped out before she had closed the door, then followed her silently downstairs. He appeared now, as if from thin air, and it was the macaw's turn to be terrified as, instead of finding his favorite victim at the end of the table, he suddenly encountered a dog that had no fear of him.

Cato had no words in his vocabulary to express his feelings on the occasion. He could only squawk, shriek, and scream as he narrowly escaped Angel's jaws. Hastily he took flight, beating his wings in a disorderly retreat. As the corgi snarled at him, Cato crashed onto the massive iron chandelier hung above the table. Gobbets of candle wax fell onto the leg of "veal" as the chandelier tipped dangerously then righted itself beneath the bird. Angel barked, and Cato screamed back in undisciplined argument.

Mrs. Spurgeon added her piercing voice to the confusion of animal noises. "Mr. Wayborn! *What* is that uncivilized beast doing in here?"

Abigail heard Cary push back his chair. In the next moment, he was down on all fours, looking under the table at her. She looked back at him as defiantly as she could through the bottom of her glass as she finished the Madeira.

"More wine, cousin?"

"Mr. Wayborn, that wicked bird belongs in a cage!"

"I'm inclined to agree with you," he said, cursing under his breath as he bumped his head on the table. "Would you be so kind as to take the dog out? I'll manage the bird. Or are you frightened of dogs as well?" As he spoke, he shoved the snarling corgi under the table.

"No, indeed," said Abigail, scooping Angel up with real affection. "Best dog ever!"

Over their heads, they could hear Mrs. Spurgeon threatening to climb up on her chair to rescue her darling boy. Abigail crawled out from under the table while Cary emerged from the other side. Cato spied Abigail, but with Angel tucked under one arm, the tender morsel was unassailable. He shrieked in frustrated rage.

"Good boy," Abigail murmured lovingly to the corgi, stopping to pick up her plate. "Be so good as to serve me a little more veal," she told an obliging servant.

Outside, the moonlight on the snow was so beautiful that she scarcely felt the cold. The stillness reminded her of one of Mr. Coleridge's early poems, "Frost at Midnight." Content with her lot, she sat down on the bench in the shelter of the portico and shared her "veal" with Angel. "You are the best dog in the whole world," she told him very sincerely as he licked the plate.

Her guardian angel did not remain faithful to her for long. He soon caught sight of a rabbit in the distance and shot out of the portico like a cannonball, his short legs barely able to keep his head out of the snow. From the back end, he looked rather like a rabbit himself, Abigail thought, as the front door swung open.

"Cato's been captured," Cary announced, pressing a handkerchief to his badly scratched hand. "We've reached a compromise. Cato will not be caged, but he will be confined to my study. He'll be in no one's way there, and Mrs. Spurgeon can use it for a sitting room, if she likes. If you would like to come back in, I think I can vouch for your safety."

"Thank you, but I don't mind the cold. I'm quite happy where I am."

He looked out towards the woodlands beyond his lawn. Icicles hung in the branches, chased in silver by the moonlight. "The Frost performs its secret ministry, unhelped by any wind," he murmured.

"I didn't think you liked Coleridge," she said, surprised.

He sat down on the bench across from her and leaned forward. He hadn't come out to talk poetry with the girl. "Look here," he said abruptly. "What would you do if the Spurgeon sent you away? Where would you go?"

"What do you mean?" she asked, puzzled. "How could she send me away?"

"She's awfully fond of that bloody bird, and he certainly hates you, my dear. I think it very likely she'll be sending you back to London as soon as the roads are cleared up."

"You seem to think Mrs. Spurgeon has some power over me."

He looked at her sharply. "Is she not your employer?"

Abigail's mouth fell open.

"There's no shame in finding employment as a companion. Mrs. Spurgeon is a waking nightmare, but she *is* respectable. Come, come, Miss Smith," he said impatiently. "Now is not the time for false pride. We're cousins, after all. I know you don't have much money. I know your father is the rudest man in Dublin. Are you running away from him? Is that it?"

"My father is not the rudest man in Dublin," Abigail exclaimed, startled.

"I expect the title is passed from man to man with great frequency."

"My father is the best man I know!" she said. "I am not a servant, sir. I am not in danger of—of losing my place. I don't require any assistance from you. And I'm not Irish."

"You are—forgive me—socially awkward, sexually backward, and a glutton for whisky. But if you tell me you're not Irish, naturally, I take your word for it," he said, shrugging.

"That is very good of you, I'm sure!" said Abigail, climbing to her feet.

"Don't go on my account," he said pleasantly, "unless, of course, it's time for Mrs. Spurgeon's foot-bath."

"I told you, I'm not her servant," said Abigail, growing red in the face.

"Then stay," he invited her. "I think we ought to be friends, don't you? You're not still sulking because I kissed you? I said I was sorry. Can't you get over it?"

Abigail bristled. "No, you didn't. You never said you were sorry. You were stupid and rude. Just the sort of rude, stupid person who'd put French windows in a house like this!"

"You know," he said thoughtfully, "you really ought to be thanking me."

"Indeed?"

"I seem to have cured you of your stammer," he pointed out.

Abigail looked away angrily. He *still* had not apologized.

"Tell you what, cousin. I'll let you make it up to me

tomorrow. There's going to be ice skating down at the Tudor Rose. Go and fetch your second best pair of boots."

"And why would I do that?" she snapped.

"I couldn't ask you to spoil your best boots," he patiently explained. "The blacksmith's going to put skating blades on them. Go on. Hurry up. I'll wait for you here."

"You actually expect me to go to a skating party with you?" she said incredulously.

"Yes, of course. You couldn't possibly go to the inn without an escort. Run and get your boots, there's a good girl. I haven't got all night."

"I am not going skating with you," said Abigail. "I don't even like skating. Or you!"

"I'll teach you to like both," he said kindly. "It'll be fun. And I promise not to kiss you, if that's what you're worried about. I'll be a perfect gentleman."

Angel suddenly bounded into the portico and dropped a dead rabbit at Abigail's feet. "Augh!" she said. Angel looked up at her, puzzled by this strange reaction to his handsome gift.

"I hope you like rabbit stew, cousin."

"You can always tell Mrs. Spurgeon it's veal," she said tartly.

No doubt insulted by their lack of enthusiasm, the proud little corgi picked up his rabbit and dragged it away, leaving a bloody trail in the snow.

Cary sighed. "Would you like to buy a dog, Miss Smith?"

"Good night, Mr. Wayborn."

She was gone. Feeling underappreciated, Cary started for the gatehouse. He had scarcely progressed ten feet in the knee-deep snow when he heard a window opening behind him, followed by a piercing whistle that elicited a sympathetic howl from the corgi.

Cary nearly laughed aloud as a pair of leather boots

with their laces tied together came flying out of the open window, landing at his feet in the snow. Angel abandoned his grisly prize to investigate the new arrival. By the time Cary retrieved Abigail's boots, the window had closed and there was no sign of Miss Smith.

"She can't resist me," he explained to Angel, who had been thoroughly unhinged by the girl's flying shoes and was rushing here and there in the snow, barking, in case other shoes got similar ideas. "No woman can."

Chapter 6

Cary awoke the next morning in such a cheerful, springtime mood that the sight of snow outside his window startled him. The sagging bed had left him with a stiff neck, the fire had died of damp in the night, and the stone walls of the gatehouse were like blocks of rough-hewn ice, but nothing could shake his sense of well-being. He put it down to the excellent dream he'd had, in which Miss Smith had been made to admit, from the church pulpit, no less, that his kisses in no way reminded her of the nocturnal order of Chiroptera. She'd then apologized to him privately and in the most delightful manner. Her contrition was so touching that he generously had allowed her to make amends. She'd proved to be surprisingly good at making amends.

One handsome concession deserves another, he decided. He went outside for a bowl of fresh snow. After melting it over his smoking fire, he resolutely took up his razor. Miss Smith had tossed her shoes out of the window to him, and the least he could do was shave off the beard she found so offensive. Then they could go skating, and this time, when he kissed her, there would be no talk of bats.

In walking to the village, he discovered that the worst of the snow had been cleared from the road. This was good; he'd be able to drive Miss Smith to the Tudor Rose, giving his cousin the opportunity to admire his horses as well as his own skill in handling them. He whistled all the way to the blacksmith's, then strolled to the Tudor Rose to order his breakfast while the smith modified Miss Smith's boots with skating blades. The inn's back garden, which went down to the banks of the frozen river, was already filling up with skaters. Cary took a seat at one of the planked tables outside and watched a group of children skate. Mr. Temple, the well-meaning young curate, seemed to be in a position of authority over the energetic youngsters. He greeted Cary with deference; when the Vicar of Tanglewood Green shuffled off the mortal coil, the living at the parsonage would be in Mr. Wayborn's gift.

When Cary had eaten, he collected Miss Smith's skates at the smithy, hung them about his neck by their laces, and headed home. As he crossed the stone bridge that marked the edge of his property, he was surprised to see Miss Smith herself on the riverbank. She was sitting on a rock that had been hewn into a rough bench, a red horse blanket spread underneath her skirts, and she appeared to be drawing or painting on a lap desk. Though she had only apologized to him in a dream, he found he had quite forgiven her. He waved to her, but she pretended to ignore him, a useless subterfuge as she obviously was painting the bridge under his feet. As he crossed the bridge and trotted closer, his own short-legged dog bounded out of the snow and barked at him.

Miss Smith could no longer ignore Mr. Wayborn's approach. Indeed, the way she stared at his clean-shaven face was very gratifying to his male pride. He walked straight over to her, bent at the waist, and planted a firm kiss on her mouth before she knew what was what. He just couldn't resist. Predictably, she blushed.

"Good morning, Cousin!" He grinned at her, doffing his hat for good measure. "I see your guardian Angel has been with you all this time."

The kiss had happened so fast that Abigail couldn't be sure it had actually happened at all. He would have to be a madman to simply walk over to her and kiss her, she decided. Then again, she would have to be mad to imagine such a thing. As she could scarcely ask him to clarify matters—"I beg your pardon, sir, but did you by any chance just kiss me?"—she decided her best course of action was to ignore the entire disgraceful episode, real or imagined.

"He . . . was waiting for me when I came out," she stammered.

"There's something different about me," he prompted her. "The old ornament of my cheek hath already stuff'd tennis balls, to paraphrase Shakespeare."

"What?" she said, unable to comprehend him.

"I have shaved my beard."

"Oh, I see," she said, resolutely returning her attention to her work. She was painting in watercolors and melted snow. The paintbox set on her lap was very new and clever. The lid was designed to convert into a miniature easel, and there were tiny china dishes for water and for mixing colors. She wore gloves with the fingertips snipped off, the better to grip her brushes.

He looked over her shoulder at the picture she was painting. She tilted her head instinctively, as though afraid to leave her neck exposed to him. "Not going very well, is it?" he said compassionately. "Your bridge is in grave danger of falling down, cousin. Had I seen your picture beforehand, I should never have used said bridge to cross yon river."

Painting a winter-white landscape was certainly a challenge, but Abigail felt she had a good command of the problem she had set for herself. "But I'm not trying to paint the bridge, Mr. Wayborn," she told him.

"In that case, you have succeeded handsomely, and I withdraw all criticism."

Abigail tried to explain. "I've given myself a test. I'm trying to capture the light by painting only colors and shapes, not things. The bridge is of no interest to me."

"Well, it's of interest to me," he said. "It's my bridge. As for colors, it's all white today, even the sun and the sky. Perfect day for a skating party," he hinted.

"No, you're wrong," said Abigail. "There's scarcely any white at all, when you look carefully. There are grays and blues, violets, and purples, and even yellows."

"Purple snow? My dear Miss Smith, have you been out here tippling whisky?"

Abigail angrily put her brushes away and closed up her paintbox, not caring that her picture was still wet. Why was it she had such difficulty explaining even simple things to him? She hated explanations, anyway; she would much rather be left alone. "It's time I went back to the house," she announced. "I've not had my breakfast."

"I've had mine already," he said. "Have yours while I look for my skates. I think they must be in the cupboard under the back stairs, with the fishing tackle. We've not had a hard freeze like this in five years."

"Your skates are hanging around your neck," said Abigail, dropping her paintbox. The lid fell open, spilling tubes of paint onto the snow. She hastily began shoving everything back in.

"These are not my skates," he told her, kneeling down to help her. "They're yours."

Abigail gulped. His face was just inches from hers and she was now certain she must have imagined that kiss. There was no possible way this beautiful man would ever kiss her again after her absurd behavior on the previous day. She imagined it would be quite a different experience if he did, now that his beard was gone. She could actually see his lips.

"*My* skates?" she stammered. "I haven't any skates."

He scowled at her. "You haven't changed your mind about going skating with me? Look here, I deliberately postponed my morning business to take you skating."

She stared at him in surprise. "I can't think why. I never agreed to go skating with you."

Cary began to laugh; the girl's pretense was so outrageous. "You certainly did!"

Abigail summoned her dignity. Handsome or not, he wasn't going to get away with lying and bullying. He was not her father, after all. "I said no, Mr. Wayborn," she said, employing more icy civility than he thought strictly necessary. "By that I meant absolutely not, under no circumstances, and out of the question."

"You may have said no, absolutely not, under no circumstances, and out of the question," he conceded. "But then you whistled for my attention and tossed your shoes to me from the window! This is what's known in the Royal Academy of Science as a contradiction."

Abigail gaped at him, infuriated. "I think perhaps your vanity has caused you to hallucinate, Mr. Wayborn! You know perfectly well I did no such thing."

Cary grimaced; in his dream, she'd been nothing but sweet, rational, and compliant. "I have the shoes to prove it," he pointed out. "They hang about me like Mr. Coleridge's albatross!"

"My shoes!" Abigail exclaimed in dismay. "You've put blades on them, too. How dare you go into my room and take my shoes! Who do you think you are?"

"Go into your room?" he repeated, his face growing hot. "You tossed them out of the window at me, you little . . ." He caught himself in time. "You led me to believe we had an appointment, then you dash all my hopes with buckets of cold water."

"I daresay you will find someone else to go skating with you!"

"But I want *you*, cousin," he said, in his best sincere manner.

"You'd be just as happy to escort Mrs. Nashe," she accused him.

The justness of the charge caused him to lose his temper. "Possibly even happier," he said coolly. "But I shouldn't mind taking you instead."

Abigail's face turned red as a broiled tomato. She began to stammer. "You insufferable . . . conceited . . . vile . . . Shall I tell you what I really think of you?"

"Don't I look interested?"

"If you were a painting," said Abigail, her eyes flashing, "I could sit and stare at you all day long with the greatest of pleasure."

"Thank you, Cousin. That is most gratifying."

"But you are not a painting!"

"No, I'm not," he politely agreed. "I never was."

Silently fuming, Abigail grabbed her paintbox and stalked towards the house as fast as her long skirts and the snow would permit her to go, leaving her blanket behind on the rock. Cary did not deign to pick it up. Nor did he open the door for her when she achieved the portico; but he did whistle a pleasant tune as he waited for her to do so. Abigail tucked her box under one arm and stormed inside.

"I did not invite you in, sir," said Abigail, already halfway to the staircase door as he made his way to the big fireplace in the entrance hall.

His lip curled. "I'm paying a morning call to my tenant, Mrs. Spurgeon. Besides," he added, pointing to Angel as the corgi hopped onto one of the fireside chairs, "I have to collect my dog. Don't let me keep you, Cousin."

She didn't. She closed the door firmly behind her and he could hear her heavy boots on the stairs. He sighed. Why he should want to kiss a girl who walked like a gouty Cumberland carriage horse was beyond him, but he could not deny that it was so.

He was joined shortly thereafter by Vera Nashe. The widow was looking extremely fetching in a clinging gown of sheer black muslin layered over white. He wanted to kiss her, too. She so graciously returned his pleasantries that he even entertained a short-lived hope of renewing their flirtation.

"Do please forgive my unseemly outburst of last night," she said, looking at him through her dark lashes as he bent over her hand. "I'm quite ashamed of myself."

"My dear Mrs. Nashe," he began fervently.

She did not allow him to finish. "I'll tell Miss Smith you're here to take her skating," she said, snatching her hand away. "She will be delighted, I'm sure."

Cary grimaced. "I've already informed her myself, Mrs. Nashe. But she says she will not go. Could I not persuade you to go in her place?" He gave her his most charming smile.

Mrs. Nashe's injured eyes reminded him that it was neither politic nor polite to ask one female to take the place of another, and he silently cursed himself. "I don't mean to imply that you and Miss Smith are interchangeable," he said, stumbling from one blunder into another.

She gave him an inscrutable smile. "No?"

"Rather, I would be as glad of your company as I would be of hers. Gladder still."

The compliment seemed lost on Vera Nashe. "Can you not persuade *Miss Smith* to go?" she gently inquired. "It would do her good, I think, to be amongst other young people. She is shy, of course, but not timid.

We cannot allow her to live like a hermit crab. I depend upon you, sir, to draw her out of her shell."

No woman had ever fobbed Cary Wayborn off onto another, and he didn't like it. His glorious morning was fast becoming a grim nightmare.

"I don't know how to draw our hermit from her shell without being snapped in two by her claws," he said, trying not to show Vera how much her rejection had stung his pride.

"I daresay you'll manage," Vera told him. "I quite consider I've done my part by tossing her shoes out of the window. I see you had blades put on. The rest is up to you, sir."

Cary stared at her. "*You* tossed the shoes?"

Vera laughed softly. "Forgive me. I heard the two of you talking outside. I could tell the poor girl wanted to go skating with you, but she was determined to allow her pride to get in the way of a good thing. Poor Miss Smith. When she met you in London, I'm afraid she mistook you for Sir Galahad, the most gentle, perfect knight of the Round Table! It was quite a blow to her when she discovered her idol had feet of clay."

"I perceive that Miss Smith has been confiding in you, madam," Cary said stiffly.

She raised an eyebrow. "The kiss? Yes, she told me. Do go easy on the poor child, Mr. Wayborn! I daresay all she knows of men could be fitted into a nutshell, and when a girl is in a state of helpless innocence, a kiss is quite enough to sweep her away. As I'm sure you know."

Cary frowned. If word got out that his kiss had been mistaken for a bat's clumsy attack, he would very quickly become a laughingstock. Months of cursed celibacy would stretch into years, until, out of sheer desperation, he would be forced to wed one of the plump Mickleby girls.

Vera left him with a friendly warning. "You have

about twenty minutes to make your escape, Mr. Wayborn, if you wish to do so without meeting my mistress. Mrs. Spurgeon is a puzzle Evans and I put together twice a day, and it takes us precisely twenty minutes to do it. She's just getting out of bed now."

The image of the Spurgeon's Herculean proportions climbing out of his bed caused Cary to shudder uncontrollably. He doubted he'd ever be able to sleep in that bed again without thinking of the lady's manly shoulders and sweaty, powdered cleavage. Quickly, he rang the bell for a servant, and issued a summons for Miss Smith.

Once it was revealed that Mrs. Nashe was the shoe-throwing culprit, Miss Smith would be forced to ask his forgiveness for accusing him of taking her shoes. It would then be child's play to convince her to go out with him. An inexperienced skater, she would naturally be forced to cling to him on the ice, which would afford him ample opportunity to make himself agreeable. In any case, he infinitely preferred Miss Smith's scorn to Mrs. Spurgeon's disgusting familiarity.

As he waited for the young woman, he became aware of a flurry of activity going on elsewhere in the house. At first the sounds were faint; he heard feet moving back and forth on the floor above him, going up and down various staircases. Voices mumbled behind this door and that. Finally, the hall door opened and Miss Smith came in wringing her hands. She had taken off her cloak. Her green plaid dress clashed resoundingly with her butterscotch hair, and her boots made a lot of noise. Angel ran to greet her.

Cary was struck again by his own physical reaction to her. She was not at all his usual sort of girl, and yet the attraction was inescapable. Not even her ugly dress could put him off. She glanced at him, looked away, and paced up the room, turning indecisively.

"May I be of some assistance to you, Cousin?" he inquired pleasantly.

Miss Smith looked at him. Clearly, she would have preferred eating a dog's dinner to speaking to him. "Mr. Wayborn, sir," she began haltingly, then halted altogether.

"I am listening, Miss Smith." He smiled at her encouragingly.

She stumbled on. "I think we must—Do you suppose you could—?"

"Find it in my heart to forgive you? Well, perhaps, but where's my incentive?"

Abigail was in too much distress to be baited. "Sir! I can't find Paggles anywhere," she said. "Would you be good enough to instigate a search of the house and grounds?"

"You would like me to instigate a search for Paggles?" he said slowly.

"Yes. Sir, I beg of you—"

"Certainly," he replied, getting to his feet. "You had only to beg. It would be helpful, however, if you could tell me what a paggle is. And how many have you let loose in my house?"

Her face whitened. "Miss Paggles is my old nurse," she said coldly.

"Just the one, then. And you have misplaced her? Pretty careless of you."

He had misjudged the extent of her anxiety. "I have not misplaced her," she shouted at him. "She was still abed when I went out. Now she's nowhere to be found. None of the servants have seen her. If she has gone out, she hasn't got her coat, nor her shoes. I wish you would take this seriously, Mr. Wayborn. She could be hurt, and it's cold out."

"Yes, all right. Steady on, Smith. Take me to her room."

"She's not *in* her room!" cried Abigail, maddened by

his insouciant attitude. "I've searched the upstairs thoroughly. If she were in her room, *I* should not be *here*."

"It seems reasonable to begin our search where the missing party was last seen," he gently explained. "She can't have gone far, and—forgive me—I think I know my own house better than you do. Take me to her room," he repeated firmly, and this time Abigail meekly obeyed.

Paggles's room was the mirror image of Abigail's room next door, down to the red and white bed hangings and the Tudor roses on the ceiling. "Ah-ha!" Cary cried, as soon as Abigail had opened the door.

"What?" cried Abigail, her heart in her throat.

"Nothing. I do find it interesting, however, that you put your nurse in the room next to yours. Most people put their servants in the attics with the spiders. Do try to stay calm, Cousin. We've never lost a Paggles at Tanglewood Manor, and we never will."

"Do you think she went through the wardrobe into my room?" Abigail inquired anxiously as he opened the big clothes press.

"Too full of clothes. A weasel couldn't get through. Besides, if *I* can't get it open—"

"But it's really quite easy, if you touch it just so," said Abigail, demonstrating how easily the back panel that separated Paggles's clothes from her own could be made to disappear.

The sibilant hiss set Cary's teeth on edge. Muttering under his breath, he went to the casement window. "Was this window open or closed?"

"Closed." Abigail rushed to the window, pressing her forehead against the thick, leaded panes in an effort to see below. "Do you think she might have fallen out?"

"Not if it was closed. She could hardly fall out, then close the window behind her."

"The wind might have blown it shut after," Abigail said defensively.

"You're right," he said, opening the casement and looking down into the walled garden. The black stalks of the rosebushes were sheathed in ice, the fountain was frozen, and a gardener's boy was shoveling snow from the path. "No sign of a broken nurse."

Abigail leaned out of the window next to him. "Have you seen my nurse?" she called to the boy. "Older woman, white-haired, dressed in a nightgown?" The reply was negative.

"You know," said Cary, closing the window, "she might have just slipped out the back door for a bit of a walk. How can you be sure she had neither coat nor shoes?"

"Because I hadn't put them on her yet," Abigail replied. "She was still in bed when I went out. She always waits for me."

He hid a smile. "And do you always dress your old nurse?"

"She can no longer do it herself," Abigail explained. "She's rather special to me, you see. She was the only servant to come away with my mother from Westlands when she married my father. She's been with me my whole life."

He suddenly snapped his fingers. "I know just where she's gone."

"Where? Tell me, please."

He caught her by the hand. "Where do old nurses go, after all?" he said, leading her down the hall to a door. "To the nursery, of course. Just as I thought," he said, opening the door. The light was very dim, but Abigail could make out a set of narrow stairs clearly intended for use by the servants. "Footprints in the dust. You're quite right, Cousin; she hasn't got her shoes."

Impatiently, Abigail pushed past him, running upstairs. The door to the nursery stood half-open. She went in, calling for her nurse. Carousel horses had been painted on the planked floor, but the light coming through the huge, cheerful windows had long since faded their bright colors. In a square of warm light, Paggles was seated in a rocking chair cradling a china-faced doll in her arms. Overwhelmed with relief, Abigail choked back a sob.

Paggles's smile, though almost toothless, was lovely with contentment. "Good morning, Miss Abby. And Dickie-bird!" she added brightly as Cary came up behind Abigail. "How good of you to visit your old nursery. Such a good boy."

"Dickie-bird?" Cary murmured in Abigail's ear. "Cousin, I must protest."

"She thinks you're Lord Wayborn," Abigail explained. "He's called Richard, you know."

"Evidently not. Evidently, he's called Dickie-bird." Cary strode forward, all charm, and took the old woman's hands in his. "Dearest, loveliest Paggles. How good it is to see you again. Why don't we take you back to your room now? Miss Smith, will you help me?"

"Who is Smith?" cried Paggles, horribly confused. "I keep hearing that name. Don't let Smith take me to the poorhouse! Mayn't I stay here with you, Dickie-bird?"

Cary looked at Abigail, puzzled.

"No one is sending you to the Poor House, darling," cried Abigail, kneeling at the old woman's feet. She felt horribly guilty; she had never expected that her assumption of a false name might frighten Paggles out of her wits. She turned to Cary. "Mrs. Spurgeon mentioned sending a servant to the—the *P.H.*, sir, and now she can't get it out of her head."

Paggles looked at her, her pale eyes clouded by confusion. "My lady?"

"My lady?" Cary murmured.

"She sometimes confuses me with my mother," Abigail explained quickly, before turning to the old woman. "It's Miss Abby, dear. And Dickie-bird is here, too. Don't you want to go back to your room now? It's nice and warm there."

Paggles shook her head rapidly. "I must stay here in the nursery. Smith cannot get me here, not if Dickie-bird won't let him," she muttered, rocking back and forth. "Where is Smith now? Gone, I hope! Oh, I'm frightened, Miss Abby."

Abigail covered her face with her hands.

"Don't distress yourself, Miss Sm . . . Abby," said Cary. "She's perfectly welcome to stay in the nursery." He found the bell-rope and gave it a firm tug. To Paggles he said quite forcefully, "No one is taking you to the poorhouse, Nurse Paggles. Dickie-bird won't let them. You're quite safe here. I shall have a fire lit, and your clothes brought to you. And, what's more, you shall have a lovely breakfast on a tray."

"With marmalade?" Paggles's voice quivered with pleasure.

"With marmalade," he promised.

"Such a good boy," said Paggles. "I knew you would not send me to the poorhouse." She squeezed Abigail's hand. "Go out and play now, Annie-Fanny. It will be teatime before you know it."

"Carpe diem," Cary agreed, pulling Abigail to her feet. "As a matter of fact, Annie-Fanny and I were just about to go skating."

"Ice skating!" cried Paggles in delight. "Do you remember, Miss Abby, when the Tsar of Russia came to London, and there was ice skating in the Park? And we rode down the slide in a toboggan. It was after the bad man was sent to Elba, but before he came back again."

"Yes, of course, darling," Abigail murmured, "but I

would not dream of leaving you now. I never liked skating anyway. I'd much rather stay with you."

"You're not proposing to stay shut up in the nursery all day?" Cary objected.

"No, my lady, you mustn't!" cried Paggles. "Go out and enjoy yourself. Mustn't fuss over silly old Paggles. I'm quite happy where I am. Make her go with you, Dickie-bird, and I shall knit you a muffler, there's a good boy."

A breathless Polly came into the room at that moment. Cary's instructions to her were so thorough that Abigail could think of nothing to add. In short order, Paggles had all of her things around her, and Cary withdrew while Abigail got her dressed. When Polly had brought up Paggles's breakfast, Abigail quietly went down the stairs to find Cary.

"Your marmalade is quince preserve," she told him, "but I daresay, she won't notice. You've made her very happy, sir. I'm truly grateful. She's a dear old thing, but she does get fuddled at times."

"I really hadn't noticed. I can answer to Dickie-bird, if you can answer to Annie-Fanny."

She couldn't help laughing. "My mother was Lady Anne Frances."

"What a pity you were not named for her. Then you would be Annie-Fanny too."

"I was named after Paggles, actually."

"I see," he said gravely. "Then you actually are called Paggles."

"No, *she* is called Abigail," the young lady clarified. "But when he was a boy, Dickie-bird couldn't say Abigail. It sort of came out as Paggles, and got stuck that way."

He looked at her with a critical eye. "Young Paggles, in fact."

"Abigail—such an old-fashioned name," she said, blushing. "My father calls me Abby."

"Your father. Mr. John Smith, I presume?"

Abigail sighed. "His Christian name is William, sir."

"You ought to have called yourself Williams, then," he said sternly. "Too late now, of course, but may I suggest we drop the Smith, at least in Miss Paggles's presence? She seems to have a morbid fear of all things Smith. Can't say I blame her. Nasty things, Smiths."

"Yes, sir," Abigail said meekly. "Thank you, sir."

He smiled faintly. "Well, young Paggles, if you hurry, I think we can still get out of the house before Mrs. Spurgeon is fully assembled. I'll give you breakfast at the Tudor Rose. Skating," he said in reply to her bewildered expression. "You. Me. Ice. Yes?"

"I don't skate," said Abigail firmly. "Sir, I never said I'd go skating with you."

"No," he agreed. "But neither did I go in your room and steal your shoes. Mrs. Nashe confessed to the fell deed not twenty minutes ago—at least, I hope it was not twenty minutes ago. It was she who whistled at me; she who threw your shoes out the window."

Abigail frowned at him. "Why would Vera do such a thing?"

"She wants you to go skating with me. So does Paggles. It's a conspiracy, in fact."

Abigail stood up straight. "Sir, as much as I appreciate your helping me find Paggles, I'm afraid that your idea of what constitutes an enjoyable activity may differ too sharply from mine to bring enjoyment to either of us."

"Good Lord," he said. "I didn't realize people actually talked like that. Don't worry, Cousin Abigail. I promise I won't kiss you again. You have my word as a gentleman. Though I should like to point out that when I kissed you, you seemed to like it."

"What?" she cried, exasperated. "I thought you were a bat."

He glared at her fiercely. "You little beast! You did *not* think I was a bat."

"I certainly did! Don't you remember? I jumped out of the wardrobe—"

"Not that," he said impatiently. "Less said about *that* the better. I mean, this morning, outside. When I met you by the bridge," he pressed as she looked at him blankly.

"So you *did* kiss me!" she exclaimed angrily. "I thought so!"

Cary's eyebrows shot up. "You *thought* so? What the devil do you mean?" he demanded. "Was there any doubt?"

"Well—"

She scarcely got the word out. He swung her around, pushed her against the wall, and drove his mouth hard against hers. Abigail froze in shock as she felt the point of his tongue urging its way between her lips. Unthinkingly, she let him in. He kissed her expertly. Unfortunately, she was so worried that she might disgrace herself by falling at his feet in a dead faint that she could scarcely enjoy herself. He left her mouth briefly and kissed her neck, his hands skimming boldly down to her waist. As she tried to speak, he claimed her mouth again. It was just as well; she had no idea what she would have said.

Cary stopped kissing her eventually, but only when they heard Polly on the stairs.

"What do you think of that?" he asked breathlessly, holding her steady.

Abigail was equally breathless. And trembling. And confused. But at least the feeling of desperate panic was subsiding, and she now had a very clear notion of the sort of man she ought to marry. A calm, plain, respectful fellow who never, ever pounced on her or threatened her peace of mind. A good-looking passionate man put far too much stress on the heart.

Cary's question had not been academic. "How was it? Vespertilian?"

"Vesper . . . what?" she stuttered.

"Vespertilian," he said, cupping her chin with his hand to keep her from hiding her eyes from him. "From the Latin *vespertilio*, meaning bat. Was it at all bat-like?"

"No, sir," she said, staring at him.

"That's a relief anyway," he said, releasing her. "Too much tongue? No, don't answer that. Just tell me you're quite sure this time that you *have* been kissed."

"Yes, sir."

"Excellent. We seem to be making progress."

"You promised you wouldn't do that again," she pointed out, rather belatedly.

"On condition that you went skating with me," he replied. "If you go skating with me, the promise will go into effect. If not, well, this is what you have to look forward to."

"That's blackmail," she objected. "Either I go skating, which I hate, or you will attack me again, which I also hate," she added emphatically.

"Attack you! I'll have you know, that was some of my best stuff," he said, annoyed.

Polly suddenly opened the door at the foot of the stairs. She looked at them in surprise, and Abigail turned red. "Hullo, Polly," said Cary, sounding quite normal. "All serene?"

Polly dropped a curtsey and said the old lady was knitting.

"Excellent," said Cary. "Look in on her from time to time, will you? There's a good girl. Miss Abigail and I are going skating at the Rose."

"Look here," Abigail said angrily. "I don't skate, and someone must look after Paggles."

Cary gritted his teeth; it was like trying to persuade a skittish horse to swallow a medicine ball. "I will teach you," he said cheerfully. "And Polly will look after Paggles."

"She could fall down the stairs."

"Polly's not going to fall down the stairs," he assured her, and Polly giggled. "And neither is Paggles. Now go and get your cloak, or I shall go straight upstairs and tell Paggles you're refusing to go. She'll be very annoyed with Annie-Fanny for hurting Dickie-bird's feelings in this callous manner. I should hate for Paggles to be upset again. Well?"

Abigail found it impossible to argue in front of the very interested Polly, a weakness he fully exploited. "I will go with you, sir," she said, "though it gives me no pleasure."

"Excellent. Who could ask for more?"

"Nor will it give *you* any pleasure," she warned, "for I really cannot skate."

"You really cannot skate," Cary told Abigail two hours later when he was helping her off the ice and back up the bank to the Tudor Rose's back terrace. The curate, Mr. Temple, jumped up at their approach and offered Abigail his seat. "You're hopeless," Cary said bluntly. "I must get you off my ice before you break it."

"I think your ice has broken *me*," she complained, gratefully accepting the curate's chair.

"I don't mind your falling down ten times a minute, Cousin Abigail," he said as she panted for breath, "but I strongly object to your pulling me down with you."

"Serves you right," she retorted, rubbing her sore ankles through her thick woollen socks. "I wanted to come in twenty minutes ago. Indeed, Mr. Temple, I didn't want to go on the ice at all, but he badgered me and bullied me until I gave in, the more fool I. He even used my old nurse against me. Was that not unkind of him?"

Mr. Temple scarcely knew how to answer; it was impolite to contradict a lady, but impolitic to cross a gentleman who might one day grant him a good living.

"What is infinitely worse, you've given the Misses Mickleby some fatal ideas," Cary complained. "They are all falling down now in the hopes I will come and pick them up."

"They are certainly falling down, but it does not follow they are depending on you, sir. They have Mr. Maddox and their brother," she added, bending down to unlace her skates.

"Let me help you." Cary was at her feet, pulling off her skates. "We are cousins, so no one can say I'm taking liberties." Mr. Temple smiled complacently, and, once again, Abigail's natural diffidence worked to Cary's advantage; she was too embarrassed to speak. Nor could she create a scene by pushing him away. Instead, she concentrated on the blue- and black-coated figures gliding along the frozen river as he busied himself at her feet.

The three plump, rosy-cheeked Mickleby girls so closely resembled one another that Abigail could not tell them apart, though she knew they were called Rhoda, Ida, and Lydia. Rhoda was the eldest. Hector Mickleby was their brother, and Mr. Maddox was his friend from Magdalen College. Both boys were nineteen and neither could hold a candle to Cary Wayborn.

"Feet hurt?" Cary inquired solicitously. Without waiting for a reply, he began rubbing the balls of her feet through her ugly black woollen socks.

Abigail closed her eyes in acute embarrassment, her face scarlet. "Stop it," she whispered through her teeth. "What will Mr. Temple think?"

"What are you implying? He'll think your feet hurt."

Happily, the curate's attention was engaged elsewhere. "There goes Miss Rhoda," he said gaily, as a

female Mickleby sat down hard on the ice, carrying Mr.
Maddox with her. The other two sisters fell in a heap at
their brother's feet, their skating blades flashing in the
sun. Hector did not enjoy handling his giggling sisters
half as much as Mr. Maddox did; he skated away with
his arms behind his back.

"Oh, Mr. Wayborn, do come and help us!" cried the
two abandoned girls in chorus.

"Do, please, sir," urged Hector, skating near to the
bank.

"I cannot leave my cousin unattended," Cary told
him, holding Abigail's boot for her.

"I will look after Miss Smith." Mr. Temple and Mr.
Mickleby spoke at once.

Abigail felt her usual panic at the prospect of being
left among strangers.

"Can you not spare me, Cousin?" Cary teased her.
"You seem alarmed. Now, don't scowl at me," he instructed. "Rather, say, 'I can spare you passionately, sir,
and just as long as you please.' *That* would be putting
me in my place. She's a queer, quiet little thing," he told
Hector and the curate. "You'll have to compose her side
of the conversation, as well as your own. She will not
match wits with anyone."

Though he doubted that skating with Miss Ida and
Miss Lydia would give him any pleasure, Cary had no
qualms about leaving her with the two gentlemen. She'd
be perfectly safe, and after an hour spent in such tepid
company, she'd be more appreciative of himself.

Hector grinned at Abigail. "You needn't fear matching
wits with me, Miss Smith! Nobody thinks I have any."

"The landlady here is famous for her clangers, if
you're hungry," Mr. Temple said, giving the younger
man a look of disapproval. "It's a local dish, a large
pastry stuffed on one side with a meat filling and on the
other with fruit."

"Hard as a door-knocker, too," added Hector.

Absurdly grateful to them for trying to make her feel at ease, when all Cary did was tease her, Abigail agreed to the simple meal. "And a half-and-half to wash it down, I think."

"Miss?"

She looked up to find the waiter staring at her. "Half mild and half bitter," she explained.

"You heard her," said Hector, snickering. "I'll have a pint of ale as well. Mr. Temple?"

The curate hesitated. He'd never been the sort to drink ale. He certainly had never drunk ale with a lady. Still, he had no wish to offend Mr. Wayborn's cousin . . .

"He's thinking about it," Hector observed derisively. "A curate can't be too careful."

"Yes, all right. Pints all around!" said Mr. Temple, growing red in the face.

The landlord came out to them in person. Scowling, he set a pewter cup on the table.

"That's the littlest pint I've ever seen," Hector objected.

"It's a *lady's* pint, Master Hector," said Mr. Sprigge banging down their clangers and ale.

Chapter 7

"What do you suppose they're talking about?" Lydia Mickleby asked Cary, holding his arm tightly. At seventeen, she had little conversation herself, and tended to fill any awkward silence by speculating about other people's conversations.

Cary glanced at the happy little group on the terrace and frowned. Evidently, the two younger men found Abigail as appealing as he did. "They seem so interested that I can only suppose they are talking about *us*, Miss Lydia," he said lightly. "Shall we eavesdrop?"

With a Mickleby on each arm, he skated closer to the bank, where frosty reeds sheltered them from the conversationalists. "It's ice cold," Mr. Temple was complaining.

"I think it's quite good cold." Cary recognized Abigail's voice.

"My teeth are chattering," Hector complained. "I'm changing to hot cider. Waiter!"

"If only I could invent a way to serve it cold on a hot summer's day," sighed Abigail. "I swear I could earn a million pounds."

"A million pounds," Hector scoffed.

"Yes, indeed, Mr. Mickleby," said Abigail. "Sometimes it's the littlest things that bring in the highest profits. Take my Christmas wrap, for example. When I was about ten, we had a bit of wallpaper left from doing over the summer breakfast room, and I used it to wrap the Christmas presents. That's where I got the idea. Very inexpensive paper, just to wrap presents in, with pretty designs. The very first year it was on the market, we turned a profit of a thousand pounds, and that's *after* Papa bought the paper mill outright. The next year we were up to five."

This was the longest speech Cary had ever heard her utter, and that it was delivered to two lesser mortals annoyed him considerably.

"F-f-f-five thousand pounds?" stuttered Mr. Temple, who was paid the handsome sum of thirty pounds per annum for making sermons and visiting the sick.

"Then this past year, I went 'round to all the London shops, and sold them the idea of offering a gift-wrapping service. Only a penny more, and the clerk wraps your package for you, right there in the shop. Of course, they bought the paper from me. I quite doubled my profits."

"You mean ten thousand pounds?" screamed Hector.

Cary had heard enough. He allowed Ida and Lydia to draw him away. He was going to have to speak to his "shy" cousin about telling such outrageous whoppers before her lies spiraled out of control. Ten thousand pounds, indeed!

But first, he was going to have to kiss her again, promise or no promise.

In the meantime, he had no objection to linking arms with Ida and Lydia to keep them from falling on the ice. The two girls idolized him, and, after being rejected by Vera and by Abigail, he needed to be idolized. As they chattered on, he skated with his eyes half-closed, enjoying the sound of their breathless female voices without attending to a word they said.

"Mr. Wayborn?"

"Yes, Miss Ida?" he murmured contentedly.

"It's Lydia. Where's Hector going with Miss Smith?"

Cary's eyes popped open. Abigail had disappeared from the terrace. He looked around and saw Hector and Mr. Temple on the snow-covered bank across from the inn. They were leading Abigail away from him, uphill, and Hector was carrying a huge serving platter.

"What's he doing with that tray?" cried Lydia.

Leaving Rhoda in the care of Mr. Maddox, Cary and the two younger girls hurried back to the Rose to change their shoes. According to Mr. Sprigge, the other members of their party were going up to the top of the Cascades, a local beauty spot, and they meant to slide down the icy stone steps on Mrs. Sprigge's pewter tray. Mr. Sprigge became exercised on the subject of trays. "If anything happens to that tray, sir, Mrs. Sprigge will not be best pleased. And then there's the bill—! Drinking like there's no tomorrow, they were," he grumbled.

After settling the bill with a shilling, Cary skidded across the river towards the opposite bank. Ida and Lydia ran after him, calling in thrilled voices, "Are we going to slide down the Cascades, too, Mr. Wayborn?"

"Certainly not," he snapped, pushing his way through the frozen reeds and up the bank.

In fashioning the Cascades, Art and Nature had combined in a marriage of dubious felicity. Once, the river had run placidly over the top of a little prominence, then down a long, gentle slope that gradually flattened out behind the Tudor Rose, until the water scarcely could be observed to run at all. Then, in the last years of the eighteenth century, the natural state of things had been judged too tame for real beauty. Turbulence had come into fashion.

In keeping with the new sensibilities, the little prominence had been transformed into a sinister cliff by the addition of a very large cut stone that resembled a step. Six more "steps" had been added on the way down, creating a dramatic series of frothy waterfalls.

The falling water was icebound now, the dark, giant steps coated in ice.

Cary could see Abigail and the two men nearing the top, struggling up the incline in the heavy piles of snow. He shouted to them, waving his arms, and Abigail waved back, her butterscotch hair standing out vividly against the pearly frost that surrounded her. He watched in disbelief as Hector Mickleby, with his unkempt chestnut hair falling into his eyes, began arranging the huge pewter tray on one of the steps. Unable to run uphill in the snow, Cary bounded up to them in a series of clumsy leaps.

Abigail was already seated on the tray when he got there, having painstakingly inched her way across the slippery step on her hands and knees, but Cary caught Hector before the young man could join her. He could tell at a glance that the boy was drunk.

"Have you all gone mad? You'll crack your silly heads open like plover's eggs."

Abigail looked at Cary in surprise. "But I have gone down the chutes in the Park, sir, in a toboggan, and those are *much* steeper than this."

Cary's surprise was not less than hers; he'd formed the idea that Hector had foisted this harebrained scheme on her, but she seemed a more than willing participant in the madness. Vera was right. Abigail was shy, but by no means timid.

"I did say I thought it was a bad idea," whispered Mr. Temple, mopping his face with his handkerchief. He seemed to be drunk too, and suffering from the worst effects of inebriation.

Abigail at least appeared sober. "Indeed, madam?" Cary asked her. "Did you go down the chutes on a bloody great tray?"

"No, of course not," Abigail calmly replied. Sitting on her platter, she felt quite safe from him. This time, *he* seemed to be the one discomfited, and she took pleasure in the rare reversal. "But, for heaven's sake, *Paggles* went with me. It's not at all dangerous, I assure you."

Cary grimly took in the frozen scene. The Cascades went down nearly twelve yards, then came the long, icy ribbon of frozen water slanting downhill. It looked like suicide to him. He wondered what Abigail would do if he ordered her to get off the tray and walk back towards him. Assuming she obeyed, she would probably slip, and break her fool neck on the steps. "Go and get a rope," he told Mr. Temple, just as that gentleman turned his head to one side, and vomited.

"Are you afraid, Mr. Wayborn?" Abigail exclaimed in astonishment.

"I'll go down with you, Miss Smith!" Hector cried recklessly. "I am not afraid."

"No," said Cary, shoving the boy aside. "I'll go."

"It was my idea," Hector sulked.

"The lady is my cousin. You can take your sisters down, if you like."

"You can take my sisters, sir," Hector sniffed. "I'll take your cousin."

"I can certainly go alone," Abigail said quickly. "It is what I intended."

Cary set one boot onto the icy step. Hector had placed the tray on the third step from the top, the widest of the seven steps. It was a far from safe feeling to be standing on iced stone.

"You'd better crawl, sir," Abigail advised him.

Cary did not reply, but concentrated on his steps as he inched towards the tray. They all watched as he crossed

the ice, not breathing until he took up a position behind
Abigail on the tray. Abigail scooted forward to give him
room, drawing her knees up to her chest. One of his
knees appeared on either side of her, and she saw that
the right leg of his trousers had split to show one brown
knee. She had not realized how very cold it was until
she felt his warmth suddenly mold itself to her body. He
seemed to fit her exactly. She felt his breath on her neck
and, unable to endure such intimacy, she pressed her
cheek to her shoulder; but he merely moved his head to
the other side.

"An English gentleman," he said in her ear, "never
crawls."

She made no reply but squirmed as he slid his arms
around her waist, his fingers splaying just beneath her
breasts. In response to her movements, the tray slid a
few inches forward, skimming across the wet, icy step,
and she went perfectly still.

"How do you like Temple and Young Mickleby?" he
asked, snuggling against her. "They're drunk as lords,
both of them. The curate and the squire's son."

"They can't be," she scoffed, looking at the two men
on the bank. Mr. Temple was down on all fours like
Nebuchadnezzar, and Hector was jeering him mercilessly. "Mr. Temple only had four pints, and Mr. Mickleby switched to cider."

"You're not counting the half-pints. I've seen the bill.
Indeed, I've *paid* the bill."

"I drank the ladies' pints," said Abigail. "And I shall
pay the bill."

"Don't argue with me, Cousin, not when we're about
to die." Cary laughed softly. The sound made the hairs
on her neck stand up. "I can't believe I'm doing this,"
he muttered.

"It's perfectly safe," she protested. "You'll see."

He squeezed her waist. "It is *not* safe. We're going to die. Kiss me for luck?"

"Certainly not," she gasped.

"No? Shall we go down together then, and meet our Maker?" Not waiting for a reply, he leaned hard forward, holding her tightly against his body as the tray slid and bumped its way down the steps, swerving this way and that. Abigail shrieked as they sailed off the last step and landed with a jolt on the smooth ice track winding down to the broad, flat river.

Cary buried his head in the side of her neck as the tray slid down the long, smooth decline, gathering speed until it slammed into a curve. She felt him gripping her body tightly between his knees, then they were out of the curve and shooting across the icy surface of the river. The tray came to a gentle stop not ten yards from the Rose's back garden.

"Well, I'm damned," Cary whispered softly. "Nobody died, after all."

"I told you there wasn't any danger," said Abigail.

"Don't tempt fate," he told her. "Just because we didn't die this time, doesn't mean it's safe. We'll certainly be killed the next time."

Abigail laughed out loud. "The next time?"

Mrs. Mickleby, the squire's wife, had braved the snow to call upon her new neighbors at Tanglewood Manor. Her ancient brougham had foundered in the snow half a dozen times, but each time the footmen had managed to free the wheels, and the lady's determination to see Mrs. Spurgeon was so great that she scarcely felt the inconvenience.

Mrs. Spurgeon immediately set her most pressing concerns to rest. The London widow was precisely as loud, as abrupt, as large, as old, and as ugly as any mother could wish. For her second day in the country,

Mrs. Spurgeon had chosen a primrose yellow gown and a long brunette wig. She looked like an aging Louis Quatorze. In short, she was not the sort of widow to tempt either Mr. Wayborn or Mrs. Mickleby's own foolish son Hector. Indeed, one wondered in what way this imposing female had ever tempted Mr. Spurgeon.

In an instant, therefore, Mrs. Spurgeon secured all her good will, but the ravishing Mrs. Nashe was not so fortunate. To Vera the squire's wife was hostile, but, as she lacked both consequence and wit, her repeated attempts to crush Vera could inflict no lasting harm. Indeed, not even the digs and demands of Mrs. Spurgeon could penetrate the pretty nurse's serenity.

"More tea, Vera." "A pillow for my back, Vera." "Do crack these chestnuts for me, Vera." "You are very dull today, Vera. You have not spoke two words together. Mrs. Mickleby must think you a half-wit."

Such treatment might have excited Mrs. Mickleby's pity had not Vera's placid calm been interpreted by the squire's lady as smugness. When Vera poured out the tea, she seemed quite the mistress, not merely of the teapot, but of Tanglewood Manor itself.

"Do you like birds, Mrs. Mickleby?" Mrs. Spurgeon asked her guest.

Mrs. Mickleby enthusiastically indulged herself on the subject of goldfinches.

"Bring Cato," Mrs. Spurgeon instructed Vera. "Miss Smith is not here to upset him. Bring his perch. Cato is an *ara macao*," she informed Mrs. Mickleby. "A scarlet macaw. I've taught him to eat with a spoon."

"But who is Miss Smith?" Mrs. Mickleby inquired, puzzled.

"My dear Mrs. Mickleby," said Mrs. Spurgeon, "I hardly know *what* she is, so it's not fair to ask *who*. I expect my son found her through an agency."

"Oh, it is a servant you mean," exclaimed Mrs. Mickleby in relief.

"If she is a servant, she's a very bad one," said Mrs. Spurgeon stoutly. "She went out very early—before I was even out of my bed—and I've not seen her all this morning. Vera tells me Mr. Wayborn took her ice skating at the village inn."

Mrs. Mickleby's alarm was awakened by this intelligence. Mr. Wayborn was a gentleman. He would not go skating with a mere servant, but he might take a paid companion; many such people were gentlewomen driven by poverty to find respectable employment. Such a woman might be forgiven for seeking to escape her enslavement by making an advantageous marriage. Indeed, Mrs. Mickleby *would* have forgiven Miss Smith, had she not already settled on the gentleman as an ideal son-in-law. As it was, she tried Miss Smith in absentia and convicted her of being a conniving and artful adventuress.

She said aloud, "Then she is a gentlewoman, at least, in spite of her name."

Mrs. Spurgeon shrugged. "Do you think so? Why, she has Portuguese friends!"

Mrs. Mickleby was horrified. "Portuguese friends? She is not . . . Oh, my dear Mrs. Spurgeon, can you assure me that she is in no way a Portuguese herself?"

"I shouldn't think so," Mrs. Spurgeon snorted. "Unless they have started making them with carroty hair and freckles. But she speaks quite proudly of her Portuguese friends at the dinner table. I don't think the Portuguese suitable for dinner myself. Gentlemen may speak of them over port," she conceded, as Vera brought in Cato on her arm. A servant followed, carrying the macaw's perch.

Vera gave Cato a cuttlebone to chew, and he made a good impression on Mrs. Mickleby. At her hostess's instigation, she offered him a chestnut and he came to take it from her hand, then returned to his perch. Cato remained quietly and aloofly engrossed in chewing, even when Abigail entered the room some time later, accompanied by Mr. Wayborn. They took no more notice of Cato than he did of them. Indeed, they did not notice anyone. They were laughing together, and Mr. Wayborn was taking the girl's fur-lined cloak.

Vera appeared amused; she quietly went on cracking her chestnuts into a pretty silver bowl. Mrs. Mickleby slowly turned purple. Mrs. Spurgeon adjusted her wig in anticipation of Cary's attentions. He saw the ladies first. His eye alighted in mild alarm on Mrs. Spurgeon's brunette curls, then he was all smiles and charm. "Good morning, Mrs. Spurgeon. Mrs. Nashe! And Mrs. Mickleby, too. Delighted! Any chance of a fresh pot of tea?"

He dutifully bent over the ladies' hands. It was his first opportunity to see Mrs. Spurgeon as a brunette, and he made the most of it, lavishing her with compliments. "But, madam, did we not agree that your delightful bird would remain in my study?" he gently chided her.

Mrs. Spurgeon pouted. "Miss Smith was out. I didn't think it mattered. He's the dearest, sweetest bird alive," she told Mrs. Mickleby in her confidential roar. "Look at him—he's an angel. Only Miss Smith upsets him. She upsets him most dreadfully."

Mrs. Nashe quietly set down her nutcracker and took the macaw out of the room.

Cary turned to introduce Abigail to his neighbor's wife, and discovered, to his exasperation, that the girl was trying to sneak unnoticed to the staircase door. "Miss Smith!"

Abigail started guiltily. "I'm just going to check on Paggles, sir," she whispered.

"I should like to present my neighbor, Mrs. Mickleby, to you," he said sternly. "I made you acquainted with her daughters and her son at the Tudor Rose. We have had the most entertaining morning, ma'am," he told Mrs. Mickleby. "You will never guess what we have been doing. Tell her, Abigail."

Realizing she could not escape the acquaintance, Abigail came back into the room and performed a wretched curtsy. "How do you do, Mrs. Mickleby?"

Mrs. Mickleby found Miss Smith's blushing humility, which she perceived as humbug, quite as distasteful as Vera Nashe's self-assurance. "And what have you been about this morning, Miss Smith?" she coldly inquired in her best grandam style.

Abigail flushed, and began to stammer. "We have been going down the Cascades, ma'am, on a platter."

"But you have failed to capture the excitement of the experience," Cary complained. "First off, it was a very, very *large* platter. We sat on it together, and bumbled, and slipped, and glided all the way down to the Tudor Rose. We could have been killed at any moment."

"I see," Mrs. Mickleby said, growing colder by the moment.

Cary quickly changed the subject. "Miss Smith lives in London, ma'am. I'm sure she'd be delighted to answer any questions Rhoda might have about her own presentation at Court."

"I assure you, sir, I am capable of preparing my daughter to meet her Queen," said Mrs. Mickleby stiffly. "It wasn't so very long ago that I was presented myself."

"Yes, of course," said Cary, "but Miss Smith lives in Town. She will have a more intimate knowledge of the theater and other entertainments, the shops, the museums, and the exhibitions. Miss Rhoda is to have a Season in London this year," he told Abigail, then turned back to Mrs. Mickleby. "I believe, ma'am, that you are planning to give Miss Rhoda a proper send-off. A going-away party. I daresay Miss Smith could be persuaded to attend. She has no aversion to a country dance, I'm sure."

Mrs. Mickleby looked sour. "I have already invited Mrs. Spurgeon," said she. "If *she* wishes to extend the invitation to include Miss Smith, I shall be happy to receive her, too."

Cary's eyes narrowed.

"I think I'd rather have Vera with me," said Mrs. Spurgeon.

"Just as you like," said Abigail, happy to be spared any gathering where the hostess so clearly did not want her. "Please do excuse me, Mrs. Mickleby. I'm delighted to make your acquaintance, of course, but I must check on my—my friend upstairs."

Mrs. Mickleby rose from her place. "I do hope, Miss Smith, that your *Portuguese friends* will not be visiting you here," she said haughtily. "This isn't that sort of neighborhood."

Startled, Abigail stopped where she was. "My Portuguese friends?"

"You spoke of them last night over the Madeira," Mrs. Spurgeon prompted her.

Abigail smiled. "Oh, I see! No, ma'am, my Portuguese friends are all . . . *bottled up.*"

"Bottled up? Whatever do you mean?" cried Mrs. Mickleby.

Cary glared at Abigail, who was laughing behind her hand. "Figure of speech, ma'am. She means they are all bottled up in Brazil," he said quickly.

"Brazil?" Abigail repeated in astonishment.

"Yes, of course," he said, looking hard at her. "Your Portuguese friends are all bottled up in Brazil, in a manner of speech. At the Court of the Emperor Joao the . . . uh . . . Sixth, is it? Where your father—Sir William Smith—serves as private secretary to the Ambassador."

Abigail's amber eyes grew wider with every lie. "My father!"

"I think you will find, Mrs. Mickleby, that my cousin

has rather a droll way of talking, which has made her a great favorite at the Court of St. James."

"Your cousin!" exclaimed Mrs. Mickleby, turning pale. "My dear Mrs. Spurgeon, you did not tell me Miss Smith is Mr. Wayborn's cousin!" she accused.

"I thought you were joking about being this young lady's cousin, Mr. Wayborn," said Mrs. Spurgeon. "You said you'd assumed the name of Smith when you sneaked into the Army."

"I did so," Cary replied. "But that was because of my Smith relations."

"Well, there you are," said Mrs. Spurgeon, turning to Mrs. Mickleby. "That explains it. They are cousins, you see," she told the stunned woman.

"Only very distant cousins," Abigail felt obliged to point out.

"Fairly close geographically," Cary retorted.

"If Miss Smith is your cousin, Mr. Wayborn, she must be related to the Vicar as well," said Mrs. Mickleby, trying to gauge the extent of her social blunder.

"No, indeed, madam. Did I not say? Miss Smith is one of my *Derbyshire* cousins. Her uncle is Lord Wayborn of Westlands."

Mrs. Mickleby cried out in pain. "I trust I have not offended you, Miss Smith," she babbled anxiously. "That was never my intention. It was not made clear to me who you are. Mrs. Spurgeon—"

"Don't blame *me*," said the former blonde. "*I* was not rude."

"You are not offended, are you, Abigail?" said Cary. "Depend upon it, Mrs. Mickleby. Nothing ever offends my cousin. She has the sweetest, most forgiving disposition in the world. I can speak for her; she is not engaged. She will gladly condescend to go to Miss Rhoda's soiree."

"I assure you, Mrs. Mickleby, I would not dream of

such a thing," said Abigail, her face scarlet with embarrassment. "I beg you to excuse me," she added, breaking for the stairs.

She ran straight up to her room, too furious with Cary even to visit Paggles. As she burst into the room, the man's dog jumped down from her bed and barked sharply, startling her, to say the least. Content to have made her heart jump into her throat, Angel returned nicely to the bed, settled down, and began chewing on something he held propped between his front paws.

Some of the anger Abigail felt for the master transferred to the dog. "You're not supposed to be up here," she said severely, dragging him down from the bed by his collar. To her dismay, the red and white coverlet was thickly coated with orange dog hair. "And what have you got in your mouth?" she demanded. "Give it to me."

Angel contritely dropped the twisted paper into her hand. Abigail smoothed it out on the windowsill. It was a letter addressed to Mr. Cary Wayborn. She ought not to have read it, but she recognized the sprawling, spidery handwriting as her father's. Mr. Wayborn, she discovered to her dismay, owed Ritchie's Fine Spirits an outstanding balance of thirty guineas for a case of Gold Label scotch purchased in the year previous. If Mr. Ritchie did not receive said sum forthwith, he would seek satisfaction by court order.

At the bottom of the page, Red had scrawled in giant letters: *Immediate Payment Due*.

Cary—she assumed it was his writing—had scrawled back: *Not Bloody Likely*.

"You said you were going to see Paggles."

Abigail spun around to see Cary in the doorway. "Get out of my room! How dare you invade my privacy?" she demanded, quite forgetting that she had just been reading his mail.

"I'm not actually in," he answered, unperturbed. "I'm

standing in the hall. I must also point out that, strictly speaking, this is *my* room, not yours. You are only renting it."

"And while I am renting it, you have no right to come in," she snapped. "How dare you make up stories about my father? Knighting him, and sending him to *Brazil*, of all places! How can you be so—so *strange*?"

He leaned against the door frame. "I had to explain your Portuguese friends somehow. *You* make up stories. Why can't I?"

"I do no such thing!" she said indignantly.

"You make up *names*, certainly. Mayn't I make up a story to go with the name? I only gave your father a little *sir*. You gave yourself ten thousand pounds' worth of Christmas wrap." He laughed suddenly. "And I'd hang on to your ten thousand pounds, too. You'll need them when Mrs. Mickleby discovers you've been knocking back pints in the local tavern with her precious son Hector. Though I daresay we can put it down to aristocratic eccentricity."

"I was not knocking back pints," said Abigail. "They were—they were *ladies'* pints. Anyway, I don't care what Mrs. Mickleby thinks of me. I don't like her either."

"Well, I care what she thinks of you," he said. "*You* may be going back to London, but I have to live with these silly people. I wish you wouldn't poison the well for me; I've little enough society as it is. A man gets lonely out here in the frozen wilderness. Now that she knows who you are—sort of—I'm sure Mrs. Mickleby will treat you with all due deference."

"I don't want her to defer to me. Why should she? I just want to be left alone."

He stared at her. "Left alone? You are quite possibly the most backwards little creature I've ever met," he said. "For starts, you're my cousin. That alone makes you first in consequence among the ladies of the neighborhood. I wouldn't allow my humblest relation to be slighted right under my nose by a mere Mickleby, and you are scarcely that."

She looked at him blankly. "First in the neighborhood? What *can* you mean?"

"My dear girl, you're the granddaughter of an earl," Cary said impatiently. "There is no one to whom you should give way."

"You had no right to expose my connection to that family," she said unhappily.

His brows rose. "'That family?' The Wayborns, you mean. And by 'connection,' I can only assume you mean your mother?"

"Lord Wayborn has never acknowledged my existence," said Abigail. "I have no right to trade on his name, when he so clearly wants nothing to do with me. And now you have made it known he is my uncle. It was very wrong of you to dress me in borrowed plumes— and just so Mrs. Mickleby would invite me to her house! I don't even want to go to her house."

"They are not borrowed plumes," Cary told her sharply. "Rather, it is your birthright. Did your mother never teach you to take precedence, girl?"

"She died when I was only five," said Abigail.

"Well, that explains it," he murmured. "I can see now you are merely ignorant of proper conduct. Ignorance can be mended. With my help, you will soon be conducting yourself in a manner befitting your rank."

"I'm sure I don't require lessons in conduct from *you*, sir," she said indignantly.

"And I'm sure you do," he said coolly.

"Indeed?" Abigail marched over to the windowsill and snatched up Red Ritchie's letter. "Here's your bill, sir! The merchant is threatening to have you imprisoned for debt."

"Where did you get this? Have you been rifling

through my things?" All traces of good humor had vanished from his face; Cary was furious.

"In a manner of speaking," she responded tartly. "I took it out of your dog's mouth."

"Quite right, too," he said, tossing it into the fireplace. "Here is its proper place."

"Sir," Abigail cried as the paper blackened on the grate, "that is a bill for thirty guineas!"

"Not anymore," he pointed out. "This Ritchie fellow's getting impudent. That isn't the first bill he's had the gall to send me. I ought to have him brought up on charges of harassment."

"But the account is overdue," Abigail protested.

"No, that's where you're wrong," he said. "There's no such thing as an overdue account. It's all nonsense conjured up by tradesmen to scare people into giving them money they haven't got. Accounts are either paid or they're not. They'll be tacking on interest and late fees next, if we don't take a stand against them. It's insufferable."

"But is your account with Mr. Ritchie paid or not?" Abigail demanded.

He frowned at her. "That isn't the point. I owe money all over London, to better men than Red Ritchie, too! But Mr. Weston isn't sending me dirty letters. Mr. Hoby ain't threatening me with debtor's prison. I simply can't get any more coats or boots from them until I settle my accounts. I accept that, and no harm done. This Ritchie fellow is an uncivilized cur. How dare he hound me like a criminal? I'm an English gentleman."

"You took a case of his scotch," she pointed out. "Has he no right to demand payment? And if you don't pay him, how are you any better than a thief?"

"How am I any better than a—!" he choked, unable even to repeat the last word. "Obviously, if I could pay him, I would. The stupid man sends me a bill every week. It's like being pecked to death by chickens.

SURRENDER TO SIN 137

Glaswegian chickens. *That*, Cousin, is one bill I shall never pay. If I had a *thousand* pounds in my purse, I would not do it. It's the principle of the thing."

"The principle!"

He stared at her for a moment, then said despairingly, "I have much to teach you, Cousin. But first, the Micklebys' party. Do you dance, or must I teach you that as well?"

"Mrs. Mickleby and I are in perfect agreement, sir; we neither of us want me to go."

"Nonsense. She mayn't have wanted Mrs. Spurgeon's dogsbody there, but she certainly wants Lord Wayborn's niece. It will be judged a resounding failure if you don't go. For starts, if you don't go, *I* can't go, and if I can't go, they may as well call the whole thing off. Poor little Rhoda will cry her eyes out."

"You may certainly go without me," said Abigail. "If I am first in consequence, as you say, then let me exercise the privilege of my rank, and stay at home."

"You have no such privilege," he told her dryly. "Your privilege is to take your place at the head of Tanglewood society, such as it is. Mrs. Mickleby will be mortified if you decline her invitation. Really, Abigail, she'll be hurt. I know that you are shy in unfamiliar situations, but shyness, you know, is no excuse for rudeness."

"I wasn't rude," said Abigail, appalled. "Pray, how was I rude?"

"Mrs. Mickleby is a silly woman. She made a blunder. It was my fault, anyway. If I had made it clear from the start that you are my cousin, she would never have insulted you. She would have fawned over you quite shamelessly. In any case, she's apologized, and ought to be forgiven. You would not want to hurt her feelings?"

"No," said Abigail. "Of course not. If you think her feelings would be hurt . . ."

"She'd be crushed," he assured her. "And, of

course, Paggles would have to be informed of your
un-Christianlike behavior."

"Very well, then!" she said crossly. "You may tell her
I accept the invitation."

"I have already done so."

Abigail frowned at him. "Have you indeed?"

"Yes, monkey, but this is absolutely the last time I do
your dirty work for you. Next time, you'll tell her yourself,
and be very gracious in your supercilious condescension."

"In my *what*?"

"It's not as easy as it sounds; being gracious and con-
descending and supercilious all at once. I'll have to
teach you; I'm quite good at it. But that is a lesson for
another time. For the nonce, I must leave you," he went
on blithely. "Strange men with hatchets are meeting me
at the Dower House—something about an elm tree.
Unless of course you wish me to stay? I could come in
and close the door. We'd be quite private, if that appeals
to you."

"No, indeed," she said repressively. "Tell me, Mr.
Wayborn, when you say I should give way to no one in
this neighborhood, does that include yourself?"

"Certainly not," he replied, grinning. "I am your nearest male relation. Also, older and wiser than yourself.
This gives me natural authority over you. I am your
guardian, in fact, and you are my ward. You must do as
I say."

"Is that so?"

"Yes; certainly. And if you had not extracted that asi-
nine promise from me never to kiss you again, I would
give you a practical proof of my power over you."

Abigail stared at him, dumbfounded.

"Speechless? Good. You talk too much. I'll see you
at tea."

Chapter 8

It was Mrs. Spurgeon's habit to retire to her room directly after luncheon and nap until tea. Abigail certainly did not seek to detain her. Vera went with her mistress, but promised to return within an hour for a game of backgammon with the younger woman. Abigail took the opportunity to visit Paggles in the nursery. When she returned to the sunny front parlor, Vera was setting up the game. "How is your nurse, Miss Smith?" she asked politely.

"Sleeping—and please call me Abigail."

"Our old women seem to be on the same schedule," Vera remarked, passing Abigail the dice cup. "Well, my dear? How deep shall we play?"

Abigail sat down reluctantly, looking out the window at the sparkling white day. "As deep as you like," was her careless reply. "But would you not rather go for a walk, Vera? I don't deny it's cold, but there's something exhilarating about walking in the snow, and, look, the sun is out. We will not have very many days like this. The snow will soon melt, and there will be no walking in the sludge."

"I'll do my walking in the summer, I thank you," said
Vera laughing. "I've not the least intention of spoiling
my shoes. I haven't as many pairs as you."

Without much enthusiasm, Abigail rolled the dice.
It was soon very clear that backgammon was not
her game. She had neither luck nor strategy. "Shall
we play cards, then?" Vera asked as she gathered up her
winnings.

"We shall have cards enough after dinner," Abigail
replied. "I should like to go up to the Cascades again,
but my cousin is gone away. It was such fun going
down."

"Why, there he is now," said Vera, looking out the
window.

"No, it is only Mr. Mickleby," Abigail said immediately. "My cousin's coat is purple."

"And what do you think of him now?" Vera asked,
smiling.

"Of Hector Mickleby?"

"Mr. Wayborn. You enjoyed his company this morning, I think."

"I don't know what to make of him," Abigail confessed. "Just when I think I hate him, he does something
kind, or silly, or just plain strange. He says that I am
first in consequence in the neighborhood. Do you think
that is true?"

"My dear, I'm sure of it. Was not your grandfather a
Peer of the Realm?"

"Yes, but what can it signify? My uncle has made it
clear he wants nothing to do with me. Indeed, I have
never met him."

Vera chuckled. "No one else here who can boast so
much. Amongst such humble neighbors, an estranged
uncle who is an earl must be counted very grand, indeed."

"Grand! I much prefer London, where I am of no
consequence whatever."

"I'm sure that cannot be. You are the daughter of Sir William Smith, are you not?"

"Good heavens," said Abigail. "You mustn't believe everything Mr. Wayborn says. He has such an odd sense of humor. It's true my mother was Lady Anne Wayborn, but my father is not a gentleman, Mrs. Nashe. He's a merchant. I don't know what that makes me. A gentle-woman, or a tradesman's daughter?"

Vera's dark eyes twinkled. "A man may take whatever rank he pleases, but a woman is only as good as her mother."

Both women started in surprise as Hector Mickleby suddenly rapped on the window with his knuckles. "Open the window, Miss Smith," he shouted, pressing his face against the glass.

Abigail obediently opened the casement. "Would you not rather come through the door?" she asked uncertainly as Rhoda Mickleby was lifted up through the window. The girl climbed nimbly onto the window seat. Abigail, who was quite unused to such events, became flustered.

"We always come through the window when Mr. Wayborn is in London," Rhoda explained, laughing as she hopped down from the seat. "You see, we haven't got a key."

"But Mr. Wayborn is not in London," said Abigail, jumping back in dismay as Hector, and Mr. Maddox, to whom she had been no more than barely introduced, each vaulted in turn over the windowsill. "He's gone to the Dower House to oversee the removal of the fallen elm."

"Oh, we haven't come to see him," said Hector. "We've come to see you!"

"Oh." Abigail felt a vague panic beginning to stir. "Mrs. Nashe," she said quickly. "These are Mr. Wayborn's neighbors, Miss Mickleby, and her brother, Mr. Mickleby. This is Mr. Maddox, Mr. Mickleby's friend."

"Backgammon?" said Hector, as Vera hurriedly put the game away. "Bit of a bore, eh?"

"Oh, Miss Smith!" cried Rhoda. "You *must* come with us to the Cascades this minute. Say you will! Hector says he won't go down with me at all, and I'm too frightened to go alone. He went down with Ida and Lydia," she added resentfully.

"Much good it did them," her brother retorted. "Mama is sending them to bed without any supper. And it's to be the last of the turtle-feast Maddox brought from London."

"But Ida said it was quite worth the punishment!" said Rhoda, seizing Abigail's hands. "Mr. Maddox has been good enough to offer to go down with me, but Hector says it would be most improper."

"So it would be," said Hector. "You ain't engaged to the man."

"Hector says if you will go down with *him*, Miss Smith, then it would be quite all right if *I* went down with Mr. Maddox. No one can say it is improper, if *you* do it. Say you will. I'm the only one who didn't have a chance to go down. It's not fair!" She pouted quite childishly.

The thought of Hector Mickleby's arms around her made Abigail feel slightly ill. "I'm afraid that's quite out of the question, Miss Rhoda," she said firmly.

"You would have gone down with me, Miss Smith," Hector said, frowning, "if Mr. Wayborn hadn't butted in. But I suppose he wants you all for himself. I might have guessed."

Abigail felt as though she had been set down in the middle of a circus performance and was somehow expected to be ringleader. "I couldn't possibly have gone down with you, Mr. Mickleby," she said. "I could only go down with Mr. Wayborn because he is my cousin."

Hector scowled savagely. "He has that advantage, and

he uses it, too! If the two of us were on equal footing, Miss Smith . . ."

Abigail was glad he did not complete his thought; the notion of Hector ever being Cary Wayborn's equal was patently absurd.

"But Miss Smith!" cried Rhoda, as the conversation turned away from her nearest concerns. "If you won't go down with Hector, then I can't go down with Mr. Maddox! And I must go down with Mr. Maddox. It's very important."

"I am very sorry, Miss Mickleby," Abigail stammered.

"No, you're not!" said Rhoda stoutly. "You don't care! No one does. It's all so unfair. You're all against me. I shall *die* if I can't go down the Cascades on a platter."

"You may go to hell on a platter for all I care," responded her brother. "Any chance of tea, Miss Smith?" he added. "Or, if Mr. Wayborn's got any rum, we could make punch."

"Nobody wants your horrid punch!" said Rhoda.

"Calm yourself, Miss Rhoda," Mr. Maddox murmured in embarrassment, smiling at Abigail. "We can not ask Miss Smith to do what she thinks improper."

His deference made Abigail as uncomfortable as Rhoda's bullying and Hector's incivility.

"In any case, your mama would never approve of such a thing, Miss Rhoda, if she has punished your sisters merely for going down with their brother," Abigail pointed out. "And your mother's wishes must be more material to you than anything which I might do or say."

Mrs. Grimstock came in at that moment to announce Mr. Temple's arrival.

"What's *he* want?" Hector snarled, flinging his body into a chair.

"Shall I bring in the tea, Miss?" asked Mrs. Grimstock.

"Yes, Grimstock," said Rhoda without Abigail's ever

realizing the housekeeper had been addressing *her*. Mrs. Grimstock withdrew, and when Mrs. Nashe left the room, murmuring it was time to wake Mrs. Spurgeon, Abigail felt utterly abandoned. She was glad to see Mr. Temple.

The tall thin man in the clerical collar seemed embarrassed. "You did say I might come and have a look at your Blake, Miss Smith. I didn't realize you were entertaining, or I should never have presumed . . ."

Hector snorted. "By that he means he followed our footprints here, Maddox," he said spitefully. "Horning in on another fellow's territory, what?"

Most people of Hector's acquaintance dismissed his rudeness as youthful high spirits, but Abigail thought him abominable. "I am not having a party, Mr. Temple," she said firmly. "And you are most welcome, sir. I hope you are feeling better?"

"Four pints only, sick as a dog," Hector explained in an aside to Mr. Maddox. "What the Vicar will say is anyone's guess."

"I'll just go and get the book," said Abigail. Any guilt she felt in abandoning Mr. Temple to the Mickleby wolves was entirely swallowed up by her own relief. In her room, she unlocked her portable writing desk and took out the illustrated *Songs of Innocence and of Experience* she had bought in London. Having located the volume, she was in no hurry to rejoin the young people downstairs. She could always claim there had been a difficulty finding the book. If she stayed away long enough, Mrs. Spurgeon would come out for her tea, and that lady's strong personality would be more than equal to the Micklebys. And if she stayed upstairs for a very, *very* long time, there was even a chance they would all take the hint and go away.

She ran up the stairs to see Paggles. There was no clock in the nursery, but, as Abigail was accustomed to having her mid-afternoon tea at the same time each day, she felt she could gauge when she might safely go back down again and not risk being alone with her "guests."

Polly came up with Paggles's tea a short time later.

"The master do be looking for you, Miss," she said, surprised to see Abigail.

"The master," Abigail repeated. "You mean Mr. Wayborn?" She picked up her book, kissed Paggles's pleated cheek, and ran downstairs. As she closed the door that blended into the hall wall, Cary Wayborn stepped out of her room. They confronted each other at almost the exact spot where he had kissed her that morning.

"What were you doing in my room?" she demanded angrily.

"Looking for you, Cousin," he replied so cheerfully she almost felt ashamed of her bad temper. "Have a look at this," he added, pulling a miniature in an oval frame from his pocket. "Found it in the Dower House. Could this be our missing Catherine, do you think?"

Abigail took it from him, but was obliged to go into her room and stand at the window to see it properly, and he followed her. "Sophia, Electress of Hanover," she said, handing it back to him. "When you *do* find Catherine of Aragon, there will be no shoulders on display, I promise. That wasn't here before," she added suddenly, noticing a little silver-gilt clock on the mantel.

"No, I brought it from the Dower House for you. You needn't thank me."

Abigail frowned. "I wasn't going to," she said. "I was going to ask you to stay out of my room. Just because we are cousins—sort of—doesn't mean you can run tame in my room."

"And I might ask you not to leave people lying about my house like discards," he retorted. "Your guests downstairs seem to think you're coming back. Shall I tell them you are hiding with your old nurse until they take themselves off? Does Paggles know her young lady is in the habit of leaving her guests unattended?"

"I wasn't hiding," Abigail said untruthfully. "I've been looking for the book I promised to show Mr. Temple."

He snatched the volume from her, then sat on the windowsill and opened it. "The Blake?" he said incredulously. "You bought it? You don't even like Blake," he complained. "You're not allowed to buy things you don't like."

"As I explained to Mr. Temple," she said primly, "sometimes I make a purchase, not for pleasure, but as an investment. *I* don't like Mr. Blake, but other people do. In a few years, it may be possible for me to sell it at a handsome profit."

He stared at her. "Sell it? At a profit? That's downright cold-blooded. If Mr. Blake were here, he'd fling you out the window for talking such rot. The man don't pour his heart and soul into his art so that you can turn a profit, madam!"

"I daresay Mr. Blake is glad of the money I paid for his work!"

"Are you always so mercenary?"

"I am practical," she said indignantly. "There's nothing wrong with being practical."

"How very odd," he said quietly, returning her book to her. "In general I feel a keen animosity for people like you. There are some remarkably *practical* people downstairs, as a matter of fact, whom I dislike rather a lot. Shall we join them?"

Abigail was puzzled. No one she had left downstairs seemed to meet the description. "To whom do you refer?" she asked, as they began making their way down to the first floor.

"Why, to your devoted admirers, of course. Hector Mickleby, Mr. Buttocks, and even poor Mr. Pimple. In your absence they have been fighting over you like a gang of thieves; more so since you cannot be equally divided among them. Miss Rhoda is quite put out."

"You needn't mock me," she said angrily. "Mr. Maddox is devoted to Miss Mickleby, Hector is a menace, and Mr. Temple only stopped by to see my rare combined volume."

Cary burst out laughing. "I'll bet you my *head* that Mr. Pimple asks you whether or no the paper of your rare combined volume comes from your father's mill!"

Abigail gasped. "Are you saying Mr. Pim—*Mr. Temple* is a fortune hunter?"

"Well, he ain't a paper mill hunter!"

"Mr. Temple is a curate," she protested.

"I can see how that might add to a young man's desperation," he replied. "Poor Mr. Pimple—he'd marry anybody, and for considerably less than your ten thousand pounds."

"Thank you very much," Abigail said tartly, outstripping him to the end of the hall.

To her relief, Mrs. Spurgeon, golden turban in place, was in possession of the teapot. More chairs had been brought into the room, and Abigail slipped quietly into hers. Rhoda instantly attempted to enlist Mr. Wayborn in her cause. "I don't see the harm," she cried passionately, "if Miss Smith will go down with Hector, Mama couldn't possibly object if I go down with Mr. Maddox. Or I might go down with *you*, sir," she added treacherously.

"I say!" Mr. Maddox protested.

"My dear Rhoda," Cary said lightly, "while I regard you almost as an infant relation, I am not, in fact, your relative. It would be unthinkable for me to go down the Cascades with you on a platter. Nor should you go with Mr. Maddox. As for Miss Smith going down with Hector—frankly, Abigail, I am astonished you would even consider such a sad breach of conduct. You are becoming an unmanageable hoyden. I shall have to write to Sir William and tell him so."

"What?" said Abigail, infuriated. "I never! I didn't."

"I am glad to hear it," said Cary. "It would be exceedingly improper."

"But Hector says he won't take me, Mr. Wayborn!" cried the unfortunate Rhoda.

"I won't," her heartless brother confirmed.

"My advice to you, young Rhoda," said Cary, "if that *is* your real name, is that you find yourself a cousin. Then you will never walk alone. Abigail and I are nearly inseparable, and yet our intimacy is entirely above reproach, because we are cousins. Why, I am in and out of her room ten times a day."

Abigail glared at him helplessly.

"I knew it," said Hector, bitterly. "No one else has a chance."

"I *have* got a cousin," said Rhoda, artless in her resentment. "But he isn't handsome like you, Mr. Wayborn. I wouldn't be caught dead on a platter with him."

"Is this the rare combined volume you promised to show me, Miss Smith?" Mr. Temple interrupted quietly, drawing his chair a little closer to hers.

"Yes, of course." Once again Abigail was grateful to the curate, and of all the gentlemen present, she decided she liked him the best. He gave her such a calm, quiet feeling. There was never any confusion of emotions with him. He was really quite safe and confidential.

"Such lovely paper," he murmured in his soothing voice as he turned the pages. "I daresay it comes from your father's mill?"

Abigail did not dare look at Cary. She knew the gray eyes would be laughing at her.

Discreet for once, Cary made no comment, but turned instead to Mrs. Spurgeon. "You don't mind, do you, Mrs. Spurgeon, if I house a few *objets* from the Dower House in the banqueting hall here? You're not planning any large parties, are you?"

She purred at him. "Of course you may put your *objets* anywhere you like."

"What sort of *objets*?" Abigail couldn't resist asking Cary.

He turned to her, pleased. "I was hoping you'd be interested, Cousin. The truth is, I need your help. There's an awful lot of stuff in that house. Trash, mainly, I fear. And, of course, the house itself will have to be pulled down."

Abigail was startled. "But surely you mean to rebuild?" she cried.

He shook his head. "What do I need a dower house for? My children will just have to refrain from turning their mama out of doors the moment I am dead. To be perfectly honest, the place is a nuisance. No one wants to rent it; it can't be sold unless I sell some land with it too, which idea I hate. It sits in the middle of my estate gathering dust and no money. I'm glad a tree fell on it. I only hope to find one or two things worth selling amid the rubble. That's where you come in, Cousin. You know all about old things."

She looked at him, wanting to say no, but knowing that she wouldn't. She absolutely adored looking through lots of old things in the hopes of finding a real treasure.

"You will help me, won't you?" he said, employing the power of a direct appeal.

Abigail bit her lower lip. "If you really don't mean to rebuild, I suppose you might sell it off bit by bit. I'd say you might fetch as much as eight hundred pounds, depending on how much can be salvaged."

"But you haven't even seen the stuff," Cary said,

puzzled. "Are you clairvoyant? Most of it's trash, I'm telling you."

"No, I mean the house itself," Abigail explained. "The doors and the fireplaces and so forth. The bricks, the stones, the paneling, the roofing slates. All that sort of thing."

"Are you actually proposing that I sell my *bricks*? To whom, may I ask?"

"To builders, of course," said Abigail. "Don't you know the housing market in London is exploding? The brickyards and the stone-cutters simply can't keep up. When we did our house in Kensington, we got almost all our stone shipped to us from Ireland, from houses they'd pulled down over there, and it was still more economical than having new stone cut—not to mention quicker. I can put you on to our builder in London, if you like."

"You're quite serious?" said Cary. "Someone will buy my old slates and my bricks?"

"And your windows, if the tree left any intact. I'm telling you, they can't put houses up fast enough for London. The population is going to double in the next ten years."

"I wish I had an old house I could pull down," Hector muttered fervently.

"Don't you dare pull down Gooseneck Hall!" cried Rhoda.

"Why, that rascal Osborne," Cary cried indignantly. "I bet he knows all about the game. Small wonder he offered to pull it down for a pittance—he means to sell it off, doorknob by doorknob, to the highest bidder. Excuse me, ladies," he said, getting to his feet. "I have some urgent business to attend to."

He paused on his way out, and returned suddenly to where Abigail was seated. "You," he said warmly, "are worth your weight in gold." He kissed her softly on the forehead.

Hector groaned and rolled his eyes.

Abigail flushed with pleasure, quite forgetting that Cary had ever done anything to annoy her, and quite forgetting that Mr. Temple was her favorite.

The first of the salvaged furnishings from the Dower House began to arrive at Tanglewood the next morning after breakfast. Right away, Abigail spotted a pair of Famille Rose jars. Sadly, one was cracked, but it was enough to make her put off her own plan to paint that afternoon, and instead she directed the rest of the deliveries. There were oil paintings and hip baths, garden implements and chairs, mirrors, and curtains, all jumbled together in interesting confusion. Vera Nashe looked into the room once or twice while Abigail was sorting, but was forced to withdraw each time by fits of sneezing. Abigail worked quietly and efficiently all afternoon, grouping smaller objects on the huge sixteenth-century banquet table of blackened oak, and making careful lists. Cary himself did not put in an appearance until late afternoon. Abigail pounced on him instantly, showing him a crate in which a jumble of kitchen crockery had been thrown with very little packing straw. "Look! Half of it's broken," she complained. "These things must be packed with greater care if they are to be sold."

Cary was unaffected. "It can't be worth much," he said, poking through the bits with a contemptuous finger. "It's only brown crockery."

"You might have sold this slipware jug for ten pounds," she said fiercely. "If the handle hadn't broken off. It all adds up, you know."

"What, this hideously ugly thing? Who'd buy it?"

"Some people collect early English pottery," Abigail explained. "In good condition, a jug like that can be quite valuable because, you see, most of them have had their handles broken off."

"And the furniture? Worth anything?"

Abigail was doubtful. "It seems to be mainly Restoration era, which is not exactly in fashion at the moment."

"Worthless then. I suspected as much."

"No, not worthless," she said. "But you wouldn't be able to sell it in London. You might try to sell it in a local auction. People do need tables and chairs, whatever the fashion. But I should advise you to store it. If it ever comes into vogue again, it might be worth quite a bit."

"The thing is," he said awkwardly, "I need money rather quickly. There's the new fencing, and I promised the tenants I'd put staircases in all their cottages, and then there's *this* drafty old pile, and I haven't yet paid for the improvements I made to the stables. How's it going to look if I don't put staircases in all the cottages, after making over the stables? They'll say I treat my horses better than my people."

"But you should get eight hundred pounds from the salvage of the Dower House," Abigail pointed out. "Possibly as much as a thousand."

"Osborne agreed to pay me five hundred; he's going to haul it all away and sell it."

"Mr. Wayborn! It's worth much more than that."

"I think I did well," he argued. "I need the money quicker, and I can't be bothered selling bricks and roofing slates. I'm a gentleman, after all. Besides, Osborne was expecting to sell the stuff. I couldn't very well cheat him."

"He was going to cheat *you*," Abigail pointed out. "He was going to make you pay to haul it away, and then sell it at a tidy profit."

"Well, I'm not vindictive," said Cary. "And it's worth something to me for him to haul it away and see to the business end of things. I wouldn't know how to sell a brick."

Abigail shook her head. "Is it worth three hundred pounds to you, sir?"

"Well, yes," he said carelessly, "I suppose it must be. But I shall have five hundred pounds in hand by the end of the week, and that's the material thing."

"Will that cover all your debts?" Abigail asked curiously.

"Lord, no," he answered, with a laugh. "I should be ashamed if a mere five hundred pounds could cover my debts. No, I live on a much grander scale than that, Cousin. But it should be enough to cover my debts in Hertfordshire, and that is all I care about."

"Not your London debts?" she murmured in dismay.

"You're not worried about that bloody Red Ritchie fellow, are you?" he asked, smiling. "I say, that's rather good, isn't it? Bloody Red Ritchie."

To her own surprise, Abigail was not angered by the insult to her father. Chiefly she was distressed by Cary's cavalier attitude. "He *has* threatened to put you in debtor's prison," she reminded him.

"I'll settle bloody Red Ritchie, you'll see," he said.

"What do you mean? Will you pay him?"

"Not a penny." His smile flickered, and his voiced became low and caressing. "Are you worried about me, Cousin?"

"Certainly not," she said as convincingly as she could. He reached for her, but this time she was ready for him. "Don't you dare kiss me!" she said, putting her hand up between his mouth and her own.

He seemed surprised. "Kiss you? What on earth made you think I was going to kiss you? I gave you my word I wouldn't, and I always keep my word."

Abigail pulled together the pieces of her shattered dignity. "I see," she said coldly. "That promise is in effect now, is it? Because I seem to recall a time when it was not."

"It's most definitely in effect now," he assured her. "My lips will never again touch yours. You have my word. However, I am not constrained from brushing cobwebs from your shoulder."

To her consternation, he did so, then proceeded to brush them from her skirts as well. "It's no good," he said, after a moment. "Go upstairs and change. I've invited someone to tea, and I want you looking presentable."

"Is it time for tea already?" said Abigail, suddenly aware of the little headache she always felt when she was late getting her tea.

"Yes. You need a clock in here. Or would you like to borrow my pocket watch?"

"That reminds me," she said suddenly. "I found a box full of old clock keys. Perhaps one of them will fit the standing clock in the hall. I'll try them after tea, shall I?"

He propelled her towards the door. "And, for heaven's sake, change out of those noisy boots," he commanded her. "You sound like the infantry on the march. You had a pair of slippers last night at dinner. Can't you wear them?"

"I shall have to borrow—" Abigail began without thinking.

"Borrow what?" he demanded.

"I shall need to go to the village," she said quickly.

"Are you trying to be mysterious?" he said crossly. "Girls with freckles shouldn't try to be mysterious, you know. Out with it. What would you like to borrow? If it's mine to give, you shall have it."

Abigail giggled. "I doubt you have any lady's stockings, sir!"

"Stockings?"

"I must have forgotten to pack mine," Abigail hurriedly explained.

"Can't you borrow from Mrs. Nashe?"

"I did," she said ruefully. "But then I tore great ladders in them. I can't ask her for another pair. They're rather expensive."

To her surprise, Cary seemed to be giving the matter serious thought. If he was at all embarrassed by the nature of her problem he showed no sign of it. "I've got some hosiery, of course, but I shall have to ask my man where he keeps it."

"Why should you have hosiery?" Abigail asked suspiciously.

He frowned at her. "What are you implying? You've seen me in evening dress. Knee breeches and white silk stockings."

"Are you proposing that I wear *your* stockings?" she asked, shocked.

"They only come to my knee, but you're so small they'll probably stop where they ought. Wherever that is," he added with an air of innocence. "I really wouldn't know what a lady's stockings get up to under her skirts."

Abigail snorted.

"Cheeky madam," he reproved her. "Go on up to your room now and change. I'll have Polly bring you my very best pair of stockings. Don't worry," he laughed as he saw her horrified expression. "I'll wrap them up; she won't know what's in the package."

When Abigail had put on Vera's stockings she had felt no intimate connection with that lady, but wearing a man's stockings, she discovered, was quite a different experience. She felt silkier, more feminine, and just a little bit naughty. As she entered the small parlor where the others had gathered for tea, she saw only Cary as he stood up and bowed. She curtsied back demurely, but their eyes met in silent conspiracy. A shiver of excitement went through her. Later, in her room, she would tell herself it had only been her ridiculous imagination, but while in the moment, she freely enjoyed the little secret they shared. It was a fine, private enjoyment, better than his kisses, which had always caught her in too much surprise to be wholly pleasing. She slipped quietly into the chair next to Mrs. Spurgeon, who was yellow-haired again after her brief turn as a brunette.

"Abigail, may I present my cousin, Sir Horatio Cary," Cary said formally.

"Oh!" Abigail exclaimed in surprise. She had not even seen the other gentleman, though he too had risen as she came into the room. She saw now that he was just a bit taller than Cary, and strikingly handsome, too, with deep cornflower blue eyes and dark gold hair coifed in a fashionable crop. He wore a small mustache and beard, rather like the one Cary had removed the day before.

"*Captain* Sir Horatio," Horatio corrected, bending over Abigail's hand. "It was my honor to end the war in command of the *H.M.S. Monarch*. I don't doubt you've heard of her, Miss Smith? And then His Royal Highness, the Prince of Wales, was so generous as to knight me."

His manner of speaking was so deliberately high-toned that Abigail felt he was attempting to belittle her. She looked askance at Cary.

"All true as far I know," he murmured, a remark which his cousin chose not to hear.

"His Royal Highness, on the occasion of his granting me my knighthood, was so kind as to condescend to present me with a small token of his esteem. May I show it to you, Miss Smith? Mrs. Nashe is admiring it at the moment," he added, and Vera instantly gave it up.

"Certainly; by all means," Abigail said politely, though she was more than ever taken aback by his pomposity. The Prince's token turned out to be nothing more than a gold snuffbox with a brown horse painted on its green enameled lid. Abigail dutifully admired the

Regent's taste, both in snuffboxes and in Knights of the Realm, and gave the little box back to its proud owner. She then felt at leisure to take her seat and drink her tea.

"My cousin tells me that you are Lord Wayborn's niece, Miss Smith," said Sir Horatio as Mrs. Nashe passed him his cup.

"Yes, my mother was his lordship's sister," Abigail replied, with her usual reticence.

"Excellent!" he said, smiling at her.

He really was an exceptionally handsome man, Abigail decided, without being attracted to him in the least. While superior to his cousin in manners and formality, he lacked Cary's warmth and charm. His very superiority awakened hostility in ordinary mortals. "Excellent, sir?" she responded stiffly. "In what way?"

"I had grave concerns, Miss Smith," he said earnestly, "when I learned that my impetuous cousin had brought in some tenants for the Dower House. Of course, if the estate had been properly managed, there would be no need of that sort of thing. We never had to take in tenants before. And now this sad business with the elm. If only you had cut it down, Cousin Cary, when I advised you to *last* winter."

"Did you do so?" Cary sounded disinterested.

"Of course I did, and so did my father; I recall it distinctly," Horatio answered. "But then you've never been one to take advice." He turned to Abigail with his charming smile. "When I heard he'd leased the Dower House, I imagined all sorts of low characters in the neighborhood. Guess my relief when I learned who you are, Miss Smith. Naturally, I have no objection to respectable people of good family occupying the house."

Cary suddenly got to his feet. "We had better go, Cousin Abigail," he said, as Abigail and Horatio looked at him in surprise, "if we are to reach the village before the shops close."

"Did you need to go to the shops, Miss Smith?" said Horatio before Abigail could reply. "Please allow me to take you. I have my gig." He looked pointedly at Cary. "I should think you would be on your way to Brisby's farm, Cary. Brisby has reported a case of swine fever."

"What am I to do about it?" said Cary.

Horatio sniffed as if such a response was no more than what he had expected. "Then, of course, there's the removal work going on at the Dower House. Quite dangerous, I should think, given the state of the roof. Why, it might collapse at any moment. I should think you have more important responsibilities than escorting this charming young lady on a shopping excursion. I will accompany Miss Smith to the village. It would be my honor."

Cary controlled his annoyance with difficulty. "Certainly. If Abigail has no objection."

"I should not wish to inconvenience Sir Captain Horatio," Abigail said quickly.

"It's *Captain Sir* Horatio," said the gentleman. "But you may call me simply Sir Horatio. And I assure you, my dear young lady, it is no inconvenience to me."

"I think I should go with Mr. Wayborn to the Dower House," said Abigail. Indeed, Horatio's pomposity had made Cary's company more desirable than ever. "To make sure things are being packed correctly," she added.

Horatio sniffed. "I should think Cary would be able to manage that much on his own, though perhaps I am wrong. In any case, I could not let you go near the place, Miss Smith. It's far too dangerous."

"Horatio is quite right," Cary said, to Abigail's consternation. "I couldn't permit you within a hundred yards of the Dower House. Besides, you *do* need to go to the shops."

"If there's an apothecary," Mrs. Spurgeon suddenly

interjected, after an interlude of extraordinary silence, "you might fetch me some of my headache powder. I do feel one of my fits coming on. Vera, help me to my bed."

"I will get my cloak, Sir Horatio," Abigail said as Mrs. Nashe helped her mistress from the room. "Thank you."

Chapter 9

"Are these not *your* horses, Mr. Wayborn?" Abigail asked, puzzled, as they stepped out through the portico and she saw the team of bays harnessed to Horatio's newly lacquered gig.

"What, those cursed old nags?" Cary exclaimed indignantly as Horatio's groom hopped down to open the door for Abigail. "I drive a team of chestnuts. These are bays. Rather nondescript bays, at that. And you've got their heads raised too high, Horatio," he added. Rushing over, he brought the near horse's harness down two notches, relieving the strain on the horse's neck.

"It's the fashion," said Horatio, considerably annoyed.

"It's a bloody stupid fashion," said Cary, moving on to the other horse. "If you must raise their heads to such an absurd degree," he went on, ignoring his cousin and speaking directly to the groom, "better to do it slowly, by inches. Let the poor beast get used to the strain."

"Hoggett! Attend me! You will raise their heads this instant."

"Don't be a damn fool, Horatio," Cary said through clenched teeth.

"Kindly refrain from using such language in the presence of a lady," Horatio said coldly, tucking Abigail's gloved hand in the crook of his elbow. "My dear Miss Smith, I do apologize for my cousin's want of conduct."

"I'll talk however I damn well please on my own front steps," Cary said angrily.

"I think," Abigail said quickly, "that your horses are very pretty, Sir Horatio. I think they're quite as pretty as Mr. Wayborn's chestnuts."

Cary's rage subsided into exasperation. "*Pretty?*" he said incredulously. "Do you know nothing about horses? Do you at least ride?"

"I've had lessons," Abigail said doubtfully. "But they move around so. The horses, I mean, not the lessons. If only they would stand perfectly still, I'm sure I could do it."

Cary sighed as if he had never encountered such a lapse in human conduct in all his life, and Abigail distinctly heard Sir Horatio's groom chuckle.

"Hoggett! I am waiting for you to raise their heads," Horatio said, undeterred from his original purpose. "Mr. Wayborn may do as he pleases with his own cattle, but I am a Knight of the Realm. I will not have my horses going about with their heads down."

"Please don't, Sir Horatio," Abigail pleaded. "Don't do it if it hurts them."

Horatio smiled at her. "My dear Miss Smith," he said, helping her into the vehicle. "I would by no means go against *your* wishes." He climbed in beside her, and the groom jumped up into the driver's seat. Cary gave them only a sullen wave as they started off down the drive.

"I believe I must have offended Mr. Wayborn in some way," Abigail said, biting her lip. "It's true I'm entirely ignorant on the subject of horses. Is it wrong to say a horse is pretty?"

"The boy is horse mad," Horatio replied, leaning back comfortably in the cushioned seat. "Always has been.

He looks down on anyone who isn't as keen as he is. I'm no horseman, Miss Smith. Why should I be, when I have lived aboard ships for more than half my life?"

Not wishing to encourage any more familiarity, Abigail did not inquire about her companion's experiences in the Royal Navy. He told her anyway, concluding his long, vainglorious narrative as they turned onto the High Street of Tanglewood Green. "One thing I learned at sea, Miss Smith," he added importantly, as he answered the respectful nod of a passerby with a careless wave of his gloved hand, "which our mutual cousin will do well to learn on land, is to care for my people properly, in mind, in body, and in spirit."

Abigail's spine stiffened. "Are you saying Mr. Wayborn doesn't care for his people?"

Horatio smiled thinly. "I am sorry to pain you, Miss Smith, but it's quite true. Upon inheriting the place from my grandmother, he spent all the income on London amusements and left his tenants to shift for themselves."

Abigail was puzzled. "*Your* grandmother, sir? But I had thought Mrs. Cary was Mr. Wayborn's grandmother, and that your father was his mother's cousin."

"That is true," said Horatio. "But my father was so exquisitely aware of the duty he owed the estate that he condescended to marry his cousin and assume the parsonage at Tanglewood Green. My mama and Cary's mama were sisters, you see. Now, my father does not agree with first cousins marrying, but, in his case, it was entirely justified. Old Mr. Cary hated my father so much that he would not have granted him the living at the vicarage otherwise."

"I see," said Abigail.

"But I was speaking of my cousin's negligence. He never lived here. If it were not for my father's efforts on his behalf, pandemonium would have ensued after my grandmother died."

"But Mr. Wayborn *does* live here," Abigail protested.

"Oh, yes, *now*," Horatio agreed contemptuously. "His creditors have run him out of London, I daresay. And what do you suppose he did, upon arriving in the neighborhood after years of absenteeism? Did he build a school? Did he put sanitary drains and staircases in the cottages? No, indeed! He renovated his stables. Horses before people, that's his motto."

Abigail squirmed uncomfortably. She hated to hear Cary spoken of so harshly, but she could scarcely defend him against charges she suspected might be true. "I believe he is trying to do better, Sir Horatio," she said unhappily. "It is not easy to change."

But Horatio was just getting started on a favorite theme. "He's a disgrace to the family, that's what he is. Singing in the church choir and giving a Christmas ball—at which intoxicating spirits were served to the lower orders—cannot atone for all his years of neglect!"

"Does my cousin sing in the church choir?" Abigail asked, momentarily diverted by the charming image of Cary in a white robe singing orisons. She assumed he had a pleasing tenor.

"It's not enough," he coldly told her as the groom brought the gig to a gentle stop.

"He does intend to put staircases into all the cottages," said Abigail, as Horatio helped her alight from the vehicle.

"Yes, Miss Smith. *All* of them. That is the other problem."

"*Other* problem? I don't understand."

"Cary is determined to make improvements to *all* the cottages." He moved closer to her and spoke confidentially. "Even the ones who don't deserve it. There is a *woman* among his tenants, Miss Smith, a very low, loose-moraled creature, I'm sorry to say. Her children bear the stain of illegitimacy. In the course of his Christian duties, my father naturally has refused her all assistance. Indeed, her character is so far beyond redemption that he had no choice but to deny her the new vaccines for her children."

"But that is monstrous!" said Abigail, aghast. "The children should not be made to suffer for their mother's transgressions, even if she is as bad as you say."

"Indeed they should not, Miss Smith," Horatio agreed, entirely missing the thrust of her words. "'Tis a great pity that, due to the mother's sin, two children have died of smallpox, and a third was born blind. But Cary refuses to turn them out. He should have more respect for *you*, Miss Smith, than to allow this vicious woman to continue living among decent people."

His priggish hypocrisy was beyond Abigail's power to understand or tolerate.

"Excuse me, Sir Horatio," she said, stopping at the door of a shop. "I must go in. Would you be good enough to wait for me outside?" She rushed into the shop before he could reply.

Quickly she purchased a dozen pairs of stockings, and rejoined Horatio on the street, where he was engaged in verbally stripping down his groom. As he saw her, Horatio instantly stopped haranguing his servant and offered Abigail his arm. After a few more errands, they returned to the gig and started back for the Manor House beneath a darkening sky.

"I hope I have not said too much," Horatio said, tucking the fur rug securely over Abigail's legs. "It was not my intention to upset you, only to warn you."

"Indeed, sir," she said, willing herself to maintain a civil disinterest.

"Do forgive my presumption," he said, his voice cloying. "Indeed, I hope that I am wrong in thinking you have formed an attachment to my unworthy cousin. Cary will be obliged to marry into a great fortune if he is to save the estate. Forgive me, Miss Smith, I know you have some ten thousand pounds, but I fear it will not be enough to clear his London debts."

Abigail could no longer pretend to be disinterested. "Are you saying my cousin is a fortune hunter?" she demanded.

Horatio sighed. "He *ought* to marry an heiress, and well he knows it. But he is so . . . so *perverse* in his habits that he prides himself on doing quite the opposite of what is fit and proper. Very likely, he will marry some penniless nobody, just to spite his family." He shook his finely coifed head. "If only the estate had been entailed! But it was *not* entailed, and the previous owner left it to his wife, of all people. My grandmother left it to Cary Wayborn. No one knows why. He never went near the place when my grandmother was alive, *and* he was most ungrateful when she offered to purchase him a commission in the Army."

"But Mr. Wayborn was not an officer," said Abigail, confused. "He had no commission."

"That is precisely what I mean, Miss Smith," Horatio replied. "Ingratitude. Cary was only eighteen at the time. He had not yet come into his money, and his elder brother refused to give him access to the funds. But Cary was determined to have his way. For the sake of the family's honor, my grandmother offered him the money to buy his colors. My dear Miss Smith, I am sorry to speak ill of my own kin, but Cary actually *declined* the offer! Instead, the ingrate ran away from University, and enlisted in the Army as a common private. A *common private*, Miss Smith! I daresay, you can imagine how degraded we all felt when we found out what he'd done."

"Your discomfiture must have been unimaginable," Abigail said, suppressing a smile.

"I have it on good authority that, while he was in Spain, he was *flogged*."

"Good God," Abigail breathed. "Flogged?"

"That is what comes of sleeping on the ground with the men, and eating from a common cooking pot . . ." Horatio shuddered delicately. "Without servants or civility! It was not fitting behavior for a gentleman. But then, Cary has always been selfish."

"I suppose," said Abigail slowly, "he wanted to serve his country. I daresay, he knew he wouldn't make a convincing clergyman. Not like your esteemed father."

"We were prepared to forgive him, too," said Horatio. "But when he came back from Spain, he was no better. Unapologetic, and as determined as ever to have his own way. When he came into his fortune, he squandered it. In less than eighteen months, it was gone. Twenty thousand pounds, mind you! But then what should happen, but that my silly grandmother should die and leave him Tanglewood. She must have gone mad at the end; that's all I can conclude."

"Mrs. Cary was entitled to leave her property as she pleased, was she not?"

Her indignation was entirely wasted on him. "You've put your finger on the heart of the matter, my dear," he said, still confident of her sympathy. "Tanglewood ought to have been entailed away from the female line. No one adores the fair sex as much as I, but, when females are free to leave property as they will, ruin and chaos is the natural result. A lady is not a fit judge of such matters."

"And Mr. Cary?" Abigail said sharply. "Do you not respect his decision to will his property to his wife? Was he not the best judge of how to dispose of his own property?"

He actually smiled at her. "What a delight it is to converse with an intelligent female!" he said. "You seem almost to guess my thoughts, Miss Smith. Of *course* that is the great evil in not having an estate properly entailed to the male line. Without the comfort of an entail, a man may be persuaded to leave all his worldly goods to his wife, or even to his daughter!"

"And, if Tanglewood *had* been entailed, would it have gone to you, Sir Horatio?"

"To my father, first, then to me, as his eldest son. My father, you see, is the son of a son, while Mr. Wayborn is merely the son of a daughter." With shocking presumption, Horatio took her hand in his. "I am telling you these things, Miss Smith, because I felt a certain natural regard for you the moment we met. I would not want the innocent niece of Lord Wayborn to fall prey to my cousin's fatal charm. I should not want you, my dear Miss Smith, to discover too late that he is a rather insincere young man. I should not want you to break your heart."

Abigail pulled her hand away. "I assure you, Sir Horatio, my heart is in no danger."

"Fortunately, you will not be bereft of more agreeable company. *I* come to Hertfordshire every Sunday to hear my father's sermon. I expect you and I will become great friends."

Abigail doubted his friendship, but she let him kiss her hand when they parted at the Manor. It seemed the quickest way to be rid of his "agreeable" company.

The next day was Sunday. Abigail did not attend services in the village. When the other members of the household, including the servants, left early for church, she had the house to herself. After giving Paggles her breakfast, she decided that her first project would be to see if any of the keys she had discovered might fit the tall standing clock in the entrance hall. She chose the very largest key to try first, and, to her delight, it fitted. She was able to open the glass door and get the clock

working again. After running upstairs to check her own
clock, she was able to move the hands to the correct
time. Her triumph was sadly lessened when she heard
how loudly it ticked; she could hear it quite clearly in
the banquet hall at the other end of the house, where she
spent the rest of the morning at work, taking inventory.
The chimes boomed impressively at the top of the
hour—like a Chinese gong. It occurred to her that the
key might have been lost accidentally on purpose.

She had just come down from checking on Paggles—
Dickie-bird's new striped muffler was progressing
nicely—when Mrs. Spurgeon, Vera, and Evans returned
from church. Mrs. Spurgeon had found the journey very
tiring; she wished to go immediately to bed.

"Oh, I am sorry," said Abigail. While she had her
doubts about Mrs. Spurgeon's need for a full-time nurse-
maid, she thought the lady appeared genuinely fatigued.
When Vera came out a few minutes later, Abigail asked
whether she thought they should send for the doctor.
Vera assured her that her mistress would be quite well
after a long rest. Unconcerned, the dark-haired woman
walked down the hall and stopped at the door to Cary's
study.

"Time to feed Cato. Evans won't go near the beastly
thing, so the task falls to me. Unless, of course, *you*
would like to do it?" Vera's eyes twinkled at Abigail.

"No, indeed," Abigail said, hurrying back to the banquet hall to continue her work. A few minutes later, a
noise, which she assumed to be the servants returning
from church, brought her out of the east wing. As she
passed the staircase, she collided with Cary, who had
come down the stairs almost at a run.

"Abigail!" He put out both hands to steady her.
"Good God, I'm sorry. Are you all right?" He looked
down at her with concern in his steady gray eyes. The

force of attraction gripped her anew, as if this were the first time she had ever seen that lean, dark face.

"I'm all right," she said quickly. "Nothing broken."

"Shall I send for the doctor?"

Abigail shook her head to clear her thoughts. He must have been inquiring after Mrs. Spurgeon's health, she thought stupidly. She had only imagined that his concern was for her. "Vera thinks all she needs is rest."

"What? I take that as a sign of delirium. Come here and sit down." He put her on the steps, and she sat down obediently. "Have you had any fever?"

"Do you mean has Mrs. Spurgeon had any fever?" she said slowly.

"Mrs. Spurgeon be damned," he said cheerfully, laying the back of his hand across her forehead. His hand felt beautifully warm. "You're quite cool, thank God, but I'm not taking any chances. You're going back to bed, and I'm having the doctor."

Abigail jumped up. "I don't need a doctor," she said firmly.

"Well, you're ill aren't you?" he demanded.

Abigail shook her head, confused. "Ill?"

"Mrs. Spurgeon said you were ill. Aren't you?"

"No," said Abigail. "No, indeed. Why would she say such a thing?"

"You were not in church," he pointed out. "Headache? I hope it's better now."

"No, I'm perfectly well," Abigail protested. "I never had headache. I don't attend Church of England services, that's all. I'm Presbyterian."

For a moment he appeared incredulous. Then he laughed aloud. "Poor Mr. Temple—he had such high hopes! This will be a great scandal in the neighborhood, Cousin," he added with mock gravity. "Worse than the Scandal of the Lady's Pint. I had no idea the Derbyshire Wayborns have turned Presbyterian."

"They haven't," said Abigail. "My mother was Church of England. My father is Presbyterian, though I must confess, we are not very devout. I believe I've been to church no more than a handful of times in my life. I don't see why you're laughing."

"I don't see why I am either," he said, sobering. "I'm going to catch hell from the Vicar. He's already after me to turn off my groom, who is Irish and a Catholic. Now, it seems, I have rented my house to a mad Calvinist maiden."

"I'm not a Calvinist," said Abigail, annoyed. "And I don't see what business it is of the Vicar's if I'm not Church of England. We do live in a free society, after all."

"I wouldn't call Cousin Wilfred's parish a free society, exactly," said Cary, laughing. "Come, I'll introduce him to you."

"He's here?" she cried, forgetting her brave words on religious freedom.

"He insisted on coming," Cary said grimly. "Horatio too."

"Oh, dear," Abigail murmured in dismay. "I wish Mrs. Spurgeon had not told them I was ill. I'm sorry if they were worried."

He looked at her coolly. "*I* was worried."

Abigail flushed hotly.

"To be fair, Horatio expressed the most elegant concern. I daresay he has no idea you're a Presbyterian. I can't wait to tell him," he added gleefully. "Shall we?"

Abigail began, haltingly, "I believe I must check on Paggles—" but Cary took her firmly in hand, saying, "Nonsense. I just looked in on her, and she is in a state of perfect happiness."

In the next moment, she was standing in front of Horatio and his father, the Vicar. Both men climbed to their feet when Abigail entered the room. Before Cary could do so, Horatio performed the introductions.

The Vicar was an elder, paunchier, bespectacled version of his son. Abigail found it difficult to believe he was responsible for denying smallpox vaccines to parish children. "My dear Miss Smith, I cannot tell you how glad I am that you are feeling better," he said in the ringing voice of a true veteran of the pulpit.

"She's not sick, Cousin Wilfred," Cary said traitorously, standing behind her. "She never was. She just don't go to Church of England services. Never has."

The Vicar's blue eyes blinked rapidly. Sir Horatio appeared quite taken aback, too. "Never goes to—!" stuttered the father.

"Surely she's not a Papist," the son said stiffly.

Abigail wished she could run away, but Cary had planted himself behind her. "No, Presbyterian," he said helpfully.

"Good God!" the Vicar whispered, staring at Abigail almost in horror.

"Cheer up, Cousin Wilfred," Cary said irreverently. "At least she's not a Druid."

"My mother was Church of England," Abigail said, hoping this might prevent the Vicar from dropping dead of apoplexy. It did seem to help; the Vicar's color began to return to normal. "My father's Presbyterian, so I've never been quite sure what that makes me. I shouldn't like to go against my father, but then again, I shouldn't like to dishonor my mother's memory."

"Oh, I see," said the Vicar, with an air of immense relief. "I daresay the matter will be decided when she marries," he went on, apparently talking to his son. "If she marries a Presbyterian, I expect she will be lost to us forever. But if she were to marry an Episcopalian . . ."

"Now, Papa," Horatio interjected, with a little self-deprecating laugh. "You mustn't try making any matches for Miss Smith."

"No, indeed," said Cary, brutally suppressing the

subject. "You are not here to find Abigail a husband, Cousin Wilfred. You wanted to see all the bits and bobs coming out of the Dower House. Well, come and have a look. Abigail has been working very hard in bringing it all to some kind of order."

The older gentleman was instantly diverted. "Yes, indeed," he said earnestly. "I do think, if it's at all possible, that our family treasures should stay within the family."

"It's a disgrace that we must even think of selling them," declared Horatio. "But if you must sell, you should at least allow the family to go through the things first. I understand you sold quite a few paintings from the Manor without telling anyone. There was a Craddock landscape I particularly wanted. We are not without means," he added, smiling at Abigail. "We can certainly afford to give you some money, Cousin Cary, if you are in desperate straits."

"I beg your pardon, Dr. Cary," Abigail interrupted. "I'd like to offer you some refreshment, but I don't think the servants have returned yet. They are walking, I think."

"Yes," said Horatio, with triumph in his blue eyes. "In former times, there was a wagon to take the servants to church. Nowadays, they must walk."

He never seemed to miss an opportunity to belittle his cousin. Abigail could only hope she had not sounded quite so pompous when she'd criticized Cary for letting some of his kitchen crockery get broken. Dismaying thought! She silently vowed never to criticize Cary again.

"Do not trouble yourself," said the Vicar, patting her hand. "I doubt there is any tea in the house worth drinking anyway. Now, as I recall, there were a number of valuable portraits . . ."

Abigail would have preferred entering the room last,

or not at all, but she was swept ahead of the three men. At first glance, the room seemed a disordered jumble of odds and ends. Embarrassed that all her hard work had not yielded a better presentation, Abigail quickly led the Vicar over to the corner where she had grouped the paintings into portraits, landscapes, and still lives. The Vicar seemed to know exactly what he was looking for.

"Here it is!" he said, summoning Horatio to help him separate one large portrait in an elaborate frame from the rest. "Cary, I'll give you ten pounds for it on the spot. I have it on me."

"I trust it's not money from the collection plate," Cary replied.

"It's a Sir Peter Lely," Abigail protested as she saw the painting. "I shouldn't sell it for less than two hundred pounds, Mr. Wayborn."

The Vicar sputtered, and Horatio loudly protested, but Abigail remained firm.

Cary eyed the portrait dispassionately. He liked pictures of pretty women, preferably innocent of clothing, and he liked pictures of horses. Beyond that he had little interest in art. "And who is Sir Peter Lely? One of my moldy old ancestors?"

Abigail's eyes widened. "Sir Peter Lely is the artist, Mr. Wayborn. The sitter, as I'm sure you must know, is Oliver Cromwell. Are you descended of Oliver Cromwell?"

Cary guffawed. "Is *that* the old regicide? What on earth is he doing in my house? And worth two hundred pounds, you say?"

"I should think," Horatio began loftily, "that since we are family . . ."

"You ought to be allowed to cheat me?" Cary finished, smiling. "Cousin Abigail says I mustn't take less than two hundred pounds for it, so, you see, I have my instructions."

"What a vile man Cromwell was," said Abigail,

shuddering. "And yet so ordinary in appearance. It makes one feel ill."

"Come now, Miss Smith," Horatio rebuked her. "Desperate times call for desperate measures. He was what England needed for the time. A strong hand on the till."

Abigail turned on Horatio angrily. "Oliver Cromwell murdered our king because His Majesty disbanded Parliament. Then *he* sat on a stolen throne, and did the very same thing. He ruled like a tyrant, murdering anyone who got in his way. What England needed! I suppose you think *Napoleon* was good for the Continent, too."

Horatio smiled tightly. "Of course I will not argue with a lady," he said with forced calm, "but I make certain that, if Miss Smith knew anything whatever of historical fact, she would agree with my opinion, which is, of course, the only reasonable opinion on the subject."

"Perhaps I'll give it to my groom," said Cary thoughtfully. "He's Irish. He'll want to throw darts at it. He can hang it up in the stables."

"It's far too valuable for that," said Abigail regretfully. "It must be sold."

"I will give you one hundred pounds for it," said Horatio. "It ought to remain in the family, as it has for over a hundred and fifty years."

"You're certainly welcome to go to London and bid on it at auction," said Cary magnanimously. "Indeed, Cousin Horatio, I hope you get it."

"Come, Papa," said Horatio coldly, drawing himself up to his full height. "He is not going to be reasonable. He cares nothing for the family."

"I'm so sorry, Mr. Wayborn," Abigail breathed, when they had gone. "I did not mean to make trouble for you with your family. But ten pounds was not a serious offer."

"No matter," he said. "They will always find fault with me. You see, they had some right to expect Tanglewood would belong to them one day. Rather unexpectedly, my grandmother left it to me."

"They have no right to criticize you. You may dispose of your property as you wish."

"And pack my crockery however I wish?" he teased her. "I deserve much of their criticism. I have been a poor landlord."

"That is in the past," she said quickly. "You are making amends now."

"If I am to make amends I shall need money." He sat down on the edge of the banquet table and picked up a small figure carved of ivory. Abigail thought it might be the queen from a chess set, but she had not managed to locate any other pieces. "Do you really think I could get two hundred pounds for the old regicide?" he asked.

She nodded. "Some people think highly of the so-called Lord Protector. You might even get more. Personally, *I* wouldn't give you five pounds for it."

He grinned. "Not even with a view of re-selling it later at a tidy profit?"

"I do have some standards, Mr. Wayborn," she said primly.

"I am glad to hear it," he said. "I was beginning to wonder about your taste in men. First you reject me—that alone shows a want of proper womanly feeling. Then you cut a swathe through the local population. Messieurs Pimple and Buttocks will never be the same. Now my cousin Horatio seems to have fallen beneath your fatal spell. Oh, and I mustn't forget poor Hector Mickleby. You see, I cannot even keep score, your conquests are so fast and furious. Who will be Cousin Abigail's next victim? Whose heart will she break next?"

"Your cousin!" Abigail exclaimed indignantly.

"So it's to be Horatio, is it? And you claim to have standards."

"I do, sir. And *he* is most assuredly beneath them."

"I daresay he had much to say about me, and none of it good," Cary said idly.

"Actually, he gave you a sterling character," Abigail replied, "though, to be sure, he meant to do the opposite."

"A sterling character," he mused. "Do you think mine is a sterling character, cousin?"

"Certainly not," said Abigail, smiling. "You are impulsive and imprudent. Your language is quite shocking at times, and of course, you do take insufferable liberties."

"You sound like Horatio," he said. "Except for the taking liberties part."

She made a face. "If you ever compare me to him again, I shall make you very sorry."

He chuckled softly. "And how would a gentle little thing like you make me sorry?"

"I'll think of something," she said smartly, and, mercifully, inspiration struck. "I could tell Mr. Weston you have got dog hair on one of his coats! That would make you sorry."

"Very sorry indeed," he agreed. "And that, I think, is my cue to take myself off for a thorough brushing."

"Oh, no," said Abigail. "I didn't mean—"

"It is not good-bye," he assured her, "but au revoir. You will see me again, and I daresay, sooner than you would like. Mrs. Spurgeon has bid me come to dinner, and I daren't refuse her anything. So we will take our mutton together—or, rather, our veal. You have no objection?"

"To your coming to dine? No, indeed."

"Good," he said, bowing over her hand. "Because she's also asked Horatio and Cousin Wilfred. It promises to be a delightful evening."

Despite her unhappy conviction that it was useless to try, Abigail wanted to look pretty for Cary that evening.

She went upstairs to try on every dinner dress she had brought with her to Hertfordshire in the vain hope that one of them had the power to transform her into a diamond of the first water. The results, which she studied at length in the mirror hung inside the wardrobe door, inevitably disappointed. Whatever she wore, she was still short in stature, freckled, and topped with curly hair. It was hopeless.

As she stood studying the effect of a saffron gown of very fine India muslin, she suddenly remembered that she still had Cary's stockings. The night before she had carefully washed them in her room, inspected them for snags and ladders, of which, thankfully, there were none, and set them out to dry at the fireside. When they were dry, she had carefully wrapped them up in brown paper. Now she composed a short note, thanking the owner for their use, and went down to find a manservant to deliver the package to the gatehouse.

As she tiptoed past Mrs. Spurgeon's chamber, in which that redoubtable woman lay snoring, she saw that the door to Cary's study was open. The beastly macaw would be able to escape if he hadn't already. She looked in cautiously, planning to close the door quickly if Cato was still safely inside. Instead, her hand froze on the doorknob.

The bloodstained corgi was relaxed at full length upon the rug, inside a ring of scarlet and turquoise feathers, his short back legs stretched behind him. With his strong jaws he was busily crunching on something. Abigail did not choose to speculate on what it might be. She could not pretend to mourn the loss of Cato, but this seemed a more painful death than he deserved.

"*Angel!*" she cried. "You bad dog! What have you done?"

Angel looked at her over his shoulder, feathers protruding from his mouth. Overcome with horror, Abigail closed the door, and ran blindly out of the house, as fast as she could, in the direction of the gatehouse, scarcely feeling the cold blowing up her saffron skirts.

Before she could knock on the door, Cary opened it and pulled her aside.

"Did anyone see you?" he asked, looking out the door quickly before shutting it tight.

She shook her head, trying to catch her breath. There was a deep, painful stitch in her side. For a moment she could not speak. "Angel . . ." she finally gasped.

"Darling!" he replied, to her astonishment. Without another word, he dragged her into his arms and kissed her.

Chapter 10

After a moment's indecision, Abigail gave in, stretching her arms around his neck, and giving him her mouth. He moaned softly. This maddening girl had never responded to him before, never opened her mouth, never returned his caresses, but now he could feel her hands clutching his hair as her small, soft body pressed against his.

It would be churlish of her to correct such a sweet misunderstanding, Abigail decided. After all, she might just as easily have been talking about him when she had said "Angel." She could scarcely deny that she adored him. Abandoning herself to his kiss, she felt his tongue gently probing her until, as if possessed by him, her own tongue began to move into his mouth. Pleasure unlike anything she had ever experienced swept through her body like a tempest, and if he had not been holding her so tightly her legs might have given way. Her terrifying shyness seemed to leave her all at once. The shock of her first real arousal was almost too much for her.

He broke the kiss first. "I knew you would come to me one day and release me from that damned stupid promise," he murmured against the silky skin of her throat, brushing his firm mouth against her leaping pulse. "I have dreamed of this moment."

"Oh," Abigail said, wishing with all her heart that this, in fact, had been the purpose of her coming. "Have—have you really dreamed of me?"

"Yes," he said. He was holding her by the shoulders, and there was a strange, dangerous light in his gray eyes that caused her heart to race. "Haven't you dreamed of me?"

Abigail simply nodded. She did not think this a conceited question at all; it seemed perfectly natural that she would dream of him, and that he would ask her about it. "We were back in Hatchard's, and you kissed my hand."

A glint of amusement appeared in his eyes. "That's very nice, monkey," he said gravely. "Now let me show you my dream." He molded the shape of her body with his hands. "You weren't wearing this in my dream," he murmured, fingering the golden brown muslin.

"What was I wearing?" she asked anxiously. "It's so difficult to find a color that doesn't clash with my hair."

"You were naked," he replied. As her mouth fell open in shock, he pulled her closer to him and began kissing her again, gently but thoroughly. "You usually are."

Abigail stared at him, mesmerized by his burning eyes. "Do you dream of me often?"

"Every night," he answered, brushing her lips with his fingertips.

"And I'm—I'm—I haven't got any clothes?"

"That is how it ends," he said. "Shall I show you how it begins?"

Abigail felt her aching bones melt at the sound of his voice. She waited for her powers of reasoning to come to her rescue, but she could neither think nor speak.

"You know what I'm going to do next, don't you?" he

said softly, and, mutely, she nodded, lifting her mouth for his kiss. "I want to feel every shiver of your body as I discover every secret. I want you to tremble when I touch you. I want you to cry out in pleasure. I want to be the one to make you a woman."

Abigail had merely expected to be kissed again, but this sounded delightful, too. She drew closer to his warmth and closed her eyes in trusting surrender.

As if in a dream, she felt his hand on her throat and then her left breast. He cupped her gently. "I have dreamed of this and this and this," he whispered, imprinting her throat with kiss after kiss. His hands slipped around her back, and then his head was on her breasts. With the point of his tongue he drew a line down the valley between her breasts, until her dress forced him to withdraw. He tugged at her gown with growing frustration, but Abigail was too lost in his caresses and her own pleasure to recognize his need. She thought everything was perfect; his dark, warm hands, his mouth. Her nipple tightened almost painfully as he drew it into his mouth, sucking it gently through the thin muslin of her gown. It was not what he wanted, but the dream of caressing her naked breasts would have to wait; he didn't want to tear her dress.

Holding her to him, his mouth glued to hers, he moved her over to the table. Still kissing her, he began drawing her skirts up. Here at least, he could feel the skin he craved. He found stocking. Very nice, white silk stocking purchased the day before, but it was not what he wanted. Abigail moaned softly into his mouth as he drew his hand up the length of her new stockings, from her ankle to her knee. He thought he would lose his mind. Above the knee, just where he ought to have found warm female flesh, he discovered drawers. Very fine lawn drawers with beautifully worked tiers, but it was not what he wanted.

Grunting now, urged on by her voluptuous response to his kiss, he sought out her most secret treasure, almost humming with excitement at the joining of her thighs. The lawn was so thin he could feel her dampness, and the texture of the tight curls, and he pressed the soft mound fiercely with his hand. Abigail responded instinctively, rocking slightly back and forth.

Cary could no longer control his desires. In the next instant, he had torn the buttons off her drawers and forced his hand inside the rent, cupping her mound. Their cries mingled together as they joined mouths. The little nest of soft red-gold hairs was sweet beyond his dreams. He felt the delicate lips opening to him, and Abigail suddenly went still.

"Cary, what are you doing?" she whispered uncertainly.

"Trust me," he answered, finding the soft bud above her entrance and stroking it gently. Abigail thought she would die of pleasure as he caressed her, at first slowly, and then with greater and greater urgency, until, pressed against his hand, she reached the pinnacle of pleasure. Watching her face as she melted under his touch gave him tremendous pleasure but it was not enough to ease his painful erection.

"I want you out of this dress," he finally growled, startling her out of the clouds of her crisis. "Where in the bloody hell are the buttons?"

Without thinking, she told him. "Here on the side."

At the same time, she became vaguely aware that he had laid her down on the rude planked table of the gatehouse, as if he meant to make a meal of her. She smoothed down her skirts with a furtive hand, and willed her breathing to return to normal. What was that strange feeling that had wracked her whole body? It had frightened and confused her, but to him it seemed a matter of course. She wanted to ask him about it, but it was evident he was in no mood for questions. He

seemed almost angry. Abigail suddenly felt she might
burst into tears.

"Why in hell's name are they under your arm?" he
asked, undoing her top button with one hand, while
clearing off the rest of the table with the other. A tin cup
bounced on the floor. He was desperate now for his own
satisfaction. Most of all, after touching her sweetness,
he wanted to see her body, her breasts, her soft belly, the
succulent fruit between her legs. He wanted full possession of her, body and soul, and he could no longer wait.
Consequences be damned.

"I have to dress myself," she explained. "I can't do the
buttons if they are in the back."

"There's an awful lot of them, and I can't guarantee
their safety. You'd better do it."

"I have no intention of undressing," said Abigail, hurt
and bewildered by the change in him. When he had
driven her wild, he had been gentle and sensitive to her
every response. Now he seemed cold, rough, and almost
businesslike.

"Fine!" he said, pushing her skirts up rudely.

Abigail thought at first that he was going to bring her
to another crisis, but he was opening her, first her drawers, and then the soft inner lips of her body, preparing
her for his first thrust. He stood between her legs, bending over her as he unbuttoned his breeches. His face was
set along grim, determined lines. His intensity frightened her almost as much as it excited her. Belatedly, she
realized that he actually meant to ravish her right there
on the table.

"No, wait!" she cried, pushing him away. "Please!
What are you doing?"

His hand stopped in the act of pulling his weapon
through the unbuttoned opening of his breeches. "What
the devil—! Isn't this what you came for?" he said, his
jaw clenched.

"No!" she said, scrambling away from him. "Certainly not."

With a stifled groan, he turned away from her and violently forced his engorged member back into the downward position, stuffing it back into his pants. He was coldly furious. He hated being teased, and he hated the sort of woman who would take a man to the very brink of ecstasy and then push him away. "You called me Angel," he said harshly. "You came running to me. What was I to think?"

"No," Abigail said wildly. "No, I didn't."

He swung around, his eyes blazing. "You certainly did, madam!"

"I wasn't calling you Angel," she said, unable to meet his eyes. "I meant the dog. I'm sorry. You were mistaken."

"I was mistaken—!" He glared at her. "You expect me to believe you meant the *dog*?"

Abigail hopped down from the table. "Well, I did," she said stubbornly.

His eyes narrowed. "So when you said 'Angel' to me in that low, husky voice, you meant Angel *the dog*? This you expect me to believe?"

"Certainly I expect to be believed," she answered curtly. "I was out of breath from running! I was not husky! You are the most horribly rude, conceited man I have ever met!"

"I certainly hope so," he muttered. "However, now is not the time to criticize one another. You came here for quite another reason, or so you would have me believe. Might a horribly rude, conceited man inquire what that reason might be, Miss Smith?"

"Angel—*the dog*—has eaten Cato," she said primly.

He frowned at her. "Do you expect me to believe that you came here—ran here—only to report that—that—"

"That your dog has eaten Mrs. Spurgeon's odious, yet rather costly, bird!"

"What the devil do I care? And you? You hate that bird."

"If Mrs. Spurgeon finds out, she will be well within her rights to demand compensation," Abigail said. "I daresay she paid fifty pounds for that bird."

"Then you really didn't come here to put me out of my misery?"

"Certainly not. I don't care three straws for your misery," she declared, smoothing down her rumpled skirts. "If you are in misery, I'm quite sure it's your own fault."

He fell silent for a moment. When he spoke again, he was resigned. "Fifty pounds. Where am I supposed to get fifty pounds?"

"He might have been a very old bird," Abigail suggested, relenting a little. "He might even have been dead when Angel—the dog—when he—Oh, it's too disgusting!"

Cary swallowed his disappointment and became decisive. "Take me to him," he said, taking his coat from the row of pegs just inside the door. He eyed her with cool detachment. "Would you like a coat, Abigail? You must be cold."

Abigail shook her head. "We'd better hurry," she said. "Mrs. Spurgeon will be getting up soon, wanting her tea. And her bird."

The unpleasant scene had already been discovered by Vera Nashe by the time Cary and Abigail arrived at the Manor. Angel had retired to the armchair in Cary's study for a post-banquet snooze, and looked the picture of domestic innocence. He had even licked the blood from his paws. Vera had collected the feathers remaining on the rug.

There was no sign of Cato's beak or his claws, but Cary assured them his dog would have no difficulty devouring even the hardest parts of the bird. "He'd eat the tables and chairs, if I let him. How do you feel about lying?" he went on to ask, looking at Vera.

The widow understood him instantly. "In a good cause, Mr. Wayborn, I'm all for it."

"Abigail?"

She jumped at the sound of his voice. "What?"

"Do you think you could tell a lie?"

"I think we must, dear," Vera told her gently. "I know Mrs. Spurgeon. She will not rest after this, until the poor little beast is put down. And he was only doing what comes naturally."

"Put down!" cried Abigail, scooping Angel up. "Oh, Mr. Wayborn, you can't let Angel be put down. It's not his fault, after all."

"Not his fault at all," Cary agreed. "Cato oughtn't to have been so tasty! Right," he went on, turning to Vera. "Open the window and place the feathers on the windowsill. With any luck, Mrs. Spurgeon will think the bird has flown its prison."

"But how could he have got out if the window were closed?" asked Abigail.

"Cato is a very clever bird," Cary told her. "He opened the latch with his beak."

"Yes," Vera approved. "That she easily will believe. Shall we leave this door open or closed? Closed, I think, or we shall have to search the whole house."

The other two conspirators agreed, and Cary followed the women out of the study.

"I must wake Mrs. Spurgeon now," said Vera, starting down the dimly lit hall.

"And I should check on Paggles," Abigail said quickly, but Cary caught her by the hand and pulled her into a room that proved to be the linen cupboard. Angel woofed softly as Cary took him from her arms and set him on the floor.

"Well, Smith?" Cary said, cornering Abigail against

the shelf. "If you can forgive this godforsaken cur for devouring a tasty bird, can you not forgive me?"

"He's not a cur," Abigail protested. "He's just a tiny bit carnivorous, that's all."

"So am I," he said, a smile playing at the corner of his mouth. "Am I forgiven?"

Abigail looked away in confusion. "I suppose . . . if you are apologizing to me—"

He laughed aloud. "Indeed I am *not* apologizing to you. You'd never forgive me if I did." He traced the line of her jaw with his finger. "What is it about you, anyway? Why can't I give you up?"

Abigail blinked at him. "Have you tried giving me up, sir?"

"Oh, yes," he replied, sending little ripples of excitement up and down her spine. "But it's like trying to square a circle. I can't understand it. I ought to despise you."

Abigail was bewildered. "Despise me? But why?"

He grinned at her. "Because I know who you are, Smith. I got it all out of dear old Paggles. She loves talking about her young lady. So, you see, I know all about your connection to Dulwich." He laughed at her expression of horror. "Now I understand why you hid behind the sales counter at Hatchard's!"

Shocked, Abigail stumbled back into the shelf, knocking some neatly folded sheets to the floor. Her thin disguise had been stripped away and she felt horribly exposed. "You know . . . everything?" she whispered, getting down on her knees to retrieve the fallen linen. "You know about Dulwich . . . and me?"

"It's the strangest thing in the world," said Cary. Gently pushing Angel away with his foot, he took the linens from Abigail and restored them to the shelf. "I hate Dulwich more than any other mortal man, but I cannot hate you. I suppose he brags about what he did to me?"

Abigail shook her head, unable to look him in the eye. "What did he do to you?"

"It was when I was in Spain. He was there with some Home Office friend of his, taking a review of His Majesty's troops in the field like a pair of bloody tourists. Well, he recognized me the moment he saw me. Thought it would be fun to order a flogging for the enlisted man."

Abigail recoiled in horror. "Did *he* do that?"

"He provoked me, until I hit him," Cary explained. "Then, of course, I *had* to be flogged. I don't blame my sergeant. We can't have enlisted men attacking civilians, after all. Then, as a *coup de grace*, after I'd been flogged, his lordship reported me to my colonel, and I was shipped back to England in disgrace. Apparently, it's a tiny bit illegal to enlist under a false name."

"And that is why you hate him," murmured Abigail, climbing to her feet.

"I didn't mind the flogging. But he ought not have betrayed me to my colonel. That wasn't cricket, if you see what I mean."

Abigail could not comprehend this apparently important male distinction. She was more upset by the flogging. Silently, she berated herself for ever agreeing to marry the man. How could she have been so thoroughly deceived? He was a monster. And what, she wondered, must Cary really be thinking of her? True, she had come to her senses in time; to her credit she had jilted Dulwich, but could Cary ever forgive her for the engagement? He claimed not to despise her, but surely, she must at least bear some taint in his eyes.

A horrifying possibility occurred to her suddenly. Could this be why Cary felt entitled to maul her at every turn? She felt tears welling up in her eyes. Had he taken such liberties, not out of passion, but merely because he regarded her as used goods? Worse yet, did he think she had allowed *Dulwich* such liberties? The very thought made her ill. In truth, the man had never even kissed her, not even when she had accepted his offer of marriage.

She couldn't look at Cary. He would be loathe to marry her, even if, by some miracle, he had fallen in love with her; surely he would be too proud to offer for a woman once engaged to the man who'd had him flogged. She also knew that if he were to kiss her again, she would be unwilling and unable to resist him. She was in danger of becoming not his wife, but his mistress, and this important female distinction added to her distress and confusion. If he loved her and wished to offer the protection of his name: bliss. If he were merely amusing himself: misery.

"Excuse me," she said, brushing away her tears. "I mustn't stay in the cupboard all day."

He stilled her with his hands, resting one on her shoulder. The other he placed flat over her breastbone, effectively pinning her against the shelf. She could feel her heart pounding, and knowing that he felt it too compounded her acute embarrassment.

"This won't take long," he said, grinning at her. "I paid you a rather irregular tribute in the gatehouse just a few minutes ago."

"Tribute!" she exclaimed.

"Shall I refresh your memory?" His hand slipped down from her shoulder, and Abigail panicked at the implied threat.

"No! Don't you dare!"

He chuckled. "Ah, then you *did* notice. You are becoming more observant. You haven't always remarked my attempts to make love to you. But perhaps you mistook me for a bat again? No? Well, that's progress, I suppose. It seemed to me—but perhaps I flatter myself—it seemed to me that at a certain point in the exercise you became rather *happy*."

"Mr. Wayborn, you have insulted me for the last

time—!" she began, seeking refuge in righteous indignation.

"You mean you were *not* happy? How very odd. I had quite the opposite impression. As I recall—correct me if I am wrong—first you began to tremble—"

"Yes—all right!" she said, stopping the embarrassing flow of words. "I was happy! That is to say, I *was* happy, briefly. But I am *not* happy now. I can only regret what . . . what happened and declare to you, sir, that it must *never* happen again."

He looked at her gravely. "I accept your apology, Smith, and, as you assure me it will never happen again, I forgive you."

"How dare you!" she stammered indignantly. "I do not apologize. I am not sorry. Why should *I* be sorry?"

"Why indeed?" he countered. "When I have given you the greatest pleasure of your life, and you have given me absolutely nothing in return."

Abigail sputtered ineffectually. "What do you expect in return, sir?" she demanded.

"I expect to be given my fair share of pleasure," he replied.

"What?" said Abigail, torn between the desire to flee and the imperative need to remain concealed forever in the cupboard. "You know perfectly well I cannot give you any pleasure! I mean—that is to say—I *should* not. It would be quite improper. It would be a *sin*."

"So it would be," he agreed. "Speaking as one who has actually studied sin at university, I can confirm your assessment. It would indeed be a sin if we were to give in to our carnal desires and despoil our bodies outside the bounds of holy matrimony. Just tell me it's a bit of a struggle for you, that's all I ask. Tell me you are at least tempted to give way to my sinful inclinations. Tell me you have sinful inclinations of your own."

"Cary, for heaven's sake—! Where I come from, we do not discuss such things."

"But I thought you came from London."

"I do. Well . . . Kensington."

"That explains it. You want me, don't you?" he persisted, his voice low and urgent. "You are not indifferent to me?"

She could not help but grimace at such a strong absurdity. "You know I am not."

"You have restored me to hope, Smith," he said. "You will not give me any pleasure, but you are not completely indifferent to me. Therefore, the courtship will continue at a brisk pace."

Before she could catch her breath, he had pulled her out of the linen closet and they were hurrying down the hall, past the staircase, and into the empty entrance hall. Though nothing definite had been decided between them, Abigail was in high spirits. "The courtship will continue at a brisk pace," he had said. Surely that was a declaration of sorts? Surely that meant his goal was marriage? If this proved to be the case, much of her anxiety would vanish.

Cary held out the package Abigail had dropped in the study. "This belongs to you, I think," he said.

"It's for you, actually," she explained. "The stockings you lent me."

"Ah," he said, tucking it inside his coat. "Did you wash them?"

"Of course."

"Pity."

"You'd better go now," she said, blushing. "Hurry!"

He leaned close to her. "You will hurry me again very soon, Smith," he predicted, "but, when you do, it will mean something remarkably different."

He pressed a chaste kiss to her cheek, then he was gone.

* * *

Dinner that evening was a quiet affair, with both Cary and his cousin Horatio sending their regrets, the captain by handwritten special delivery, Cary by word of a rumpled boy. To Abigail's astonishment, they both claimed to have been called to London on urgent business. Neither man had said a word.

"I daresay it is because of Miss Smith's Presbyterianism," Mrs. Spurgeon postulated, looking down the table with a jaundiced eye as she picked at her "veal" chop. For the evening she had chosen her yellow wig, dressed in the Grecian style, and a voluminous gown of chartreuse silk trimmed heavily in fringe, like a drawing room curtain. "What have you to say for yourself, Miss? Are you not ashamed?"

Abigail declined to apologize for her religion. Inwardly, she was smarting at Cary's unexpected departure. All her hopes plummeted. It was frightening to realize how much her happiness now depended on him, especially when he was free to abandon her at a moment's notice, without explanation. What possible business could he have in London? Between the disaster of the Dower House, his new tenants at the Manor, as well as the decline in the estate, one would think Mr. Cary Wayborn would have business enough to keep him in Hertfordshire. To say nothing of his promise that "the courtship" would continue at "a brisk pace."

What sort of husband would he make anyway? The man was a faithless spendthrift.

She picked at her "veal" in a mood of spiteful disappointment. She was so annoyed that when Mrs. Spurgeon turned the subject to the virtues of her beautiful lost bird, she nearly lost her temper and told the woman the truth. She caught herself in time. If *Cary* had devoured Cato, she would not have hesitated to expose him, but she was rather fond of Angel. Moreover, it would have been cruel to tell Mrs. Spurgeon how her

Take A Trip Into A Timeless World of Passion and Adventure with Kensington Choice Historical Romances!

—Absolutely FREE!

Enjoy the passion and adventure of another time with Kensington Choice Historical Romances. They are the finest novels of their kind, written by today's best-selling romance authors. Each Kensington Choice Historical Romance transports you to distant lands in a bygone age. Experience the adventure and share the delight as proud men and spirited women discover the wonder and passion of true love.

Get 4 FREE Books!

We created our convenient Home Subscription Service so you'll be sure to have the hottest new romances delivered each month right to your doorstep—usually before they are available in book stores. Just to show you how convenient the Zebra Home Subscription Service is, we would like to send you 4 FREE Kensington Choice Historical Romances. The books are worth up to $24.96, but you only pay $1.99 for shipping and handling. There's no obligation to buy additional books—ever!

Save Up To 30% With Home Delivery!

Accept your FREE books and each month we'll deliver 4 brand new titles as soon as they are published. They'll be yours to examine FREE for 10 days. Then if you decide to keep the books, you'll pay the preferred subscriber's price (up to 30% off the cover price!), plus shipping and handling. Remember, you are under no obligation to buy any of these books at any time! If you are not delighted with them, simply return them and owe nothing. But if you enjoy Kensington Choice Historical Romances as much as we think you will, pay the special preferred subscriber rate and save over $8.00 off the cover price!

We have 4 FREE BOOKS for you as your introduction to
KENSINGTON CHOICE!
To get your FREE BOOKS, worth up to $24.96, mail
the card below or call TOLL-FREE 1-800-770-1963.
Visit our website at www.kensingtonbooks.com.

Get 4 FREE Kensington Choice Historical Romances!

▶ *YES!* Please send me my 4 FREE KENSINGTON CHOICE HISTORICAL ROMANCES (without obligation to purchase other books). I only pay $1.99 for shipping and handling. Unless you hear from me after I receive my 4 FREE BOOKS, you may send me 4 new novels—as soon as they are published—to preview each month FREE for 10 days. If I am not satisfied, I may return them and owe nothing. Otherwise, I will pay the money-saving preferred subscriber's price (over $8.00 off the cover price), plus shipping and handling. I may return any shipment within 10 days and owe nothing, and I may cancel any time I wish. In any case, the 4 FREE books will be mine to keep.

NAME _____

ADDRESS _____ APT. _____

CITY _____ STATE _____ ZIP _____

TELEPHONE (____) _____

E-MAIL (OPTIONAL) _____

SIGNATURE _____

(If under 18, parent or guardian must sign)

Offer limited to one per household and not to current subscribers. Terms, offer and prices subject to change. Orders subject to acceptance by Kensington Choice Book Club.
Offer Valid in the U.S. only.

KN017A

I..II.I.I.I.I..I.I..II...II.I..I.II.I.I.I.II.I..II

Zebra Book Club
P.O. Box 6314
Dover, DE 19905-6314

PLACE
STAMP
HERE

Take A Trip Into A Timeless World of Passion and Adventure with Kensington Choice Historical Romances!
—Absolutely FREE!

Enjoy the passion and adventure of another time with Kensington Choice Historical Romances. They are the finest novels of their kind, written by today's best-selling romance authors. Each Kensington Choice Historical Romance transports you to distant lands in a bygone age. Experience the adventure and share the delight as proud men and spirited women discover the wonder and passion of true love.

Get 4 FREE Books!

We created our convenient Home Subscription Service so you'll be sure to have the hottest new romances delivered each month right to your doorstep—usually before they are available in book stores. Just to show you how convenient the Zebra Home Subscription Service is, we would like to send you 4 FREE Kensington Choice Historical Romances. The books are worth up to $24.96, but you only pay $1.99 for shipping and handling. There's no obligation to buy additional books—ever!

Save Up To 30% With Home Delivery!

Accept your FREE books and each month we'll deliver 4 brand new titles as soon as they are published. They'll be yours to examine FREE for 10 days. Then if you decide to keep the books, you'll pay the preferred subscriber's price (up to 30% off the cover price!), plus shipping and handling. Remember, you are under no obligation to buy any of these books at any time! If you are not delighted with them, simply return them and owe nothing. But if you enjoy Kensington Choice Historical Romances as much as we think you will, pay the special preferred subscriber rate and save over $8.00 off the cover price!

We have 4 FREE BOOKS for you as your introduction to
KENSINGTON CHOICE!
To get your FREE BOOKS, worth up to $24.96, mail
the card below or call TOLL-FREE 1-800-770-1963.
Visit our website at www.kensingtonbooks.com.

Get 4 FREE Kensington Choice Historical Romances!

💜*YES!* Please send me my 4 FREE KENSINGTON CHOICE HISTORICAL ROMANCES (without obligation to purchase other books). I only pay $1.99 for shipping and handling. Unless you hear from me after I receive my 4 FREE BOOKS, you may send me 4 new novels—as soon as they are published—to preview each month FREE for 10 days. If I am not satisfied, I may return them and owe nothing. Otherwise, I will pay the money-saving preferred subscriber's price (over $8.00 off the cover price), plus shipping and handling. I may return any shipment within 10 days and owe nothing, and I may cancel any time I wish. In any case, the 4 FREE books will be mine to keep.

NAME_____

ADDRESS_____ APT._____

CITY_____ STATE _____ ZIP _____

TELEPHONE (_____)_____

E-MAIL (OPTIONAL)_____

SIGNATURE_____

(If under 18, parent or guardian must sign)

Offer limited to one per household and not to current subscribers. Terms, offer and prices subject to change. Orders subject to acceptance by Kensington Choice Book Club. Offer Valid in the U.S. only.

KN017A

Zebra Book Club
P.O. Box 6314
Dover, DE 19905-6314

treasured pet had died. It was better for everyone to let her think the clever macaw had opened the window and flown away.

"I daresay he is halfway back to India now," said Mrs. Spurgeon, ringing the bell for the next course. "Poor darling. He will not understand one word of what the natives say."

Summoning a reserve of kindness, Abigail suggested that the window in the study be left open in case Cato should return from "India" as quickly as he had disappeared. There would have been no point in explaining that macaws come from South America.

Cary returned to Hertfordshire two days later and paid his respects to the ladies at the Manor, inquiring solicitously after Mrs. Spurgeon's bird.

"I thought I saw him go into your orchard," Mrs. Spurgeon answered, tucking a thin strand of gray hair under the fringe of her curled auburn wig. "The gardener and two under-gardeners searched for nearly an hour, but he was nowhere to be found. I daresay he has returned to India and I will never see him again."

"If so, he will be profoundly missed," Cary said tactfully, if not truthfully.

Abigail answered all her cousin's civilities with civility, but volunteered little in the way of conversation. Vera did most of the talking, compensating for Mrs. Spurgeon's malaise and Abigail's silence with a gentle inquiry. "I trust your business was concluded satisfactorily, sir?"

Cary smiled. "Indeed, Mrs. Nashe. I was able to sell the painting without any difficulty."

"Sell the painting," Abigail repeated sharply. "What painting?"

He glanced at her. "The Cromwell. I sold it."

"*That* is why you went to London? To sell the painting?"

"Yes, Smith. Among other things."

"What other things?" Abigail demanded, forgetting that she had no real right to question him. Vera Nashe raised her brows, Mrs. Spurgeon muttered to herself, but Cary only laughed.

"For one thing," he said cheerfully, "I settled my bill with that scoundrel Red Ritchie!"

"I don't see that he is a scoundrel," she sniffed. "You owed him that money. But I'm glad you paid him."

"I did no such spineless thing. Pay him? I *don't* think."

Abigail frowned. "But you said you settled the bill."

"Oh, it's settled all right," he replied. "I went to see him at his warehouse."

Abigail felt her blood run cold as she tried to imagine this encounter.

"He was less than glad to see me, especially when I gave him his Gold Label scotch back and flung his poxy bills in his rancid face, the dirty old crook."

"*What*?" Abigail jumped to her feet, then sat down again.

"I thought the old boy was going to come apart at the seams. Now I know why he's called 'Red.' It's the color of his face, not his hair. He's bald as an egg."

"How could you do such a thing?"

"It was simplicity itself," said Cary. "But then I have never been loathe to do what is right, no matter how distasteful."

"No. *How* could you do such a thing?" Abigail repeated; it was no longer a rhetorical question. "How could you return scotch you've already drunk up?"

"Well, I couldn't," he answered. "Fortunately, as it turned out, I hadn't drunk the stuff after all. My groom advised me there was a case of the foul brew in my cellar, untouched."

Mrs. Spurgeon was roused out of her melancholy.

"*Scotch* whisky? In my cellar? Mr. Wayborn, I won't allow it. Mr. Spurgeon only drank *English* whisky. Take it away at once."

"Madam, I have already done so," Cary assured her. "I have returned it to its maker. So you see, Miss Smith, the bill is quite settled."

Abigail folded her arms and glared at him. "That was *my* scotch in the cellar."

Cary seemed unable to believe his ears. "Pardon?"

"I brought it with me from London," Abigail explained. "You had no right to take it. You know perfectly well you drank yours. Cary, you *stole* my scotch!"

"Yes, of course," he murmured ruefully. "I'd quite forgotten your special relationship with the bottle. I confess it never occurred to me it might be your case of Ritchie's Gold Label. Surely, a *case* of the stuff is rather excessive, even for you?"

"I wasn't sure how long I'd be staying," she replied tartly. "I promised my father I'd take a *quaich* every day. For your information, I have not yet finished the bottle in my room."

"Ladies do not keep bottles of *liquor* in their rooms," Mrs. Spurgeon informed her.

"Where do they keep them?" Cary politely inquired. "I've often wondered."

Abigail refused to be diverted. "You stole my scotch!" she accused him. "And used it to humiliate my—Mr. Ritchie! You still owe him that money. And now you owe *me* a case of scotch as well."

Cary sighed. "How excessively awkward. Obviously, if I'd known it was *your* scotch, Cousin, I would never have touched it. Please accept my deepest apologies. If I could get it back for you, I would. As it is, would you accept cash? I believe the price was thirty pounds."

"I couldn't possibly accept money," said Abigail. "It was a gift from my father."

Cary sighed. "Then I have no choice but to confess the fell deed to your father and reimburse him for the full amount."

"Why could you not simply pay your bill?" she demanded in exasperation.

"I told you, I don't like the man," he replied. "I don't suppose your father would give me a little time to come up with the money?"

"What do you mean? You said you sold the Cromwell picture. Where's the money?"

"The fellow at the auction house would only give me thirty pounds," Cary explained.

Abigail stared at him. "Thirty pounds! I told you it was worth at least two hundred. For pity's sake, Horatio offered you a hundred!"

"Considering it was worth precisely *nothing* to me, I think thirty pounds rather more than fair," Cary replied. "Indeed, I felt like a cheat taking thirty pounds for something I heartily despise. I felt I ought to have been paying *him* to take it away."

"You are not meant to *sell* it to the auctioneer. You are meant to give it to him—"

"How very generous of me," Cary smiled.

"Then *he* sells it at auction, and *you* get the money. You pay him a small percentage."

"That hardly seems fair when he does all the work," Cary said, unperturbed. "Let us say I paid him a *large* percentage, and leave it at that. In any case, I no longer have the money."

Abigail was stunned. "How could you be so foolish and irresponsible?"

Vera Nashe tried in vain to catch Abigail's eye. "My dear Miss Smith," she murmured.

"Calm yourself, Cousin," he said lazily. "I have rid myself of an execrable painting that never gave me a moment's pleasure, and gotten a little money for it besides.

I have invested this money in a little project which I expect will be infinitely more rewarding than two hundred pounds. Believe me, I am well pleased with the bargain."

This time Abigail heeded the gentle warning in Vera's eyes, and bit her lip.

"I wish you the very best of luck in your investments, Mr. Wayborn," Vera said placidly.

He smiled. "My cousin is sure I will end my days a sad bankrupt, but while she is counting her pennies, I shall be counting my blessings. Look at her, Mrs. Nashe. Can we not guess her thoughts? 'A fool and his money are soon parted,' perhaps?"

"I beg your pardon, sir," Abigail said stiffly. "It is no concern of mine how you choose to dispose of your property."

Over the next few days, Abigail avoided Cary at all costs. She was so successful that, by the week's end, she began to suspect that her success in avoiding him was due in part to his success in avoiding her. It was a lowering thought, but as she went over their last conversation in her mind, she could scarcely blame him for not seeking her company. How shrewish and judgmental she must have seemed to him.

As she sat before her mirror brushing out her hair before bed, she told herself she did not care if he had lost his taste for her. After all, her attraction to him was scarcely based on his character. He was a hedonistic spendthrift who neglected to pay his bills. He had treated her father in an infamous manner. Without so much as a declaration of love, he had taken the liberties of a husband, and, worse yet, he gave no sign of wishing to repeat the exercise.

The courtship will continue at a brisk pace. My foot, she thought bitterly.

"Cary Wayborn, I wouldn't marry you if you were the last man on earth," she said aloud.

The face in the mirror appeared wholly unconvinced, and the voice trembled. She loved him, she knew. She loved him even though he was foolish with money, or perhaps even because of that. In her sheltered view, it took great courage and daring to live beyond one's means. Beyond that, he was the only man who had ever responded to her as a woman. To be kissed breathless by a man was quite a new and precious experience for her, and one she had never supposed would come her way. That he had shattered her lifelong tranquility in a careless manner, without any serious design on her, pierced her to the quick, but she could not hate him. She loved him to distraction, and the fact that there wasn't the least chance of her ever marrying him hurt more than anything.

Chapter 11

On the following Sunday when the others went to church, Abigail went for a long walk. The snow was melting, and the slush in the paths was liberally mixed with mud, but in the quiet solitude of the woods she found that she could think more clearly.

Her position in Hertfordshire had become unbearable, she decided. She would have to return to Kensington. If the mess with Lord Dulwich hadn't sorted itself out, she would find another hiding place. Aunt Elspeth in Glasgow seemed more desirable to her now. She resolved to write to her father. Red could scarcely object to her removal from Tanglewood, once she informed him that the house he'd leased had been rendered uninhabitable by a fallen elm. Somehow, she would forget Cary Wayborn and recover her lost tranquility.

Arriving at this decision brought her little comfort, however. She had no idea how long she walked or how far. To avoid the dirt in the well-traveled areas, she turned deeper into the trackless woods, climbing higher to the places where the snow remained untouched and the icicles in the trees might have been carved of rock

crystal. She had no fear of being lost; she could always
follow her own footsteps back; but as she emerged from
the other side of the silent woodland, she realized that
she was exhausted. There were no benches or stones
on which to sit, but, as she wandered further across a
field of snow, she found a fallen log. As she sat down,
she heard a loud noise. At first she thought it might be
the crack of a huntsman's rifle, but it was followed by
such a barrage of raps, taps, and claps that she supposed
it must be a woodcutter hacking at a tree. Perhaps she
had wandered near the Dower House and what she had
heard was the sound of workmen clearing away the
fallen elm. As the noise subsided, a man wearing an
Oxford scarf emerged from the wood. Abigail recognized him by his close-cropped thatch of barley-white
hair. It was Mr. Maddox. The young man was so deep in
thought that it was only Abigail's greeting that prevented him from stumbling over her.

"Good morning, Mr. Maddox!"

Startled, he halted in front of her and sketched a bow.
"Good *afternoon*, Miss Smith."

"Is it so late?" cried Abigail. "I only meant to go for
a short walk. I seem to have lost all track of time, Mr.
Maddox."

"Are you alone, Miss Smith?" he asked. He seemed
puzzled. "You've strayed a bit, haven't you? You're less
than a hundred yards from the top of the Cascades. Just
on the other side of those trees," he added, pointing the
way.

Abigail did not know the local geography enough to
realize this meant she had walked nearly four miles in
the slushy snow, but she was surprised to learn that the
Cascades was so near the Manor. "Is that where you're
going?" she asked the young man. "To the Cascades?"

He nodded glumly. "It's Rhoda—Miss Mickleby, that
is. She is determined to go down the Cascades on a tray

like her younger sisters did. She won't listen to reason. She won't listen to threats! I can't put her off any more. What will Mrs. Mickleby think of me if I can't stop her?" he fretted. "I'm at the end of my tether with that girl, Miss Smith."

"Mr. Maddox, you must put her off," said Abigail in alarm. "The ice will have thinned considerably in the last week. I cannot imagine that it would be safe."

He cast her a look of annoyance. "I know perfectly well it's not safe," he said. "Just try convincing *her* of that. I had no idea she was so irrational. I'd like to wash my hands of the silly nit. But the thing is, Miss Smith, I made a sort of pledge to her, if you see what I mean."

Abigail's eyes widened. "You mean you are engaged to her, Mr. Maddox?"

He shuddered. "And she still wants to go to London! I told her she ought to give one of her sisters the chance, but she won't hear of it. Now all I can do is hope she finds someone she likes better. Then she might release me."

Abigail pitied him. Without knowing Miss Mickleby well enough to determine her character, Mr. Maddox had committed himself to her. Now he was beginning to realize the extent of his mistake, but was trapped by honor in the unhappy engagement. Fortunately for her, women were not bound by such strictures, and she had been able to break with Dulwich.

"I am very sorry for you, Mr. Maddox," she said sincerely. "But you cannot leave Miss Mickleby at the Cascades when she is likely to injure herself."

"Well, she hasn't got a tray," he said. "I told her I'd go and get her one, just to put her off. She promised not to do anything foolish until I return, if one can trust a word she says. I say, Miss Smith! Would you come with me and talk sense to her? She might listen to you."

Abigail doubted this very much, but she could not refuse Mr. Maddox's appeal.

They found Rhoda sulking against a tree. "You abandoned me," she accused her young man. "What's *she* doing here?" she added petulantly as she saw Abigail.

Mr. Maddox's lips thinned. "Do please forgive Miss Mickleby's rudeness, Miss Smith," he said angrily. "She's a sullen, ill-mannered child. I've no doubt that when she grows up, she will be a sullen, ill-mannered woman."

Two hot spots of color appeared in Rhoda's plump cheeks. "Where's the tray, John?" she demanded. "I have been waiting here these two ages at least."

"Couldn't find one," he retorted.

Her lip curled in scorn. "You promised," she complained. "You're perfectly useless!"

Though ordinarily shy, Abigail was incensed by Rhoda's gall. "Now, look here, Miss Mickleby," she said sharply. "You will stop this nonsense right now."

"You stay out of this," Rhoda snapped.

"Indeed, I won't," said Abigail. "Mr. Maddox is right. You are behaving like a naughty child. I know your mother has forbidden you to go anywhere near the Cascades."

"*You* did it! You all did it, except me. It's not fair, I tell you!"

"*My* mother didn't tell me not to," Abigail pointed out. "In any case, it's no longer safe for anyone. The ice is melting. If it were to break, you would certainly drown."

"Perhaps I *should* find a tray," Mr. Maddox said darkly.

"Coward!" Rhoda replied. "I'm not afraid."

"If you persist in this nonsense," Abigail said sharply, "I shall have no choice but to—to write to my mother's friend, Lady Jersey!"

The threat effectively terrified Miss Rhoda. "Oh, Miss Smith! You wouldn't!"

"I certainly shall," Abigail stoutly lied. "And you know what that means. No vouchers to Almack's. When you get to London, you will be shunned by all decent society. You might as well not go to London at all, if Lady Jersey is against you."

Rhoda darted forward and clutched her arm. "You won't set her ladyship against me, will you, Miss Smith? Dear Miss Smith! Kind, thoughtful, generous Miss Smith."

Mr. Maddox turned his face away in disgust.

"Well, I won't," said Abigail. "If you go straight home, and never even think of disobeying your mama again."

"I'll see that she gets home," said Mr. Maddox.

"I'm not speaking to *you*, John Maddox!" said Rhoda, knocking into the young man as she stomped past him. "I wish I'd never laid eyes on you. I consider you a traitor and a talebearer! You had no right to tattle on me to Miss Smith. I hate you!"

"When we are married, I shall make you very sorry for that," said Mr. Maddox.

Rhoda swung around. "Married?" she shrieked, her eyes bulging. "I shouldn't marry you, John Maddox, not if you were the last man in England! I'm quite finished with you. You were only *practice* anyway. I want a *real* London beau."

To her extreme annoyance, the young man threw back his head and laughed. Rhoda sputtered indignantly. "I shall find a better husband in London!" she shrieked.

"No doubt," he said cheerfully, taking her firmly by the arm. He grinned at Abigail. "Miss Smith, if you follow the river for half a mile, you will come to a little bridge. Follow that path, and it will save you an hour's walk in the woods."

"Thank you, Mr. Maddox," Abigail said gratefully.

Rhoda Mickleby snatched her arm away from her

escort, and marched to the east, towards Squire Mickleby's estate, excoriating Mr. Maddox in a shrill voice as she went. Now free of any obligation to marry the girl, the young man seemed to take great pleasure in the young woman's diatribe, chuckling almost continuously, which only served to deepen her anger.

Abigail followed the river north, guessing that the bridge Mr. Maddox had mentioned must be the one where Cary had discovered her painting. Her feet ached, but she forced herself to go on, eager to get away from the tiresome sound of Rhoda's voice as quickly as she could.

She had just come within sight of the bridge, and the rough-hewn stone bench on the bank, when she heard a dog barking. Two pointed ears appeared above the brown, bedraggled reeds on the other side of the river, followed by a pair of round black eyes and a long foxy nose. Abigail stopped in her tracks. She liked the corgi, but she had no desire at present to see his master. Angel howled joyously. "Hush!" she whispered urgently. "Hush, Angel! Go away!"

The corgi took this for a welcome and threw himself off the bank, landing with a smack in the middle of the frozen river. Instantly, more than a dozen white cracks appeared all 'round the dog as the ice began to break. Horrified, Abigail recognized the sound she had heard earlier. It was not huntsmen or woodcutters. Up and down the river, the ice was breaking.

The corgi's impact had cracked the ice under him, but not broken it. "Angel!" Abigail cried. "Angel, stay! Stay!"

Heedless of the command, the determined corgi scrabbled for a foothold, growing increasingly desperate as the ice cracked under him. His hindquarters went under first as a patch of thin ice suddenly gave way under his weight.

Abigail screamed for help as the corgi slipped under

the ice. To her relief, Angel's head reappeared. His front paws paddled at the edge of the ice, breaking off more and more of it, until he was swimming in a hole, struggling to keep his head above water.

Abigail watched helplessly from the bank. She knew that, if she tried to help, the ice would never hold beneath her weight, but she couldn't bear to watch the little beast drown. She broke off a long, thin branch from a nearby tree, and, with a prayer on her lips, she surged down the bank on her hands and knees. The ice close to the bank held, but as she crept out onto the river, she sensed it fracturing under her knees. To distribute her weight more evenly, she dropped onto her stomach and inched forward like a worm, swinging the stick across the ice towards the dog. For what seemed like an eternity, she crept forward, praying silently, until the end of the branch was within reach of the dog.

"Get the stick, Angel," she panted softly, moving the branch back and forth to entice the dog. "Come on, boy. Chew it. You love to chew. It's very tasty, I promise."

Without even a groan of warning, the ice beneath her simply disappeared, plunging beneath the river, and carrying her down with it before snapping in two. Abigail's mouth filled with icy water, and the weight of her winter clothing pulled her down. The current was unexpectedly strong beneath the deceptive tranquility of the ice. She felt herself swept and dragged along by its force. Later, she would realize that the savage current had saved her; had it not been for its strength she would simply have been dragged to the river bottom by the weight of her skirts. But for now she was skimming beneath a layer of ice, fighting for her life.

Abruptly, the current drove her into an unmovable object, pinning her against it. Flailing around in a frenzy of panic, she was able to break the ice above her head. She surged upwards into the hole, but she was unable to find anything to hold onto, and went under again. The vicious current was again her friend, pushing her up when her weight sought to bring her down. This time, as she came up, her hands flailed against something that did not give way when she grasped it. Its sharp edge cut into her palms, but she refused to let go. For the first time, she felt the cold air crystallizing on her wet face and head. "Angel!" she cried out in anguish.

The hole she had created was not big enough to allow her shoulders through. With just her head and hands above water, she clung to the spur on the rock, vomiting water as the current continued to pound her lower body.

All at once she knew where she was. The current had carried her all the way back to the Cascades, and she was clinging to the top step without being able to see over it. She tried to pull herself up, but the ice in which she was wedged refused to budge. By contorting her body, she was able to work one arm and shoulder through the opening, but that was all. The edge of the stone step cut into her armpit. Beneath the water, her foot probed the stone, and found a chink. Instinctively, she pushed her foot in as far as it would go. Her teeth chattered uncontrollably as the water in her brows and lashes froze over. She wasn't going to drown, she realized. She was going to freeze to death.

Faintly, as if from a great distance, she thought she could hear Angel barking.

"Abigail!"

It was Cary's voice, but she could not see the speaker. She had just decided she must have hallucinated it, when Cary's dark head appeared above her. As he edged onto the step on all fours, the sight cut her to the quick.

"Oh, Cary—you're crawling," she murmured inanely.

His eyes blazed. "You damned fool! You might have been killed!"

"Angel was drowning," she protested. "I had to—"

"That bloody beast!" he said savagely. "Remind me to strangle him."

"He's drowned," cried Abigail.

"Not he," Cary snorted. "Who do you think brought me here? Frightened the life out of my horse. Now give me your hand. I'll pull you up."

Abigail bit her lip. "Cary, don't. You'll fall!"

"That's my lookout. Your hand, Abigail."

"Couldn't you get a rope or something?" she stalled.

"I haven't got a rope," he said, assuming an air of patience. "And I'm not leaving you here while I toddle 'round to the shops and buy one. Your hand. Quicker, if you don't mind."

She gave him her hand. The instant he grasped it, she knew everything would be all right. She wasn't going to die. Strength and warmth seemed to flow through his fingertips into hers.

"Good God, your hand is like ice," he muttered, his face grim.

Having no leverage, he began to pull her up by the main strength in his arms. Abigail cried out as the ice broke around her shoulders. Cary squirmed forward and, catching her under the arms, tried to lift her out of the water. Abigail tried to pull her shoe out of the chink in the rock beneath the water, but couldn't. She heard Cary cursing.

"Wait," she cried. "My foot is caught."

Just as she spoke, her shoe gave way, and her body sailed out of the water and landed painfully on the top step. Cary's grip on her broke as he fell backwards. Unable to regain his balance, he rolled with a series of thuds and curses down to the fourth or fifth step. Abigail couldn't see him. She screamed his name, but there was no reply, not even an echo.

* * *

Some time later, she felt warm. She could hear voices murmuring around her, humming like bees. She forced her eyes open, and Vera Nashe's face swam before her. "She's awake," someone said, but it was a lie. Consciousness slipped away again.

Suddenly, a finger lifted one of her eyelids, and then the other. Just as suddenly, the finger disappeared, and darkness closed over her again. Her body careened restlessly. At times it seemed to be hurtling through space. At other times, she felt herself to be in bed. She became uncomfortably warm, then unbearably hot. She woke up, as if from a nightmare, by sitting upright and opening her eyes. Her skin was sticky with sweat, and her heart was pounding.

She was in her room at Tanglewood Manor; she recognized the Tudor roses painted on the ceiling. A fire was blazing on the hearth. For a moment, she was mesmerized by the dancing flames. She could not remember her dream, though she was sure it had been a nightmare. She could not understand why her head ached and why her body felt bruised all over. The palm of her left hand itched. Her hand was bandaged. Unwrapping the bandage, she found a nasty looking cut sealed with tiny silk stitches.

Vera Nashe quietly entered the room, and some of Abigail's confusion lifted, though it was still very hard to think. It had not been a dream. She had cut her hand at the Cascades. She had nearly drowned in the river, and Cary had fallen in his attempt to rescue her. If he was dead, it was entirely her fault. Tears spilled from her eyes. "Mr. Wayborn?"

Vera smiled. "So you are awake, my dear. We've been so worried about you."

Abigail could barely hear her; a sound like the roar of a waterfall was in her ears. The dryness of her mouth made it difficult to speak, but she managed to croak, "Is Cary all right?"

Vera seemed very far away, and Abigail was faintly surprised when the other woman took her hand; she had seemed much too far away to do that. "Yes, yes," she said soothingly, wrapping a fresh bandage around Abigail's palm. "Mr. Wayborn is expected to make a full recovery. I'm much more worried about you. You were in the water such a long time."

"Was he badly injured? May I see him?"

She tried to swing her legs out of bed, but Vera was too strong for her. "You mustn't get out of bed. Doctor's orders. Don't worry about Mr. Wayborn. He's a few bumps and bruises, but he's young and he's strong. He'll be fine. You, on the other hand, have had a bad fever."

She turned up the lamp at the bedside and Abigail stared at it. Questions occurred to her, but then slipped away. It was difficult to focus. "Where is he?" she finally asked.

Vera smoothed Abigail's hair back from her damp forehead. "He's right next door, resting comfortably. I've just given him his medicine. Now I shall give you yours." As she spoke, she took out a dropper filled with scarlet liquid and emptied it into a glass of water. The scarlet drops swirled through the clear liquid like dancing feathers. Vera held out the glass. "Laudanum," she told her cheerfully. "It will take away the pain."

"I'm not in pain," Abigail whispered. The red drops looked revoltingly like blood.

"You will be, if you don't take your medicine," said Vera, smiling. "And if you don't get better, you won't be allowed to see Mr. Wayborn."

Abigail took the glass. As a child she had once had a toothache, and Paggles had rubbed a little laudanum into her gums, but the effect had been nothing like this.

A cloud of foggy pleasure seemed to press down on her, almost paralyzing her limbs.

"Sleep," Vera commanded, and the word echoed in the room long after she had gone, growing louder instead of fainter, until Abigail could not bear it. The feeling of euphoria became almost suffocating, frightening, drowning her ability to think. Convinced that something was very wrong, Abigail tried to call out, but she could scarcely hear her own voice. Vera was gone, and Abigail was sure no one would come.

She got out of bed, but her legs trembled so violently that she was forced to her knees. She began to crawl across the planked floor to the door, but the room seemed to lengthen into an almost endless tunnel. She could barely see the door at the end of it, and when, after a herculean effort, she reached it, it was locked. Looking back the way she had come, she saw the room had changed. It was no longer a place of safety. Strange black and gold shapes darted in and out of the firelight, and the air was thick with smoke. A whispering wind seemed to blow in the room, agitating the curtains of the bed. "This is not real," Abigail told herself firmly. "The fever has disturbed my mind."

It was her last coherent thought. Her vision blurred, and feeling blind and dizzy, she groped her way to the nearest shelter—the wardrobe—and climbed inside, parting the dresses hung on the rod and secreting herself among them. The door banged shut, and Abigail was safe inside in the dark.

This particular wardrobe had a secret. She tried to remember who had told her that. She had a feeling it was someone very important. She pushed hard against the back of the wardrobe and the wall slid away. Abigail tumbled out into a different place.

"Ups-a-daisy," said a familiar voice, as two strong arms seemed to pluck her out of thin air and set her on

her feet. The wardrobe door banged shut, and she was
suddenly standing in a room the exact mirror of her
own. Two hands turned her around, and she found herself face to face with a flesh-and-blood Caravaggio.

Cary's skin gleamed like copper in the firelight. He
was completely naked. His skin was the same warm
bronze all over and his male part was badly in need of a
few fig leaves. Cary himself seemed completely unaware of his uncovered state, and Abigail felt decidedly
guilty for imagining him like that. All the same, she
couldn't take her eyes off of him.

"I was beginning to think you weren't coming," he
murmured, folding her in his arms. The warmth of his
naked body seemed to pass right through her skin, and
all at once, he was kissing her and she was kissing him
as if it were the most natural thing in the world. It didn't
shock her at all to realize that she was naked, too. They
might have been Adam and Eve in the Garden of Eden.
After all, it was a dream. In the dream her body fitted
his exactly.

"Angel!" she murmured breathlessly, as his mouth
wandered hungrily down her neck.

"Don't worry about the dog. The dog is fine. You
might worry about me, however," he went on petulantly.
"After all, I nearly died. Saving you, you ungrateful
little baggage."

"But I meant you," she said fervently, clinging to him.
"I meant you. It was always you. Cary, I was so afraid
you were dead. You're not, are you? You're not a ghost?"

"Do I feel like a ghost?" he asked, taking her hand
and guiding it to the center of his chest, where his heart
beat reassuringly.

"No," she admitted. "You feel alive."

"If I were mere fallacy of vision, could I do this?"

Abigail had never thought of herself as a person endowed with a powerful imagination, but now she could

imagine anything and everything. She could taste him
as he kissed her. Honey and whisky. She could feel the
muscles of his arms hardening around her like bands of
iron. She could even imagine the way he smelled, like
shavings of cedarwood left on a warm grate. She could
hear every sweet word he murmured. He was invested to
the hilt in each and every one of her senses. She could
see, hear, smell, taste, and touch nothing else. It was as if
she were possessed by him. Not content to melt her from
without, he had moved in, under her skin, melting even
her bones. The barest whisper, the tiniest flick of his
tongue, had the power to permeate her entire body. There
was nothing to do but cling to him, offer herself to him.

"If I were a ghost, could I do this?" Cary scooped her
up in his arms and carried her to the bed. Abigail closed
her eyes and fell into a cloud of feathers, landing softly
in the warm nest, but when she opened her eyes he was
still there. Grinning devilishly, he climbed onto the bed
after her, his legs tangling with hers. "Look at me," he
said, slapping his hard, flat belly. "Did you ever see a
more corporeal being in your life? Feel that. That's all
muscle, my girl."

Abigail had never seen a naked man before, only stat-
ues, and the cold white marble sculptures of Canova had
not prepared her for the splendor of this living man. As
if compelled by a higher power, her small hands reached
for him. Against his golden brown skin, they looked a
travesty, small, pale, freckled. His torso was like carved
marble covered in warm, brown velvet. He moved as
unself-consciously as a satyr in the woodlands, and
smiled at her indulgently as she stroked him tentatively.

"You do seem real," she whispered. Yet, she knew, he
could not be. She was imagining this magical creature,
as she had imagined the whispering wind on the other
side of the wardrobe. Except that this was so much
better than any dream she had ever before experienced.

Real or not, it was impossible not to touch him. Indeed she could not get enough of him. His muscles, finer than any carved in marble by human hands, leaped as she trailed her fingers over the contours of his torso. Surely, not even Cary, the man she adored, could be so perfect.

As if reading her thoughts, the hallucination said proudly, "Madam, you will search in vain for a soft spot on this body. Not an ounce of fat or weakness will you find anywhere. Hard riding and hard wenching have been the making of me," he added, winking at her.

Obviously, her dream had modeled his fine body on those of the figures she had seen in sculpture gardens and museums, inventing for her the perfect man, a lover who could only live in her imagination. As she imagined, so he was. But why had she endowed him with that odd, truncheon-like object between his finely muscled legs? She'd never seen one of those on a statue. And why, oh, why did he have to talk like a conceited braggart? The real Cary, of course, probably *did* live a life of idle dissipation, wenching and drinking and gambling, but such realism had no place in her dream. The real Cary made her nervous. So nervous that, despite her intense attraction for him, she always felt an irresistible desire to run away from him.

"It's not fair, you know," she said wistfully. "You're so beautiful. It turns me into a complete idiot. I wish I were beautiful like you. I wish I could make someone feel about me the way I feel about you. Not fair, Cary."

He chuckled softly, and gently pushed the curls out of her eyes. "And I wish you could see what I see, my beautiful Smith. Dearest, loveliest Smith. If you were slathered in slippery honey, I vow I could swallow you whole. Where did you get such pretty peaches?"

"Don't," she begged. "Don't make a joke of it. It makes me sad."

Instantly, he became what she wanted, intense and serious. His eyes were warm. "What do you need from me?" he asked gently.

"Just love me," she said helplessly, tears standing in her eyes.

Because this was a dream, he understood her perfectly, while the real Cary would have tormented her into hysterics. Instead, they communicated like two angels, by thought, by a touch that was scarcely physical it ran so deep. Because this was wholly imaginary, Abigail was neither shy nor awkward. The feelings that he aroused in her did not frighten her. They seemed natural, as if she had been making love to him a thousand years. Because he had made her body with his hands, she could not be ashamed of it. For the first time in her life, she felt beautiful, desirable, worthy. His dark, magical hands melted all barriers between them, caressing the soft peaks of her breasts, cupping her soft bottom as he drank the sweetness flowing from her like a river of honey. Her body melted slowly, like wax in the sun, while he supped like a cloud of lazy bees. At first everything was drowsy and golden. He drew her in, trapping her senses in a charm of easy pleasure, before together they began the slow, maddening ascent to a joy so cruel, so fleeting, and so intense that it sears as much as it pleases.

He was masterful, this man she had created. She imagined that he kissed and caressed her for hours, neglecting no part of her. The faintest touch, a kiss whispered behind her knee, the flick of his tongue, a chuckle, could magnify the pleasure she felt as his hand quietly and firmly caressed her between the legs. As though swimming through a tide, her body strained to meet his, and like wild water broken up by immortal rock, she moaned softly as she broke in his arms. He knew exactly how to give her the most pleasure. Time and again, he brought her up the scale, then back down, releasing her too soon, until she was writhing like a wounded thing. Each time, she thought she had reached the end of the world, but each time he would take her a little further, into some new, intoxicating realm, higher and higher, until finally, her body could bear the strain no longer. The last scrap of Abigail melted away and the scent of honey filled all the world. She drowned in it, weeping hysterically, exhausted. She could imagine nothing more. "Perfection," she breathed, sinking almost into unconsciousness.

Cary chuckled softly, proud of himself. In the darkness, he crouched over her, his mouth swollen and red. Curiously, she touched it with her fingertips, feeling the words as they emerged from his lips. "That, my sweet, is only the beginning."

His teeth flashed like a wolf's. The hard gleam in his eye startled her. Suddenly, she was Abigail again. Frightened, shy, awkward, *stupid* Abigail. In that moment she truly despised herself. She could not even *dream* properly. Even in dreams, the lusty smile of a lover threw her into a blind panic. She sat up and tried to cover herself, but he was lying on the sheets, displaying himself quite shamelessly. She began to babble, hoping he would show mercy and let her go before she embarrassed herself further by bursting into tears.

"Look here, Cary," she said quickly. "I know this is going to sound a tiny bit odd, but there's something in my room. It whispered at me. It—it frightened me. If it finds us here . . . I'm afraid of what it might do." She jumped out of bed and, unable to get the sheets away from him, ran naked to the door. Somehow, he got there before she did. "It's locked," he informed her, leaning against it, the picture of insouciance.

"How do you know?" she demanded, panting. "You haven't tried."

"I know," he said, blocking the way with his body.

"Cary, you have to let me go," she pleaded.

He grinned incorrigibly. "If you like knobs, I've a nice one here for you."

Outraged, Abigail momentarily forgot her anxiety. "It's not a knob," she rebuked him. "It's a lovely branch with a lovely plum on the end."

"And do you like plums?" he asked solicitously.

He was standing in front of her now, so close that his sex knocked gently on her belly. He took her shoulders in his hands, which was a good thing since Abigail no longer trusted her legs to support her. He whipped her around and suddenly her back was against the door, the length of his body pressing her against it.

"I tell you there's something nasty in my room," she repeated, trembling. "You don't understand. I only came to tell you—No, that's not right. I didn't even know you were here."

"Didn't know I was here," he scoffed. "That's rich. I know exactly what you came for, Smith, and you're going to get it if it takes me all night. Look what you've done to me." He took her hand and drew it slowly down his body. Abigail moaned as she felt what she had not dared to touch before. It was hotter and harder than any other part of him. "Feel what you do to me. Obviously, I'm in no condition to be teased. Give me an answer now. Yes or no?"

"But what if it comes through the wardrobe?" she asked anxiously, even as, driven by instincts she did not know she had, her hand closed over the hot, solid shaft of flesh.

"I understand your apprehension," he replied, "but, really, it's not that big." He tried to encourage her hand to stroke him rather than hold him so passively, but Abigail missed the signal. Thinking he was pushing her away, she slowly withdrew her hand.

"I meant the thing in my room," she said unhappily, believing he no longer wanted her.

"What about it?" he said, frowning at her. "Look, if you want to go, go. Try the knob."

Abigail looked at him, not moving. "It's locked," she whispered.

He groaned as she took hold of him again. "Abigail, you are driving me insane," he said in a strangled voice. "I beg of you, make up your mind, put me out of my misery. For God's sake, let me have you." He cursed as he again tried to teach her to stroke him and she again withdrew her hand. "This is absolutely the worst dream I have ever had!" he exclaimed.

"Y-your dream?" she stammered. "There must be some mistake. This is my dream."

He looked at her so fiercely that she trembled. "No, monkey," he said firmly. "This is my dream. My dream. I make the rules. I say we stop talking and go to bed at once." Looking quite determined, he drove her ahead of him to the bed, Abigail stumbling back nervously.

"Surely this is my dream," she protested, even as her legs gave way and she fell backwards into bed. Hurriedly, she crossed her arms over her breasts.

"Mine," he replied shortly, leaning over her to uncross her arms.

"But how do you know it's your dream? How do you know it's not mine?"

"If this were your dream, Smith, I strongly suspect we'd be wearing clothes and doing something sadly respectable," he whispered, bringing his mouth swiftly down on her breast like a hawk seizing a dove. She gasped as his teeth grazed her tender nipple.

"Ordinarily, I'd agree with you," she said, struggling to breathe. "But, Cary, something very odd has happened to me. I seem to have developed an unquenchable physical desire for you. I'm sorry, but there it is. I keep wanting to touch you, wanting you to touch me."

"Very odd," he agreed. "Considering you keep pulling away from me, you little tease!"

"You keep pushing me away," she accused angrily, sitting up.

"Bollocks. You—" He caught his breath as her hand closed over him a little too tightly for comfort. "Gently, if you please. I am not pushing you away," he explained. "I want you to move your hand." This time, he caught her hand before it flew away. "Move it," he clarified, "not remove it." Covering her hand, he taught her the caressing motion. As she caught on, he closed his eyes and groaned softly. "There now. If this were your dream, would we be doing this? Would your little hand be moving up and down in this charming way?"

Abigail bit her lip. "But we often do things in dreams we might not otherwise," she pointed out. "If you knew what I was thinking right now—feeling right now— you'd run."

"Would I indeed? You interest me strangely."

"I want to do such things to you, things I could never ever do in real life. But here, in this place, there doesn't seem to be anything to stop me," she said, stroking him lovingly.

He grunted, rocking back and forth on his heels as he stood before her. "I have changed my mind about the talking. You may speak at will, my dear Smith."

"You see?" she said, fascinated. "I can't stop touching you. It's as if I have lost all trace of my moral upbringing. I seem to have no inhibitions left at all. I want to rub myself all over you like a cat." To her own amazement, her body did just that.

Cary could bear no more. He fell on her, growling, "Definitely my dream."

Abigail swallowed hard as his weight pushed her deep into the feather mattress. "Are you sure? Because—"

"I am thinking of a number, Smith," he announced abruptly, raising himself up on his elbows. "One to ten."

"Why?" she asked, puzzled, and a little hurt. "It seems like an odd time for arithmetic."

"I am thinking of a number," he repeated severely. "If this is your dream, you will know what that number is. Wrong!" he cried triumphantly when she guessed seven.

"Just a moment," Abigail said, scrabbling farther into the bed as he made a wild grab for her. She stopped when she reached the headboard of carved black oak. "*I* am thinking of a number, too. If this is *your* dream, sir, tell me: what is that number?"

He laughed softly, crawling after her. "My dear girl, *you* are not thinking of a number. You are thinking about rubbing yourself all over me like a cat."

Abigail gasped. "How could you possibly know what I'm thinking?"

"You told me," he pointed out. "Besides, women don't think about numbers when they are in bed with me."

"No," she sighed.

"Therefore it is my dream."

"Yes."

It was bad enough to be naked in one's own dream. But to be naked in someone else's was absolutely scandalous. Abigail could feel her whole body blushing. Even by the warm glow of the firelight, her freckles stood out atrociously. She jumped for the bed curtains and hid behind them. "Cary," she said fretfully. "Can you see me right now? As I am, I mean?"

"Every delightful freckle," he said, pursuing her to the bedpost and catching her in his arms, getting an armful of crewel-work for his trouble. "You've even got them on your bottom." As he spoke, he was trying unsuccessfully to extricate her from the red and white curtains. Abigail refused to let go, bunching the material tightly in her hands. "You're acting very strangely tonight, Smith," he complained. "In fact, you're letting me down. Is this the same woman who, only moments ago, gave in to my most secret and depraved desires? Good God, if I've had you once, I've had you twenty times. Now you suddenly turn up shy. Not fair, really."

Abigail's heart sank. "Who is this woman?" she demanded. "Why didn't you ask *me* to give in to your most secret and depraved desires?"

He scowled. "Look here! I can still put you over my knee and paddle your behind! I've done it before, and I'll do it again. Remember?"

"No. You're obviously thinking of someone else," she said angrily. "Which is actually a bit rude, if you stop and think! How would you like it if I started thinking of another man right here in the middle of your dream?"

"I am not thinking of anybody else," he snapped. "I am thinking of you, Smith, whoever you are. I dream of you every night. It's always been you, and you bloody well know it."

"Really?" said Abigail, delighted. "You dream about me? Like this, I mean?"

"Certainly not. In my other dreams, you were much nicer to me. I ask you, is this how you show your gratitude? By hiding in the curtains?"

She gasped. "You expect me to be grateful? You made me tell you I want to rub myself all over you like a cat," she reminded him. "How will I ever be able to look you in the eye after this?"

"That was wrong of me," he gracefully admitted. "But, on the other hand, I did save your life," he pointed out. "You were well on your way to freezing to death in the river when I happened along in your time of need. Now I'm in a time of need, Abigail. You could save me."

Abigail was instantly contrite. "Oh, I am sorry. You did save my life, didn't you? You were so brave. I was so frightened. And then you fell." Her eyes filled with tears.

"Yes, yes. I was incredible," he said impatiently. "And I deserve to be rewarded."

"Naturally, I want you to have a nice dream. But what can I do?"

He stared at her. "What can you do?" he repeated incredulously. "Didn't you just say you wanted to do things to me? Rub yourself all over me like a cat. Your words, not mine."

"Your dream, not mine! You *made* me say that," she corrected him. "I do want to make you happy. You've no idea how much. I just don't know how. I don't mean to be ungrateful. I've had a lovely time in your dream. I really have. Nicer even than what you did to me at the gatehouse, because *that* was real, and it frightened me to death."

He sat down on the bed and went perfectly still. "Are you frightened of me, Abigail?"

She shook her head vehemently. "I just don't know what to do, that's all. I'm afraid I'll make a mess of things. You're so beautiful," she added rather helplessly. "I wish I could make you happy. If you could just tell me . . . show me . . ."

He groaned suddenly. "Don't tell me you're a *virgin*? Not again."

Abigail said furiously, "Of course I am! What do you take me for?"

"I was hoping to take you for a very naughty girl," he retorted. "Now it seems I shall have to start all over, from the very beginning. Yes, the *very* beginning," he added ruefully, glancing down at his naked body. "Conversation is not good for the Prime Minister, you know.

It weakens his resolve. He begins to think it would be better just to go to sleep."

"I only want a hint," Abigail said tartly. "If it's too much trouble . . ."

"No," he said quickly. "He's a resilient fellow, and I don't mind sharing with you my vast stores of erotic knowledge. You know I don't. But when a woman falls into a man's dream completely innocent of clothing, it raises the old expectations, if you see what I mean." Abruptly, he yanked the bed curtain loose from the tester, and pulled her down to him, curtains and all. "This will not be like the gatehouse, Abigail," he warned, "where I gave my all, and you ran off like a frightened rabbit."

She flushed angrily. "I did not—" she began, but her eyes fell before his. "I was a frightened rabbit," she admitted. "I'm sorry, Cary. It won't happen again. I promise."

He sighed, searching for her slim, freckled body in the curtains. "Very well, Smith. I forgive you. The Prime Minister forgives you, too. I will show you the way to heaven, but this is absolutely the last time. No more frightened virgin. After this, I expect you to be perfectly shameless in your pursuit of carnal pleasure, at least with me. Agreed?"

"I'll do my very best, Cary," she said sincerely, as he slipped under the curtain with her.

"That's all I ask of you, Smith."

Abigail willed herself to become pliant again in his arms, to please him. Cary was not adverse to taking his time. Slowly and gently, he unwound her tightly coiled nerves. But this time, he would not allow her to float away in a dream. He aroused her but refused to satisfy her. This was about his satisfaction, the satisfaction she had denied him for far too long. He issued urgent commands to her, sometimes quite harshly. He seemed to require something from every inch of her body, her arms, her legs, her hands, her mouth, even her voice. Abigail was too enthralled by the greediness of his body to worry about the shortcomings of her own. Knowing that she could please him as he had pleased her made her dizzy with power. She was not experienced, but she was selfless, tireless in her effort to please him.

Cary had never been so aroused in his life. The slow blossoming of her shyness pleased him more than the clever handiwork of any courtesan, however skilled. Any man could receive pleasure from such a woman, but to have shy, trembling Abigail loving him, surrendering to her own womanly desires for the first time, drove him almost to madness. Soon the tyrant's commands became the soft pleas of a lover. Cary clung to her as helplessly as she clung to him.

"Love me, Abby. Oh, love me. Don't stop loving me," he begged.

Cary wanted her, but more than that, he needed her.

"You're heaven," he whispered, as he entered her.

She gasped in awe as he filled her. She could not possibly have imagined that feeling of blissful belonging coupled with a sharp physical pain as he destroyed her virginity. He heard her gasp, but the fire in him was blazing too hot for caution. As her discomfort dissolved beneath a wave of divine pleasure, he swung in and out of her in a frenzy until the fire was quenched, and he lay still. Like an exhausted babe, he nuzzled her breast.

Abigail could not bear the thought of his leaving her. "Oh, no," she moaned, tightening around him instinctively. "Love me again. Don't stop."

His dark head suddenly lifted, and she saw the gleam in his eye. It no longer frightened her. "You asked for it," he said roughly.

Chapter 12

The voice was very difficult to hear because there was a terrible droning roar reverberating in Abigail's skull; nonetheless, she recognized that it was Cary's voice, telling her to wake up. "Cary," she murmured weakly, fighting her way back to consciousness. The closer she came to waking, the more she was aware that her body felt bruised all over. It would have been easy to slip back into sleep if he hadn't been calling her. He sounded panicked. Something was wrong. They were back at the river. She had to help him.

"Cary, don't," she moaned. "You'll fall!"

"*Wake up*," he commanded, hauling her to the side of the bed and planting her feet on the floor. Abigail started to fall backwards, but he seized her by her hands, flinging her arms over his back. She thought he meant to carry her away from the river, but instead he began wrapping her in a sheet. She was in a bed somewhere. "Abigail, you must get back to your own room before we are discovered," he said, rapidly slapping her cheek. "Do you understand?"

She blinked at him. He seemed to be weaving before

her eyes. His dark hair was rumpled. "Do please stop moving about," she whined. "My head aches so."

"Yes, darling, I'm sure it does," he said, taking her face in his hands. She suddenly realized that she had been the one weaving, not him. Now that he was holding her still, her eyes could focus. She could see that he was naked to the waist. She was also naked under the linen sheet, and there was a suspicious pain between her legs.

"Listen to me, Abby," he said urgently.

"What are you doing in my room?" she demanded suddenly.

"It's not our fault," he said. "Do you understand? We thought it was a dream."

"Get out of my room!" she said, panicking.

"It's my room," he told her gently. "You came to me, Abigail."

Abigail turned white. She suddenly remembered things that could not possibly have happened. Not in England. Certainly not to her. "It's not what you think!" she protested wildly. "There was something in my room. I was frightened. My door was locked. I had to come through the wardrobe. I didn't mean . . . I don't remember what happened after that," she said so fiercely that he knew she was lying.

"I'm afraid amnesia isn't going to answer," he said gravely. "It's pretty damned obvious what we've been up to. You must be in some considerable discomfort."

Involuntarily her hands pressed into her abdomen. His member had penetrated her up to the navel, and she had the pain to prove it. "I'm sure I don't know what you mean."

"It's not your fault, monkey," he told her gently. "It was the opium."

"What opium?" she cried in horror.

"There's opium in laudanum. It can have a strange effect on the mind. The lines between fantasy and reality become blurred. People have been known to behave in ways they might not ordinarily. I think we meet the case." He smiled at her. "Surely it wasn't all bad?"

"I told you I don't remember," she said stubbornly.

"Of course not. Neither do I." Incredibly, he chuckled.

"I don't see anything amusing in our present situation!" she said angrily. "You're a man. You can do what you like. No one censures you. But I am ruined!"

He tried to appear sober, but failed. "Don't worry, Smith. I'll marry you."

Abigail felt nauseous. Yesterday she would have been elated by an offer of marriage. But this was hardly an offer. More of an off-hand remark. He was actually laughing.

"What choice do we have?" he went on. "You're ruined now. It's not our fault, but the fact remains: you are ruined. We should be married at once."

"I must go," said Abigail. "I cannot be found here."

"You're right about that," he agreed. "Allow me," he said, opening the wardrobe door for her. Carefully averting her face, Abigail pushed her way through the clothing to the other side. As she stepped out, she felt a sharp tug on the end of the sheet in which she was wrapped. "I'm going to need the sheet back, if you don't mind," he said cheerfully.

She let him have it, and hurriedly found something else to put on. "Not that horrible green plaid again," he said, poking his head through the clothes. "This one."

Abigail snatched the blue dress he pushed toward her and yanked it over her head.

"Miss Smith?" Vera Nashe was standing in the doorway. She sounded surprised.

Abigail slammed the wardrobe shut.

"I'm surprised to see you out of bed," said Vera, hurrying over to her.

"I was just getting dressed," said Abigail, unable to look the other woman in the eye.

Vera felt her forehead. "The fever's broken. That is excellent. The doctor is here to see you. He'll be pleased with your progress, I think."

Abigail blushed. Her chief physical complaint at the moment was a raw pain that began between her legs and extended up through her womb. "I'm rather tired, if you don't mind," she said. "Could he return later, do you think? I—I have a dreadful headache."

Vera chuckled. "Are you trying to say you are not *well* enough to see the doctor? But, Miss Smith, that is precisely when you *ought* to see the doctor."

Abigail had no answer for this. She was obliged to sit on the edge of the bed while the doctor felt her pulse and listened to her heart. Kindly Mr. Carmichael reminded her of every other doctor whom she had ever met. He checked the whites of her eyes. He made her stick out her tongue while he looked down her throat. The soreness in her belly seemed to intensify. What if Cary Wayborn had done her a permanent injury? It seemed possible, even likely, given the amount of pain, and the very strange things they had done together like two frenzied animals. Mr. Carmichael might be able to allay her fears, but, of course, confiding in him was entirely out of the question. She would die of shame if anyone knew.

"Young woman, you are in the pink of health," he told her at last. "A few bumps and bruises, but those will heal. Next time, stay out of the river."

The doctor collected the bottle of laudanum from the bedside table. "Good heavens, Mrs. Nashe!" he cried, aghast. "How much did you give the young person?"

"Five drops, five times," said Mrs. Nashe. "Just as you said, sir."

"I said one drop five times, five drops in total!" cried

the doctor. He looked at Abigail in astonishment. "We are very fortunate the young lady suffered no ill effects."

"Yes," Abigail agreed faintly. "Very fortunate indeed."

Cary was judged well enough to return to the gatehouse, and, for the next several days, Abigail kept to her room. However, she could not remain cloistered forever. By the week's end, she was persuaded to go downstairs and receive visitors from Gooseneck Hall.

Hector Mickleby had little to say for himself, but Mrs. Mickleby and her eldest daughter more than made up for his silence. After eliciting from Abigail every detail of her near drowning, they turned to the happier subject of Rhoda's impending removal to London. Rhoda had clearly been given instructions upon pain of death to mind her manners.

"Where shall I go first, Miss Smith—Astley's Amphitheater or Covent Garden?" she asked Abigail, with every appearance of being interested in the latter's opinion.

Abigail gave a distracted answer, her attention divided by the sudden appearance of Angel, who came bounding into the room ahead of his master. Knowing that Abigail could scarcely avoid him in such a setting, Cary went straight to her and took her hand. "He insisted on coming to see you," he explained as the corgi hopped onto Abigail's lap and began gnawing the lace at the edge of her sleeve.

Cary stood back and looked at her in amusement. "He's really your dog now," he said. "After all, you saved his life. I would certainly have let him drown."

Rhoda giggled. "And *you* saved Miss Smith's life. Does she belong to you now, sir?"

Cary's teeth flashed. "She does indeed. And I belong

to Nathaniel Brisby, for it was he who hauled me off the bottom step of the Cascades."

"Only think, Mama," cried Rhoda. "If Miss Smith hadn't stopped me, I might have gone down the Cascades with that silly Maddox boy, and been horribly drowned. It was too bad of Mr. Maddox to suggest such a thing! Why, if I had drowned, I should never have been able to go to London. And *that* would have been a great pity."

"For *you* perhaps," Hector said sullenly. "Miss Smith, I should like you to know that if *I* had been at the river on that fateful day, *I* would have been the one to rescue you. And I should not have fallen over doing it."

"Thank you, Mr. Mickleby. When do you go to London, Miss Rhoda?" Abigail asked, doing her best to ignore Cary, who stood nearby, teacup in hand, a sardonic smile on his lips.

"Week after next, Miss Smith," she said, her eyes sparkling.

"Then I shall be at home, too," said Abigail. "I'm going back to London. I've already written to my father. He's sending a chaise for me next Monday."

"Oh!" said Mrs. Mickleby, leaning forward eagerly. "Is Sir William back from Brazil?"

"Yes," said Abigail, after a small hesitation. "He is back, and I am going home."

Rhoda's brow furrowed. "You're still coming to my party tomorrow, aren't you?"

"Of course she's coming," said Hector. "She's promised me the first two dances."

Rhoda's face fell. "You hadn't forgotten?"

"No, of course not," said Abigail quickly. "I wouldn't miss it for the world."

Cary set down his cup. "If you do intend to go, Abigail, I insist that you get plenty of rest. You look tired."

"Yes," Rhoda agreed very sweetly. "You don't look

rested at all, Miss Smith. I'm sure I shall never appear so haggard in company until I am ten years married."

Mrs. Mickleby took Cary's hint. "Do be quiet, children," she said, climbing to her feet. "It is high time we were going. Miss Smith, we leave you to your rest."

"Yes, you must rest," Rhoda said kindly. "And I shall send you a cucumber from Gooseneck Hall. If you place two slices over your eyes for an hour, I'm sure those unsightly pouches will be quite carried away!"

"Thank you, Miss Rhoda."

"Do please give my best regards to Mrs. Spurgeon," said Mrs. Mickleby on her way out. "I hope she will be well enough to attend, though I understand she has not been the same since the disappearance of her marvelous bird."

Cary went out with them, but returned a moment later.

"So Mrs. Spurgeon keeps to her room, does she?" he said, chuckling. "I have an aunt who is the same. Whenever anyone has the temerity to acquire a real illness, my Aunt Elkins suffers all the torments of a jealous heart and must prove herself sicker still by keeping to her room."

Abigail was busy poking the stuffing back into a hole in her upholstered chair.

"Now, Angel," Cary said sternly.

"He didn't mean to eat the cushion," said Abigail. "I must have dropped some crumbs."

"I meant you," he said, parting his coat tails and taking a seat. "What's all this nonsense about you going home? This is your home now, or it soon will be."

"I'm returning to London," she said. "There's nothing you can do about it."

"Don't be a fool, Abigail," he said impatiently. "What will you do in London? Meet some nice young man and deceive him into marrying you? What will you tell him on your wedding night when he discovers your secret?"

Abigail gasped. She had not thought him capable of such cruelty.

"Do you expect Mr. Husband to be delighted to discover that he is not your first lover?"

Abigail covered her ears with her hands. "Shut up!"

"But perhaps he will be more understanding when you tell him how you crawled into my room, naked as a savage, and threw yourself into my arms."

Abigail jumped to her feet, startling the corgi. "It was the laudanum," she said, balling up her fists. "I should never have—it would never have happened otherwise."

"Ah, yes," he laughed. "The laudanum defense. And what of our revels in the gatehouse? The linen closet? And, don't forget, under the stairs. Were you also taking laudanum on those occasions?"

Abigail glared at him.

"What an understanding fellow Mr. Husband is! I should very much like to meet him. Indeed, I intend to. If the poor man suffers any lingering doubts, I feel sure I can silence them forever. I daresay he will be pleased to know it was I and not some rude fellow who first taught his wife the joys of the marriage bed. But perhaps I know him already?" He smiled mockingly. "Hector Mickleby? Excellent choice of a victim, Smith. I doubt the little greenhorn could tell the difference between a plucked and an unplucked pullet."

"I think you're disgusting," she said coldly. "I'm sure you know the way out," she added, leaving the room with what dignity she could muster.

"Take the dog," he called after her, maddeningly calm. "I'll call for you tomorrow at six. Wear something pretty. You have stockings? Dancing slippers?"

Abigail stopped in the doorway. "*What?*"

"Miss Rhoda's going-away gala," he reminded her. "Remember, you promised Hector the first two dances."

"You needn't take me," she said sharply. "I can go with Mrs. Spurgeon and Vera."

"I have a sneaking suspicion Mrs. Spurgeon will be too ill to attend. You can scarcely go alone. It will look very odd if I don't take you. People will think we're hiding something."

She closed the door with an angry slam. The insufferable man evidently found the situation highly amusing in every respect. Without seeing any humor in her predicament whatsoever, Abigail knew that Cary was right. She was ruined, and he was the only man in the world whom she could ever marry. The pain in her womb, which she had thought permanent, actually had vanished quickly, but her virginity was gone forever. She could scarcely compound the shame by marrying an unsuspecting male who had every right to expect his bride to be a virgin. Even Hector Mickleby deserved better than such a cruel deception.

She had two choices. She could marry Cary, or she could die an old maid. She didn't want to die an old maid, of course, but she couldn't imagine a happy future with Cary. Not when he casually said things like, "Don't worry. I'll marry you." Not when he didn't love her.

How different things would be if he loved me, she thought sadly as she carried the dog up to meet Paggles. All her present doubt and misery would be swept away. She would share his insouciance. She might even be able to laugh about their present situation.

"You look different today, my lady," said Paggles. Looking up from her knitting, she smiled brightly. "Being married seems to agree with you."

Abigail was suddenly weary of everything, especially of being mistaken by Paggles for her long-dead mother.

"Try to remember, Paggles. I'm Abigail. Anne was my mother."

"That is what I told Dickie-bird," the old lady replied, "but I don't think the dear boy understood me. He seemed to think you were his sister. But you're not. You're his niece."

Abigail suppressed her impatience. At least Paggles was in good spirits and her health, judging by her rosy cheeks and bright eyes, seemed actually to be improving. It was not her fault that her mind was going. "I wish you hadn't told Dickie-bird about Lord Dulwich and me," she said. "Though I don't suppose you did any harm."

"That is what I couldn't make him understand," said Paggles. "Knit one, purl two. He seemed to think that your Mama was Lady Dulwich, that became Lady Inchmery when the old earl died. But that was one of the Bolger sisters, though I can't think which one."

Abigail frowned. "Cary thinks my *mother* married Lord Dulwich?"

Paggles blinked at her. "Who is Cary, dear?"

"Dickie-bird, I mean."

"Not *your* Lord Dulwich," Paggles explained patiently. "Your Lord Dulwich is far too young to have married your mama. This would have been *your* Lord Dulwich's papa. He's Lord Inchmery now, but he would have been Lord Dulwich in your mama's day."

"So Ca—Dickie-bird—thinks that *my father* is Lord Inchmery?" cried Abigail. "And that Lord Dulwich is— is my *brother*?"

"You haven't got a brother, dear," Paggles pointed out. "Your mama had brothers, though. Perhaps that is what you are thinking of. Your uncles."

"What a hopeless muddle! He doesn't know who my father is at all!"

"It is not a hopeless muddle," said Paggles, annoyed.

"I have just explained it to you, miss! And your father is Cedric, Lord Wayborn. Or rather, was. He is dead now, poor lamb."

"No, Paggles," Abigail moaned. "Cedric was my *grandfather*. I'm Abigail! And my father . . . has just come back from *Brazil*!"

"Now you're just talking nonsense," Paggles said disapprovingly. "Brazil, indeed!"

"I'm sorry, Paggles," Abigail sighed. "Of course, you're right."

Paggles seemed mollified. "Now then," she said, pointing at Angel, who had found an old wooden toy to chew. "Who cut off your fox's tail? I don't like foxes as a rule, but it seems rather cruel to cut off their tails."

"It's not a fox, darling," she said wearily. "It's a corgi."

Abigail spent the best part of the next day deciding what to wear to Rhoda's ball, trying on nearly every dress she had brought with her, excoriating herself for not bringing this gown or that from London. Nothing seemed suitable, nothing seemed to fit, nothing looked good on her. When she went down to tea, Vera smiled sympathetically.

"Trouble deciding what to wear?"

Abigail blushed. "What gave it away?"

"You're wearing four different necklaces," Vera pointed out.

"It's hopeless," said Abigail. "I never was any good at putting myself together. I always look . . . *wrong*, no matter what I do."

"May I advise you, Miss Smith?" Vera suggested gently.

"Mrs. Nashe, I would be so grateful if you did."

"Please, it's *Vera*. Now, the garnets scream 'aging

dowager,' though I imagine you would look absolutely charming in a garnet-colored velvet redingote."

"I haven't got a garnet-colored velvet redingote."

"The pearls are magnificent, but let us not be ostentatious. Ditto the canary diamonds. Keep in mind this is only a little country ball. The first rule of fashion is mustn't overdo."

"I suppose the emeralds are all wrong, too," said Abigail miserably.

"No, indeed. They are small, tastefully set, and obviously of the very highest quality."

"I have matching earrings," Abigail said, brightening.

"Good. Have you got an emerald green dress? Never mind," Vera said quickly, as Abigail's face fell. "I have one. I shall lend it to you."

"You're so kind," said Abigail. "But I couldn't take your dress. What will you wear?"

"I shouldn't think I'm going," Vera replied. "Mrs. Spurgeon has declared her intention of staying home this evening, and, of course, I have a great deal of packing to do if we are to return to London on Monday. I can't leave Evans to do it all on her own."

Abigail flushed in embarrassment. "I suppose it was high-handed of me to announce our return to London so abruptly. Of course, Mrs. Spurgeon need not go if she doesn't wish it."

"Actually, I think it will do her good. I'm worried about her. You must have noticed how lethargic she has become, how quiet and reserved. In short, how unlike herself."

"If you think she is really sick—" Abigail began, becoming concerned.

"She is homesick," said Mrs. Nashe, allaying her fears. "The sooner we get back to London, the better."

"Yes," Abigail agreed emphatically.

Vera smiled. "Let me bring madam her tea, then I shall help you dress. I have an idea for your hair."

* * *

At ten minutes of six Vera stood back and admired
her handiwork. Abigail too was pleased. The green
dress made her hair appear more golden than red, and
Vera had dressed it in the Grecian style, with bands of
thin green ribbon threaded through the tamed curls. "I
never thought of using curling tongs," Abigail said in
wonder. "My hair is so curly to begin with."

Vera presented her with a little tin of pomade. "Remember, a little of this goes a long way. Use it sparingly,
and you won't have to worry about your curls looking
frizzy or unkempt."

"Thank you, Vera. You're my fairy godmother, that's
what you are." Impulsively, Abigail hugged the older
woman.

Vera seemed embarrassed. "Run along now. He'll be
here any moment. And if he doesn't pay you a thousand
compliments, he'll have to answer to me."

Abigail knew that, thanks to Vera, she was looking as
pretty as she possibly could. She reddened with pleasure
when she thought of Cary's reaction. Perhaps, if he
thought her pretty, he would find a more flattering way
to solicit her hand. It was too much to ask that the green
dress would make him fall in love with her, of course,
but a few compliments would go a long way towards
smoothing her badly damaged pride.

To her dismay, Cary hardly looked at her. His greeting was barely cordial, and he helped her into the carriage without a word. Almost before she was settled in
her seat, he tapped the roof with his stick and the carriage shot forward on its way down the drive.

He sat opposite her, pinning her to her seat with a
withering stare.

"We're not taking your—your bays?" she timidly
inquired.

"Chestnuts."

"No, thank you. They make my throat itch."

He glared at her and she went down under a wave of fresh humiliation. "Oh, you meant your horses," she said miserably. "I thought you meant . . . well, *chestnuts*. It's Sir Horatio who's got the bay horses."

"Captain Sir Horatio," he corrected her stonily. "Here," he said, tossing something into her lap. Abigail saw that it was a shoehorn carved of tortoiseshell.

"What's this?" she asked, puzzled.

"It's a shoehorn," he informed her. "In case anything flops out of that ridiculous dress, I thought you could use my shoehorn to shovel it back in!"

In affronted silence, Abigail pulled her shawl tightly around her.

"But perhaps I should give it to Hector instead so that *he* can shovel you *out* of it!"

This could not go unanswered. "You—you—!" she stammered, growing red in the face.

"You look like an orange-seller—complete with oranges!" he complained.

"For your information," she snapped, "these are not *my* oranges!"

"Oh, I know that, miss!" he retorted. "No one knows your oranges better than I! Or should I say *musk-melons*?"

Abigail was crushed by this display of contempt. "I borrowed some padding. I had to. The dress wouldn't fit me otherwise."

"I've heard of borrowed plumes, but borrowed breasts? What are you doing with a dress two sizes too big in the bosom, anyway? Doesn't your modiste have a measuring tape?"

"I borrowed this dress from Vera," she said tearfully. "It matches my emeralds. You weren't supposed to notice my oranges! You were supposed to notice my hair."

They went along without speaking for a while, listening to the sound of the horses' hooves as the carriage jogged along briskly. "I'm sorry, Abigail," he said after a moment. "Your hair does look . . . pretty."

"Thank you," she said sullenly.

"I've always preferred peaches to oranges, that's all."

She threw the shoehorn at him. She wondered why he had such a thing in the carriage at all, but now was not the time to satisfy an idle curiosity. Now was the time to ignore the insufferable man. It was going to be a long, miserable evening.

The horses clopped along the road.

"Married in orange," he suddenly murmured. "What's the rhyme for that? 'Married in white, you have chosen right.' 'Married in blue, your love is true.' 'Married in red, better off dead.' But what do they say about orange?"

"Nothing rhymes with orange," Abigail said repressively.

"What about green?" he persisted. "Married in green . . . your love is obscene?"

"Ashamed to be seen," she coldly corrected him.

"Well, we know you're not ashamed to be *seen*," he remarked. "Not from the waist up, anyway." He paused politely, leaving Abigail room to wittily retort. "I suppose it could be worse," he went on airily, as Abigail opted for cold silence. "It might have been yellow. 'Ashamed of your fellow.' You're not ashamed of me, are you, Abigail?"

She looked at him directly. "Will you kindly stop talking, Mr. Wayborn? I am not in the least interested in anything you have to say."

"Cream," he said. "Married in cream, your life will be a dream. You ought to have worn cream, Abigail. Or ivory. Your life will be live-er-ly."

"That doesn't rhyme," she snapped. "And, for the last time, I'm not marrying you. I should rather die an old maid!"

He lifted a brow. "Maid? I don't think so, my girl."

"I hate you!" was her considered and intelligent response, at which he took out his flask and slung back a mouthful of whisky. "You're drunk," she accused.

"Want some?"

The carriage came to a sudden stop and a splash of whisky flew out of the flask and landed on Abigail's borrowed oranges. "Perfect!" she cried. "Now I smell like a distillery."

Cary was profuse in apologies and handkerchiefs, all of which Abigail pushed away.

"Married in whisky. Sounds pretty risky."

"At least I can now get away from you," she answered, flinging open the door and jumping out. The footman leaped back just in time.

Abigail plunged blindly down the path, oblivious to her surroundings. She heard Cary walking behind her, whistling, and then she heard the carriage rolling away. She came to an abrupt stop. She had reached the covered gate of a long stone wall. A square stone house loomed on the other side, set in what appeared to be a country garden. There was a single candle burning in the lower window. Otherwise, the house was dark.

She had never been to Gooseneck Hall, but she was certain this was not it. For one thing, it would have been ablaze with light and music if a party were underway.

"What is this place?" she demanded. "Where has the carriage gone?"

He answered her questions in reverse order. "The carriage will return shortly. This is the manse at Little Straythorne." He went past her and opened the gate for her. "It's the rector's house. Sorry, I don't know the Presbyterian word for it."

"I know what a manse is. Why have you brought me here?"

"Because it was no good asking Cousin Wilfred to

marry us," he patiently answered. "He thinks Presbyterians are cannibals or witches, or, possibly, cannibal witches. But this fellow here will marry us for a mere ten guineas, which I have in my pocket, in actual guineas."

"I told you, I'm not marrying you," she repeated. "Cary, you can't just kidnap me and force me to marry you. This is England, after all."

"No, I can't force you to marry me. I know that. But you must admit that I *have* succeeded in kidnaping you. Look at you. You're completely kidnaped."

Abigail's mouth tightened. "You had better recall your carriage, sir. I am expected at Gooseneck Hall. When I am missed—"

He grinned at her. "What sort of a kidnaper do you think I am? Naturally, I sent your regrets to Gooseneck Hall. I've thought of everything. Gooseneck thinks you're at Tanglewood, and Tanglewood thinks you're at Gooseneck. We're in the ether, Smith. We can do anything."

"It's not funny!" she lashed out at him.

"No, it isn't," he agreed. "It's deadly serious, and you had better make up your mind to be reasonable, my girl. We made love, Abigail. There are consequences. I'm sorry if you don't like it, but we *must* marry. You can't marry anyone else. If you don't marry me, what will become of you? An old maid, my arse! You could be pregnant. Have you thought of that? There's nothing else to be done."

She turned her face away from him. "Do you think I don't know that? But must you be so horrid about it? So unfeeling?"

He grasped her by the shoulders and forced her to look at him. "Unfeeling? I am being *practical*, Abigail," he told her harshly. "Reasonable. Sensible. Responsible. In short, all the things you complain I'm not. Here I am, being practical, and you don't like it. Too bad!"

"You're not practical, Cary Wayborn," she sobbed.

"You're a complete cabbagehead! If you *were* practical, which you are *not*, you'd know we *can't* be married here. It's not our parish, and we haven't had the banns called."

"That's where you're wrong, monkey," he retorted. "I've got an Archbishop's license in my pocket, and I've got your ring, too. It's the Cary emerald. I got it out of the family vault when I was lately in London."

Abigail stared at him. "But that was last week," she said in a small voice. "That was before—before—Oh!"

"You may well say, 'Oh,' you ungrateful little baggage." He pulled a small leather box out of his pocket and opened it. The large, square-cut emerald gleamed in the moonlight.

"You wanted to marry me then?" Abigail cautiously inquired.

"I did think about it," he admitted, "but you weren't exactly nice to me upon my return. You said a lot of hurtful things. You called me foolish and irresponsible. I decided to cut line."

Abigail's heart sank. Once he had wanted to marry her, and she had spoiled everything by hurling insults at him. "And now?" she asked quietly, afraid of the answer.

He looked away. "Now we have no choice," he said flatly. "We must marry. Unless, of course, *you* mean to be foolish and irresponsible? You must admit, it is the only practical solution. God knows, I don't want you on my conscience."

Abigail felt sick, but at the same time, she knew that he was right. She could not return home to her father as if nothing had happened. She could not play the part of a marriageable young lady ever again. It would be a ghastly fraud.

The door of the manse opened and a tall, gaunt figure appeared, holding a candlestick aloft. "Hurry," said Cary grumpily. "Before I change my mind."

Abigail followed him meekly.

Cary signed the registry first, then handed her the pen. "Sign your name, Abigail," he told her curtly, "and this is the last time you will ever write it. From now on you are Abigail Wayborn, do you understand? You are no longer a member of that family."

He paid the vicar of Little Straythorne as Abigail placed her name under his. The carriage was waiting for them in the moonlight. Abigail was overcome with a sense of doom as she climbed inside. No marriage with such a miserable beginning could ever end happily, she was sure. Knowing that they might have been happy if she hadn't spoiled everything only added to her torment.

Cary took the seat opposite her. "You look utterly miserable," he observed. "Not very flattering, considering this is our wedding night."

Abigail glanced at him. "You look fairly grim yourself."

"Do I?" He drank deeply from his flask. "Drink?"

Abigail took it from him gratefully. The Irish whisky gave just the combination of warmth and punishment she felt she deserved. She drained it.

Cary began pulling off his left boot. "For heaven's sake, cheer up," he said crossly. "Try and look happy when we arrive at Gooseneck Hall. Where's the shoehorn? I need it to put my dancing pumps on. I'm sorry, but I refused to be married in dancing pumps. I married you in my last pair of Hoby's boots. Remember that."

"Gooseneck Hall!" she cried, suppressing a hiccough. "Cary, I couldn't."

"As good a place as any to announce our marriage," he said with forced cheer. "Try smiling. You remember how to smile, don't you?"

"No!" said Abigail, panicking.

He stopped struggling with his boot. "Just turn up the corners of your mouth, like so."

"No, Cary, we cannot announce our marriage. I forbid it."

He scowled. "Are you seriously proposing we keep it a secret?"

"No, we couldn't do that. But I must tell my father first." She hesitated. She couldn't be sure if, in his eyes, being Red Ritchie's daughter was any better than being Dulwich's sister. As for being Dulwich's former betrothed . . . it didn't bear thinking about. "Cary, about my father—"

He held up his hand. "Don't worry about your father. I'll tell him. I'll write him a letter. You needn't see him at all."

"Not see him?" Abigail felt a sudden cold fear. She had not considered this before, but, as her husband, Cary now had near absolute power over her in the eyes of the law. He would be well within his rights to prevent her from seeing her father, if he so wished. He could hold her prisoner, if that was his desire. And, of course, he was legally entitled to the use of her fortune. And her body. In fact, it was now legally *his* fortune and *his* body, to do with as he pleased.

"Cary, you would not prevent me from seeing my own father?" she asked, hating the note of pleading that crept into her voice. "You would not be so cruel."

He seemed surprised. "Do you want to see your father?"

"Yes, of course, I do. I love my father very much. And he deserves to hear about—about *this* from me, face to face."

He smiled sardonically. "Then by all means, you must tell him about *this* face to face."

"I shall go home on Monday as planned, and I shall tell him then."

"Would you like me to go with you?"

"No," she said quickly.

He shrugged. "Just as you please."

"You don't understand. He always wanted me to marry well."

"And this you have not done?" he said coldly.

Abigail realized she was offending him at every turn, and making a bad situation worse. "Please understand, Cary. My father very much wanted me to marry a title. He spent a fortune on my education, my clothes. I had lessons in everything. Dance lessons, piano lessons, singing lessons, art lessons, lessons in French, Italian, and German, even lessons in walking and talking. And I was never good at any of it."

"You walk and talk."

"This is going to hurt my father," said Abigail. "He had such ambitions for me."

"I'm not precisely a bootblack, you know," he said, fuming. "So what if I haven't got a title? I am a gentleman. I have an estate. But Tanglewood is too small for him, I daresay."

"Do you expect him to rejoice in your debts?" Abigail returned.

"Bugger your father," he said violently. "If you wish to go on seeing him, do so. But you needn't ask him to Tanglewood. He will not be welcome under my roof."

"You can't be serious!" Abigail protested. "He's my father, Cary."

"What about Dulwich?" he demanded. "Surely you've no desire to see him again?"

"No, indeed," she quickly assured him. "I never want to see *him* again. Cary, there's something I must tell you about Dulwich. My father—"

"I've heard enough about Dulwich and your father, madam," he interrupted. "Not another word on the subject, I beg you. You may see whomever you like when you are in Town. Only, do not bring them here, and do not force me to listen to any account of people whom I so thoroughly despise. Also, I shall make it clear through my attorneys that I will accept no consideration from your family. Nor should you."

"What, nothing?" Abigail cried in astonishment.

"Not a ha'penny," he said firmly. "I trust, madam, that you can live within two or three thousand a year, because that is all your husband can provide."

"But I have some money of my own," she said. "My father still manages it, of course, but it is mine outright, settled on me when I came of age. You would not require me to return it, simply because you dislike my family?"

He frowned at her. "No one is going to *rob* you, if that's what you mean. You'll have your money, madam, don't worry."

Abigail retreated into silence. He had succeeded in making her feel small and mercenary.

Cary knocked on the roof, and when the driver opened the panel he gave curt instructions for them to be conveyed back to Tanglewood Manor. "At least," he said sullenly, as the panel slid closed, "there is no need for you to pretend to be happy, Mrs. Wayborn."

"Cary, I'm sorry," she said desperately. "I know I've ruined everything."

"I wouldn't say that," he said briskly, but Abigail's glimmer of hope quickly died when he added, "It was fairly well doomed at the start. Perhaps it was a mistake to sell my Cromwell in order to buy that silly license. I thought you'd be nicer in bed than the Lord Protector, but I suppose there's not the least chance of my claiming the rights of a husband now."

Abigail's eyes flew to his face. "What do you mean *now*?"

"I didn't mean precisely *now*. I had no thought of ravishing you here in the carriage." He looked at her in growing amusement. "Perhaps I should."

Abigail knew her face was scarlet, but, despite her

embarrassment, her skin prickled with excitement. If he wants me, she thought, then perhaps all is not lost. It was not the same as true love, of course, but at least it was something.

"Since you will not permit me to announce to the world that I am your husband, I cannot spend the night with you. Either we consummate our union in secret or not at all."

Abigail bit her lip. "Then you would wish us to have a real marriage?"

"If by 'real marriage' you mean one that includes the physical congress of our two naked bodies, I'd say you have the situation well in hand. Yes, Abigail, I do intend to be a rather impertinent fixture in your bed. Are you prepared for life with a demanding partner?"

Abigail swallowed hard. "Is that why you married me?" she asked evenly. "Because you wish to make love to me again?"

"Not in the least," he replied. "I haven't the slightest wish to make love to you again."

"Oh!" said Abigail, thoroughly confused.

"I thought I was clear," said Cary, pulling off his white gloves. "Making love to you again would be a shocking waste of our talents. What I propose is that we do it repeatedly, perhaps even incessantly, for the first week or two, starting now."

Chapter 13

"I like to begin slowly," he said, sliding onto the seat beside her. He kissed her with surprising tenderness, finding her lips and coaxing them open with the point of his tongue. But while his mouth dallied with hers, his hands contradicted his words. They moved over her body hungrily, stripping the padding impatiently from the bosom of her borrowed gown. "With you I do not always succeed. You do make my blood run fast. Ah, there you are," he breathed, finding her small breast.

Abigail sucked in her breath, wondering if she could ever become accustomed to such intimacy with a man, even this man, whom she adored. In the next moment, both his hands were inside her dress, and then the dress itself was down around her waist. She guessed he must have vast experience undressing women in fast-moving vehicles. Rather a depressing credential for a husband, she reflected gloomily.

"Drawers," he muttered unhappily, as his hand worked its way up her leg under her skirts.

"Only *you* would wear drawers at such a moment."

Abigail began to babble as he tore through the buttons

on her silk drawers. "It isn't going to be like—like it was that night, you know. *I'm* not like that. It was the laudanum. It made me behave—it made me feel—" She gasped as he suddenly entered her with his finger. She flinched, but the pain she feared never materialized. It felt, not pleasant exactly, but warm and natural. Instinctively, her muscles contracted around it. "I never did any of those things before."

"I should bloody well hope not," he replied, dragging her further down on the seat so that her head rested on the cushions.

She looked up at him as he fitted himself between her legs. "You're bound to be disappointed," she said fearfully, her body taut with anxiety.

He looked down at her as he slowly opened his evening breeches at the front. "Perhaps *you* will be disappointed," he remarked as he freed his fully aroused member.

Abigail squeezed her eyes shut, bracing herself for the inevitable first thrust, longing for it almost as much as she dreaded it. "If it is only one tenth of what I felt before, I shall not be disappointed," she breathed.

"How much do you remember of that night?"

"I remember everything," she whispered, shamefaced.

He laughed softly, then, to her astonishment, he slipped to his knees, burying his head between her thighs. She clapped her legs together just seconds too late, and there was no dislodging him. It was so acutely personal, she was not sure she could bear it at first, let alone enjoy it. He kissed her first through the silk of her drawers, then as, little by little, the tension in her muscles relaxed, he parted the silk and pleasured her with his tongue, feeding hungrily, as Abigail, unable to resist him any longer, raked her fingers through his hair. Oblivious to everything else, she pursued the coming crisis and cried out in relief when it burst within. It was not the laudanum, she realized. It was Cary. He was magic. He could make her feel in ways she had not thought possible.

She opened her eyes and smiled at him dreamily. He caught his breath, unable to resist the look on her face, that of a woman given over completely to sexual desire. The scent of her intoxicated him. "For God's sake, take me in your hands and guide me home before I disgrace myself," he begged, falling on her like some wild beast.

Abigail had no idea how he could ever disgrace himself, but she quickly did as he told her, forcing the head of his erection into her tender entrance.

Slowly he filled her, touching her to the womb, delighting in the response of her body. He moved in concert with the gently swaying carriage, so perfectly in contact with her most sensitive part that Abigail was carried away almost instantly on another tide of bliss. Her second crisis proved too much for him, however. "Forgive me," he murmured in her ear as the very last of his willpower gave way amidst her seductive little whimpers. He gathered her legs over his hips and plunged into her again and again. Abigail at first was mindful of the proximity of the coachman, but as his thrusts drove her relentlessly to the peak of pleasure, a savage, broken cry fell from her lips. Cary roared as he emptied himself into her clinging body, then retreated to his side of the carriage. "I did not mean to do that," he murmured. "My poor darling. You deserve so much better."

Abigail was too emotional to find words. She was married. Her husband, the man she was bound to body and soul forever and ever, was a man so depraved that he actually had ravished her in a carriage. Worse, he had made her like it. She was certain the coachman had heard her crying out at her zenith. Compared to their last encounter, this had been quite brief, yet the effect had been just as powerful upon her senses. Unquestionably, she would have been quite willing and able to do anything he required of her. She doubted she could have stopped if the coachman had actually opened the trap to inquire why the young lady was screaming. And she hadn't the excuse of opium. *Perhaps*, she thought hopefully, *I'm as bad as he is.*

There was scarcely enough time to straighten their clothes before the carriage came to a stop. "Disappointed?" he asked politely as she stuffed the pads back into the borrowed dress. He looked so cocksure that for a moment Abigail deeply resented him. She was nowhere near him in shameless depravity, she realized sadly. He seemed satisfied, too, which gave her hope for the future. If she could please him in this way, even if he did not love her, perhaps they *could* forge a happy life together.

Trembling from head to foot, she did not trust herself to speak. She shook her head. She would just have to try harder, that was all. She had no choice. She would have to be everything he wanted. Do everything he wanted. Because if he ever went elsewhere for love, she would die.

Cary brought her safely inside the house and placed her in the care of Mrs. Nashe before bidding both ladies good night. "Tell me everything," Vera said eagerly, the instant he had gone. "I've never seen your eyes so bright, my dear. I perceive you were a great success."

Abigail wished for the thousandth time that she was not such a blusher. "Perhaps a small success," was all she would allow herself to say. Pleading exhaustion, or headache—her head was so full of Cary, she couldn't be sure of what she was saying—she ran upstairs to her room.

"What kept you?" Cary asked. He was sitting on her

bed, entertaining the corgi with one of the cravats he had removed from his neck. He had already removed his boots and his stockings, and, with his brown calves and bare feet on display, he looked more than ever like a gypsy prince. Abigail stared at him, once again a little frightened by the powerful physical attraction she felt for him. Would she ever get used to this? She stared at him in dismay. What she desperately needed at that moment was time alone. Time to sort out her wrecked feelings, time to digest the enormity of what she had done, time to devise a plan for winning her husband's heart. Time to curl up in a ball and cry like a baby.

"You might want to close the door," he said. "You're letting in a draft."

She hastily closed the door. "How did you get up here so fast?"

"It's my house, monkey. I've got keys and architectural plans. A man can always get into his own house. Surely I am not unwelcome in my lady's chamber?" he added mockingly.

After what had transpired in the carriage, she could scarcely pretend an outraged modesty. She could always be alone tomorrow. All at once it occurred to her that many men in his position would not have felt obligated to marry her at all. They certainly would not have insisted on it, after the way she behaved. And if he was making light of it, at least he did not treat her with contempt. Her heart swelled with gratitude. He might not love her, but he was a true gentleman. She could always trust to his honor. "You're most welcome, sir," she said humbly. "I did not expect to see you here, that's all."

He stood up and began unbuttoning his peacock blue waistcoat. "Indeed? If your purpose was to keep me at arm's length, I'm afraid you've gone about it all wrong!"

She smiled shyly. "But I have no wish to keep you at arm's length."

"Then you have succeeded," he said, grinning as he hauled his shirt over his head. "Aren't you going to get undressed, Mrs. Green-ashamed-to-be-seen? A man shouldn't have to fight with padded bosoms and buttoned-up drawers on his wedding night. At least, not twice."

He shoved the corgi off of the bed and stripped off his breeches. It was completely unfair that she was so shy and he wasn't shy at all, Abigail reflected. It was inhuman. Even beautiful people ought to be possessed of a *little* modesty.

"How can you be such a nudist?" she asked, exasperated. "And so brown all over?" she added as he bent to pull back the covers, giving her an excellent view of his copper-brown backside.

"I lie out by the river in the summertime," he explained, bundling up his clothes and tossing them on the chair. Angel, his master's cravat in his mouth, hopped onto the warm clothes and settled down to enjoy his heavily starched snack.

"What if someone were to see you naked?" Abigail asked, horrified.

"Lucky them," he carelessly replied. He lay down on the bed, and stretched out with his arms folded behind his head. Almost as much as she loved him, she envied him for his complete lack of self-consciousness. "Hurry up, Abigail," he commanded. "I wish to see you in all your glory, un-upholstered, wearing only your blushes."

"Freckles, you mean," she said ruefully.

"I like your freckles," he responded. "Show me these freckles of which you speak. I would study them at length, and praise them, and kiss them."

She wasn't about to give him a show of freckles or anything else. She opened the wardrobe and hid behind one of its doors as she undressed. Her best nightgown felt cool against her skin. As her head emerged from it,

she caught sight of a book resting on the bottom shelf.
She picked it up and closed the wardrobe.

Cary had gotten under the covers. He looked at her
curiously. "Story time?"

Abigail sat on the edge of the bed with the book in
her lap. "Cary, I must thank you."

"Must you thank me in a nightgown? I prefer to be
thanked in the nude."

Abigail persevered. "I know you did not have to
marry me. It was especially kind of you after I rejected
you so many times. I was so foolish. Indeed, I don't
know what I would have done if you had not married
me. Because I do want a home of my own, and children,
someday."

"You left out husband," he pointed out. "You want a
husband, don't you?"

"Of course. One can't very well have one without the
other, can one?"

"Not everyone is as conscientious as you, my dear
Smith," he said, smiling. "All in all, I'd rather be married for the purpose of creating legitimate issue than
simply to cover up the fact that we took too much laudanum and behaved rather badly."

"Then you want children, too?"

"Dozens. I want our nursery to look like an orphan-
age, in fact," he replied. "Does that alarm you, Smith?"

"Not at all," she assured him. "I had no brothers and
sisters myself. I was rather lonely."

"That you will never be again. I promise."

Almost unable to bear the warmth of his gaze, Abigail took a deep breath and held out the book she had
removed from the wardrobe. "This is my wedding present to you, Cary. It's not much, I know. But I didn't
know I was going to be married tonight, did I?"

"Ah, the Blake," he murmured, taking the book from
her with a smile. "Indeed, it would have been cruel of

you not to give it to me, when you are only waiting for it to appreciate, whereas I appreciate it already. But I've no Wordsworth or Coleridge for you," he added, leaning forward to kiss her cheek. "What can I give you?"

Abigail twisted the emerald on her hand. "You've given me so much already. This beautiful emerald. Really, it was so good of you to marry me at all."

"Nonsense," he said roundly. "You caught me at just the right time in my life, Smith. I was withering away in exile when you found me. I was so starved for female companionship that Mrs. Grimstock was starting to look good to me."

"Is that what you mean by 'withering away?'" she said angrily. "Lusting after poor Mrs. Grimstock? She'd leave your employ if she knew."

"That was only when I first came into Herts," he explained. "By the third or fourth month, I gave up. I resigned myself to a cold bed. I bought a dog, sort of. Indeed, I was well on my way to turning into one of those crusty old bachelors who sit by the fire and talk to themselves when you burst into the scene. In another month or two, I'd not have been fit to marry anyone. Celibacy is not my natural state, you know. It was having a warping effect on me. I believe I even behaved rather badly when we first met."

"When were *you* ever celibate?" Abigail wanted to know. "Do you expect me to believe you don't keep a mistress somewhere?" The moment she said the words, she wished she could have them back. She sounded like a shrew.

Cary frowned. This was not exactly how he envisioned spending his wedding night, but perhaps it would be better to clear the air and give Abigail what reassurances she needed. "Where, for example? Cousin Wilfred watches me like a hawk."

"London, of course."

Cary snorted. "Alas, I can no longer afford to keep a mistress in London. So you see, Smith," he went on playfully, "marriage was the only answer to my unhappy predicament. I couldn't really see Grimstock putting up with any nonsense."

"But you might have married anyone," Abigail said. "You need not have married me."

"True, true," he agreed with his usual modesty. "But I could never make up my mind. Just as well you made it up for me."

"I did not mean to trap you," Abigail said, distressed.

"Not at all. You did me a favor coming through the wardrobe in your skin. It made choosing a wife so simple. No more lonely nights. No more talking to myself. No more involuntary celibacy." He had thought she needed reassurance, but now it occurred to him she might have another reason for these inquiries. "You would not wish me to keep a mistress, surely?" he asked sharply. "Are you trying to put me off?"

"No," she answered, so loudly that the corgi uttered a faint woof of surprise. "I hope you will never be sorry you married me. I believe I can make you happy. I shall try."

"You may find it difficult," he warned.

She forced herself to look him in the eye. "Anything you want, Cary, whatever it is, I shall do it for you gladly. I will never deny you anything, I swear. If it is in my power to give you, it's yours. *I'm* yours. I will always submit to your—your needs. I will never complain. I don't want you to keep a mistress. I don't want to share you with anyone. I will do anything you ask of me."

"Fascinating," he murmured. "You can still blush while making the most indecent proposal ever made me by a woman. Well, Smith. Fortunately for your womanhood, I am a man of truly modest needs. Ten times a day is all I ask."

"T-t-ten times?" she echoed faintly, turning quite pale. "A day? Every day?"

"Paltry, I know. But we must make allowances for the fact that you are a novice, my dear. In no time, I make sure, you will be servicing me twenty or thirty times a day. But ten will do me for now." He grinned broadly.

"Cary, I—"

"Upside down to start, of course, before breakfast, usually, though not always. Then, right side up, just for a change. Then sideways, backwards, and forwards, in quick succession. What is that, five? Halfway there. Time for lunch."

"Oh, you're not serious," she breathed, turning bright pink.

His eyes widened. "You seem disappointed, Smith. Now *I'm* blushing. Yes, of course I'm joking. I'm not a monster, Abigail."

"Don't make fun of me," she said softly.

He seized her hands. "I can't help it, Abby. I'm an ass, and you might as well know it now. When I'm nervous, I make stupid, flip, impertinent remarks that probably make you want to slap me. I blame Eton."

Abigail stared at him in astonishment. "Why?"

"Why? Well, I was rather small for my age. The other boys—"

"No," she impatiently interrupted. "Why on earth would *you* be nervous?"

"For that I blame you," he explained. "You're obviously nervous, and that in turn makes me nervous. I try to make you laugh, but that only seems to make it worse for you. You're so tightly wound up I fear there's no unwinding you. You're different from any other woman I've ever known. I never know where I am with you."

"I don't mean to be different," Abigail cried, horrified. "I can change."

"I don't want you to change, you maddening little

baggage," he explained. "I just want us to get to a place where I don't frighten you to death. Don't draw away from me when I touch you," he added softly. "I can't bear it."

"Do I do that? I don't mean to, Cary. I'm just so nervous."

"After my behavior in the carriage, I can't say I blame you," he said ruefully. "Indeed, I wouldn't blame you if you sent me packing."

"The carriage?" Just thinking of that passionate encounter made Abigail breathless. If only she had not been so worried about the coachman overhearing them, she might have succeeded in pleasing him. "You were wonderful in the carriage," she told him humbly, and made a silent vow never to shrink from him again, no matter how nervous she felt. It was stupid and selfish, and, she was beginning to understand, it made Cary think she did not want him.

He grinned sheepishly. "You should see me in bed."

"Perhaps I will," Abigail replied. "Someday."

"God in heaven," he said, grinning. "Smith has made a joke." He held the covers up for her as she quickly joined him, then they were together in the warm nest.

His hands claimed her instantly, but unhurriedly. There was no doubt of his arousal, but, clearly, there would be no repeat of the quick, hard onslaught she had enjoyed in the carriage. A lazy, teasing pleasure began building up in Abigail's blood. In money matters, he might be hopelessly impractical, but he was a diligent and masterful lover. One can't have everything. Indeed, truth be told, she was glad he had at least one imperfection. Snuggled safe under the covers, she reached for him.

"It's always the quiet ones," Cary chuckled, cupping her small breasts, enjoying the rose-pink nipples that hardened under the thin material of her gown. When

Abigail lost her shyness she became the most respon-
sive woman he had ever bedded. She awakened and then
fulfilled his most powerful desires in a way no other
woman ever had. Socially awkward and self-effacing
she might be, but in bed at least she was the perfect
partner.

He murmured playfully as he began rolling up the
hem of her nightgown, "He comes and passeth through
sphere after sphere; First her sheets, then her arms, then
anywhere."

He put his hand on "anywhere," and she marveled
that her body did not even flinch as he probed and ex-
plored. Just hours ago she would have thought such intimacy too shocking to be contemplated, let alone
endured. Now she merely opened herself as wide as she
could, drawing him on with a greed that took her own
breath away. This wanton lady could not be Abigail
Ritchie. Abigail Wayborn was quite a different matter,
however. She reminded herself that there was no sin in
joining with the man who was now and forever her husband, but parts of her refused to believe it. It felt sinful
to let go so utterly.

"Was that Shakespeare?" she asked him idly, trailing
her nails across his brown skin.

"Donne," he corrected.

Abigail giggled. "Surely we are just getting started?"

"It *is* a bit early in the evening for Donne," he agreed,
laughing aloud.

Her gossamer gown, which was bunched up around
her thighs, was soon rendered entirely transparent by his
sweat mingled with hers. "Are you sure you are not too
tired?" he asked once, but when she shook her head, he
did not ask again, marveling at the way her small body
took him in a second time with the same thrilled response. "You will suffer for it in the morning," he
warned, but she would not let him go. A temporary ache

of the womb seemed a small price to pay for this incomprehensible bliss. She actually would have consented to a third encounter, but Cary refused. "*I* should be sore in the morning," he murmured, making her laugh.

Afterwards, as he slept, she stroked his rich black hair, wondering if it would ever turn gray. Surely not, she decided, as she floated into sleep. Surely she had married an immortal.

The corgi woke her before dawn by jumping on the bed. The fire had died down, and Cary was moving about in the dark, hunting for his clothes. "See with what simplicity this nymph begins her golden days," he greeted her poetically.

"Hmmm?"

"That's Marvell, you marvellous creature."

"Cary, what *are* you talking about?"

"Thus have I had thee, as a dream doth flatter, in sleep a king, but, waking, no such matter," he recited, smiling down at her. "Except, of course, this time I am still a king, and you are still mine."

The words thrilled her. Whatever else troubled their fledgling marriage, she had no doubt of his desire for her. They were as compatible in the bedchamber as they seemed to be incompatible out of it. "Was that more Marvell?" she asked teasingly. "Or Donne?"

"Well, I'm finished, if that's what you mean. No, monkey, it's Shakespeare. Sonnet Eighty-seven. Don't you Presbyterians read the classics?"

Abigail sat up in bed and stretched. "What time is it?"

Cary sighed, pulling on his breeches. "But at my back I always hear Time's winged chariot hurrying near," he complained, pushing the rest of his attire through the wardrobe. "The girl will be here any moment to build up your fire. I swear, when the world knows I am your husband, I shall keep you between those sheets for five straight days, but for now . . ." He knelt over her on the bed and planted a kiss on her forehead. "Farewell! Thou art too dear for my possessing."

Abigail had no Shakespeare to give him in return, so she kissed his mouth, pulling at his lower lip with her teeth. He did not seem disappointed.

The morning passed in a blur. Mrs. Spurgeon appeared at breakfast in a lace cap and iron-gray curls, complaining of numerous ailments, to which Vera murmured sympathetically. Abigail scarcely heard them until Mrs. Spurgeon's voice suddenly intruded upon her thoughts.

"I sometimes think I hear his voice, his dear sweet voice."

Abigail was startled. "Whose voice do you mean, Mrs. Spurgeon?"

"Why, Cato's, of course," the older woman replied. "Haven't you been listening? I see him in my dreams, and when I wake I think I see him there on his perch, just for a second. But it is just a dream. Is the window open, Vera?"

"Of course," Vera said soothingly.

"The window must always be open, in case he should return. I do not think I can leave this place on Monday, not without my darling boy."

"But you must!" said Abigail, before Vera's signal silenced her.

"My poor, darling boy," Mrs. Spurgeon murmured disconsolately, as if she had not heard Abigail's outburst. Abigail felt a stab of pity for the woman. She hardly seemed the same robust, domineering harridan who had driven poor Paggles out of the carriage on the day they had met. The loss of her bird had hit the lady very hard.

"I'm so sorry, Mrs. Spurgeon," she said guiltily.

"You never liked him," she spitefully replied. "It's all your fault he flew away!"

"There, there, madam," Vera interceded, patting Mrs. Spurgeon's hand and soothing her agitation. "It is no one's fault, I'm sure." She whispered to Abigail, "Perhaps it would be best if you went for one of your walks, dear. There's no sense in antagonizing her."

Stung, Abigail went upstairs to put on her cloak and gloves. Before coming into Hertfordshire, she had never thought of herself as being capable of inspiring strong feelings in her fellow creatures, but Mrs. Spurgeon had been shaking with rage. For her part in Cato's untimely demise, Abigail felt horribly guilty. Angel, however, suffered from no such complexity of feeling; he was eager for a walk. As she stepped onto the porch, she saw Cary coming up the path, his purple coat more neatly brushed than his dark hair, which was falling into his eyes.

He stopped to pat the dog on the head, a difficult operation as the dog's head was continually moving as he jumped up and down excitedly.

"Going for a walk?" he greeted Abigail. "You've anticipated me. I was just coming to invite you for a chaste little stroll in the woods." Abruptly, his face changed. "What's the matter? I thought you were happy when I left you."

"I was," Abigail said quickly. "I still am. It's Mrs. Spurgeon. She misses her bird frightfully. Sometimes I think—Do you think we ought to tell her the truth?"

"Certainly not," he answered, taking her arm and leading her away from the house. "Unless, of course, you wish to cause her more pain. Believe me, it is far kinder to let her believe Cato merely flew away, than to tell her the truth." He kicked a clod of half-melted snow mixed with mud in Angel's direction. "Disgusting beast. He wasn't even sick. That bird went down his gullet as smoothly as a warm bowl of milk, beak and all."

Abigail, remembering the bird's shrieking voice, shuddered involuntarily.

Angel blundered off in the direction of the woods. "Let him go," Cary instructed, steering her across the muddy lawn to a stand of birches. "There's a little private path I would like to show you."

A quarter of an hour later, they were standing at the back door of the stone gatehouse. Abigail was more flattered than surprised. "You know why I brought you here," he said, tilting back her head so that she was forced to look at him. It wasn't really a question.

"Yes," she said happily.

"Good," he grunted, fitting his key in the lock. "I don't usually bring young ladies here in the middle of the day, but, since you are my wife, I will make an exception in your case."

Abigail went in before him. "I am not in the least interested in what you usually do," she told him primly as she stood in the cold hall.

Cary chuckled as he closed the door. "Hang your cloak on the peg," he invited her, helping her out of it. "Nothing borrowed from Vera, I see," he said approvingly as he eyed her blue dress. "Everything present and correct."

The hall opened into a poky room dominated by a brick fireplace. In the center of the room, which served as both kitchen and sitting room, was a long deal table and two chairs. To one side of the fireplace was a ladder leading up to a loft. The fire had been built up, Abigail guessed, in anticipation of her arrival.

Her eyes went to the ladder. "Do you expect me to climb up there with you?"

"If you insist," he answered, herding her towards the loft with his body. "I was going to offer you a cup of tea, but if madam is inclined towards another lesson in wifely conduct . . ."

Abigail started up the ladder, giggling. At the top she was obliged to crouch down to avoid banging her head on the low ceiling, but the narrow bed had a real eiderdown mattress and a quilt lovingly pieced together from tiny, vibrantly colored squares of satin.

True to form, Cary threw aside his clothes and arranged himself on the bed in readiness. "Usually," he drawled, "the lady gives me a moment to gather my thoughts before she pounces on me. But I suppose a wife must be permitted a few liberties. Pounce if you must. I shall bear it as best I can. Incidentally, I think you'll find that removing all clothing will greatly increase our mutual satisfaction."

Abigail tossed her head as best she could while bending almost in half. "I told you I don't care what you usually do with your tarts," she said smartly, hauling up her skirts and climbing onto the narrow bed. In a moment she was straddling him. "I mean to institute a few reforms."

"Such as no drawers, perhaps?" he said, finding the nest of hairs between her thighs. It felt to his curious fingers like a ripe peach drenched in honey. "Now that was a necessary reform indeed, my queen. You are exactly right to remove all obstacles from the path of progress."

"I cannot take all the credit," said Abigail. She gasped as his long finger slid into her swollen center, then went on, "My most trusted advisor, after a long and thorough investigation, exposed the scandalous practice of wearing drawers for what it was—a cruel and unnatural impediment to men in carriages everywhere."

"Good man, this advisor of yours," Cary approved. "You are fortunate to have him."

"I am well aware of my good fortune, sir," she answered, sweeping her hand down his smooth belly until she found his hot, stiff member. "I receive excellent advice and my prime minister is forever at my beck and call."

"He certainly is," Cary agreed gruffly.

"And such a handsome fellow, too," she murmured, teasing the head of his prime minister shamelessly. "So dependable, always ready for action, though perhaps just a bit hot-headed, but I don't mind that."

Cary could endure no more teasing. "For God's sake, Abigail!" he muttered, drawing her down upon him by the hips. "Is this any way to treat a public servant?"

Abigail collapsed into giggles as he slid deep inside her.

Cary heaved a deep sigh of relief. "You were made for me," he murmured. "Surely you were made for me."

The sudden knocking at the door was most unwelcome. The queen and her top advisor were seriously displeased and the prime minister suffered the worst of all possible setbacks in his career. "Bloody hell," Cary growled, rummaging on the floor for his breeches.

The knocking continued, accompanied now by a peevish female voice. "Cary Braedon Rutherford Wayborn! I know you're in there! Open the door this instant."

"Juliet interruptus," Cary snarled.

"Perhaps she'll go away," Abigail suggested hopefully.

"Not her. Have you seen my shirt?"

"I suppose it's one of your tarts," Abigail said, handing it to him.

"Hardly," he retorted. "My tarts have better manners. That annoying female happens to be my sister, Juliet." As Abigail's eyes widened in terror, he smirked. "How clever of you not to get undressed, my dear. Why don't you go down and open the door to your new sister-in-law? She will be most eager to make your acquaintance."

"Cary!" Abigail whispered harshly. "Why didn't you tell me your sister was coming to Hertfordshire?"

"I had no idea she was coming," he answered calmly. "Try not to panic, monkey. There is a back door, remember? She's fairly insinuating, but even she can't be in two places at once."

In her haste to descend the ladder, Abigail nearly fell. Cary pushed her unceremoniously down the hall. "Remember the path through the woods?" he asked, forcibly putting her into her cloak. "Follow it until you come to the orchard wall. The gate's open. Walk through the orchard—there should be no one there this time of year. When you come out of the orchard, you will see a door straight ahead and to your left. Here's the key."

Abigail took it from him, repeating these instructions to herself.

"Immediately inside, you will find a staircase to your right. There's a door at the top of the stairs. The key is in the box on the table next to the door. It has a purple ribbon tied to it. You should be able to find your way to your room from there. Hurry, monkey—the harpy is growing impatient." Closing her fingers around the key, he gave her a quick kiss and propelled her out the door.

Abigail scampered into the woods, disappearing just as Juliet came around the side of the house and saw her brother. She was dressed in white furs and her patrician face was set in a scowl. "There you are!" she scolded him. "Didn't you hear me knocking?"

"I daresay Cromwell heard you knocking," he said.

"Who?" she demanded, pushing past him. Her gray eyes scanned the interior of the gatehouse as she moved further into it, apparently missing no detail.

"Cromwell. Perhaps you've heard of him? First, he murdered King Charles because he was a nasty tyrant. Then he gave us the Rump Parliament, followed by the Bare Bones Parliament, and finally he dissolved Parliament altogether and just became a nasty tyrant, too."

"He's dead," said Juliet, unimpressed. "He couldn't possibly have heard me knocking. What were you doing sneaking out the back door?"

"You frightened me," he explained. "I thought you were a bill collector. I was about to make a run for it."

Juliet lifted a brow. "In your bare feet?"

"Indeed. But enough about me. I want to hear all about you," he said amiably, herding her to the table. "You might begin by telling me what you're doing here."

Juliet sat down at the deal table. Pulling off her gloves, she gave the teapot an experimental touch. Cary took the hint and put the kettle on. "Horatio told me a tree fell on the Dower House. Indeed, he couldn't wait to tell me. Anyone would think you had carelessly dropped a tree on your own house, the way he talks of it. He said you were living here in the lodge. I didn't believe him. Cary, it's no better than a hovel, a pot shed!" She looked around wrinkling her slender nose.

"It has its good points," he said mildly, "namely a roof and four walls. I had to give the tenants the Manor House. There was nothing else to be done. You will like them. They are sound, respectable people."

"I hope so," said Juliet. "It will be exceedingly awkward for me to share the house with them if they are not respectable."

Cary took the seat opposite her. "I beg your pardon?"

"I said—"

"I heard what you said. You can't seriously be contemplating a stay at Tanglewood. What does Auckland say? Is he here with you?"

Two bright spots of color appeared in his sister's cheeks. "Never mind what he says. It's all finished between Ginger and me. Cary, I've—I've broken my engagement!" She promptly burst into tears.

Like all blue-blooded Englishmen, Cary hated tears. "Look here!" he said sharply. "Pull yourself together." He provided his sister with a tea towel and commanded her to dry her eyes.

Juliet made a choking attempt at speech.

"I'm sorry," Cary said impatiently. "You were saying . . . ? Blub? Blub? Blubber-blub?"

Juliet took a deep breath. "I might have known you'd take his side," she said resentfully, then reversed herself in the next moment. "I was so sure you would take my part. I knew, of course, that *Benedict* would blame everything on me, but, Cary, I did think that *you* would come to my defense."

Cary frowned. The mention of his elder brother made the situation seem serious. "Benedict knows about this?"

"Not yet," she admitted. "I thought it best to leave town."

Cary went to collect the whistling kettle. "So . . . who else knows of your spat besides me?" he asked his sister.

"It's not a spat," she said severely. "I've broken it off. I'm now officially a jilt."

Cary found two crockery mugs while Juliet prepared the tea. Thankfully, his sister seemed past all blubbering. She drank her tea so calmly that Cary made the mistake of believing her to be rational. "If I were you, I'd high-tail it back to London and patch things up with Auckland," he suggested.

Juliet slammed down her mug. "Patch things up?" she fairly howled. "Haven't you been listening to me? I'm finished with him. I can't, and I won't, marry a man who doesn't trust me."

"Auckland doesn't trust you?"

"He's been listening to petty gossip," she said contemptuously. "He's beastly jealous of Mr. Rourke. Last week, he threatened to cut him off financially if I don't stop seeing him."

Cary raised both brows. "The *actor*?" he exclaimed incredulously.

"Exactly," said his sister triumphantly. "What sort of man is jealous of a mere actor? I find the whole thing insulting. So what if I visit him backstage in his dressing room?"

"Excuse me, miss?"

She squared her shoulders. "You men visit actresses all the time," she said defensively.

"For God's sake," Cary said irritably. "The man has every right to be annoyed. An actor's dressing room is no place for a respectable young female. Have you lost your mind?"

"I enjoyed his performance at dress rehearsal so much that I was compelled to present him with a basket of oranges," she coldly replied. "It was infinitely respectable, I assure you. Lots of people were there. Besides, I *have* to see Mr. Rourke. We're working on a new play. Ginger knows that. He even approved all the expenses. Now he runs about Town accusing me."

"Accusing you of what exactly?"

She shrugged. "Yesterday was the absolute last straw. He saw me coming out of the Albany with Mr. Rourke. The things he said to me—"

"What the devil were you doing at the Albany?" Cary demanded.

She started up indignantly. "A better question might be what was *Ginger* doing at the Albany!" she snapped. "He was supposed to be at home sleeping. Instead, he was out in the middle of the night spying on me, following me. It's too despicable. I will not be spied upon."

Cary caught her roughly by the wrist. "You were at the Albany with Mr. Rourke in the middle of the night? Small wonder Auckland don't trust you!"

She returned his steely gaze belligerently. "If he loves me, he ought to trust me no matter what I do," she declared. "I will not be questioned. I will not be accused."

"The guilty often object to such things," he said, releasing her arm.

"I am not guilty, you ass," she said. "I had a very good reason for being at the Albany that night, and it had nothing to do with poor Mr. Rourke. I didn't even see him until it was time for me to leave, and then he was good enough to help me. I had a veil on, so I daresay he didn't even know who I was."

"Juliet, I'm your brother and I don't believe you," said Cary.

"Thank you very much, sir," she said tartly. "I see you have forgotten, and so has Ginger, that there are other gentlemen besides Mr. Rourke who have rooms at the Albany."

"I see. You were visiting *another* gentleman. Why, that's perfectly all right."

She tossed her head impatiently at his sarcasm. "Our cousin Horatio has rooms at the Albany," she reminded him. She fumbled angrily in her pockets, then placed a small object on the table. "There! Now don't you feel ashamed of yourself?"

Cary immediately recognized the little snuffbox with the racehorse enameled on the lid. "You *stole* Horatio's snuffbox?" he cried in outraged amazement.

"Well, he wouldn't give it to me," she snapped. "Naturally, I stole it. And a thankless job it was, too! He never lets it out of his sight, you know. I had to hide under the bed and wait for him to come home. He sleeps with it under his pillow, for heaven's sake. It's too ridiculous."

"It certainly is," Cary agreed. "What did Auckland say when you told him all this?"

She sniffed. "I shouldn't have to explain. It's quite his own fault if he got the wrong idea. He ought not have been spying on me. He ought to have trusted me. After all, I'm perfectly innocent."

"I'm afraid I cannot agree," he said, picking up the snuffbox.

She had the grace to blush. "The stealing was all Ginger's idea. You were there; you heard him. He said someone ought to take Horatio's snuffbox and throw it

in the Thames. If he'd only behaved better, we might
have had a good laugh."

"I daresay Horatio isn't laughing. Ridiculous or not,
that snuffbox was a royal gift, and he's dashed fond of it.
He's probably in Bow Street right now, hiring Runners."

Juliet did not seem to hear him. "Instead, he accused
me of betraying him. So naturally I said if he kept up
his nonsense I should have to break our engagement.
Then he said . . ." Her lower lip began to tremble. "He
said . . . 'Madam, I wish you would!'" she whined.

"Blow your nose," Cary told her with a marked absence
of brotherly sympathy.

Abigail turned an abrupt corner on the gloomy
narrow stairs and banged her forehead painfully on the
low ceiling. Reaching up to steady herself, she scraped
her palm on a nail jutting from the wall. She went up the
last few steps on her hands and knees. A tiny round
window admitted just enough light for her to make out
the door and the little table beside it. She was forced to
take the box over to the window to examine its contents.
While poking through the jumble of keys looking for
the one with a purple ribbon fastened to it, she made an
unexpected discovery. She sucked in her breath as she
fished out the miniature in its tiny gold frame.

"Catherine of Aragon," she breathed excitedly,
cradling the treasure in her bleeding hand. Quickly, she
located the necessary key. The door opened onto a
brightly lit hall. Once her eyes adjusted to the bright
light, she was able to find her way back to her room
without difficulty.

As she rushed to her dressing table, her anxiety at
being presented in short order to Cary's sister was compounded by her appearance. Her dress was smudged
with dust from the stairs and plastered with leaves from

her flight through the woods. There were cobwebs in her curly hair. A marble-sized swelling had appeared on her forehead where she had bumped it. She looked like a frightened scullery maid.

Hurriedly, she washed, changed into a fresh dress with a modest neckline, and brushed her short hair. Satisfied that she at least looked like a *clean* frightened scullery maid, she crept downstairs. Mrs. Spurgeon seemed to be stirring in her room; Abigail heard Vera and Evans murmuring behind the door. She quietly made her way to the picture gallery and was engaged in adding Catherine of Aragon to the collection of miniatures in the curio table when a piercing voice suddenly assailed her.

"You put that back this instant or I shall alert the whole house!"

Abigail was so startled that she dropped the glass lid of the case on her hand, crushing her fingers. She cried out in pain.

"Serves you right," said Juliet Wayborn. "Grimstock! Grimstock, come at once!"

Chapter 14

Abigail turned to see a tall young woman in a very elegant black and white striped dress trimmed in fine lace. Unmistakably she was Cary Wayborn's sister. She had the same gypsy tint to her skin, though she evidently never bronzed it by bathing in the sun. Her wide charcoal gray eyes were very like her brother's, as were her patrician nose and firm chin. Her mouth was wide and feminine, and her hair was simply dressed. Her manner was imperious.

Abigail cradled her injured hand. "I wasn't taking anything out," she said timidly. "I was putting something in."

"Nonsense!" said Miss Wayborn. "I saw you stealing that miniature."

Abigail turned pale, but her eyes snapped angrily. "I was not stealing!" she said stoutly.

The housekeeper arrived, wringing her hands.

"Grimstock," said Juliet Wayborn. "I just caught this person stealing from my brother. I think we'd better have the J.P. Send Jeremy."

"I was not stealing," Abigail said evenly. "Miss Wayborn is mistaken. Fetch Mr. Wayborn here at once."

Poor Mrs. Grimstock hesitated.

Juliet found this intolerable. "Do as I say, woman! Or it will not be well for you."

Mrs. Grimstock scurried away, and Abigail rounded on Juliet angrily. "You have no right to threaten my servants, Miss Wayborn."

Juliet laughed unpleasantly. "*Your* servants?"

"Yes," Abigail said icily. "I have rented this house and all its contents from Mr. Wayborn. For the duration of the lease, they are my servants, and I will not permit you to abuse them."

"I see," said the other lady. "I collect you are the famous Miss Smith?"

"I very much doubt that I am famous."

"I do exaggerate," Juliet admitted graciously. "My cousin Horatio mentioned you in passing. I have been given to understand that your mother was one of the Derbyshire Wayborns. Is that correct?"

Abigail bristled at the other woman's skepticism. "Yes."

"And . . . *which* of the Derbyshire Wayborns was she?"

"Anne," said Abigail, growing more annoyed by the minute.

"Indeed. And your father is a diplomat," Juliet murmured. "How very curious that I could find no trace of you in London, Miss Smith."

"As I said, Miss Wayborn, I am not famous."

At that moment Mrs. Grimstock returned, not with the Justice of the Peace, but with the master of Tanglewood Manor. Cary looked delightfully rumpled in one of his purple coats. "Hullo," he said cheerfully, ignoring the poisonous animosity hanging heavily between his sister and his secret bride. "I see you've met our cousin, Miss Smith. Cousin Abigail, my sister Juliet."

"Miss Smith was just helping herself to a few of your miniatures," Juliet said sweetly. "You may want to count them, Cary. It's the only way to be sure she's put them all back."

Cary had never seen Abigail in such a temper. She looked positively dangerous.

"Are you accusing Abigail of being a thief?" he said sharply. "That's a bit cheeky, coming from you."

Juliet glowered at him. "I know what I saw."

"I found Catherine of Aragon," Abigail said angrily. "I was just putting her in the case when Miss Wayborn walked in and began accusing me."

Cary smiled. "You found poor old discarded Catherine!" he exclaimed, walking over to the case. "Well done, monkey."

Abigail spared Miss Wayborn a single cold glance. "I found her in a box under a pile of old keys," she told Cary. "The glass is cracked, but I don't think it will affect the value if you have it replaced."

"There, Juliet!" he said. "You couldn't have been more wrong. Cousin Abigail has just completed my collection. Thanks to her, I now have Henry the Eighth, all his wives, and all his children."

"How nice for you," Juliet said indifferently.

"I think you owe Abigail an apology," he said sternly.

"I beg your pardon, Miss Smith," Juliet said coolly, adding a sullen curtsy.

"Naturally, I accept your apology," said Abigail stiffly.

"Excellent," said Cary. "She's not so bad, once you get to know her."

"Indeed," said Juliet.

"I'm sure she isn't," said Abigail.

The ladies spoke simultaneously. Still acting in concert, they both turned to Cary with outraged expressions.

"Right," Cary said stoutly. "So that's all sorted. You're going to be great friends. I just know it. Juliet's going to be staying here a few days, Cousin Abigail. I hope that's all right. She won't be in the way, and, of course, you're going to London on Monday."

"Oh, you're *leaving*?" Juliet said sweetly. "What a pity. I was *so* looking forward to knowing you better, Miss Smith. It's not right for cousins to be strangers, don't you agree? But, of course, *we* are strangers no more. Now that I am aware of your existence, rest assured I shall take a lively interest in all your affairs."

Cary laughed nervously. "Juliet, you're too good. Isn't she too good, Abigail?"

"Why, she's positively angelic," said Abigail, assuming a bland tone.

Juliet's eyes flashed. "I should like to go to my room now." She swept out of the gallery like an indignant queen.

Abigail glared at Cary. "'She's not so bad, once you get to know her?'"

"I meant her, of course."

"Too right you meant her!" she snapped. "Must she stay here? We seem to have taken an instant dislike to one another."

"As long as the dislike is cordial . . ."

"Cary, really!"

"She's going through a difficult time," he told her. "She's just broken her engagement to the Duke of Auckland, and she's utterly miserable. Surely you can put up with her for two days. I promise to have her out of here before you return from London. When *do* you mean to return?"

Abigail was easily distracted. After all, Juliet was nothing when compared to the coming ordeal with her father. Red Ritchie wasn't likely to be pleased to learn that his only child had married, without his knowledge

or consent, a highly unsuitable man. "I suppose . . .
Tuesday or Wednesday. Perhaps sooner, if my father
disowns me completely."

"Would you like me to go with you?"

Abigail grimaced. "No, Cary. He isn't likely to be
swayed, as I have been, by your good looks and your
charm."

He shrugged. "Tuesday or Wednesday, then. Scarcely
enough time to put in any French windows," he observed.

Abigail laughed.

"And if Juliet won't go back to London, I can always
send her to our brother in Surrey. She's really his responsibility. He's the eldest. In any case, I fully expect
her lord to make his way here and reclaim her."

"Do you think so?" Abigail asked doubtfully. "When
she has jilted him, and hers is not the sweetest of tem-
pers? Perhaps he is relieved."

"I collect you've never met the Duke of Auckland,"
Cary said laughing. "It's all a big misunderstanding. I'm
sure it will turn up right in the end. But, if for some
reason she's still here when you return to take your
rightful place as mistress of Tanglewood, you can
always have the bailiff toss her out."

"Oh, no," said Abigail quickly. "I wouldn't do that. I
mean, she is your sister, after all. I suppose," she added
reluctantly, "I can tolerate her impertinence for a short
time."

Miss Wayborn made herself especially tolerable
throughout teatime by having hers on a tray in her room.
But Abigail's temper flared when she went upstairs and
discovered Polly removing her belongings from her
room. "What are you doing?" she demanded.

Polly the maid's face was pale, and she didn't dare
speak aloud. "Miss Wayborn says she must have your
room, Miss, to put her maid in," she whispered. "I
tried—" She broke off and shook her head rapidly as

though to clear an unpleasant memory. Abigail guessed that Miss Wayborn had ruthlessly suppressed Polly at the first sign of disobedience.

Juliet herself stepped into the hall, sending Polly scurrying away with an armful of Abigail's clothes. "Ah," she said sweetly, "Cousin Smith! As you can see, I've just about got my maid settled in the room next to mine, but there were a lot of frumpy old garments hanging in the wardrobe. Perhaps you might care to go through them—you might find something better than that gray sack you're wearing. I did see a bright green plaid that would *so* become you . . ."

Abigail remembered that Cary particularly disliked that dress. "Those are *my* things, Miss Wayborn," she said quietly, "as I am sure you know."

Juliet widened her eyes. "*Your* things?" she cried. "Oh, Cousin Smith! What you must think of me. But, you know, I *have* nearly got Fifi settled in. It would be so inconvenient to shift things around *now*, and since you're leaving us on Monday, perhaps forever . . ."

Abigail swallowed her pride. After all, she had no desire to occupy the room next to this spoiled creature. "I shouldn't dream of inconveniencing your maid," she said. "Indeed, she is quite welcome to take my room. I'm sure she will be very comfortable, and, of course, very close to her mistress, which is the material thing."

This calm, rational response did not sit well with Juliet, who was clearly spoiling for an argument. "You needn't toad-eat me, my girl," she said softly, "for it won't get you anywhere. My brother may be starved for company out here in the country, but he's not so desperate as you seem to think."

"I beg your pardon," said Abigail.

"Come, come. I too can put on a face of outraged innocence. We both know you're after him. I had a full report from my cousin Horatio." Juliet tapped her hairbrush thoughtfully against her hip. "I'm only telling you this for your own good, my dear. My brother has a talent for making silly young girls fall in love with him, but if you think he will ever return your feelings, you very much mistake the matter. Why, he's practically engaged to my dear friend, Lady Serena Calverstock, who is a woman of impeccable breeding and good fortune. She's also very beautiful and elegant. So you see, you are wasting your time here. You had much better stay in London, where you may very likely attract an offer from a professional man—a doctor or a lawyer. Possibly an architect. But my brother is a gentleman. He would never disgrace himself by marrying a nobody."

"My mother—"

"Don't embarrass yourself," Miss Wayborn advised her. "You may have my brother convinced, but you will never convince me. There *was* an Anne Wayborn, but there's no mention of her marriage in *Burke's*."

"That's only because her family didn't approve of my father."

Juliet held up her hairbrush. "Don't misunderstand me. I think it's very clever of you to have reinvented yourself in this charming way. As a Wayborn, I'm flattered. I have no intention of exposing you. I even wish you happy hunting. But you will not get your hooks into my brother. On that I am firm. My advice to you is go to London and take what you can get."

Now secure of the upper hand, Juliet went into her room, smiling, and closed the door.

Fuming, Abigail moved into the nursery with Paggles.

At dinner, Miss Wayborn dominated the conversation, deflecting Cary's every attempt to draw the other ladies into the talk. Abigail unclenched her lips only to admit morsels of food and refused to look at either her husband or her sister-in-law.

"Do you remember So-and-so?" Juliet would ask her brother.

"Of course," Cary would say, then turn to his other guests. "So-and-so is such-and-such."

"Well, he got himself into the most devilish awful scrape!"

The scrape of So-and-so would then be described in some detail. When So-and-so was either extricated from his scrape or simply exhausted, Cary would attempt to change the subject. Juliet would interrupt with important news about another so-and-so.

At last, as the savory was brought in, Juliet took notice of the other ladies—or at least two of them. Abigail she ignored, but she listened sympathetically to the story of Mrs. Spurgeon's lost macaw, and gravely agreed that he was a very brave and intelligent bird. Then, still ignoring Abigail, she turned to Mrs. Nashe with a few polite questions.

"Haven't we met before?"

Vera demurred. "I don't think so, Miss Wayborn. We don't exactly move in the same circles."

"I'm sure I've met you before," said Juliet, staring at Vera, who was clearly made uncomfortable by the attention.

"My sister thinks she knows everyone," Cary said apologetically. "Mrs. Nashe is the widow of a young Army lieutenant," he quietly explained.

"No, I know what it is," Juliet said, smiling triumphantly. "You're Kate Hardcastle!"

"I believe Mrs. Nashe's Christian name to be Vera," said Cary.

"Yes," Mrs. Nashe said quickly, casting him a look of gratitude. "And my maiden name was Fletcher, not Hardcastle."

Juliet laughed. "Don't be silly! I mean you were Kate Hardcastle in *She Stoops to Conquer*. I saw you on stage. Oh, it must have been two seasons ago now. Mr. Rourke was in the role of Tony Lumpkin. I never missed a performance."

Mrs. Nashe appeared mortified. "I'm no actress, Miss Wayborn," she stammered. "I am a respectable widow."

"Are you quite sure you're telling the truth?" Juliet demanded.

"Juliet!" Cary said harshly.

"What? Didn't you ever see that play? What was the actress's name? I wonder what became of her after *She Stoops*. She seems to have disappeared."

Abigail unclenched her lips. "I believe you owe Mrs. Nashe an apology," she said coldly.

Juliet cast her a look of scorn, but muttered unconvincingly, "I beg your pardon, Mrs. Nashe, but the resemblance *is* very striking."

Abigail did not find this satisfactory. "You must forgive poor Miss Wayborn," she told Vera gently. "She has just broken her engagement to the Duke of Auckland. I'm sure no one blames her for being ill-tempered in such trying circumstances."

Juliet turned savagely on her brother. "You *told* her? Cary, how could you?"

Cary cast Abigail a look of strong reproach, but his bride remained unrepentant. As his sister continued to berate him, Abigail rose and put down her napkin. "Shall we have some music in the sitting room?"

The following day was Sunday. Mrs. Spurgeon claimed to be too ill to attend services, and Juliet refused to climb out of bed. Only Vera appeared when Cary called to take the ladies to church. Vera went back to her room for her gloves, which gave Cary and Abigail just a few moments together. "Where were you last night?" he demanded in a whisper. "There was a strange woman in your bed, possibly French."

Abigail's mouth fell open. It had never occurred to her that he would steal into the house with his sister under the roof. She had seriously underestimated his audacity, if not his lust. "Cary! *Juliet's maid* is in my room."

He was laughing. "Yes, I know. I met her. Delightful girl. I daresay it was not a new experience for the mademoiselle. She seemed quite *blase*, if that's the word I want."

Abigail's blood ran cold, then hot. "Cary, you didn't!"

"I had to," he said innocently. "She expected a real presentation of the gifts."

Abigail did something she had never done before. She hit a man as hard as she could. The blow landed harmlessly on his shoulder.

"What was I supposed to do?" he said, laughing. "Say, 'Sorry, thought you were Smith,' and steal away? I had to think of your reputation. I did it for you, monkey."

Abigail glared at him. "You had better be joking, monkey," she snapped.

"Well, I am, of course," he admitted. "I think I managed to convince her I was looking for Mrs. Spurgeon. It was deuced embarrassing. And the poor prime minister! I told him he would be paying his respects to Her Majesty. He was quite looking forward to it. Guess his surprise when he suddenly found himself addressing his remarks to an alien government."

In spite of herself, Abigail smiled.

"Will you meet me later?" he asked, lowering his voice further still.

"Cary, I can't," she whispered.

"But you're leaving me tomorrow," he pointed out.

"The prime minister has something needful of the Queen's review. It's in the national interest."

With very little coaxing, Abigail gave in, as he knew she would. "After luncheon," she promised as Vera returned with breathless apologies and French gray gloves.

Monday morning came far too soon. Even though she was leaving much of her clothes at Tanglewood, and even though Cary had agreed that Paggles should not make the journey to London, there was still last minute packing to do, and to Abigail's vexation, she could not find her little writing desk, which, in addition to her writing supplies, contained a number of personal effects she wished to keep with her. After thoroughly searching the nursery, it occurred to her that it might have been left in her old room, now occupied by Juliet's maid. Muttering under her breath, she went down to retrieve it.

The hall was dark. Both bedroom doors were closed. Angel was under the table, gnawing assiduously at something propped between his paws. Abigail set down her candle and knelt down, half crawling under the table. "What have you got there?" she asked pleasantly. "More picture hanging wire? A rusty old nail, perhaps?"

She had previously discovered him chewing on both these things. Angel gave up his prize with a faint woof of complaint.

Abigail climbed to her feet and dried it off with her handkerchief. The lid of the little snuffbox was intact. It showed a pretty racehorse painted in enamel on a green background. The bottom half of the box, which appeared to have been made of fine gold, had been crunched in by the corgi's powerful jaws. Abigail recognized it instantly; Captain Sir Horatio Cary had made such a point of showing it to her and everyone else.

"You bad dog!" she exclaimed. "Angel, how could you?"

Angel appeared hurt and perplexed by the stern tone of her voice.

"Never mind," Abigail sighed, wrapping it up in her handkerchief and slipping it into her pocket. "I'll take it to London, and see if it can't be repaired."

"Who are you talking to?" inquired a supercilious and unmistakable voice. "What are you doing under the table?"

Abigail climbed to her feet, bumping her head in the process and turned to face Miss Wayborn. The patrician girl was clad in a quilted velvet robe of royal purple. "I was just saying goodbye to the dog," Abigail murmured as Juliet critically eyed her plain russet-colored traveling costume. "I wondered if your maid is awake yet?" Abigail went on. "I believe my writing slope was left behind when I quit the room so unexpectedly."

"I'll get it," the other woman said coolly. "We can't have you forgetting anything."

"I assure you I won't," Abigail replied.

"Is this it?" Juliet asked a moment later.

"Thank you," said Abigail, glad she had remembered to lock her traveling desk. She didn't put it past the insufferable Juliet to read her private letters.

"Forgive me for not seeing you off," said Juliet. "But as you can see I'm not dressed. I'll wave to you from the window, shall I? Goodbye."

Abigail was the last to enter the coach. "If she is not gone when I am back," she quietly told Cary, who was pretending to check the trunks fastened behind the coach, "I believe I shall have the bailiff, after all, if only to preserve my sanity."

He chuckled softly. "I'm going to miss you, Smith.

Until you return to open Parliament, Mr. Prime Minister will be just a shadow of his former self."

Abigail blushed.

"Goodbye, Cousin Smith!" Juliet cried sweetly, leaning out of an upper window and waving a large silk handkerchief in emphatic farewell.

"I mean it, Cary," Abigail whispered as Cary escorted her to the carriage door and helped her inside. "I want her out." She angrily settled into the seat next to Vera and pulled the rug over her knees.

Angel suddenly darted between Cary's legs, in an ill-advised attempt to jump into the carriage. Cary hoisted him up and plopped him in Abigail's lap. "Better take him, Smith," he said crisply. "He'll only howl inconsolably the whole time you're gone."

By the time the coach turned up the drive, the corgi was contentedly nibbling on Abigail's gloves.

The morning journey passed pleasantly, with Mrs. Spurgeon sleeping almost the entire way. Abigail set her chaperone and the nurse in Baker Street in time for luncheon, then went on to Kensington alone. At the mansion, the butler informed her that her father was awaiting her in the Chinese drawing room. Abigail went straight there, pulling her bonnet strings as she walked.

She burst through the black and gold lacquered doors, then came to a sudden halt. Red Ritchie was not alone in the vast salon crammed with every possible example of chinoiserie.

"I beg your pardon!" she stammered, as the two men turned to look at her. Abigail's father was considered tall, but the red-haired man with him was a giant. He wore rumpled clothes and a scowl on his face. He wasn't handsome. As Angel darted into the room, however, Abigail saw what must have been his saving grace: a boyish grin that could not fail to charm. "A corgi!" he cried. "Haven't seen one in years."

In the next minute, he was down on the carpet, playing with the dog.

"Abigail!" cried Red Ritchie, waving her in. "May I present to you his noble grace, the Duke of Auckland?"

Abigail regarded the ugly giant in astonishment. *This is a duke?* she thought, watching him impersonate a Pembroke Welsh corgi. Then: *This is Miss Wayborn's duke?*

The Duke climbed to his feet and made a rather awkward bow. "Please, call me Geoffrey," he said in a pleasant northern burr.

"Fifi?" Juliet inquired rather casually as her maid was artfully giving her hair the naturally windswept look, "have you seen that little green snuffbox? I can't seem to find it anywhere. It's rather important," she added, suppressing a catlike yawn.

Thirty minutes later, Juliet was in a panic. Together, she and her maid tore the room apart in a wild search for the missing box that turned up empty. By the time they had finished doing the same to Fifi's room, Juliet had reached a conclusion.

In the absence of his tenants, Cary was again master of the Manor. His sister found him in front of the fire in the main hall, cracking nuts over his newspaper.

"Someone has stolen Horatio's snuffbox," she announced.

Cary peacefully removed the meat from the nutshell and popped it in his mouth. "Not someone," he retorted. "*You.*"

"No, you ass! I mean someone else has stolen it—from *me!* I think we both know who."

Cary's eyes narrowed. "Who?"

"That Smith person, obviously. If I were you, I'd check on your miniatures."

Cary leaned back in his chair and looked at her. His sister was pacing up and down the room. "That's absurd," he told her sharply.

Juliet paid no attention. "Well, she won't get away with it! I shall track her down and make her give it back!" She ground to a halt in front of him. "What is her address in London?"

Cary flushed.

"Don't you know?" she demanded impatiently. "Good Lord! How did you find these people? You didn't—you didn't *advertise?*"

"No, of course not," he said irritably. "They came highly recommended by a Mr. Leighton, a friend of Cousin Wilfred's, an attorney, I believe. Look here, you may as well know that Abigail—Miss Smith—well, hang it all! For starts, her name is not Smith."

"Really? I am all astonishment."

"Her father is Lord Inchmery, which makes her . . . Dulwich's sister." He squirmed as he revealed this highly unpleasant information. "But that's not her fault, obviously, and her mother *was* a Wayborn. She died when Abigail was very young."

Juliet sighed. "Oh, you poor man," she said softly. "She *has* got you all twisted, hasn't she? For starts, Lord Dulwich has no sister. I know this for a fact because I have never met her."

"That is scarcely proof of anything. You never met Napoleon, but I am fairly sure he exists."

"For middles," she went on relentlessly, "Lady Inchmery was a Bolger before she married, and *not* a Wayborn. You can look it up in any peerage. Oh, and she's very much alive, is Lady Inchmery. I know because I *have* met *her.*"

Cary frowned. "Abigail is not a thief."

At this moment, Mrs. Grimstock came into the room wringing her hands. "Oh, sir!" she cried. "The silver!"

"What about it?"

"It's gone, sir!" she wailed. "I thought Polly might have taken it upon herself to polish it, but I might have known she hadn't. When did she ever take it upon herself to do a lick of work when she could lay about? Every knife, fork, and spoon—gone!"

"Oh, dear," Juliet murmured archly. "Not the spoons."

Cary looked as though he had sustained a sharp blow to the solar plexis. "And the miniatures?" he asked faintly.

Chapter 15

Mr. Tom Waller of the Bow Street Runners leaned across his desk and tapped the side of his nose knowledgeably as he heard the Wayborns' complaint. "Sounds like a Soapy Sue," he declared. "A confidence trickster of the female variety. Very cunning. She made off with the family plate, you say?"

"Yes," said Cary, fidgeting with his stick. "All the household silver, and some rather valuable miniatures. The silver can be melted down; I don't expect ever to see it again."

"I was rather fond of Grandmama's punch bowl," Juliet chided her brother. "If I'd known you were filling the house with confidence tricksters, I should have stolen it myself."

"But the miniatures, Mr. Waller," Cary went on. "I should imagine there aren't very many dealers in London who specialize in that sort of thing. That would be a good place to start."

Waller grimaced. "She'll have a buyer all worked out in advance. Or else she'll sit on the merchandise until the search goes cold. Then she'll sell them off one or two at a time."

"I was given to understand they were more valuable when considered as a group."

"And who gave you that understanding?" Juliet demanded. "Soapy Abigail, that's who! Cary, how could you be so foolish? I thank God that the Cary emerald is safe in the family vault here in London. I don't doubt she would have taken it as well."

This was too much for Cary. He groaned aloud.

Juliet turned pale. "Oh, Cary, you didn't! I suppose you *showed* it to her, and kept it in an unlocked drawer where anyone could get it." She shook her head in disgust.

He looked at her guiltily. "No. It's much worse. I gave it to her."

Juliet's eyes narrowed. "What do you mean *you gave it to her?* You can't have done. Oh, you mean you lost it to her at the card table? I make sure she cheated!"

"No," Cary repeated significantly. "I gave it to her."

"Do you mean . . . do you mean that you are *engaged* to this person?" Juliet shrieked.

Cary felt a wave of nausea so severe that he was forced to close his eyes for a brief moment. "I am," he said quietly, "deeply committed to her."

Juliet lapsed into a shocked silence.

Tom Waller's eyes widened in surprise. "Oh, is *this* gentleman the victim?" he asked. "Forgive me, Mr. Wayborn, I had formed the impression that you were acting on behalf of an elderly relative. That's the usual way of things. The Soapy Sue targets an elderly single gentleman starved for female attention. A little bit of beauty, a few smiles, and she's got him eating out of his hand. That's when the fleecing begins. I never heard of a handsome young gentleman like yourself being a victim."

Cary's devoted sister laughed derisively. "She wasn't

even pretty, Mr. Waller," she revealed. "*I* saw through her, of course, but my poor brother was completely taken in."

"She was the loveliest creature I ever beheld," said Cary, staring moodily into space. "Her eyes were like amber. Her hair was the color of a Venetian sunset. And her skin is sprinkled with gold."

Juliet shook her head sadly. "*Freckles*, Mr. Waller, and a frightful shock of orange hair."

"Sometimes it's the plain ones that is the deadliest," Mr. Waller said compassionately. "Them that has no beauty has got to rely on brains. Now, they usually pretend to have some claim on the old gentleman."

"She's supposedly our cousin," Juliet said eagerly. "Total lie, of course, but just plausible enough to fool my halfwit brother."

Mr. Waller went on, "Maybe there's a sick old mother, or auntie?"

"There's a Paggles," Cary revealed reluctantly.

"A what?" Juliet demanded, wrinkling her nose.

"Her old nurse, a septuagenarian of fuddled wits, whom Miss Smith has left on my hands. On the positive side, she *is* knitting me a lovely green muffler."

Mr. Waller pursed his lips. "I would say, sir, that 'Smith' is not the lady's real name."

"Of course it isn't," Juliet snapped. "Look here, what about my snuffbox? Cary, I'm sorry that you were stupid, and that you let yourself be taken in by this preposterous female, but *I* have done nothing to deserve this. Mr. Waller, it is of the utmost importance that you find the thief and get me back my snuffbox. Naturally, I shall pay to have her prosecuted."

"Juliet!" Cary objected. "She'd be transported or hanged."

Juliet looked at him, puzzled. "Yes. And?"

Cary glared at her. "Moreover, if you did prosecute

her—which you won't—certain *inconvenient* facts about that bloody snuffbox are bound to come out. *Miss Smith* mayn't be the only one hanged as a result."

"Don't be silly," Juliet scoffed. "Horatio would never pay to have me prosecuted."

Mr. Waller shuffled through some papers on his desk. "Yes, I thought that snuffbox sounded familiar," he murmured. "Gold, enameled, with a brown horse painted on the lid."

"Yes, that's the one," Juliet said eagerly.

"A gentleman reported just such a snuffbox missing only yesterday. He swears it was under his pillow when he went to sleep Saturday night, but in the morning, it was gone."

Juliet had the grace to blush. "How very curious," she murmured. "When you *do* find the snuffbox," she went on hurriedly, "you must bring it to *me* immediately, and not to this other gentleman. I shall, of course, compensate you. Let us say . . . *twice* your normal fee?"

Mr. Waller's eyes glinted appreciatively. "I understand, Miss Wayborn. I'll find your Soapy Sue, don't you worry. I'll get you your snuffbox."

He seemed a little too eager for Cary's taste. "Now, she's not to be harmed," he said firmly. "If you do apprehend her, I just want to talk to her. You are not to be rough with her. If she is harmed, I shall be very angry, Mr. Waller. Do you understand?"

The Runner shrugged. "Just as you like, sir. Kid gloves, sir. I understand completely. I'll treat her like the runaway daughter of a royal duke. Never fear. You'd be surprised, though. Some fellows pay a little extra to see 'em roughed up a bit, if you see what I mean. I've got a good description of the thief. Is there anything else you can tell me about her? Anything that might help me in my search?"

"She likes poetry and old houses," said Cary.

"And Scotch whisky!" said Juliet. "My maid found a bottle in her room. Oh, and she's got a gray cloak trimmed in the most exquisite silver fox you ever saw in your life. I suppose she stole that too, or else got some fuddled and lonely old man to buy it for her. She'll have it on her back when you catch her, I don't doubt."

"Now that I think of it," murmured the Runner, "I do recall a girl who answers that description." He found another sheaf of papers and shuffled through them, occasionally pausing to squint at the writing. "Ah, here it is. Different name, of course." He lowered his voice confidentially. "Lord D——'s diamond ring went missing. The thief was a wily little redhead."

"Lord Derby!" cried Juliet. "She flies pretty high, I must say."

"No, not Lord Derby," Waller hastened to correct her. "Another Lord D."

Juliet accepted the challenge. "Dorchester? Durham? Darlinghead? Doncaster? Devize?" She ticked them off on her fingers. "Who have I forgotten?"

"Dulwich," Cary said grimly, squeezing his eyes shut. A hell-broth of conflicting emotions battled for control of him. The loss of his possessions infuriated him, but the loss of Abigail had ripped his heart out. He had trusted her, and she had repaid him by stealing from him. He was enraged and humiliated by her betrayal. These feelings were natural.

Unnatural was the overwhelming fear for her safety and the powerful desire he had to protect her. If Dulwich found her first, she would certainly be hanged for stealing his diamond. The thought of Abigail in danger was enough to throw him into a blind panic. "No wonder she hid behind the counter when she saw him," Cary muttered. "She'd stolen his bloody diamond."

He remembered the stark terror in her eyes when she had first spied Dulwich on the day they met. Yes, he had to protect her. The silver, the miniatures, even the bloody Cary emerald . . . these were of no importance to him. Suddenly, nothing mattered to him but saving Abigail.

"I remember that," Juliet was telling Mr. Waller. "I was away from Town at the time, but there was some sort of scandal. This girl was supposed to have been an heiress or something. She deceived Lord Dulwich just as she deceived my poor brother."

"Masters of deception, they are. Or should I say mistresses?" Mr. Waller laughed bibulously. "These shady underworld tricksters is better than any actress in Drury Lane. Some of them *is* actresses, as a matter of fact. Why, there was one little cockney passing herself off as a Portuguese countess, if you like, and for twelve years no one was the wiser."

"Lord Carlowe's mistress," Juliet said knowledgeably.

Cary scarcely heard the chatter. He was thinking hard, trying to remember any information Abigail might have inadvertently revealed that might now give him a clue as to her whereabouts in London. At Hatchard's Bookshop, she had claimed to have been waiting for her father, but could that have been a lie, too?

Juliet started in surprise as her brother suddenly shot out of his chair. "Come, Juliet, we're going," he said curtly, putting on his hat.

"What on earth—!" Juliet squawked as he pulled her out of her chair. "I was talking to Mr. Waller! He has such interesting stories."

Cary grabbed his sister by the arm and propelled her out the door. Juliet protested loudly until her brother lowered his voice and spoke in her ear. "I know how to find her."

"You do? How?"

"Quiet!" he snapped, pushing his way through the crowded waiting room. He did not speak again until he took up the reins of his team of chestnuts outside.

Wistfully, he thought of the girl who couldn't tell a chestnut from a bay.

"Well?" Juliet demanded. "Where is your doxy with Venetian sunset eyes?"

"They know her at Hatchard's," he said. "The clerk was remarkably solicitous. And if her name isn't on the list for Mr. Coleridge's new book, I'll eat my boots."

Juliet scowled. "Why couldn't you tell the Runners that? It's their job to go chasing after people like her. I'm tired. I've got a headache, and I want my tea. Take me to Park Lane."

Cary lost his temper. "Juliet, could you please for two minutes stop behaving like a spoiled brat? Honestly, I'm ashamed of you!"

Juliet gaped at him.

"I have no intention of letting Bow Street Runners anywhere near Abigail. We have to find her before Dulwich does. If he finds her first, she's as good as hanged!"

"She deserves to hang," Juliet sullenly pointed out. "She's a bloody thief."

"I don't believe she stole his diamond," Cary said angrily. "I believe he gave it to her."

"You think she tricked him the same way she tricked you? Disgusting."

"Nobody tricked me."

"How can you say that? What about your miniatures? Your silver? My snuffbox?"

"I don't give a toss about those bloody miniatures," Cary declared grimly. "Ditto the silver. As for the snuffbox . . . your possessive pronoun is sadly incorrect. It is *not* your snuffbox. She may be a thief, but she's not the only one!"

Juliet was indignant. "I may be a thief, but I am *not* a Soapy Sue! I don't break the glass in people's curio cabinets. I don't go about the place cozening lonely old bachelors—like you—who are starved for female companionship."

"No," he retorted. "You merely hide in the furniture, then sneak out in the middle of the night and steal things while your victim sleeps."

"Precisely! How *can* you compare my harmless little prank to her shameless larceny?" she demanded. "This girl has bewitched you with her freckles. You're not thinking clearly."

"I don't care," he replied as he negotiated his way out of the Strand and into St. James's. "I don't care what she's done. I will not see her life cut short by Pudding-face Dulwich. Besides which, I gave her my ring to some purpose. I made a pledge to her and she to me. By God, she will honor that pledge."

Juliet gasped. "You *don't* mean you still intend to marry her after all she's done?"

"I don't expect you to understand," he said. "I certainly don't."

"You're in love with her," Juliet accused him angrily. "You priceless ass! The girl's a common thief. God only knows where she comes from. God only knows how many men she's swindled. Quaking old men, too. Disgusting!"

"I don't care where she comes from. I don't care how many men she's swindled. I love her. I don't say it's convenient," Cary added apologetically. "But there it is."

"Well, it's not convenient at all," Juliet said sulkily. "What will our brother say? A thief for a sister-in-law? He wants to be Home Secretary, you know."

Cary could not help but chuckle as he pictured the reaction of his strait-laced brother, Sir Benedict Wayborn. "He believes in reform," he told his sister. "I'll reform her."

As it was still quite early in the Season, traffic in Piccadilly was relatively light. Cary was able to drive up the street and stop at Hatchard's. After helping his sister alight from the curricle, he instructed his groom to walk the horses up and down. He did not expect his business to take up much time.

To his relief, the senior clerk was on duty in the quiet shop. "May I help you, sir?" Mr. Eldridge asked politely, looking up from the morning receipts. "Madam," he added, giving Juliet a courteous bow.

Juliet seemed to forget the purpose of their errand. "Have you got anything new from Mr. Walter Scott?" she asked eagerly. "I heard—"

Cary pushed his sister aside. "I'm looking for a girl, Eldridge. Well, not just any girl. *The* girl, if you see what I mean. I came in with her the last time I was here, perhaps two weeks before Christmas? The shop was very busy."

"Yes, sir."

"Good. You remember."

Mr. Eldridge's eyes were hooded. "I remember the shop was busy, sir. Christmas is always a busy time for us."

"But you knew this girl," Cary insisted. "It's the girl who invented Christmas wrap."

Mr. Eldridge shook his head in apparent bewilderment. "Nobody invented Christmas wrap, sir. Christmas wrap has always been."

"I tried to tell him," said Juliet. "The girl is such a liar."

"Titian hair, brown eyes. About so high?" Cary held his hand up even with his shoulder.

"I'm sorry, sir," Mr. Eldridge said with regret.

Juliet tapped the counter. "What about curly orange hair and a complexion completely obliterated by freckles?"

"She hid behind your counter, for God's sake," said Cary. "You must remember, Eldridge. You showed her the Blake, the combined volume of *Songs of Innocence and of Experience*. And, after I left, she bought it."

"That would be a very rare book, sir," Mr. Eldridge politely observed. "Very rare indeed."

"Good Lord, Cary, what if she *stole* the book, too?" cried Juliet.

Cary scowled at the clerk. "Look here, Eldridge! Are you implying that my—my cousin stole your book?"

Mr. Eldridge appeared genuinely shocked. "Certainly not, sir."

"All you must do, then, is check your records and tell me who bought the book."

"I'm afraid that is confidential information, sir."

"Indeed! When Lord Dulwich came in, demanding you put him on the list for *Kubla Khan*, she jumped behind the counter. Surely you remember *that*?"

"I recall no such incident, sir. It sounds highly unlikely."

"Perhaps if I paid my bill?" Cary suggested acidly. "Would that stir your memory?" Fishing in his pocket, he came up with an embarrassing assortment of copper and silver coins.

"I'm sorry, sir. I don't recall anyone of that description, and our patrons do not venture behind the counter. It simply isn't done. As for the Blake . . . I'm afraid we can not divulge the identity of any of our patrons. I'm sure you understand."

"Mr. Wayborn?"

Cary whirled around to see Abigail herself standing behind him in her fox-trimmed cloak. "I thought it was you!" she exclaimed in triumph. "Your purple coat gave you away. And the . . . er . . . dog hair," she added, brushing at his shoulder with one gloved hand. "I did not expect to see you here." Observing Juliet, who was staring at her, open-mouthed, she dropped a polite curtsy.

"Smith!" said Cary, staring at the girl. She looked so decidedly unlike a Soapy Sue that he felt a little ridiculous for ever harboring the slightest suspicion against her, let alone actually hiring a Runner to bring her to justice. Surely no actress could ever blush so charmingly at will, and with such an air of innocent pleasure. He found himself smiling back at her, recalling the heavenly moments he had spent with her arms wrapped around him. Desperately he wanted to kiss her. "You're . . . you're looking well."

Abigail was positively glowing. Not even Juliet's presence could dampen her simple enthusiasm at seeing the man she loved. "It's all right, Mr. Eldridge," she said quickly. "I am a little acquainted with this gentleman."

Mr. Eldridge hastily scooped up Cary's coins from the counter. "Oh, was *this* the young lady you were looking for, sir? I must have misunderstood you. She was here the whole time."

"Fancy that," Cary said dryly.

A cloud crossed Abigail's face. "You were looking for me, Mr. Wayborn?" she inquired anxiously. "Is something wrong? Is it Paggles?"

"Paggles? Oh, no. Paggles is perfectly content," he assured her. "My new scarf is nearly as tall as I am, and still growing. No, I came to London for quite another reason. I . . . I heard *Kubla Khan* was finally out."

"Oh, for heaven's sake," Juliet muttered.

"You really *do* like Coleridge," Abigail said, beaming. "I always suspected you did, no matter what you said about him. It *is* out. I've just gotten mine." She closed her eyes and recited. "'In Xanadu did Kubla Khan/ A stately pleasure-dome decree:/ Through caverns measureless to man/ Down to a sunless sea.'" She opened her eyes and smiled at him.

"Not bad for an inebriate," he admitted.

"It's very short," she said, opening her book and leafing through it. "I have to admit, I'm a bit disappointed. Only fifty-four lines! I can't help thinking he might have come up with fifty-five if he'd only tried a *little*."

"It's my fault," said Cary. "I have poisoned you

against him. Try to think of him as he was when you read the 'Mariner' for the first time."

"Or 'Frost at Midnight,'" said Abigail.

"Excuse me," said Juliet, unable to contain herself a moment longer. "This is all very cozy, and very interesting, I'm sure. But I can tell you, Miss Smith, *I* didn't come here to discuss poetry with you. I only want to know one thing." She put a strong hand on Abigail's arm. "*Where is my snuffbox?*"

Abigail was startled. "*Your* snuffbox, Miss Wayborn? But I had thought—Is it not Sir Horatio's snuffbox?" Perplexed, she looked to Cary for some assistance.

"Never mind that," Juliet snapped. "Where is it?"

"Well, it's quite ruined, I'm afraid," said Abigail.

"What?" cried Juliet.

"Angel—the dog—simply crunched it up. I'm so sorry! I didn't know it was yours, you see. I thought the Captain must have left it . . . When I got to London, I brought it directly to Mr. Grey in Bond Street, but he said it was quite beyond repair."

"Do you expect me to believe that *the dog* ate my snuffbox?" sneered Juliet.

"You don't know him," Cary said quickly. "That dog is quite capable of eating any number of snuffboxes. I've known him to eat doorknobs, kitchen ladles, and an entire macaw, including the beak. If Abigail says he ate it, I'm sure he did."

"He didn't actually swallow it," Abigail clarified. "He was chewing on it under the table just outside your room, Miss Wayborn, when I came down to collect my writing slope."

"You never said a word about it at the time," Juliet complained.

"I didn't know it was yours."

"No, indeed!" said Juliet. "You simply disregarded

the distinction between *meum* and *tuum* and put it in your pocket."

"I tried to have it repaired," said Abigail. "Was I wrong?"

"I'm sure you did exactly right," said Cary. "Juliet's just upset."

"What about the miniatures?" Juliet demanded. "My brother's silver? I daresay the dog ate all that as well! And my grandmother's punch bowl, too!"

"What *can* you mean?" said Abigail, becoming angry. "Are you accusing me of stealing a punch bowl? Cary, what is she talking about?"

"Don't seek to enlist my brother in your campaign of deceit!" said Juliet. "I know you tricked him into giving you that emerald, you—you thimble-rigger!"

Cary restrained his sister. Her volume was arousing unwelcome attention from the bookseller's other patrons, who, fortunately, were small in number. "I gave Abigail that emerald," he said sternly. "We are not concerned with the emerald. Look here, Smith. No one is accusing you of anything. But did you, for any reason, take the miniatures with you when you left Tanglewood? To have them repaired or valued or cleaned, perhaps?"

"No," said Abigail slowly. "Gold acquires a very rich patina over time. Cleaning them would diminish their value considerably. Am I to understand, sir, that you think I stole your miniatures, your sister's snuffbox, and your grandmother's punch bowl?"

"No, of course not."

"Ha!" said Juliet. "That's not what you said in Bow Street!"

Abigail turned pale. "Bow Street?"

Cary sighed. "Abigail, they're gone. All the miniatures. As well as the household silver. Everything but two candlesticks—and they, I think, are only plated."

"Good heavens," Abigail murmured.

"And *you* took them!" said Juliet. A finger encased in yellow kid pointed at Abigail. "The Runners have a name for women like you; you're a Soapy Sue. You may as well know, Miss Smith, that we've hired Runners to catch you. Enjoy your freedom while you can, *Cousin*. You'll soon be in the dock before a magistrate with a black kerchief on his head!"

Abigail looked at Cary in astonishment. "Is that true?" she asked, horrified. "Do you believe me to be a thief, sir? Have you come to London to bring charges against me?"

"Abigail, I didn't know what to think," he admitted wretchedly. "You were gone . . . and the silver was gone . . ."

Abigail was mortified. "I see," she said coldly, blinking back tears. "Well, I don't know where your miniatures are, Mr. Wayborn, or your punch bowl, but I *can* give you your emerald back. Except I left it with Mr. Grey," she added, stamping her foot in exasperation. "When I was there earlier, he happened to notice that the stone was a bit wobbly. Here is the receipt. You are welcome to claim it any time you please."

He refused to take the scrap of paper she pulled from her velvet reticule. "Don't be absurd, Abigail. I gave you that ring. My feelings are unchanged."

Since she had no idea what his feelings were, this scarcely comforted her.

"Thank you, Cousin Abigail," said Juliet, snatching the receipt. "I'll be sure to collect it. Heaven help you, if it's not there."

Abigail smiled at her coldly. "And you may have this as well, Miss Wayborn," she said, proffering a small gold box with a green enameled lid. "Mr. Grey was unable to repair yours, I'm sorry to say, but he furnished me with a replacement."

Cary and Juliet stared at the box in her palm. "By God," said Cary. "It looks just like it."

"It *is* just like it, unless yours was engraved. Mr. Grey has many more in stock."

"In stock?" cried Juliet, taking the box for a closer inspection. "I'll have you know this snuffbox was a royal gift from the Prince Regent himself. It can't be replaced. This *must* be the original."

"It certainly isn't," said Abigail, removing a screw of brown paper from her bag. Unraveling it, she disclosed a few bits of twisted gold and cracked green enamel. "Here is the original. I really did think it was your cousin's box. His was also a gift from the Regent."

"How many more has Mr. Grey in stock?" Juliet asked slowly.

"A thousand, I think, or very nearly."

"A thousand?" Juliet repeated incredulously. "Did she say a thousand?"

Abigail fastened the snap on her reticule. "Yes, I did," she said crisply. "Apparently, the little brown horse on the lid was meant to win all sorts of races five years ago, but, instead, he fell down and broke his leg. The Regent had ordered a thousand snuffboxes made, but in the end, His Royal Highness neglected to buy them. Poor Mr. Grey's been stuck with them ever since. I've advised him to start giving them away free with a purchase of at least fifty pounds." She drew in a deep breath. "Mr. Eldridge, would you send for my carriage, please? I should like to leave now."

"How is it free if it costs fifty pounds?" Cary argued. "Sounds like a swindle to me."

Abigail frowned. "Indeed it is not a swindle, sir. The gift with purchase is simply a way to—Oh!" Her explanation was cut short by an apparent sudden need to examine the floor behind Hatchard's sales counter.

"What on *earth* is she doing?" Juliet demanded as

Abigail scurried behind the sales counter. "Has she gone mad? Cary, the girl's an imbecile!"

"My Lord Dulwich!" Mr. Eldridge warmly declaimed. "How very pleasant it is to see your lordship again. And your ladyship," he added, looking up from the pile of sales receipts he had been studying with great interest while eavesdropping on Abigail's conversation.

"Impertinent wretch," said his lordship. "How dare you address me?"

Taking Mr. Eldridge's pen from him, Cary began to write something on the back of a sales receipt. Mr. Eldridge looked at it and nodded, snapping his fingers for a junior clerk.

As he wrote, Cary glanced over his shoulder at Dulwich and the lady decorating his arm. "Ah, Puddingface! You *did* tell me you were engaged to marry a highly undesirable female of no breeding, little beauty, and vast fortune. May I wish you joy, Lady Dulwich?"

Lady Serena Calverstock's elegant ivory face broke out in ugly red hives at the sound of his voice, and Dulwich's hands shook with fury. "How dare you insult Lady Serena?" he rasped. "As it happens, I was talking about quite another female. Lady Serena has not yet consented to become my wife, though I live in hope, naturally."

"Then I have indeed insulted her ladyship!" said Cary, beginning to laugh. "I imagine it is unpleasant to be called Lady Dulwich under any circumstances, but to be called so before one's time . . . *That* is an indignity I would not inflict upon any creature. Do forgive me." Cary bowed with perfect correctness.

Lady Serena frostily ignored him, and turned to greet her friend Juliet with a little moue of disappointment. "Oh, you've got yours *already*, dear Juliet," she pouted, showing off a little snuffbox remarkably like the one Juliet held in her hand. "I don't even take snuff, but when I saw it, I couldn't resist. What a good joke! Horatio has made himself so detestable these last few weeks, pushing his little royal gift under everyone's nose. What did you buy, Juliet?" Serena scarcely paused for an answer. "I couldn't find anything I liked at the fifty pound mark, so I was obliged to buy this horrid little bird's nest brooch for seventy pounds. Dully found a rather lovely gold toothpick holder, but it was only forty-seven pounds, so he was obliged to buy the gold toothpicks as well, for ten pounds more. But at least his was a practical purchase. We're all going to bring them to the Carlton House Ball tonight, after the play, of course. *You* cannot go to the play, of course, dear Juliet, but will I see you at the Regent's ball?"

"Why can I not go to the play?" Juliet demanded, her gray eyes narrowing dangerously.

"Gift with purchase, my foot. I told you it was a common swindle," Cary muttered across the counter, apparently to Mr. Eldridge's feet, just as a phalanx of junior clerks appeared to screen Abigail's departure from the shop by means of the back door. To further distract attention from Abigail's escape, Cary strolled over to a nearby shelf and pretended to select a book. Lord Dulwich glowered at him in helpless rage.

Meanwhile, Lady Serena blinked at Juliet. "Why can you not go to the play? My dear, it's opening night for *Antony and Cleopatra*! And there's been so much talk about you and Mr. Rourke. I'm sure it is all untrue, and so I tell anyone who dares say a word against you in my presence, but, really, if you *were* to go to the play, you must know it would be a ghastly scandal. Worse than your *last* scandal, I'm afraid, when you dressed up in your brother's clothes and raced his curricle all the way to Southend." Serena pressed her hand dramatically to her bosom. "I'm afraid Auckland would never forgive you if you went to the play tonight, and it would be seen as a confirmation of all the rumors about you. But there's no reason you can't go to the ball. I haven't quite decided on my costume. What are you going to be? Roman or Egyptian?"

"I was not aware that you were acquainted with Lord Dulwich, Serena," Juliet said coldly. "Rather, I was under the impression that you shared our disdain for him."

Lord Dulwich sniffed. "Lady Serena and I are very dear friends, Miss Wayborn, and, unlike *you*, her ladyship is quite above reproach. I don't wonder your *mesalliance* with the Duke of Auckland has come to naught. The man's well rid of you, and he knows it. I shouldn't be surprised if he married someone else within a sennight."

Juliet frowned. "Cary? Are you going to let this cretinous oaf talk to me?"

"I'm sorry if you're not entertained, Juliet," Cary replied, turning the pages of his book. "Throughout my dealings with Lord Dulwich, I have tried to make him more interesting, but, as you see, he has thwarted my every attempt."

Dulwich's temper snapped its fragile leash. "You dare insult me! You may cower there behind your sister all you like, but it won't save you from my wrath!"

"Oddly enough, the most telling characteristic of the common bore is his determined and risible belief that he is, in fact, *interesting*," said Cary. "Ask a bore if he is a bore and his answer will invariably bore you. Go on. Ask him."

"Lord Dulwich, are you a bore?" Juliet politely inquired.

"You think you're so witty, Wayborn!" Dulwich snapped. "Well, you're not. So there!"

Lady Serena closed her eyes in embarrassment.

"You see?" said Cary, closing his book before it disclosed to him how to make a steak and kidney pie. "It's like the plague of locusts, except with *boring*." He offered Juliet his arm. "Come, sister. Let us run away before his lordship puts us to sleep."

"I see he has already put Serena to sleep," Juliet smugly observed.

Chapter 16

At the back door of the bakery a few doors down from Hatchard's, Abigail thanked the clerk who had escorted her there and pressed him to take half-a-crown for his trouble. "Thank you, Miss!" he said brightly, opening the door for her.

Abigail was promptly knocked back by the large, imposing figure emerging from the shop along with a wave of heat from the ovens. The clerk prevented her from falling, but there was a terrible explosion of muffins, followed by an explosion of curses from the owner of the muffins.

The bookshop clerk started up angrily. "Mind your language; there's a lady present!"

"You mind the bloody lady," the dark figure retorted in a strong north country accent. "And you mind my bloody muffins, too!"

To Abigail's dismay, she recognized the man who towered over her like a giant. What confounded bad luck! She dreaded having to explain herself to this relatively new acquaintance.

"I'm terribly sorry, your grace," she said breathlessly,

brushing bits of muffin from her cloak. "I did not see you there. Your muffins . . . Do please allow me to replace them for you."

"They were right out of the oven," complained the Duke of Auckland.

"Oh, I am sorry, your grace," cried Abigail.

"Why, it's Miss Ritchie," said the Duke, bending his head to look her in the face. "As I live and breathe! It *is* Miss Ritchie, is it not? The one with the corgi?"

"Yes, your grace," Abigail admitted. "It's so kind of you to remember."

"It was only yesterday I met you," he replied. "I'm not senile. And I told you to call me Geoffrey, as I recall, when your father gave me permission to call you Annabel."

"Abigail."

"Abigail," he agreed easily. "So let us not stand on ceremony. Besides which, I hate being graced. Is this your servant? You might tell him to close his mouth."

"No, sir—um—Geoffrey. This is the clerk from Hatchard's. He was good enough to escort me here. Thank you," Abigail added, pressing another coin into the young man's hand. "You'd better be getting back now."

"Yes, I'll look after her," said the Duke, taking Abigail's arm and leading her inside the hot bakery. "Now then, my dear, what would you like? I'm afraid those were the last of the gooseberry muffins. What's fresh, boys?"

One of the flour-dusted apprentices grinned at him. "Back for more already, sir?" he said with a cheekiness that took Abigail's breath away. But the Duke evidently was not one for jealously preserving the distinctions of rank.

"There's been a tragedy," he replied. "I dropped 'em.

And, before they hit the ground, the dogs and the rats had eaten 'em." Leaving Abigail for a moment, he peered into the ovens. "These currant buns are rising quite nicely," he remarked. "I'll have these, if you don't mind."

"And something for the lady?" inquired the cheeky one. Abigail was relieved that he at least recognized her as a gentlewoman.

"Annabel?"

Abigail did not bother to correct him. "Nothing for me, I thank you."

"You must have one of these," the Duke insisted. He was loading hot cross buns into his pockets. He handed Abigail one, the warmth of which she could feel through her kid gloves. "Shall we go out the front or the back?" he asked her, around bites of his own bun.

Abigail wished she could tell the whereabouts of Lord Dulwich. Nor was she entirely sure that she could bear another encounter with the odious Juliet Wayborn. The alley seemed the only safe place for her. "The back, please."

To her relief, the Duke accepted this unorthodox egress without comment. Abigail stepped into the alley, and, blowing on her bun to cool it a little, took a nibble from one side.

"Well, Annabel? Where shall I escort you?" he asked. "Back to Hatchard's?"

"Oh, no!" she said immediately.

"Yes, terrible place, Hatchard's," he agreed. "You'd think they would have given up on selling all those benighted books by now, but every time I go there, there's just as many as the time before. I wonder they would even go on trying."

"I like the shop," she said quickly, "but there's someone there I'd rather not see, if you see what I mean."

This did not seem strange to him at all. He merely nodded. "I prefer the peace and quiet of the alleys as well. Now, I don't think I can take you all the way back to Kensington by back ways, but I *can* get you to Hyde Park Corner, if that's where you've left your carriage."

Abigail sighed. "No, actually. I sent for my carriage. They're bringing it 'round to the front of Hatchard's. He's bound to hear them call out my name. Oh, dear! What shall I do?"

Fortunately, the Duke was the decisive, action-oriented type. He dragged her around the corner, saying, "You'd better get to your carriage before the footman goes into the shop."

Abigail balked at the alley's edge, however. Peering into the street, she saw that her carriage had not yet arrived, but that Lord Dulwich, with an exceedingly elegant female in tow, was just exiting the bookshop. "It's *him*," she breathed, ducking back into the alley.

The Duke gave Piccadilly a brief survey. "Ah, Dulwich," he nodded. "I could tell you stories about that narsty bugger. For starts, he's called Pudding-face."

"Yes, I know," said Abigail.

He leaned comfortably against the wall and munched his currant bun. "And I have it on good authority that last year, right on this very street, in broad daylight, he knocked a girl down, and he didn't even stop to help her regain her feet."

"I was that girl, sir," Abigail admitted ruefully.

"You? But weren't you engaged to him?"

"I broke it off. Is he—is his lordship still there?"

He gave the street a quick scan. "Seems to be waiting for his carriage. Serena ought to have her head examined. For starts, that hideous green bonnet is so big her neck could snap at any moment. Aren't you going to look?" he asked Abigail in some surprise.

Abigail shook her head.

"Julie always looks at hats," he said a little wistfully. "She mocks them mercilessly. Almost never wears a hat herself. But then she has such nice hair. Like a setter's ears." The Duke suddenly scowled. "Do you mean to say that Dulwich deliberately knocked you down in the street *because* you broke your engagement? Why, that's infamous, even for him!"

"Oh, no," Abigail quickly corrected him. "I'd not yet broken the engagement."

He gave a snort of laughter. "So the bloody fool knocked his own fiancée to the ground."

Abigail shuddered. "Sir! Please don't call me that."

The Duke was laughing. "What a good joke! One almost feels sorry for the stupid ass! There he is engaged to your lovely one hundred thousand pounds, and what does he do? He knocks you down in the street! He probably still wonders why you broke it off!" He threw back his head and roared so loudly that Abigail was afraid Dulwich would hear him.

"I beg your pardon!" she said softly. "But you are mistaken. I haven't got a hundred thousand pounds."

"Well, that's what your father offered *me*," he said, "but then, Dulwich is only a viscount, though he does stand to inherit the earldom. I'm a full-fledged duke."

"*What?*" cried Abigail. "Has my father offered you money to–to—?"

"I was not offended," said the Duke. "It was like this. I'd ordered a lot of drink, you know, for the wedding party. Did you know I was once engaged?"

"Yes, sir."

"Well, the vile girl broke it off, so I had to cancel a lot of things, including your father's scotch. He was good enough to return my deposit, although he somehow persuaded me to take it in scotch, instead of cash. We got

to talking. I had no idea there was so much money in
drink! Though, I daresay, it stands to reason. People *do*
drink, after all."

"Sir," Abigail interrupted. "Did you come to an
agreement with my father?"

"I said I'd think about it. Although I must tell you,
Annabel, I'm none too keen on marrying a girl who was
once engaged to Pudding-face. I have my pride, you
know, and I don't really need the money. But his scotch
is deuced good. Now, I don't want to hurt your feelings!"
he quickly added, clearly misunderstanding her sigh of
relief. "I'm sure you're a very nice girl and all that, but—
and I hinted at this to your father—if you want a title,
there are plenty of penniless earls who'd be glad to take
you. We'll find you a nice one, don't worry."

Abigail's mouth worked helplessly.

"You mustn't really expect to get a duke, you know,"
he said, laying an avuncular hand on her shoulder. "Not
that I don't admire your ambition, Annabel . . ."

Abigail found her voice. "I am not in the least ambi-
tious, sir, I assure you! It's true that my father has always
wanted me to marry a title, but, for myself, it is of no
consequence. I haven't the least interest in marrying a
title, thank you very much."

"What?" He chuckled. "Do you mean to say you've
ruled it out?"

"In a manner of speaking," she said, hiding a smile.

"What? Not even a baron? You are determined to
marry a mister? But don't you think you would enjoy
being, say, Duchess of Auckland? Eh?"

"No, sir, I would not. I don't mean to hurt your feelings, sir," she added quickly. "But I shouldn't like being
a duchess at all. For starts, I should hate going to Court.
I should infinitely prefer to live quietly in the country,
and raise pigs or chickens or something like that."

A grin softened his craggy face. "You'd be as bad a duchess as I am a duke. Julie was all wrong, too. She'd have spent all her time putting together amateur theatricals and haunting the theater. I suppose it's all for the best. But won't you miss the theater out there in the country with Mr. Pigs-and-Chickens?"

"I don't really like going to the theater," she admitted. "There's such a crush to get in."

"There is, isn't there?" he agreed. "Then, when one finally *does* get in, it's so loud one can scarcely hear the performance!"

"And when the people in the pit don't like the play, they behave so abominably. They *shout* at the actors. Sometimes, they even throw things. I think it's very bad, don't you, sir?"

"That's chiefly what I like about it," said the Duke. "In fact, I'm going tonight just to throw cabbages at Mr. David Rourke. My man's been poking through the neighborhood ash bins all morning."

Abigail stared at him. He sounded quite serious, but he couldn't be. Could he? "Don't you like Mr. Rourke?" she asked him nervously. "He gets good reviews."

"Not from me, he don't."

"You don't really mean to throw things at him, do you?"

"I certainly do," he said stoutly. "It's opening night. *Antony and Cleopatra*. I daresay, he thinks he's going to have a long run! And so he will. I shall run him out of England!"

Abigail frowned. "If it's opening night, sir, how do you know you won't like the play? It might be very good."

"I don't care if it is!" he declared angrily. "Rourke's finished. You ought to come with me, Annabel," he went on. "How's your bowling arm? There will be tomatoes, as well. Great fat, juicy, rotten ones. How I should like to mash them all into that pretty Irish face of his."

Abigail was appalled. "Sir! Mr. Rourke is perhaps no Edmund Kean, but—"

"Who the devil is Edmund Kean?" he demanded. "Another Irishman of Juliet's?"

"In any case," Abigail said hastily. "I cannot attend the theater with you tonight, sir. My father is taking me to Carlton House. It's some dreadful masquerade ball, I'm afraid, but the Prince Regent was kind enough to invite us—"

The Duke snorted. "In exchange for a lot of free scotch, I don't doubt!"

"Well, yes," Abigail conceded. "That's generally how it seems to work."

"I'm going to the Regent's ball as well," he informed her. "But it's not until after *Antony and Cleopatra*. The Prince will be attending the performance, you know. Rumor has it Mrs. Archer is his new mistress. She's Cleopatra, you know. Oh, I'm sorry! Am I allowed to say 'mistress' in front of you?"

"You just did," Abigail pointed out. "Twice."

"So I did. And you didn't faint, so I must be in the clear. In any case, the ball is being held afterwards. All the actors and actresses will be there—except for Mr. Rourke, who will be too covered in filth to go anywhere ever again—except Ireland. Tell your father I have engaged to escort you from the theater to the ball. He can have no objection to such a scheme."

"I'm sure he would be delighted, your grace, but, really, I—"

"Dulwich is gone," he interrupted her to report. "I think this must be your carriage now."

"Yes, that's it, thank you," she said, taking his arm. She supposed a more spirited girl would try to dissuade the Duke from putting his childish plan into effect, but she only wanted to get away from him.

There was no sign of Cary in Piccadilly. Had he gone into the bakery to find her? She would have to rid herself of one very large Duke before she would be free to search for him. When she remembered how badly Cary had treated her, she wasn't sure she wanted to see him again anyway. At least not for a while.

"Thank you, sir," she said, turning to her escort. "I can manage very well from here."

"Nonsense," he replied. "I'll see you home. I'm not doing anything."

Her heart nearly stopped as the door of the bakery swung open and two people came out.

Cary was so near to her that she could have reached out and touched his purple coat, but he was looking up the street as he put on his hat.

"She must have gone back into Hatchard's."

"She's gone, Cary," Juliet replied crossly. "Along with your emerald and your miniatures. With any luck we'll never see her again. Now I want my tea."

Furious with herself for not speaking up, Abigail mutely wondered how many years it would take before the sight of this particular man lost its power to strike her dumb. Her companion, however, suffered from no such diffidence.

"You!" he roared like a mad bull. "What fiend conjured you up from the depths of hell?"

Brother and sister turned to look at them in amazement. Cary did not seem to have heard the Duke. The way he looked at her made Abigail's knees melt. She quite forgot that he had practically called her a thief. "There you are, monkey," he said softly. "I thought I'd lost you."

"You certainly don't let the grass grow under your

feet," Juliet observed. "But I expect you are quite in the habit of making friends in the street. It's how you met my brother, I believe."

"I met your brother at White's," the Duke retorted.

"No one was talking to you, Ginger," said Juliet. "No one even knows you are there."

"I just met his grace coming out of the bakery," Abigail blurted. "Quite by accident. He was good enough to escort me to my carriage."

Cary quirked a brow. "Only just met, and already walking arm in arm," he remarked. "Pretty fast work, Geoffrey."

"Oh, no," Abigail said, flustered. "We met yesterday. I meant to say that we—that *I* bumped into him, literally, in the alley. I ruined his muffins, I'm afraid."

"I see," said Cary rather coolly, she thought.

"They told me you'd left town," said the Duke of Auckland, glowering at Juliet. "I ought to have known it couldn't be true. I couldn't be so lucky."

Juliet tossed her head. "You know, Ginger," she said coldly, "if you keep eating muffins at all hours, you will soon be too fat to sit a horse properly. Your curricle already lists dangerously to one side when you get into it. I should hate to see you overturn."

"Muffins," he said scornfully. "It's a *bun*, you tart. Trust a tart not to know the difference between a muffin and a bun."

Abigail gasped. "You . . . You mustn't . . ." she stammered. "I wish you wouldn't speak to Miss Wayborn like that, sir. It's very wrong."

"Who asked you?" Juliet said resentfully.

"You're quite right, Annabel." The Duke seized Abigail's hand in his giant paws and patted it protectively. "I shouldn't talk to her at all."

"Annabel!" Juliet and Cary both spoke at once.

"Sir, it's Abigail," Abigail said, growing red in the face.

The Duke snapped his fingers. "Oh, that's right. Annabel was your mother."

"Anne. Anne was my mother."

"Anne. Yes, of course. I beg your pardon. I hadn't thought of it before, but I suppose you must be cousins to these people."

"Only very distant," Abigail said faintly.

"*Very*," Juliet agreed. "Ginger, do you mean to say you *know* Anne Wayborn?"

"Are you talking to me, madam? Yes, I know Anne Wayborn. That is, I know *of* her. She and my mother were very dear friends."

"Were they?" Abigail exclaimed in astonishment.

"Of course, when your mother married your father, my mother was forced to end the association, but things were different in our parents' time," said the Duke. "Mama always regretted giving up your mother. My father, however, was inflexible on the subject. I did think that, when the old earl died, that the new earl would treat you better. This would be your uncle, Annabel."

"Abigail!" Juliet snapped.

"Sorry. I keep doing that. Abigail."

"It's all right, sir. I would just like to go home now, if I may."

"Just a moment," said the Duke. "Let me finish. It's a very funny story. I asked your uncle why he was so hard about your father. Do you know what he said?"

"I'm sure I can guess," Abigail said, wincing.

"No, you can't. He said, 'I don't care three straws who Anne married, but she never should have taken my old nursey with her when she left. *That* I will never forgive.'"

"What, Paggles?" said Cary, chuckling.

"What's a paggle?" the Duke asked, puzzled.

"She's a who, not a what," Cary explained. "Paggles is Dickie-bird's old nurse."

"Then the little thief really *is* our cousin," said Juliet, clearly appalled.

"Only very distant," Abigail said firmly. "Now I must beg you all to excuse me. My father will be wondering where I am."

"Don't forget our engagement!" said the Duke, rather loudly. "I'm taking your cousin to the theater this evening," he told Miss Wayborn. "Who knows where it will all end?"

Abigail's head was beginning to ache. "Sir," she began unhappily. "It was very good of you to ask me, but I—"

"I don't suppose you'll have the nerve to show your face there," said the Duke. After a moment of confusion, Abigail saw, to her relief, that he was now addressing Juliet.

"Of course I shall be there," Juliet replied. "It's Mr. Rourke's opening night. I wouldn't miss it for the world. Why, Ginger? Is there some reason I *shouldn't* be there?"

"No, you *should* be there," he snarled. "I'm glad you're going to be there."

"Depend upon it. I shall be!"

"I'm glad!"

"Good!"

"I'm glad because tonight I'm going to give Mr. Rourke the Boo," he shouted.

Juliet's eyes flashed and her composure suffered a sharp decline. "You wouldn't dare!" she spat, trembling from head to foot with rage.

He laughed bitterly. "Wouldn't I? I've got baskets of

rotting vegetables waiting at the ready. I'll give your precious Mr. Rourke a salad he won't soon forget."

Juliet stamped her foot. "I'm warning you, Ginger, if anything happens to Mr. Rourke, on stage or off, I swear I'll—I'll—!"

"You'll do what?" the Duke taunted Juliet with evident glee. "Jilt me? You've already done that, madam! Think of it, Julie. Your favorite Irishman, covered in slimy cabbage leaves and rotten tomatoes. I wish you much joy of him!"

"If you *dare* to throw cabbages at Mr. Rourke, *I* will throw him roses," Juliet hissed. "*Red* roses. *Heaps* of them. I swear I will."

"You'd do that to me?" The Duke's lip curled. "Yes, of course you would, you serpent. Well, you won't have a seat in my box, I can tell you. You'll have to catch as you can in the pit with the rest of your kind. No one will remark on your being alone. Harpies *are* solitary creatures, after all."

Juliet was white with fury. She caught Cary's arm for support. "My brother will be escorting me, of course. We have our own box. Isn't that right, Cary?"

Abigail looked at him with interest. "Are *you* going to the play, Mr. Wayborn?"

He looked back at her. "Are you?"

Abigail bit her lip. "I suppose I could if . . . if you are," she said. "Only, I wish no one would throw anything at poor Mr. Rourke."

"Oh, you like him too," the Duke muttered.

"Not at all," Abigail protested. "I don't think anyone should throw anything at anyone."

"What an excellent suggestion," Cary remarked. "Why don't we call a truce? We'll all go to the theater tonight, and no one will throw anything at anyone."

"What about the ball after?" said the Duke. "Am I allowed to throw things at the ball?"

"If you do," said Juliet, "I shall *kiss* him."

"I am engaged to go to the Carlton House Ball afterwards, too," Abigail said quickly, "and . . . and my father will be there. I should very much like to introduce you to him, Mr. Wayborn," she added a little doubtfully. "That is, if you would care to—to meet him."

"All right, monkey," he said softly. "I should very much like to meet your father. You shall have your truce. Juliet? Geoffrey? Pax?"

"I will if *he* will," said his sister.

"I will if *she* will," the Duke snapped back.

"Excellent," said Cary. "If only the Congress in Vienna had been so agreeable! May I escort you home, Cousin Abigail?"

"Oh," she said regretfully. "Thank you, sir, but this is my carriage."

"What? That giant blue thing with the silver spokes?" Cary's eyes twinkled. "I thought it was the nation's mail."

Juliet's head swivelled around. She seemed quite taken with Abigail's carriage.

Conspicuously new, it was painted a deep royal blue with sterling silver handles on the doors. The two footmen were in black livery trimmed in silver, with blue and silver cockades on their black tricorns. While understanding that it was far too grand for a mere tradesman's daughter, Abigail was cautiously proud of it.

"*This* is your carriage?" Juliet asked, with a peculiar inflection.

"Yes, Miss Wayborn. Is something wrong?"

"Not at all," said Juliet tightly. "It's a very elegant vehicle, I'm sure."

"I don't know horses very well, so perhaps these are

no good," Abigail said doubtfully. "I do hope my father didn't pay too much for them."

"The horses are perfect, Abigail," Cary assured her. "A very handsome equipage altogether. Just big, that's all. I shouldn't think it very convenient for driving about Town. Why, you must bounce around in there like a pip in a rattle."

"Not at all; it rides very smoothly."

"They're Cumberlands, ain't they?" said the Duke, squinting at the four horses.

"Yes, of course they're Cumberlands," Juliet said crossly. "You know perfectly well they are Cumberlands, you priceless ass."

"Pax!" he roared at her.

"You broke it first!" Juliet shrieked.

"All I said was they were Cumberlands," he grumbled. "How's that breaking the truce?"

Her gray eyes narrowed to slits. "You know how, you scaly fiend!"

The Duke groaned. "Come, Abigail. There's no talking to your gruesome cousin when she's like this." He nearly wrenched the beautifully polished door of the carriage off its hinges.

"Do be careful!" cried Abigail.

"Thank you, Ginger," Juliet said, jumping up the steps into the carriage before Abigail.

The Duke stuck his shaggy red head into the carriage and snarled at her. "What do you think you're doing, Miss? This ain't your carriage."

Juliet looked past him and smiled coldly at Abigail. "You can set me down in Park Lane, can't you, Cousin Abigail? I'll give you tea if you do."

Her arrogance took Abigail's breath away, but, at the same time, she hardly knew how to refuse. She did not wish to appear rude, even though Juliet clearly had no similar scruples, and Park Lane was only a little out of her way. All the same, she would have preferred sharing her carriage with Mrs. Spurgeon's nasty macaw, dead or alive.

"I've got my curricle, Juliet," said Cary, leaning into the vehicle. "There's no reason to trouble Cousin Abigail."

"Hadn't you better get back to Bow Street, Cary?" Juliet said impatiently. "We wouldn't want a *certain person* being dragged away in chains during Cleopatra's lament, now, would we?"

"Damn!" said Cary under his breath. "Yes, I'd better go and call them off."

Abigail frowned. "Did you *really* hire Bow Street Runners to hunt me down?"

"They're very discreet," he said cheekily. "Really, you're nobody until you've had the Runners after you. Unfortunately, they do have a nasty habit of getting re-sults. I'd better go before they snatch you off the street. Geoffrey?" he called to the Duke. "Do you have your grays out today? If not, I'd be happy to set you down in St. James's."

The Duke was watching Juliet arrange her skirts so that they fell in neat rows on either side of her. "What? No, I'm on foot." Abruptly, he clambered up and threw himself onto the seat opposite Juliet. "Could you set me down in Berkeley Square?" he asked Abigail. "It won't be out of your way."

Abigail realized with a sinking heart that she would be obliged to bid farewell to the one she could not do without, while being forced to keep company with the two she could most easily dispense with. She could scarcely contain her frustration.

"Your carriage is too big," Cary informed her, laugh-ing. "That's your trouble. You could carry about the entire Oxford University Cricket Club in that monstrous thing." He kissed her hand with disappointing celerity. His smile was equally quick. "Until tonight, then, monkey? It should be an interesting evening."

"Cousin Abigail?" Juliet inquired shrilly from within the carriage. "Are you coming with us or not?"

To Abigail's relief, Miss Wayborn chose to punish her jilted suitor by maintaining a haughty silence. The Duke seemed content to glower at Juliet. For her part, Abigail looked out of the window.

The Duke broke the silence. "I'll call for you at six then, Miss Abigail. No, better make that half past five. It's a long way to Kensington and back."

Juliet wrinkled her nose. "Do you live in Kensington, Cousin Abigail?"

"Yes, Cousin Juliet, I do. It's quiet. I like it there." She smiled at the Duke. "But you needn't call for me at home, sir. I am happy to meet you at the theater. I'm sure it would be much more convenient if it were so. I have my own carriage, after all."

"Yes, we know," Juliet said dryly.

"That's awfully decent of you," said the Duke, taking Abigail's hand. "My, how considerate *some* young ladies are."

"Well, young ladies with their own carriages can afford to be considerate," said Juliet sweetly. "And such a nice carriage it is, too. I particularly like this cobalt blue leather on the seats. How do you like the leather, Ginger?"

He frowned down at the leather cushions. "I know it, don't I? I've seen it before."

"It's Italian," said Abigail. "Specially ordered."

"Indeed?" said Juliet. "How very nice for you."

"Thank you," Abigail said uncertainly. "I daresay it *is* rather too big for me."

"Where did you get it?" Miss Wayborn inquired politely. "Colfax, of course."

"I'm not sure," said Abigail. "My father bought it for me while I was away. He got a good deal on it. Originally, it was ordered by a nobleman for a certain lady, but there was a rift between them of some sort, and when it was delivered, he refused it."

The Duke suddenly sank down in the seat, emitting a long animal moan. "Oh, God, Julie, I'm sorry!"

"So you should be," she said icily. "I shall never forgive you. Never!"

"Damn and blast, I *knew* I recognized those Cumberlands! Look here, Annabel—Abigail—I'll just have to buy the bloody thing back from your father."

Juliet laughed bitterly. "Do you expect me to believe that *her father* bought this carriage? You gave it to her! Admit it! You gave it to her just to hurt me. Well done, Ginger!"

"Oh, Miss Wayborn!" said Abigail. "Is this—was this meant to be *your* carriage? I'm so sorry. I had no idea."

"I suppose you're his mistress!" she said. "Well, there's no accounting for taste!"

"You take that back!" said Abigail. "My father bought me this carriage."

"It's true, Julie. Colfax sent it to me, but I sent it back."

"Well, that doesn't mean he can turn around and sell it to someone else," said Juliet.

"That is exactly what it means!" Abigail argued. "A great deal of work went into this carriage, Miss Wayborn, though you do not realize it. Every part of it was custom-made, down to the tassels on the curtains. Is Mr. Colfax to get nothing for his hard work, just because the two of you are bickering like . . . like Oberon and Titania?"

"Look here, Julie," said the Duke, "I'll buy it back from the man. If you stop a moment at Auckland House, Abigail, I can write you a note on my bank for fourteen hundred pounds."

"Is that what you were going to pay for it?" exclaimed Abigail. "Oh, well done, Papa!" she murmured. "He got it for seven hundred."

"Seven hundred?" The Duke scowled. "Why, that bloody thief, Colfax! He was charging me twice that!"

"Well, it *was* a custom order," said Abigail. "Not everyone wants an enormous coach and four with blue doors and silver wheels . . . and seats that fold down into beds."

"Julie! Do the seats fold down into beds?"

"I thought it would be convenient for our long trips to Auckland in the winter," Juliet said primly. "You snore when you sleep sitting up."

"And, of course," Abigail went on hastily, "the crest on the doors had to be painted over. I think Mr. Colfax was grateful that anyone bought it."

"I shall buy it back," said the Duke. "It was meant for you, Julie, and you shall have it. I apologize for the misunderstanding. I'll give you a bank note, Abigail."

"You will have to speak to my father, your grace," Abigail demurred. "*I* can't engage to sell it to you. It was a gift. I'm sure you understand. Besides, I'm going to need it tonight, if I'm to go to the theater. I should be more than happy to . . . to collect Miss Wayborn and bring her to the theater with me."

"How very good of you, Cousin Abigail," Juliet drawled. "How *kind* of you to offer to take me to the theater in my very own carriage."

"I beg your pardon, Miss Wayborn, but it is *my* carriage. Bought and paid for."

"On second thought, *do* come and collect me," said she. "It will be nice to have such a big roomy carriage.

We can bring some of the actors with us to the Carlton House Ball."

Abigail cringed in horror. "Actors? In my nice clean carriage?"

The Duke was incensed. "Rourke? Rourke in my carriage? I don't think so, my girl!"

Juliet shrugged. "Why not?"

"So you can show him how the seats fold down?" he roared.

Juliet's eyes flashed angrily. "Perhaps I will!" she snapped.

"Do it!" he said. "And I shall drop this carriage on your head!"

"I hate you!"

"Berkeley Square!" cried Abigail, looking out the window just as the carriage drew up to the shining marble facade of the Duke's town house.

The Duke jumped out and viciously kicked his hat across the road. His face was very white. "I'll see you tonight, Abigail. If you happen to have any nice juicy garbage hanging about you in Kensington, bring it along!"

"Park Lane," Abigail told the footman. "*Quickly!*"

"I cannot make you out at all, little Abigail," said Juliet, leaning back in her seat as the carriage jogged westward to Park Lane. "Either you are a spineless little fool or you're an artful little she-devil. Did your father really buy this carriage? Who *is* your father, anyway? Not Sir William Smith of Brazil, I'm sure. I see from this receipt that you are called Miss Ritchie. I never saw that name in DeBrett's, but I think I saw it on the bottle in your room."

Abigail's head ached and her nerves were badly frayed. "Miss Wayborn," she said coldly, "did you happen to have ordered a dining table and chairs from

Mr. Duckett in Jermyn Street? Ebony, with gold and ivory inlay?"

"Why does one ask?"

"No reason," Abigail said sweetly.

"You nasty little thief!" Juliet snarled. "What else have you taken from me?"

Abigail drew herself up. "You *did* tell me, did you not, that I should go to London, and take what I could get?"

Suddenly, and rather unconvincingly, Juliet seemed overcome by the swaying of the carriage. As they arrived in Park Lane, she stood up in the carriage, then sank back into her seat with her handkerchief pressed to her mouth as the servants scrambled to open the door. Abigail privately thought her a terrible actress, but she said solicitously, "You are unwell, Miss Wayborn. Do let my servants summon your servants."

Juliet opened her eyes. "No, indeed. I'm quite well now. This frigate of a carriage makes one a bit seasick, that's all."

"Perhaps you should stay at home and rest this evening," Abigail kindly suggested.

"No, I must go to the theater," Juliet said crossly. "People will think me a cowardy custard if I don't go. You *will* come and collect me, won't you, Cousin Abigail?" she went on, half-pleading, half-commanding. "It's so dreadfully important that I arrive in a proper carriage."

"But if it makes you seasick—" Abigail began.

"As you can see I am quite recovered," Juliet snapped. "And we *have* got a truce, haven't we? You would not break your word, when my poor brother has such faith in your honesty?"

"No, indeed," Abigail mumbled reluctantly.

Fully recovered, Juliet fairly bounced down the steps. "I wouldn't really let actors sit in the carriage, you know," she said gaily. "Why, it's brand new!"

The servant closed the door, and Abigail slipped down in her seat, blowing out her cheeks in a massive sigh of relief. "What a horrid creature!" she said aloud. As the carriage turned onto Kensington Road, she opened the miniature bar Juliet had so thoughtfully instructed Mr. Colfax to set into the door, and poured herself a long nourishing *quaich* of Ritchie's single malt.

She felt, somehow, that she had earned it.

Chapter 17

Cary was checking his watch with such frequency and such irritation that he almost missed Mr. Waller leaving his office accompanied by a prosperous looking man in plain, dark clothes. A passing Runner, chancing to remark, "Aughternoon, Mr. Waller," caused him to look up. "Look here, Waller," Cary called out irritably, jumping to his feet in the crowded anteroom. "I've been waiting for you nearly two hours."

Mr. Waller's eyes widened in surprise. "Why, here is Mr. Wayborn now. What a fortuitous concourse of atoms, as the poet says."

"I'll say it's fortuitous," Cary snapped. "Half of London's atoms have gone ahead of me! There's not even anything to read while one waits, not even the *Gazette*."

"Well, it's not a circulating library, Mr. Wayborn, sir," Mr. Waller pointed out.

"Quite." Cary was at the point of urging Mr. Waller back into his office when the Runner's companion suddenly addressed him.

"Mr. Wayborn," he said, his tone both deferential and

businesslike. "This is a matter of some delicacy and no little embarrassment for me. I'm sure you understand."

Cary studied the other man. Being of middle height, weight, and coloring, he had virtually no outstanding characteristics. All the same, Cary was certain he had never met the man in his life. "Who the devil are you?"

The man blushed rosily. "I beg your pardon, sir! Forgive me; we have never met. I'm Mr. Leighton." He seemed a little puzzled that his name meant nothing to Cary. "I'm an attorney," he elaborated. "My mother-in-law stayed in your house when she was lately in Hertfordshire. Mrs. Urania Spurgeon?"

"Oh, yes, of course," said Cary. "Mr. Leighton. How do you do, sir? Forgive me. My thoughts were a thousand miles away. I did not immediately recognize the name. Mrs. Spurgeon is well, I trust?"

Mr. Leighton winced. "She's never exactly in the best of health, sir. I'd say she is as well as can be expected. But the household is in an uproar, you see."

"I see," said Cary, though he really didn't. He was afraid that Mr. Leighton might turn out to be one of those people who take great pleasure in laying all their troubles at the feet of the nearest gentleman. "Well, if there is anything I can do . . ." he murmured vaguely.

"But sir! It is *I* who may be of some assistance to *you*."

Mr. Waller was more specific. "Mr. Leighton has recovered some of your stolen property, Mr. Wayborn, sir. Shall we step into my office?"

Abigail found her father in the banquet hall of their Kensington house. The elaborate grandeur of the ebony table and chairs was perhaps out of step with the neoclassical mural on the walls that depicted rosy cupids playing various musical instruments while Venus and

Mars picnicked at the foot of Mount Olympus, but, since there had never been a banquet held here, and there probably never would be, Abigail was content to indulge her father in his colliding tastes.

Red Ritchie was engaged in directing the work of a young draftsman whose task it was to meticulously draw each and every new object that came into the house; Red insisted upon thoroughly up-to-date inventories of all his possessions.

Red welcomed his daughter's interruption. "Abby, love! What did you buy? Higgins will draw it for you, won't you, Higgins?"

"Only a book," said Abigail. "But I think I might have a buyer for the new coach, Papa."

"But I wanted *you* to have that carriage, Abby," Red complained. "It was meant for a duchess. All right, Higgins, run along. That's enough for the day."

Abigail waited for the young man to depart. "The buyer is very motivated. He offered me fourteen hundred pounds. That's twice what you paid, isn't it?"

Red's expression underwent a radical change. "Oh, well done, Abby!"

"I knew you'd be pleased. He'll come and see you tomorrow, he said."

"I wanted to get you something special for your birthday," he said wistfully. "I may have to ask this fellow for more money. Do you think he would pay two thousand?"

"Almost certainly," Abigail said, smiling. "He seems to want it very badly."

"Then I might buy you a nice little phaeton for your birthday," he said, rubbing his hands together gleefully. "You could drive me to the warehouse of a morning."

Abigail felt a stab of guilt. Soon she would be leaving her father's house forever. Then he would live alone in his enormous Kensington mansion where no one ever visited him, and she would be miles away in Hertfordshire. How could she possibly tell him that she was planning to abandon him for a feckless young wastrel who didn't pay his bills? His practical Glaswegian soul would neither understand nor forgive.

"I suppose I could learn how to drive," she said, trying to sound cheerful.

"Of course you could," he said warmly. "Won't you look smart in your new phaeton, Abby! Just like one of these aristocratic ladies." Suddenly, he smacked his forehead with his open palm. "Wouldn't that have been something, if I'd only thought of it sooner? I could have had a Roman chariot made for you! Then you might have arrived at Carlton House in style! I wonder," he mused, "if I promised Colfax a fortune . . . He might have something on the lot that could be modified . . ."

"No, Papa," Abigail said firmly. "Even if you could, I could never learn to drive in one evening. It would not be so stylish if I overturned!"

"You are right," he agreed, chewing his lower lip. "I ought to have gotten you driving lessons before. But, you know, in your mother's day, respectable young ladies never took up the reins for themselves. It's quite a recent development."

They went into the sitting room at the back of the house for their tea, which consisted of sandwiches and single malt, followed by hot, buttery scones. The tall French windows looked out onto the back garden, which had always been Abigail's special project. It made her sad to think that her last view of it should be a winter view, with very little of spring's promise in evidence.

"I shall be leaving for Carlton House in very short order, I'm afraid," her father told her at the end of the meal. "I want everything to be perfect for His Highness. I wouldn't put it past those idiots at the warehouse to misdirect the deliveries, break half the bottles, and drink the other half themselves! If all goes well, Abigail, and the Regent is pleased, we'll have the royal mark on the bottle, see if we don't. That will give us just the boost we need."

"I'm sure His Highness will be pleased with everything," said Abigail, frowning. "But . . . do you think we need a boost, Papa? Has there been a decline in revenue?"

He brushed crumbs from his waistcoat. "Naught for you to worry about, Abby."

Abigail bit her lip. "I did hear you were threatening some delinquent accounts with debtor's prison. That can't be good for business. Gentlemen don't respond as they should to such threats. Has custom fallen off so sharply that you are having to ask the gentlefolk to pay?"

Her father looked at her sharply. "Who've you been talking to?"

"No one," she stammered. "It was just something I heard."

He stood up angrily and shoved his chair to one side. "I couldn't help it, Abby! I saw his name on the books. One of your hoity-toity cousins, by God. One of those high-and-mighty Wayborns! After the way they treated your poor mother, God rest her soul, I'll be damned if I extend any credit to that race of hypocrites. Not a farthing! Oh, they took my money quick enough when I married Anne, then turned their backs on her as if she'd been a leper!"

"But those are the Derbyshire Wayborns," Abigail said quickly. "Mr. *Cary* Wayborn is from Surrey. He's nothing to do with Mama. It's a completely different branch of the family."

"Well, he's an insolent young pup," Red grumbled. "He wears an earring, for the love of God. What is he, a pirate? He wants a beating, if you ask me."

"Papa!" she protested. "He's my cousin, after all."

"You don't know him, Abby. He's a worthless young

man without a penny to bless himself with, and he wouldn't know good scotch if he sat on it. He couldn't pay his bill, so he returned an entire case of single malt, untouched! What sort of a man orders a case of good whisky and then doesn't drink it?"

Abigail debated telling him that it was really her own scotch that Cary had returned, but she lacked courage. In any case, it would not improve her father's opinion of the man she'd married. "He's a gentleman, Papa. You know what they're like about getting bills. And you sent him several, I believe, with red ink all over, as if he'd been an innkeeper or something."

"You seem to know a lot about it," he said, swinging around to glare at her.

In a way Abigail was glad she had aroused his suspicions; it encouraged her to tell him what she might otherwise have been too cowardly to reveal. "Well, I have met him actually. We are distantly related, you know."

For a moment Red observed his daughter as she sat twisting her hands together, unable to meet his gaze. "Met him? Met him how?"

"I stayed at his house in Hertfordshire," she replied, trying to sound casual.

He stared at her. "What? Abby, I rented you a perfectly good house."

"Yes, sir. You did. It was Mr. Wayborn's house. Did Mr. Leighton not tell you?" she quickly added, hoping to deflect some of Red's growing annoyance onto the attorney.

"He did not. He said it belonged to some clergyman friend of his, a Dr. Cary."

"You must have misunderstood, Papa. Dr. Cary is Mr. Wayborn's cousin, but he does not own the estate. It's a very handsome and extensive property," she went on, choosing details most likely to impress her father, "encompassing several rich farms and many beautiful, productive orchards. The house is the most charming example of a Tudor manor I have ever seen. It has been in Mr. Wayborn's family for hundreds of years. He is very well-respected in that part of the country."

Red grunted. "So he owns a bit of land, does he? I daresay it must be entailed, or he would sell it off to pursue a life of unfettered extravagance."

"Indeed it is not entailed," Abigail was happy to inform him. "It was left him outright by his grandmother. I believe it is something in the neighborhood of ten thousand acres. As you know, Hertfordshire is some of the richest farmland in all England."

"If he's so rich, why doesn't he pay his bills?" Red demanded.

"You offended him, Papa," she said gently.

Red snorted unpleasantly. "Did Mr. Weston offend him too? And Mr. Hoby? As far as I can tell, the only place the man's paid up is Tattersall's."

Abigail suppressed a smile. Of course, Cary *would* pay for his beautiful horses, and let everything else go to the devil. "How would you know that, Papa?" she asked suddenly, as an unpleasant thought entered her mind.

"No one has ever returned so much as a thimbleful of my scotch," he grumbled. "This arrogant pup returned an entire case! Naturally, I made it my business to buy up all his debts in London. You say I offended him. Well, he offended me! Nothing will content me until I see him in debtor's prison."

Abigail gasped. "Papa, you *can't*!"

"No, I can't," he glumly agreed. "For they wouldn't sell me his debts. Not a one of them from Jermyn Street to Bond. Not even your friend at Mr. Hatchard's shop. They all seem to think he will make good one day."

Abigail's heart swelled with pride. "What does that

tell you, Papa? They *know* Mr. Wayborn is a gentleman. No matter what he owes, they will not betray him."

Red was unmoved. "What does it tell me?" he snarled. "He's got you all fooled, that's what it tells me. I had ample time to take Mr. Wayborn's character when he returned my scotch. Very high-and-mighty he was in his purple coat, too! He said my Glaswegian swill wasn't fit to be drunk by English gentlemen!"

"You should not have sent him all those bills, Papa," she blurted without thinking.

"You take his side against mine?" Red bellowed, incensed by his daughter's disloyalty. "You hardly know the man. Well, I may not be a fine gentleman like Mr. Wayborn, but I *am* your father, Abigail, in case you've forgotten. And I didn't raise you to be a lady so's you'd look down your nose at me."

"I'm sorry, Papa," she said quietly. "I'm not looking down my nose at you. It's business. What you did was not good for business. No gentleman would ever tolerate such treatment from a tradesman. You could only succeed in provoking him. What is the first rule of business?"

Red looked away. "Never make a decision based on emotion."

"I know you did it because of Mama, and I love you for that. But Mr. Cary Wayborn is not to blame for what the Derbyshire Wayborns did to Mama. And you can't blame him for being angry with you when you went out of your way to offend him."

Red made no reply.

"I also had an opportunity to take Mr. Wayborn's character. I thought him very . . . gentlemanlike," said Abigail, conveniently forgetting Cary's frequent lapses in propriety when he was alone with her.

Red flung up his hands incredulously. "Gentleman-like? God and Highlanders, child! The man's got an earring. Oh, I daresay he makes a lovely lady's lapdog. I daresay he knows how to make himself agreeable to women. Did he make himself agreeable to you?"

Abigail knew she was now on very dangerous ground. "He was a very attentive landlord and host," she said cautiously. "He . . . dined with us occasionally."

"Did he? I shall have to send him a bill for those dinners!" said Red. "Come to think of it, I had Leighton pay out half a year's rent. As you are certainly not going back to that house, I shall demand a refund."

"You don't care about the money," she accused him. "You're just being vindictive."

"If I didn't know better, lass, I'd say you were smitten with him."

"Papa, please." Abigail's face was red as fire.

"Great God!" he choked. "That's it, isn't it? The impertinent wretch has been making love to you! Mark my words, child. A man like that is only interested in one thing from a girl like you."

"Well, some men are very passionate," she stammered defensively.

"I was talking about your fortune!" cried Red, appalled.

Abigail realized she had made a critical error. "If his view is marriage, I see nothing wrong with that," she added quickly.

"So his view is marriage, is it?" Red tucked his hands behind his back and took a stroll about the room. "I'll just bet it is. Oh, Abigail! How could you be so foolish? The man is an obvious fortune hunter."

"He doesn't know I have a fortune," she protested. "He thinks I'm somebody called Smith. He hasn't the least thought of marrying into a fortune."

"That is what all fortune hunters say!" her parent responded derisively. "Depend on it; he has found you out. He's plotting to get his hands on your money. My money!"

"That is not rational," she pointed out. "If he knew I

was your daughter, and he was a fortune hunter, he would have paid his bill. By no means would he have returned your scotch."

Red was hard-pressed to explain Cary's behavior. "He must be trying to throw us off the scent," he said, after a moment. "Oh, my poor lass! Has he imposed on you very badly?"

"Mr. Wayborn is not a fortune hunter," she said firmly. "If anything, he does not care *enough* about money. His family have all pressed him to marry a rich wife, for the good of the estate, but he refuses."

"Good," said Red. "In that case, I need not worry. You are quite safe from him."

Abigail was stung by her father's sarcasm. "He is too proud to marry for money."

"He has convinced you, I see. Tell me, when he discovers your dark secret, do you imagine his pride will *prevent* him from marrying you? Perhaps he has other, less amiable qualities which will make the arrangement palatable to him. Such as greed, perhaps?"

For once, Abigail refused to be cowed by him. "You think him a mercenary, but you do not know him. He has many fine qualities. Indeed, in some ways I think he is quite heroic. Did you know that, when he was only eighteen, he left University and enlisted in the ranks? He fought in Spain for nearly two years. He might have been killed."

"I wish he had been! That he should not have lived to trifle with my child!"

"Do you not think it heroic?" Abigail insisted. "He might easily have stayed at Oxford and never known a moment's danger."

"What does it signify, child?" he said impatiently. "*You* don't need a hero. You are not standing in the path of an advancing army. The only danger you are in is the danger of making a foolish match. What you need is a steady, sensible, dependable fellow with a good head on his shoulders, plenty of money of his own, and, of course, a title. You owe it to yourself, you owe it to your mother, and you owe it to me. After all, I have invested a great deal in your upbringing, your gowns, your jewels, and your education. I have spared no expense. I will not see you throw yourself away on something as paltry as a *hero*."

"You think I ought to have married Dulwich instead, don't you?" Abby cried. "Well, he *was* a fortune hunter. You were going to pay him fifty thousand pounds!"

"A bargain price! Don't forget, he stands to inherit an earldom when Lord Inchmery dies. I don't mind fortune hunters, Abigail, provided the man has something to offer in exchange. A man with a title needn't be ashamed of holding out for a rich wife. Nobody likes to see an impoverished earl, after all. It hurts the whole country. Dulwich turned out to be all wrong for you, but that doesn't mean we give up. It was your mother's wish that I return you to the sphere she was forced to quit when she married me. I promised her."

"Mama would want me to be happy," she protested. "And I am convinced she would not hold Mr. Wayborn in contempt. For that matter, he is her relation. He is a gentleman. His brother is a baronet. And if his estate is not perfectly solvent now, it will be in my power to make it so. When you married Mama, you performed a similar service to her father, I believe."

This proved to be her most incendiary statement thus far. "How dare you compare your sainted mother to this worthless scoundrel? I swear to almighty God, Abigail, if you marry this man over my objections, I shall have no choice but to cut you off. When I said I'd not extend him a farthing in credit, I meant it. He'll never see a penny from me, living or dead. I'll make certain he knows it too. I daresay his interest in you will take a little turn when he hears *that*."

Abigail closed her eyes. Here was the rift she had dreaded more than anything, but now that the blow had fallen she felt curiously calm. There was nothing more to fear. "I have money of my own, Papa," she said quietly. "I am twenty-one. I am free to choose my own husband, surely. That is the law. Naturally, you are free to do as you please with your own money."

This was not the reply Red had expected. In all her life, Abigail had never seriously opposed him. Any difference of opinion between father and daughter had always been settled in his favor with very little fuss. He found her sudden show of determination quite disturbing.

"Abby!" he said plaintively. "I cannot believe you are quarreling with me over this worthless young man! We who never quarrel, but are as close as father and daughter can be. You have always been the most dutiful of daughters. I can only take this as a sign of the man's unhealthy influence over you."

"We never quarrel, Papa, because I always give in," she answered with the same eery calm that threatened his peace in a way tears and hysterics would not have done. "And I have always given in because I want you to be happy."

"And now you no longer care if I am happy, is that it, lass? I'm only your father."

"I'm sorry if you are unhappy, sir," she said, amazed by her own indifference.

"Abigail, you will not defy me!" he railed. "You may be twenty-one, but I am still your father. I know what is best for you. When you have had time to reflect on this regrettable business, you will see that I am right. You will thank me for keeping you from making such a bad bargain."

"Marriage is not a bargain, Papa."

"No, it is speculation! Would you put your entire future at risk simply because a good-looking man paid you a little attention? I know the sort of man he is, too: so conceited he can never rest until every girl in the room is in love with him. I suppose you think he loves you."

Abigail sighed. No, she could not claim that Cary loved her. He had never said so.

Her father sensed capitulation in her sigh. "Don't be too unhappy, Abigail," he said with a relish she could not help but despise. "You are not the first girl to be taken in by that chancy young man, I'll warrant. But he will soon be got over. I will buy you the prettiest phaeton I can find. You shall have driving lessons, and a pair of snow-white high-steppers or high-flyers or whatever it is you young people call horses these days."

Abigail's shoulders slumped in despair. Undoubtedly, her continually meek acquiescence to his wishes over the years had given her father the impression that he could always bully her into submission or else buy her cooperation with expensive gifts. She could not blame him for thinking to do so now. Nor could she see any way to break out of the lifelong trap. To continue to argue now would only lay her open to more bullying and more presents, and the end result would be the same. Once his mind was made up, Red was implacable. She had never known him to change his mind; he had certainly never done so due to her influence.

She would have to run away.

Relieved as he was that Abigail had capitulated after such a disconcerting show of spirit, Red was nonetheless sorry for her disappointment, and willing to lay out any amount of money to secure her return to happiness. "Now you are back in London, there is no end to what we can do," he wheedled. "I have not taken you to Vauxhall in some months. And at the end of the season, it will be in my power to take you abroad if you like."

Abigail was frankly astonished. "Abroad!"

"Yes. Now the war is over, why not?"

"You would not take me to Wiltshire to see Stonehenge, even though you promised."

"I had thought Florence or the Black Forest, but if you prefer Wiltshire, I have no objection. And, this time, should my business keep me in London, I shall engage a chaperone for you. Then you may go anywhere you like."

The sudden image of Mrs. Spurgeon among the chateaux of the Loire Valley, demanding an English Beaujolais of the maitre d'hotel, caused Abigail to smile.

Red was moved by that tiny smile to even higher flights of generosity. "I will give you an allowance of ten thousand pounds," he declared. "And we shall never speak of this unhappy matter again."

"No," she agreed. "It does seem rather pointless to try."

"Why, I begin to think you meant to give him up all the time," he remarked suddenly, to her immense consternation. "You sly thing! You only pretended more affection than you felt when you saw you could get carriages and trips abroad out of your poor father, Scotsman though I am. But that is all my fault. I gave away too much of what I felt."

"As you say, we shall never speak of it again," she said, getting up to quit the room.

"Yes, yes," he murmured contentedly. "Run along up to your room and put on your costume. I shall have to leave within the hour, and I don't see why you shouldn't accompany me to Carlton House. No one will object if you amuse yourself on the grounds as we prepare for the event. You will see them light the torches in the gardens. I am told it is a magnificent sight."

Abigail paused on the threshold. "No," she said clearly.

His good humor vanished instantly. "No?" he echoed

in an awful tone. "Abigail, there has been enough foolishness, I think. You will do as I say, and you will do it at once."

"I forgot to tell you," said his daughter. "The Duke of Auckland has invited me to see the play tonight. He asked for the honor of escorting me to Carlton House afterwards. Was that not very kind of his grace?"

"The Duke of Auckland?" he cried. "Why did you not say so before? Small wonder you gave up Mr. Wayborn so easily, when you may have a duke dangling on the line."

"Then do I have your permission to go?" she asked.

"Yes, of course! But I have not engaged any tickets for you!" he cried.

"The Duke has his own box, Papa," she told him. "I am his guest."

"Oh, yes, of course. I do forget sometimes that I am not the *only* rich man in the world. Of course you must go, Abby, love. I may see you a duchess yet!"

"That is not very likely, sir."

"Give it time," he urged. "He's taking you to the theater, isn't he? That's something. At the very least, you'll meet his friends. People will see you in his company and think the better of you for it. He must know all the lords of the land. I'd be just as happy to see you a marchioness or a countess. Pray, do not feel you must marry the Duke if you find you do not like him."

Abigail did what she had been longing to do for some time; she ran away.

At least her father had not sought to impose an Egyptian costume upon his pale, freckled, strawberry-blond daughter. Abigail's Roman costume began with a long, simple, high-waisted tunic of fine white linen. The sleeves of the tunic were not sewn but rather pinned together at the shoulders and again at the elbow with golden brooches that looked like miniature bunches of grapes. Over this she was to wear a deep purple velvet palla, richly trimmed in gold fringe. The palla was meant to be artfully draped over one shoulder, but, as the heavy material kept slipping, Abigail decided to leave it in the carriage during the play. She wished she could do the same with the gold kid sandals; they laced halfway up her calves and were exceedingly uncomfortable. She pinned her short curls up in a style she told herself was at least Greek, if not Roman, and added a wreath of laurel leaves made of beaten gold. As a final touch she found a beautiful old set of agate cameos and put them on—a bracelet, earrings, and a necklace she could not recall ever having worn before. Her appearance, when she checked it in the mirror, was ever so slightly ridiculous, which is what one wants when one attends a masquerade.

The enormous coach with blue doors and silver wheels arrived in Park Lane at six o'clock on the nose, to be immediately filled by Miss Wayborn's servants with huge quantities of hothouse roses. The heavy scent was overpowering, and there was scarcely enough room for Miss Wayborn to sit when she arrived in person some twenty-five minutes later dressed as a young and seductive Cleopatra. Her long dark hair was decorated with gold coins. Her eyelids had been painted peacock blue, and her eyes and brows were lined heavily with kohl. Her dress was composed of ephemeral layers of finely pleated gold linen, and at her neck was an enormous gold collar encrusted with lapis lazuli scarabs. On her feet were curved gold slippers.

Abigail could only stare. If not precisely beautiful, Juliet was easily the most terrifying, dazzling creature she had ever seen. She had meant to cordially inquire whether Miss Wayborn was feeling better, but the banal words died in her throat.

"You're late," Juliet informed Abigail, giving her costume only a cursory glance. "But at least you had the sense to come as a Roman matron."

"I was here at six," Abigail protested indignantly.

"Well, you ought to have known my servants would need time to put my roses in," Juliet replied as the carriage got underway. "Now there will be a terrible crush at the front entrance."

Abigail winced. "You don't really mean to throw all these flowers to that actor, do you?"

Juliet looked at her with long, inscrutable Egyptian eyes. "Well, that all depends, doesn't it, on what *he* does with his cabbages?"

"I'm quite sure his grace does not really mean to throw cabbages at Mr. Rourke."

Juliet looked at her contemptuously. "Of course he won't, you stupid girl. Because *I* have brought roses."

Somehow Abigail suppressed the urge to throttle her sister-in-law.

As Juliet had predicted, the throng of pedestrians and carriages at the front of the theater was beyond belief. Juliet rapped sharply for the driver, and, when he opened the panel, she instructed him to go around the back way. "It's always like this when the Royal Family crawl out of their palaces," she told Abigail. "What do we buy them palaces for, if not to keep them in? I'm convinced they only come out to spoil it for everyone else."

Abigail felt an undignified excitement. "Will the Queen be here, do you think?"

"Certainly not. No, tonight is the Prince Regent's night out. He's not much to look at, if you ask me, but my aunt swears he was dead handsome in his youth. Ah, here we are."

Juliet jumped out, the coins in her hair clinking like bells. Immediately, she began snapping her fingers for servants to transport her roses into the theater. Abigail exited the coach with greater caution. They appeared to be in a dark, deserted alley.

A door opened ahead of them, pouring light and noise onto the street. Juliet's roses began filing into the building, the heads and bodies of the servants carrying them scarcely visible behind the wall of scarlet and white blooms and green leaves.

"Come along, Cousin Abigail," Juliet commanded. "Come and meet Mr. Rourke."

Chapter 18

At first Abigail could discern nothing in the confusion. The place looked as though someone had begun building a scaffold in the middle of it, then abandoned the project abruptly. People wearing a multiplicity of costumes, mostly Egyptian or Roman, milled about to no purpose that Abigail could see. A group of young women, scantily clad, with flowers in their hair, was singing in one corner, and, though there were plenty of men about, none seemed to be paying the girls the slightest attention. "What is this place?" Abigail asked.

"Isn't it exciting?" said Juliet. "You're behind the stage. Ever been before?"

Abigail mutely shook her head. It was much too loud and busy to suit her. A large man naked from the waist up except for a large papier-mache mask in the shape of a jackal's head suddenly loomed over her, pushing her out of the way. Laughing, Juliet pulled Abigail around a corner and down a narrow set of stairs crowded with actors and dancers who all seemed to be coming up at once in their dazzling costumes. Then they were in a long, bare hall lit by sconces.

Mr. David Rourke was in his dressing room applying greasepaint to his famous face. On stage he was considered handsome, but in the lamplight he looked grotesque to Abigail. He was dressed for his role as Marc Antony in a purple toga, and not much else. His hair had been cut short in the Roman crop he had made fashionable. A golden breastplate and a short scarlet tunic, which he would wear in later scenes in the play, waited on a dressmaker's dummy in one corner. When the actor stood up to greet Juliet, Abigail saw that he was not tall. She did not find him very attractive, but then, she reflected, few men could measure up to the physical perfections of Cary Wayborn.

The Irishman had no lack of confidence, however. He boldly kissed Juliet on both cheeks in the continental manner. "My dear Miss Wayborn!" he said while Abigail cringed in the corner next to a large box covered in a scarlet cloth. "I wish I could put you on stage, just as you are, but, alas, my Cleopatra is old and fat."

He spoke without any trace of brogue, and yet Abigail thought he could never be mistaken for an Englishman.

"Mrs. Archer is scarcely that," Juliet answered him demurely. "I wish I could go on stage, too, Mr. Rourke, but that would never do. It's so unfair. We just came to tell you to break a leg."

To Abigail's horror, the famed actor suddenly looked at her. She felt like a rabbit that has suddenly been spotted by a hungry lion. She wasn't even sure how she had gotten into this stuffy little room in the first place. Now she wasn't quite sure she would ever be permitted to leave. Mr. Rourke's kohl-lined eyes were pale, but whether green, blue, or gray she could not tell. His smile was crocodilian. She thought him the least trustworthy person she had ever met.

Mr. Rourke bowed, but, to her relief, he made no attempt to kiss her continentally, or even to shake hands.

"And who is this charming creature? Another devotee of the theater?"

"This is my cousin, Abigail. Tell Mr. Rourke to break a leg, Abigail."

Abigail blinked at Juliet, bewildered.

Mr. Rourke smiled, creasing his painted cheeks. "You must tell me to break a leg so that I shall have good luck in my performance tonight," he explained.

"I see," Abigail said slowly. "It's all backwards, then."

"Yes. If you were to wish me luck, the theater gods would surely turn against me."

"In that case," she said. "I hope you fall and break *both* your legs. And your arms, too."

Mr. Rourke laughed. "I think she's got it, Miss Wayborn. Now get her out of here before she breaks my neck. Enjoy the performance," he added as Juliet dragged Abigail away.

"I'm sure I will," said Abigail. "No, I beg your pardon! I'm sure I *won't.*"

Juliet lost her grip on Abigail's hand as they went back up the stairs. Abigail could just make out the back of Juliet's head as she struggled against the flow of bodies. By keeping those glittering gold coins in sight, she was able to navigate through the worst of the traffic. But at the top of the steps a huge wall painted to resemble a battlefield in Syria was suddenly pulled across her path. When it was gone, so was Juliet. Frantically, Abigail scanned the crowd. There were dozens of young women in Egyptian-style dress, but none of them was Juliet.

A shout began at one end of the room, and, gradually, a hush fell over the crowd.

"Places, everyone!" someone shouted with authority.

The famed Mrs. Archer, surrounded by her women, a crown of peacock feathers on her sleek head, suddenly floated past. As Abigail stood on tiptoe to see the "real" Cleopatra, a man suddenly blocked her path.

"Are you Octavia's understudy?" he asked suspiciously.

"No, I'm Abigail," she answered without thinking.

"There is no Abigail," he said, frowning, as he consulted his playbook.

"I'm not in the play," Abigail explained. "I'm meant to be watching the play from a box. I'm lost, you see. Could you show me the way? I can pay you," she quickly added as the man turned away. A gold sovereign secured his interest, but she pulled it away quickly as he made to snatch it. "You'll have it when you take me to the Duke of Auckland's box," she said firmly.

"Lucky for you, I don't go on until Act Three," he muttered. "This way."

As it happened, it was not necessary for him to conduct her all the way to the Duke's box. The Duke was waiting for her at the top of the carpeted stairs. The red-haired giant still was not handsome, but he had evidently taken great pains with his appearance. He wore a black evening coat with white satin breeches and buckled shoes. His waistcoat was a beautiful silk and silver pattern. "There you are, girl," he said gruffly as Abigail paid the man from Act Three. The Duke's rough North Country accent was an odd contrast to Mr. Rourke's polished English.

"I hope you break your legs," Abigail called after her native guide, as the Duke dragged her towards his box. The box was like a miniature theater in itself, screened from the corridor by heavy red velvet curtains. The Duke impatiently went before her. Abigail took a deep breath as she entered. The time had come for her to tell the horrible Miss Wayborn just what she thought of her. This time she would really do it. She would not be timid.

She began with a very firm apology.

"I beg your pardon, Miss Wayborn, but, really, you must own that it was very wrong of you to leave me behind stage . . ."

She trailed off as her eyes adjusted to the dimly lit box. She was addressing a small collection of red velvet chairs. "Where is everyone?" she asked the Duke.

"Over there," he darkly replied.

Abigail followed his outstretched finger with her eyes. Cary and Juliet Wayborn were in a box almost directly across from theirs, on the opposite side of the theater. Their gilded box was filled with huge bouquets of roses. Juliet was seated in the forefront, and her brother was standing behind her. Like the Duke, Cary was not in costume, but wore correct evening dress. Abigail caught her breath as she realized he was looking directly at her. The longing to be with him and to feel his arms around her was very strong.

"But I thought we were all to share a box, sir," she cried in dismay. "What are they doing over there? And what," she added with a grimace, "is that disgusting smell?"

Grinning at her, the Duke stepped over one chair to sit in another. "Good news," he declared proudly. "My man was able to find some *potatoes*. I think they've got the famine, too."

"You mean the blight," Abigail said severely.

"Blight. Famine." The Duke shrugged carelessly. "The important thing is that they will remind Rourke of dear old Ireland and hasten him on his way back there. Sit down, my dear. Mind your step."

Abigail delicately skirted a few baskets of malodorous kitchen offal to take the seat next to him. "You don't really mean to throw things at Mr. Rourke, do you? It's too cruel!"

"*She* brought her roses, I see," he darkly replied.

Abigail looked across. Cary was motioning to her. Hesitantly, she waved back.

"Look at her, the worthless jade. I swear she only makes herself so bloody gorgeous to give me fits. That's actually your uncle's box, you know. I could have her tossed out at any moment. She hasn't even got a bloody ticket!"

"My uncle's, sir? Lord Wayborn's, you mean?"

He nodded, his eyes fastened on Juliet, who seemed to have eyes only for the stage, even though the curtain had not yet lifted. "Earl Wayborn is not yet come to London from Derbyshire, I'll warrant, and she's helping herself to his property in the poor man's absence. I daresay if he were to show up unexpectedly, she'd just casually murder him and throw his carcass over the side. Why does her brother keep waving at me? It's bloody annoying."

"I think he's waving to me, sir."

"Just ignore him," the Duke advised. "He's harmless. Keep your eye on *her*. *She's* the troublemaker. And if she wants to start a war, I shall be happy to oblige her! I've got bushels and bushels of vegetables, and I'm not afraid to use them."

At that moment the Prince Regent arrived, eliciting a standing ovation from his subjects. Abigail nearly fell out of the box trying to get a look at the future king. His Royal Highness was perhaps a bit past his prime, a bit bloated, but to Abigail he was like something out of a fairy tale. As he settled into a prominent seat behind the orchestra pit, the house lights were brought down, the stage lights were brought up, and the curtains rose to reveal Cleopatra's palace at Alexandria, where Antony, once a great general, had become the pet of Egypt's queen.

Cary did not wait long. Before the second scene was done, a servant brought a note to the Duke's box on a silver salver. The Duke snatched it before Abigail could move. "'Meet me at the top of the stairs. Yours, etc.,'" he read contemptuously, and tossed it into the nearest basket. "Not bloody likely! As though I should be taken in by such an obvious trick. Trying to get your brother to lure me away, so that you can throw your roses behind my back, eh?" His voice rose as he called to Juliet across the theater. "You'll have to do better than that, my dear!"

Cary pointed at Abigail, then walked his gloved fingers across his open palm.

"Perhaps I should go and see what he wants," Abigail said slowly.

"Good idea," said the crafty Duke. "Keep him occupied. Don't let him out of your sight. I'll watch *her*. But be careful, Abigail. She's up to something. I know it. I can feel it in the air. And that brother of hers could very well be in on it. He never liked me."

"I'll be very careful, sir," Abigail assured him, picking her way out of the box.

It was all she could do not to cry out when she saw Cary coming towards her from the other end of the corridor. A servant passed them carrying a tray of wineglasses, but she did not care. She ran to him and flung her arms around his neck. Relief flooded through her body as he embraced her. She held him as tightly as she could. His coat, which she could now see was not black but a very dark aubergine, smelled strongly of roses. She could only hope she did not smell of decaying spuds.

"Oh, my poor darling," Cary murmured in her hair. "What you must be suffering with that oaf." Behind her back, she could feel him peeling off his gloves. In the next moment his warm hands slipped around the nape of her neck. Guiding her face up to his, he began to kiss her very softly, as if afraid of injuring her. Abigail shivered at the barest contact between his skin and hers.

"He's filled the box with onion skins and rotting

cabbages and black potatoes," she complained. "It's unspeakably foul. And your sister is an absolute menace."

"Well, it's all right, now," he said, covering her mouth with his own and working her back into the curtains lining the wall, which he proceeded to pull around them as he continued kissing her. At first Abigail kissed him back passionately, but as the kiss deepened and she felt his hands stray to her breasts, she began to pull away. Blinded to everything else in his pursuit of pleasure, Cary trailed fiery kisses down her neck and his hands moved firmly down the front of her belly, drawing up her linen skirts in his fists. "I've missed you, Smith," he murmured huskily. "You have no idea how much I want you right now." He caught her hand and drew it to the front of his trousers. "Look what you've done to me."

Abigail snatched her hands away.

This Cary could not fail to notice.

"I thought perhaps you might want to talk to me," she said tartly, pushing her way out of the velvet curtains. Fortunately, at that moment, the corridor was empty. "Remember talking? It seems to me that all you ever want to do is . . . is *maul* me. I should like to think we might have *some* conversation sometime."

"What shall we discuss?" he asked. His voice was light but he was frowning. "How do you like the play so far? Do you think it will rain?"

Abigail was suddenly very angry. It seemed to her that she had been enduring abuse all day, from his sister, from her father, and from the Duke. From him she had expected comfort. But theirs, she reminded herself, was purely a physical relationship, at least on his side. Suddenly, she couldn't bear to be just a desirable body to him.

"Am I supposed to forget that you called me a thief?" she snapped. "Just because you kissed me? Well, you are not *quite* so fascinating as you seem to think."

"I was working up to an apology," he said in an injured voice.

"Oh, yes?"

"You threw your arms around *me*, Smith," he pointed out. "You started it. I was simply minding my own business. I had a lovely apology all worked out, in fact, and then you . . . you ruined it by attacking me with your amazingly soft little—"

"Augh!" said Abigail.

"Easy for you to say," he observed without rancor. "Here," he added, pulling a flat blue velvet jewel box out of his pocket. "I brought you something."

Abigail thought she would burst into tears. This was her father's way of making amends, and she detested it. "Cary, you can't just buy me a present and think all will be forgiven."

"I didn't," he said. "Why on earth would I buy *you* a present? They're yours, I think."

Puzzled, and suspecting a trick, Abigail opened the box. "My pearls!" she exclaimed. "What on earth are *you* doing with them?"

"I'm returning them to you, of course. Didn't you know they'd been stolen?" he asked, with considerable amusement.

"I've got a lot of pearls," she said defensively. "I don't actually like the clasp on these ones. Did I leave them at your house, then? Why do you say they were stolen?"

"Because, Smith, they *were* stolen, along with my grandmama's punch bowl and an assortment of other plunder, which has also been recovered. Would you like me to mind them for you?" he asked presently, observing her rather ostentatious set of Italian cameos. "Your neck seems pretty well decorated at the moment."

"Does this mean you caught the thief, and got it all back?" she asked as he pocketed her pearls again.

"That's wonderful, Cary. It is. I didn't mean to snap at you."

He laughed. "No, monkey. The thief remains at large. But when I went back to Bow Street, there was Mr. Leighton, turning in all my silver and your silly-clasped pearls."

"Mr. Leighton! *My* Mr. Leighton?"

"I hadn't realized he was your own personal Mr. Leighton, but, yes. Apparently, the thief was a member of the unhappy man's household. Namely, one Evans."

"Good heavens!" cried Abigail.

His mouth twitched. "That's just what I said."

"Mrs. Spurgeon's maid? How dreadful! And she took my pearls from my room? How very impertinent."

"Never mind your pearls, Smith. You've got them back. What about my miniatures? They easily discovered my silver and your pearls in the culprit's room. But they didn't know about my missing miniatures, and she was allowed to pack her trunk and leave the house."

"They let her get away?" Abigail said incredulously. "A proven thief?"

"Naturally, they turned her off without a character. I'm sure your personal Mr. Leighton didn't want to go through the trouble and expense of a trial. *I* certainly don't. And I wouldn't care to see the old girl hanged either. Would you?"

"No, of course not. But she might be transported to Australia! Your miniatures, Cary," she said unhappily. "They were worth so much money."

"I don't care three straws for those miniatures," he declared. "I never even looked at them before you came to Tanglewood."

"I'm surprised you even bothered to come to London to report them missing!"

"I didn't."

"What are you talking about?" she said impatiently.

"Of course you did. You went to Bow Street and hired the Runners, didn't you?"

"Not to find my bloody miniatures, you silly woman. I hired them to find *you*." He leaned against the wall and casually examined his fingernails. "When I thought you'd cleaned me out and you weren't coming back, it was the not coming back part that upset me. I thought I was never going to see you again, Smith. It's been a pretty rough couple of days for me, in fact, what with you appearing and disappearing like a mirage in the desert."

Abigail's breath caught in her throat.

"Of course," he went on, "the instant I saw you in Hatchard's, I realized you couldn't possibly have stolen my silver. My only excuse is that I've never been in love before, not really, and it's hard to think clearly when one is in love. What I thought was up, seems to be down, and all the rest of it is just topsy-turvy. All I knew for certain was that, if there was the slightest possibility you meant to leave me forever, I had to do something desperate."

"Cary," she gasped. "Are you saying that you love me?"

"Without much success, apparently. It's bloody hard to say, isn't it? When one means it, that is. When one doesn't mean it, it just sort of rolls off the tongue. Have you noticed that?"

"No," she said. "Are you in the habit of saying it when you don't mean it?"

"I shouldn't call it a habit," he said defensively. "But I admit there have been occasions when I have said it merely to avoid the appearance of being a complete cad."

"I see," said Abigail, biting her lip. "I wish you wouldn't say it then."

"What? I love you?"

Abigail shuddered. "Don't say it again, please. It's not something I care to hear."

"Really?" He seemed amused. "Most people seem

to like hearing it. *I* certainly do. Let me be sure I understand you. You *don't* want me to say that I love you ever again?"

"Yes," she said firmly.

"Yes, you *do* want me to say that I love you?"

"No, I don't."

"Well, of course you don't want me to say I love you *now*. That would be repetitive. But, perhaps, at some later date? On Thursday, if you are not otherwise engaged?"

"No, Cary. Never," she said through gritted teeth.

"All right, Smith. I solemnly swear never to tell you I love you on a Thursday. But, wait. What if your birthday falls on a Thursday? Surely I may tell you I love you on your birthday?"

He was actually laughing at her.

"You are *never* to say you love me again," she said furiously. "Ever. Not on any day of the week. Not on my birthday. Not on *your* birthday either," she added as he opened his mouth. "Never again, Cary. If you do, I shall *hit* you!"

"What about . . . *je t'adore*? *Te amo*?"

"Not in any language!"

"Then you ought to have said *jamais*. When one is determined to talk rubbish, one should always do so in French."

"Don't you dare say I am talking rubbish. You're the one talking rubbish."

Abigail turned on her heel and walked away. She did not get very far. He was suddenly in front of her. "Tell me, Smith. Have you ever stood your ground in a fight? Or do you always run away?"

"I don't want to fight with you," she said, forcing herself to stand still.

"No, indeed," he murmured. "You merely want absolute power over my vocabulary. So far, you wish to strike 'I love you' and 'rubbish' from the lexicon, the two mainstays of any civilized conversation between married people."

"It's all a joke to you, isn't it?" she said angrily.

He folded his arms and looked at her with mocking gravity. "I'll tell you what, Smith. If you can give me one good reason why I shouldn't tell you I love you whenever I please, I'll consider it. I don't take commands, but I like to think I can always be persuaded by a rational argument. If you've got one, let's hear it."

Abigail lifted her chin. "Because you don't."

"I don't what? Come now, Smith. You wanted to talk. Let's talk."

"You don't love me, Cary," she said, forcing the words out. "It hurts me to hear you say it when I know you don't mean it. It rolls off your tongue, I know, but I'd rather not hear it, if you don't mind. And I don't *need* to hear it, if that is what you think. I know that ours is not that sort of marriage."

He drew back. "I see. And 'rubbish'?"

"What?" she said sharply.

"As I understand it, your primary objection to my saying 'I love you' is that I don't mean it. Is your objection to my saying rubbish *also* that I don't mean it?"

"No, *that* I think you mean. I'm sure *everything* I say is rubbish to you."

"You can't have it both ways, Smith. You can't object to my saying one thing because I *don't* mean it, then turn around and object to my saying something else because I *do*. It leaves me nowhere to go, if you see what I mean."

"Very well!" she said crossly. "I don't care if you say 'rubbish.' Say it as much as you please. But you will *not* tell me you love me when you don't mean it."

"My dear Smith, that gives me leave to say it whenever

I like," he said, laughing. "Is that not what you hoped
to avoid?"

A young man suddenly appeared in the corridor and
hailed Cary in good-natured, affable, slurring speech of
little sense and long duration. "That Cleopatra woman
has got her bubbies half out, so Mama has sent me to
fetch lemonade," he concluded. "May I get you some,
Wayborn? Some for your lady friend?"

"Not now, Budgie," Cary growled at him. "I'm telling
the woman I love that she is, in fact, the woman I love.
It's what you might call a private moment."

"Oh, well done," the young man murmured, studying
Abigail with interest. "Would you like some lemonade,
miss? I'm just going now to fetch some for my mama,
so it's no trouble."

Abigail was staring at Cary and did not hear him.

"I say! I know you, don't I?" Budgie slurred, scratch-
ing his head.

Abigail glanced at him. "Certainly not," she said
sharply. "Do go away."

"You heard her," said Cary. "Biff off!"

"Oh, right. I'm just getting lemonade," he explained,
biffing off with surprising skill and speed, almost as if
he had biffed before.

"Cary, do you mean it?" she asked carefully. "You're
not just teasing me?"

He raised an eyebrow. "That would be rather cruel,
don't you think?"

"Yes, it would be."

"I love you," he repeated, looking down at her. "You
believe me, don't you, monkey?"

Abigail felt her insides melting and tears welling up
in her eyes. "Yes, monkey, I do."

"Good," he said curtly. "Because I'm never going to
say it again as long as I live. It's too bloody hard on my
nerves." A smattering of applause from inside the

theater distracted him. "Look here, that's the end of Act One. I'd better take you back to Auckland."

The Duke spared Cary and Abigail only a very cursory glance. "You're in the enemy camp now, Cary," he grunted as Abigail took her seat. "Are you a spy or a traitor? Julie seems to think you are a traitor," he added a little gleefully as, across the way, Miss Wayborn turned her jeweled head away with an angry toss.

"I am neither, sir," Cary replied, covering his nose with his handkerchief to ward off the heavy odor of rotting cabbages. "I am remaining neutral in the quarrel between my charming sister and yourself. To that end, I think it only fair that I divide my time evenly between you."

"Are you going to watch the second act with us?" The Duke rubbed his hands together. "That ought to roast her pride nicely."

Abigail turned in her seat to look at Cary. "Yes, do stay."

"Perhaps a trade?" Cary suggested. "I'll sit here with Abigail and you have a go at Julie."

The Duke snorted. "Oh, yes! And whilst I am making my way over there, she blows kisses at Mr. Rourke! I didn't come down with the last shower, you know. Besides, my vegetables are here. You're welcome to stay, Cary, but I'm not moving."

Cary's eyes were laughing. "I cannot leave my sister alone. There's no telling what she'll do. But I will see you again very soon, Smith," he added, bowing over Abigail's hand. "Perhaps I might procure you a glass of lemonade at intermission?"

She had to be content with that.

"Well?" said the Duke, when he had gone. "What did he want?"

"I could not find it out, sir," she answered. "Perhaps if I met him again . . ."

Anxiously, she watched the opposite box until Cary appeared in it. Juliet turned away from the traitor with a ferocious scowl. On the stage, the prodigal Antony made his excuses to Caesar in Rome, and some of the play seemed to penetrate the Duke's intense concentration on his estranged lady. "Listen to that pretty fellow, Annabel! 'I am not married, Caesar.' You see what a lover he is! He's perfectly willing to give up Cleopatra and marry that wretched Octavia creature, just to grease his path with Caesar. That's an Irishman for you."

"You mustn't confuse Mr. Rourke with the character he is playing," Abigail protested. "They are not one and the same, you know. For one thing, Antony is not Irish."

"It's Cleopatra I feel sorry for. *She* thinks he loves her, poor little mite."

Abigail suddenly jumped to her feet, upsetting a basket of potatoes.

"Mind the garbage, if you please!" he said, annoyed.

"Oh, I beg your pardon," she said breathlessly, scooting for the exit. "But Mr. Wayborn has just left the box."

"Has he? Go and see if you can find out what Julie means to do at intermission."

They met in almost the same place and dove into the curtains immediately. "I've missed you so much," he whispered, pressing her against the corridor wall.

"It's only been two scenes," she protested, laughing. "Antony hasn't even met Octavia."

"It's not me," he explained. "It's the prime minister. He needs to see the Queen on a matter of great national interest."

Abigail squirmed as his tongue tickled her ear. "Is that not perhaps an exaggeration, sir?"

"You tell me," he muttered, placing himself in her hands.

Abigail was as shocked as ever by the intimacy, but her hand closed around the stiff warm flesh instinctively. The madness of unbridled lust welled up in her. It was useless to resist it. "Not here, please," she begged. "Anyone passing by would know what we're doing."

"What do you have in mind?" he said in a strained voice.

"My carriage is outside," she said shyly. "The seats fold down."

Cary burst out laughing. "Very civilized, I'm sure. But we'd never make it. Come with me," he said, grabbing her hand. Holding up his trousers with the other, he burst out of the curtains with her and they took off running down the hall, to the considerable surprise of a small conclave of theater attendants who were throwing dice on the landing.

Cary led her quickly and stealthily into the dark interstices of the theater. The next thing Abigail could tell with any certainty, she was in a small dark room. He pushed her up against the door and kissed her hard, holding her there with his body while he used his hands to strip off his coat. "The couch," he said urgently. "For God's sake, lie down for me."

Almost as distracted as he was, Abigail managed to find the lumpy sofa and had shoved some of the clothes piled on top of it out of the way before he caught her around the hips. She realized he was going to take her from behind, as he had done the night they had both taken too much laudanum. She remembered this method with ravenous pleasure.

Suddenly he groaned. "Drawers, Abby?" he said roughly, turning her about to face him. "What are you trying to do to me?"

"Sorry!" She jumped up and slipped the pantalets off hurriedly. The next moment he was lodged as far into her as he could go. As one person they fell to the couch, panting madly, his head on her breast. "Say you love me," she begged. "Say it again."

"I love you," he said over and over again as he drove into her, turning the blood in her veins to wine. Her pleasure was so intense that for a brief moment she slipped away. When she came to, Cary was kissing her gently. The storm had passed for him as well, and his dark body was quiet and warm in her arms. "You like that, don't you, monkey?"

She could feel him inside her still, stirring softly, without urgency. "Yes, I like it. Say it again," she begged him. "I love to hear it."

"Yes, indeed. It's very nice to hear, isn't it?" he said, beginning to withdraw.

"No, not yet," she murmured, squeezing him between her legs. Knowing that she wanted him again so soon aroused him. The drugged sound of her voice, the light, flowery scent she wore coupled with the deeper, animal smell of their lovemaking spurred him on. "Love me," Abigail urged over and over again, her head lolling from side to side. "Say you love me."

But she never said the words herself, he noticed; no matter how wild with pleasure he drove her beautiful, soft body, Abigail's heart remained locked away from him. Knowing that there was a part of her he could not touch filled him with sorrow, a sorrow he would never share with her because he knew that if Abigail guessed he was unhappy and why, her accommodating nature would lead her to pretend a love she did not feel. That would be infinitely worse.

"I don't think I shall ever get enough of you," he murmured, drawing away from her reluctantly. "But then we've never had any worries in the bedroom, have we?"

"No, indeed. You always make me so happy." As she spoke, she knew that words were inadequate to describe her feelings. When their bodies were joined, she was in a continual state of bliss, but, when they parted, doubts of his love and fears of her own inadequacy assailed her. The only thing she could be sure of was her own love for him, which left her in a hideously vulnerable position.

"I wish we had more time." Cary was already hunting for his clothes. "But Antony is due for a costume change any moment now. I shouldn't like my wife to be caught in an actor's dressing room." He looked at her, a faint smile touching his lips. "Your crown is a bit askew."

"Antony?" she echoed, as he set her to rights. "Is this Mr. Rourke's dressing room?" Looking around she saw the familiar suit of Roman armor on the dressmaker's dummy. Mr. Rourke was going to need that very soon for his meeting with Pompey at Misenum. Abigail hastily left the couch to help Cary dress. "Oh, dear God," she cried in dismay. "What beasts we are! The poor man! His dressing room!"

"I daresay this isn't the first time Mr. Rourke's covert has served such a purpose," Cary remarked dryly. Pulling his shirt over his head, he added, "This is absolutely the last time we part, Abigail. I've had enough sneaking around."

"So have I," she said fervently.

"We'll go to the Regent's bloody masquerade. I'll explain everything to your good father. With any luck, he'll disown you on the spot. Then I can take you home to Tanglewood, and make love to you properly in our bed. How does that sound?"

"Perhaps it would be better if we didn't go to Carlton House at all," she said quickly. "I tried to talk to my father this afternoon. Cary, he hates you. Very likely he *will* disown me. We may as well go to Hertfordshire and just send him a message."

Cary frowned at her as he buttoned his trousers. "Run away, you mean? And spend the rest of our lives jumping behind counters when we see him in Town? No, Abigail. I shall tell him to his face that you are my wife. After all, he cannot hate me personally. Everybody loves me. I admit I *did have* something of a reputation in my youth. Drinking, gambling, making a general nuisance of myself. If your papa is a staunch Presbyterian gentleman—"

"Oh, he isn't," she said quickly. "I daresay he's not been in a church above five times in all his life. And he's not a gentleman. You might as well know it. He's in Trade."

He chuckled. "You mean he really *does* own a paper mill?"

"Among other things, yes."

He smiled at her fondly as he put on his coat. "My dear Smith, you don't actually think I give a damn about all that? I'm married to *you*, not your father. If he doesn't like it, he'll just have to jump in the Thames, that's all. For myself, I don't care who your father is. It could be bloody Red Ritchie for all I care."

Abigail nearly choked. "Do you mean that?"

He was rapidly knotting his cravat with the aid of Mr. Rourke's mirror. "Of course I mean it. Do you think Mr. Rourke would mind if I borrowed one of his costumes for the ball?" he said, picking up one of the actor's scarlet cloaks from a box in the corner of the room.

"Beaks and claws! Beaks and claws," a raucous and horribly familiar voice suddenly shrieked in the dark corner.

"No, it can't be!" Abigail breathed, her chest tightening.

Chapter 19

"Abby, get behind me," Cary said grimly as the voice continued squawking from inside the box. "Show yourself, sir!"

Crouching down, Abigail saw that it was not a box. It was a birdcage. The red cloak had been covering it. "It's not a man," she cried. "It's *Cato.*"

"It can't be." Cary joined her on the ground. "Cato's dead."

"Drawers, Abigail!" the macaw screamed at her.

Abigail turned white. "It *is* Cato, I tell you. Cary, he *knows*! He knows what we've been doing in here. You've got to get rid of him."

"Darling, this is irrational. Cato is dead. My dog ate him."

"Ride me sideways!"

"How dare you!" said Abigail, shaking her fist at the creature. "I *never* said that!"

"Well, don't look at me," said Cary, laughing.

She climbed to her feet. "Cary, he knows too much. You'll have to get rid of him."

"It's only a bird, Abigail," he told her sharply. "It

doesn't *know* anything. It's got a brain the size of a dried pea. It won't remember a blessed thing once we've gone."

"Only a bird, Abigail!"

"For God sake's, Cary, you've taught it my name!"

"Well, don't teach it mine," he snapped.

"Cary Wayborn, if you really do love me, you'll get rid of that bird."

"Get rid of it?" he said, flabbergasted. "Are you seriously suggesting that I *murder* a bird? Because it knows too much?"

"Cary, it knows my *name*. It heard us . . . coupling."

"Darling, you're not thinking clearly. There are lots of Abigails in the world. If the bloody thing does happen to say your name, Rourke will never know it's you."

"He *will* know it," said Abigail. "Your sister introduced us. I didn't want to come here. She made me. I told you, she's a menace. It's all her fault!"

"The best way to manage Julie is to push her down the stairs right away. After that, she's mild as milk." Now fully dressed, Cary knelt down to study the problem in the cage. "I suppose I *could* take him outside and let him fly away," he said reluctantly. "We'll scotch the bird, not kill it. All right, Lady Macbeth?"

"Yes, all right," she agreed breathlessly.

"You'd better get back upstairs before Auckland sends out a search party. I'll come 'round at intermission with some lemonade." He smiled at her. "Then, who knows? Perhaps I'll see you again in Act Three."

"You're not taking him out of his cage?" she cried in alarm as he reached for the bird.

"Don't worry. I can handle him."

Abigail shuddered. "Please wait until I'm gone. You know I don't like birds."

She dashed out of the room and closed the door behind her. There was no one in the hall, but, as she reached the top of the stairs a pair of men stepped out of the shadows, startling her.

"I beg your pardon," she breathed. In the next moment she was caught roughly around the waist. One man stuffed a cloth in her mouth and the other forced a huge burlap sack down over her head. Kicking in rage, she was lifted bodily off her feet and carried outside.

Cary, leaving Mr. Rourke's dressing room just a few minutes later with Mr. Rourke's macaw tucked inside his coat, noticed nothing amiss. Whistling softly, he let Rourke's macaw into one of the carriages outside, then wandered back into the theater.

"Where's Abigail?" he asked Juliet when he returned to their box. The Duke was sitting alone in his box across the theater.

"Where is my lemonade?" his sister responded crossly. "You were gone long enough."

Cary sat down, then stood up abruptly. "It's nearly intermission. I'm going to have a word with Auckland. I'll be back directly."

"What does she want now?" the Duke greeted Cary without the least civility.

"You'd have to ask her that," Cary replied. "I'm looking for Abigail."

The Duke never took his eyes off of Juliet. "She went to meet *you*, didn't she?"

"Yes, she—" Cary broke off, frowning. "You mean, she hasn't been back at all?"

"How can you let your sister out in public dressed like that?" The Duke caught Cary's arm. "She's going to meet Rourke at intermission, isn't she? Look, he's going off-stage now, the little pest. Can't you do something?"

Cary shook him off irritably. "I'm going to find Abby."

He spent the remainder of the play hunting for Abigail in the bowels of the theater, berating himself for having left her to make her way back to the Duke's box alone. She was nowhere near as familiar with the theater as he was, and had evidently gotten lost. Moreover, there were also highly disreputable people who hung about in theaters, preying upon the young actresses. In her Roman costume, Abigail might very well have been mistaken for one of them. As he described her to person after person, all to no avail, mild apprehension grew into panic.

When the play ended, to thunderous applause, the areas backstage filled with celebratory actors and their admirers. Caught in a throng on the stairs, Cary suddenly came face to face with David Rourke. Though still in costume, the Irishman had wiped most of the greasepaint from his face. He appeared to be in high spirits.

"Have you seen a girl about so high with butterscotch-colored hair?" Cary shouted above the din of laughter and gaiety from the crowd.

"Yes, your sister introduced us before the show!" Rourke shouted back.

"No, I mean, since then." As he shouted, Cary was being swept farther away by the pressure of the crowd.

"I'm missing a bird myself, sir," Rourke bellowed. "Scarlet macaw! Have you seen it by some chance?"

Cary was spared the embarrassment of having to answer by the sudden silence that descended oppressively over the throng on the stairs. The Prince Regent had come to congratulate his particular friend Mrs. Archer, preceded by an entourage of Home Guards.

The people on the stairs, Cary amongst them, were obliged to squash up against the walls. With no room to bow and scrape, the Regent's loyal subjects could only murmur, "Highness," and bow their heads as he passed.

"I know you, don't I?"

Cary looked up to find that the plump and bored fellow with heavily rouged cheeks was addressing him. "Your Highness is very kind," he replied courteously.

"You're the one with those pretty bay horses."

Cary gritted his teeth. "Chestnuts, Your Highness."

"Yes, of course. Your cousin's got the bays."

"Yes, but he hitches their heads up too high," Cary replied.

"He does, doesn't he?"

The Regent passed languidly on, and, before anyone else moved, Cary was able to escape up the stairs and continue his search. At long last, he found an actor who claimed to have conducted a young woman to the Duke of Auckland's box.

Full circle.

He made his way back to Auckland's box, going against the grain of the departing crowd, only to find that the Duke, presumably with Abigail, had already left the theater en route to Carlton House. Looking across the theater, he saw that Juliet had gone as well. Outside, the attendants assured him that the Duke of Auckland's carriage had been among the first to leave. There was nothing to do but go on to the Regent's residence alone. By walking, he escaped the crush of a hundred carriages all leaving the theater at once.

A guard was taking tickets at the gates of the Prince's residence, but this did not offer Cary much trouble. "Look here, Guard," he said, assuming an angry tone. "You've let that fellow in without a ticket! He looks like an assassin to me."

"What fellow? Where?"

Cary caught his arm before he dashed away. "No, no, no. You must never leave the gate unattended. I'll take care of him. In the future, be more careful, or I shall have to report you."

"Yes, sir! Thank you, sir!" the guard called after him gratefully.

A cursory glance around the front gardens established that neither Abigail nor the Duke were lingering among the shrubbery; the red-haired giant and the small girl with butterscotch hair could not have escaped his notice. At the main entrance to the house, he was stopped by the Master of Ceremonies. "I'm afraid no one is to be admitted inside without a costume, sir."

"Well?" Cary snapped. "Where *is* my costume? I was told it would be here, waiting for me. This isn't my first ball, you know. What sort of game are you running?"

"I beg your pardon, sir," the man stammered. "If you step right through that door, you will find the men's room. Attendants will assist you in finding your costume."

"I should bloody well hope so," Cary growled. He stepped through the door and helped himself to the costume of a captain of the Praetorian Guard.

"Whom shall I announce, sir?" the Master of Ceremonies inquired solicitously.

Cary looked past him into the crowded ballroom where Romans and Egyptians were crushed together in desperate gaiety. "I think I'll go incognito tonight. It *is* a masquerade, after all," he murmured, handing the man his brass helmet. "Hold this for me, would you?"

He spent an hour circling the balcony over the main room, but there was no sign of Abigail or the Duke. Remembering her dislike of crowds and confusion in general, he made his way to the back gardens, which were extensive and included a number of artificial streams and lakes. The carefully plotted acres offered thousands of secret spots ideal for conducting any number of illicit activities. Cary's temper began to fray.

The farther into the garden he went, the more annoyed he became. Occasionally stumbling across pairs of panting lovers did nothing to improve his temper. What the devil was Auckland thinking, bringing Abigail into these lonely paths? Auckland was desperately in love with Juliet, of course. In his company, Abigail would be safe from unwanted advances, Cary told himself. But he could not be easy in his mind until he found her.

The sharp cries of a frightened woman suddenly rent the air. Already running towards the sound, Cary saw a man and a woman struggling on the ornamental bridge arching over the man-made stream in the distance. The woman was dressed like Cleopatra in a column dress of finely pleated white linen. A beaten gold headdress reminiscent of a bird slipped from her long black hair as she tried to break the desperate grip her attacker had on her wrists. Her attacker was a bald man. In his bottle-green coat and dark breeches, he looked decidedly out of place. He actually had Cleopatra by the hair.

The woman called Cary by name as he approached. "Oh, Mr. Wayborn, thank God you are come! This madman came out of nowhere and attacked me."

Cary's dislike of Serena Calverstock did not extend to allowing her to be forcibly abducted by uncouth and balding Glaswegians. "What the devil do you think you're doing?" he snarled, shoving Red Ritchie hard against the balustrade. "Put your hands on this lady again, and I shall make you very sorry."

"That woman has taken my child," Red shouted, struggling to get past Cary. Cary stood firm. "They are holding her for ransom, sir, and this woman is part of the plot."

"I believe he is mad," declared Serena, reclaiming her golden headdress. "I was only walking across the bridge, when he attacked me. My hair, Mr. Wayborn! I thought he was going to pull it out by the roots. I know nothing of any kidnap."

"I can prove what I say is true," cried Red, producing a scrap of paper from his waistcoat. "This obscenity was left for me at my warehouse."

Cary squinted at it in the torchlight. Fortunately, the ransom note had been written in large capital letters. "We have your daughter. If you ever want to see her again, bring your diamonds to the Orient Bridge at Carlton House. A lady dressed as Cleopatra will meet you there. Give her the diamonds, and your daughter will be returned to you unharmed."

Serena gasped. "Monstrous! May I see?"

Cary frowned at Ritchie. "What diamonds?"

Ritchie showed him a hefty velvet bag.

Cary was skeptical. "Do you always carry bags of diamonds around with you?"

"Of course not," Ritchie snapped. "I had to go all the way to my banker's to fetch them out of my vault."

"And you just happened to have a bag of diamonds in your vault?"

"Of course," said Serena. "He's Mad Red Ritchie! Aren't you, sir? Everyone knows about your diamonds. He bought twenty thousand pounds' worth," she told Cary, "just to prove his daughter wasn't a thief. Can you imagine?"

"No, he can't," Red sneered. "He hasn't got two pennies to rub together."

Serena took possession of the ransom note. "This is despicable," she declared. "I've heard of such goings on in the back alleys of Naples, but this is England. Mr. Wayborn, I insist that you do something. Miss Ritchie must be in terrible danger."

"I have been waiting for hours," said Ritchie. "This wee hussy's the first person to set foot on this bridge, and, as you see, she's dressed as Cleopatra."

"So are any number of people," Serena pointed out

calmly. "I'm very sorry for you, Mr. Ritchie, but I am not your Cleopatra."

Red clutched Cary's arm. "Sir! If you help me get my child back, I will give *you* the diamonds. You could use the money, don't deny it."

Cary bristled at the insult. "Sir, you are addressing an English gentleman, not a Hessian mercenary," he said coldly. "I don't actually charge a fee for rescuing kidnaped children. I'll get your daughter back for you. You can keep your bloody diamonds."

"She's all I have in the world," said Red. "I don't know what I'll do if I don't get her back. We had a terrible argument this evening . . . about *you*, as a matter of fact."

"About me?" said Cary, lifting a brow.

"She thinks I offended you with all those bills. She said it was not good business practice. But, sir, I thought you were one of the Derbyshire Wayborns. To them I extend no credit." He shook his head sadly. "I wish I could take it all back. They wouldn't . . . they wouldn't hurt her, would they?" He looked forlornly at Lady Serena.

"Mr. Wayborn will help you," she declared. "He's very capable, you know. He won't let anything happen to your daughter. Indeed, he won't. Will you, sir?"

"Certainly. I think the best thing for you to do is wait on the bridge for the kidnaper's accomplice," Cary told Ritchie. "I will conceal myself a short distance away and catch this woman when you hand over the diamonds. She will be able to tell us where your daughter is."

"I don't care about the diamonds, sir. I just want my little girl back."

"Then do as I say quickly! Someone's coming," Cary observed, pulling Serena away with him. "We'd better hide. The accomplice will not come if she sees us here."

He herded her off the bridge as fast as he could and

pushed her into a hedge to one side of the path. "It's only Ponsonby and that beastly Coryn woman," she said, peering through the leaves as a pair of Romans passed Red Ritchie on the bridge. She glanced at him with her violet eyes. "I don't know what I would have done if you hadn't come along, Mr. Wayborn. The man wouldn't listen to a word I said. I really think he might have killed me."

Cary shifted uncomfortably. It was fairly unpleasant squatting in the bushes dressed as a Praetorian Guard. The air was cold, and his tunic was very short. "I certainly hope this woman comes soon," he muttered. "There's someone I have to meet."

"You were not always so averse to sitting in the moonlight with me," said Serena.

His back stiffened. "If you are determined to reminisce, shall we recall together how I came to be so averse, madam? No? Then let us sit quietly and hope the wretch comes soon."

If only Abby were here, he thought morosely, hanging about in the hedges would not be such a trial. There were any number of things they might do to make the time go faster.

Abigail was thrown down on something soft. Through the loose burlap covering her face, she detected light. There were footsteps. Voices murmured, then a door closed. Sensing she was alone, she began wriggling out of the sack. In the process, she rolled off of her perch and onto a soft carpeted floor. The carpet, she saw as she climbed to her feet and stepped out of the sack, was a very fine Aubusson.

She was in a richly appointed bedroom lit by huge gilded candelabra hung with glittering crystals. She had been thrown upon the huge satin-covered bed. From this she had slipped to the floor. The walls were paneled in purple silk with gilded moldings. Clearly she had been kidnaped by someone of wealth, if not taste. There was only one person she could think of who would do such a thing. In all the world she had only one enemy. Lord Dulwich.

A quick investigation of the room told her that the doors were all locked, and the drop from the windows would be neck-breaking if she attempted to escape in that way. Her kidnapers, however, had neglected to remove the poker from the huge marble fireplace. Abigail hastily stuck it into the fire to make the pointed tip good and hot.

She did not have long to wait. Soon she heard the key turning in the lock. The tip of the poker was bright red as she swung it as hard as she could at the shadowy figure that entered the room. The scream of pain and the smell of burning flesh was highly satisfying to her. The man fell to his knees, his hands pressed to his face.

"Serves you right," said Abigail. "Would you like another?"

"Please don't hurt me!" screamed the Duke of Auckland.

"Good God, sir! I'm so sorry!" cried Abigail, falling to her knees beside him. "I thought you were Lord Dulwich. Has he kidnaped you as well?"

He stared at her, his face the color of ashes. "What the devil are *you* doing here?"

Without thinking, Abigail ran to pull the servants' bell. "I don't know, sir," she said, fumbling for a handkerchief, which she pressed to the burn slashed across the Duke's cheek. "I was brought here against my will. They put me in a sack. I think at one point I was put in the box under the driver's seat of somebody's carriage! It was excessively uncomfortable."

The door opened quietly and a tall servant entered the room. "You rang, your grace?"

The Duke climbed to his feet. "Bowditch, you confounded idiot! How could you bungle such a simple thing? Look what she did to me!" he added, peeling back Abigail's handkerchief to show his wound. "Just what I don't need. A scar on my pretty face."

Abigail's mouth fell open. Bowditch took advantage of her shock and relieved her of the poker. "But I saw her with my own eyes, your grace!" the servant protested. "The young woman was coming out of Mr. Rourke's dressing room."

The Duke's green eyes bulged. "What? You saw *this* girl coming out of Rourke's room?" He stared at Abigail, appalled. "*You* were in Mr. Rourke's room? You? You and *Mr. Rourke*? I'm shocked. I don't know what to say. You'd better explain."

"*I* had better explain!" cried Abigail. "*You put me in a sack*!"

"I didn't do anything. *He* did!" responded the Duke, pointing at his servant. "And it wouldn't have happened at all, if you hadn't been where you shouldn't, doing God knows what with that actor. I'm ashamed of you, girl. You seem like such a quiet, well-behaved young lady. Why, you're nothing but a strumpet! What happened to Mr. Pigs-and-Chickens? David Rourke is about as far from a quiet life in the country as you can get. I'm going to tell your father!"

"How dare you!" cried Abigail furiously. "How dare you call me names? You *kidnaped* me, you beastly man. You and your nasty servant. This is—this is your *bedchamber*! Are you in the habit of kidnaping women and imprisoning them in your bedchamber?"

"Don't flatter yourself, my girl," he growled. "I meant to kidnap Juliet. Only she didn't go to Rourke's room, did she? No, it was you. It was you all along. *You're* Rourke's mistress, not Juliet. Julie's innocent. Do you hear me, Bowditch? She is innocent!"

"I am *not* Rourke's mistress, you impertinent wretch," Abigail cried indignantly. "For God's sake, the man's an actor. I do have some pride, you know."

The Duke scarcely heard her. "All this time, I thought Julie was in love with him," he murmured. "And all this time my darling girl was only protecting *you*. *You* were with him that night at the Albany. You're Julie's cousin. Naturally, she was concerned that Rourke had seduced you. It's just like her to come to the aid of a foolish relative. She must have gone there that night to free you from his clutches." His green eyes narrowed contemptuously. "But you like his clutches, don't you?"

"Sir," she said coldly. "I have never been to the Albany in my life. I scarcely know Mr. Rourke. What you are suggesting is revolting to me."

"Then what were you doing in the man's room at the theater?"

Abigail's face was red as fire. "I was there with someone else. My *husband*!"

He glowered at her. "But you're not married."

Abigail blushed. "Well, it's a secret. I haven't yet found the courage to tell my father, you see. When I came home yesterday, there you were. He so clearly wants me to make a brilliant marriage, I didn't have the heart to tell him."

The Duke stared at her. "So there really *is* a Mr. Pigs-and-Chickens?"

"Yes, of course there is," she said proudly. "We're very much in love."

"She could be lying, your grace," said Bowditch.

380   *Tamara Lejeune*

"No, she isn't." The Duke walked across the room and sat on the bed. "I was grasping at straws. No, I'm back where I started." He looked up at Abigail with tears in his eyes. "Do you think she loves him? Do you think your cousin Juliet is in love with Mr. Rourke?"

"He's not even handsome, if you ask me," said Abigail.

"Do you think that *I'm* handsome?" he retorted. "Before you walloped me in the face with the poker, I mean? She loved me once, in spite of my looks."

"Sir, I've only seen them together once, but, really, I don't see how—"

"When?" he said sharply. "When did you see them together?"

"I didn't mean to imply anything!" Abigail stammered. "It was perfectly innocent. She introduced me to him backstage, before the play. She told him to break his leg, you know."

His eyes lit up. "Then they are on the outs. This could be my chance."

Abigail winced. "I'm told it means good luck to theater people."

The Duke sighed. "This is hopeless," he moaned. "I thought if I could just put her in a sack and bring her here, she would realize how much I love her!"

"Oh, yes?" Abigail said politely.

"If she made a mistake, if she still loves me . . . I swear I could forgive her anything. But she doesn't even want my forgiveness. I've lost her, haven't I? She loves *him* now. He has beguiled her with Shakespeare, and my beastly jealousy has ruined all."

In spite of everything, Abigail was overwhelmed with pity for the suffering giant. It must indeed be torture to love an arrogant, spiteful woman like Juliet Wayborn. "Sir," she said gently, "I realize I only met

Miss Wayborn two days ago in Hertfordshire, but it seems to me—"

The Duke lifted his head. "Hertfordshire? Julie wasn't in Hertfordshire two days ago. Two days ago, she was with Rourke at the Albany."

"She arrived in the early afternoon at her brother's estate," Abigail explained.

"Julie was at Tanglewood on Saturday?"

"Yes, sir. I'd been staying there since all this unpleasant business with Lord Dulwich."

"I did hear she'd left Town," he said thoughtfully. "I suppose she only came back today to see Rourke," he added bitterly. "In his triumphant return to the stage!"

"Not at all, I assure you," said Abigail, happy that she could at least relieve him of this painful assumption. "She came back to Town to find *me*, as a matter of fact. Not Mr. Rourke. It seems I'd taken her snuffbox—accidentally, of course. The dog had chewed it up a bit, you see. I thought I could bring it with me to London and have it repaired. I didn't know at the time that the box belonged to Miss Wayborn."

"It doesn't. Julie don't take snuff."

"No, I don't think she does," Abigail agreed. "But the snuffbox is very special to her. It was a gift from the Prince Regent himself. Surely you must have seen it before."

"No, you're thinking of her cousin Horatio," the Duke said impatiently. "He's the one with the ruddy snuffbox. The Regent gave it him, and he's forever making people look at the bloody thing. Little gold box with a green lid, and a picture of a horse on it?"

"Yes."

He shrugged. "Horatio's. Now he claims someone stole it. I hope someone has. I hope the thief throws it in the Thames. I would consider it a public service."

"The Captain has one just like Miss Wayborn's, I know. He showed it to me several times when he was visiting his father. That's why I never suspected the one I found was Miss Wayborn's. I just assumed it was the Captain's. I didn't know there were two of them."

"There aren't two of them," he said irritably. "That's what I'm trying to tell you."

Abigail was becoming rather irritated herself. "Actually, there are hundreds of them, as it turns out. But I am talking specifically of the one given to Miss Wayborn by the Prince of Wales. That's the one the dog crunched up, only I thought it was *Horatio's*, so I took it to London to be repaired. Only it couldn't be repaired. So I had it replaced instead. I gave Miss Wayborn the replacement this afternoon in Hatchard's, just before I met you, sir. I should have known that Sir Horatio would never have left his precious snuffbox behind in Hertfordshire."

"No, he didn't," the Duke said slowly. "I just told you it was stolen from him. He's been crying about it all over Town since . . . since Saturday. Even got the Runners on the case."

Abigail did not know what to say.

"Were Julie and Horatio in Hertfordshire together?" he asked her.

"No, sir," she said. "When Miss Wayborn came, he'd already gone back to London."

"The Regent gave him that snuffbox when he was knighted. Julie never had one. He's got rooms at the Albany, too. Do you see what this means?" He jumped to his feet. "By God! She wasn't with Rourke at all. She was in Horatio's room."

Abigail was embarrassed. "Oh, dear. Do you think she is in love with her cousin and that he gave her his snuffbox?"

The Duke laughed aloud. "Julie in love with Horatio? Not in a hundred years! Horatio give away his snuffbox? Not in a thousand. He sleeps with it under his pillow, the booby. She must have had to wait in his room all night for a chance to steal it. Oh, my poor darling."

"She accused *me* of stealing it from *her*!"

"She was perfectly innocent the whole time!" The Duke sat down on the bed again. His moment of happiness seemed to have passed him by. "Oh, God, what have I done? She'll never forgive me. I've spied on her. I've accused her of betraying me—with an actor, of all things! I think I even called her a strumpet."

"And all this time she was only a thief," Abigail dryly observed.

He was on his feet again. "I've been a jealous fool. I must find her. I must find her at once. There is not an instant to lose." He stopped in his tracks as Abigail pointedly cleared her throat. "Look here, Annabel, I'm dreadfully sorry about all this. My man can take you back to the theater now, if you like."

"I beg your pardon," said Abigail. "But I don't much like the look of your man! In any case, the play must be over by now, and I am expected at the Carlton House Ball. Or do you think I always dress like this?"

He raked his hands through his wild red hair. "Julie will be there as well. With Rourke hanging about her, I don't doubt. Oh, God! What if I've driven her into his arms with my confounded jealousy?"

"I shouldn't think so," said Abigail kindly. "I don't know her very well, but it seems to me, she'd be much too proud to carry on with some actor."

He did not seem reassured. "I must change into my costume," he said miserably. "May I offer you a glass of wine while you wait?"

"Certainly not," said Abigail. "You may offer me a *quaich* of scotch, however."

Cary and Serena had been waiting for a seemingly interminable time (Praetorian Guards have no pockets for pocket watches), when a tall man with red hair wearing the purple-edged *toga praetexta* of a Roman senator suddenly peered over the hedge.

"Hullo, Cary! May I join your party?"

As Serena spun around to see who had stumbled upon their hiding place, the Duke of Auckland's face fell. "Oh, it's you, Serena. I thought you were Julie. She's Cleopatra, too. Cary, have you seen Julie? She must be here somewhere. No one can find her!"

Cary pulled him down next to them in the shrubbery. "Is Abby not with you?"

"She was. But we saw Dulwich, and she took off like a frightened rabbit. She's odd, have you noticed? Always scampering off. I don't think she sat for two minutes together during the whole play. Now she tells me she's secretly married to some sort of pig farmer. I doubt her husband would approve of the way she kept sneaking off to meet *you*."

"You *left* her?" Cary snapped. "She's out there alone?"

"Well, I couldn't very well run after her," said the Duke. "People might think I was chasing her. If it got back to Julie, I'd be well and truly in the basket. Anyway, I'm off! I've got to find Julie. Glad to see you and Serena have made up and all that. I'll leave you to it."

Cary held his arm with an iron grip. "Look here, there's been a spot of bother. Red Ritchie's daughter has been kidnaped."

The Duke shuddered. "Don't say 'kidnaped.' It's such an ugly word."

"Indeed? What do you call it when ruffians make off with a man's child, then send him a ransom note demanding a fortune in diamonds?"

"Precisely," said the Duke. "*That* is what I call kidnaping."

"Right now I've got to find Abigail," said Cary. "If Dulwich finds her first, there could be real trouble. I need you to stay here and watch that bridge, Geoffrey. Ritchie's all set to hand over the ransom to some woman dressed as Cleopatra."

"Julie's dressed as Cleopatra," he said, brightening up.

"I seriously doubt my sister is in the kidnaping line," Cary said impatiently. "Now, whatever you do, don't let this woman get away. She's going to lead us to Ritchie's daughter."

The Duke was puzzled. "Has Ritchie got *two* daughters?"

"No, just the one, and the poor thing's been kidnaped. Look, I haven't time to explain. Which way did Abby go? I've got to get to her before Dulwich finds her. It's very important."

"Last I saw of her, she was running past the Italian fountain," the Duke said. "You know, in the grove with all the dolphins."

"Who is this Abby person?" Serena demanded of the Duke as Cary sprinted off down the path. "And what on earth happened to your face?"

Cary had not gone ten yards when he ran into Budgie, the young biffer from the theater. Budgie was now attired in what appeared to be a bed sheet and on his narrow head was a wreath of artificial grapes. The large macaw on his shoulder squawked. "Ah, hullo!" the young man slurred. "Look what I found in my carriage after the play."

"Yes," Cary said distractedly. "I put it there. I thought it would be a good joke."

"Oh, it was," Budgie assured him. "Mama nearly died of fright. If you're looking for that girl you were with at the theater, I just met her in the Italian grove. A vestal virgin, is she?"

"I swear to God, if you so much as touched her—"

"Good Lord, Wayborn!" Budgie cried, backing away. "I'm no poacher. Besides, the bird frightened her away. She called it Cato. Do you think that's a good name for a bird?"

Cary pushed past him without answering.

Abigail crouched down beside one of the large stone dolphins lining the crushed gravel path and found the iron lever fitted into its base. She could hear Dulwich's sandals crunching on the pebbles. The fool had chosen to wear the short leather skirt of a Roman gladiator and his legs were pathetically pale and skinny. "Abigail?" he called out.

Abigail pulled the lever down as hard as she could. A jet of water shot from the mouth of the dolphin in a powerful blast that struck Cary full in the face. Too late Abigail saw that the legs were not skinny and white, but rather toned and bronzed.

"Oh, darling, I'm so sorry," she cried, darting out from her hiding place. "I thought you were Dulwich. He thinks I took his diamond. Only, I didn't. I swear."

Cary shook water from his hair and eyes. "You thought I was *Dulwich*?" he sputtered.

"Well, I couldn't see you properly. I was hiding."

"I know. Abby, if Dulwich finds you, he will have you arrested. Come quickly."

"Are we going to meet my father?" she asked, apprehensively. "Oh, Cary! Not yet. Not just yet. I need to talk to you first."

"Not now, Smith," Cary said grimly, taking her by the arm. His stride lengthened purposefully and she struggled to keep up. "There's something I've got to take care of. You know that fellow I owed money to, Ritchie?"

She gulped. "Cary . . ."

"His daughter's been kidnaped. I told him I'd help him. The kidnapers are sending a woman to collect the ransom. Come on!"

"But I haven't been kidnaped," she cried, running after him. "Well, I mean, I *was* kidnaped—briefly—but there wasn't any ransom. It was all a silly mistake."

"What are you talking about? Of course *you* haven't been kidnaped. Good Lord, if you'd been kidnaped, I'd be in a blind panic right about now! I suppose that's why I feel I must help the poor fellow. There will be time enough for me to meet your father."

"Cary, you don't under—aaaaaaargh!" Abigail let out a shriek as a blast of icy cold water suddenly drenched her from head to toe. Lord Dulwich stepped from behind one of the stone dolphins with a wicked-looking gladiator's sword in his hand.

"Now then," he said roughly. "Where is my diamond, you little thief?"

"I don't have it! I swear!" Abigail cried, wiping water out of her eyes. "I sent it back to you, you—you—you great horrid Pudding-face!"

Dulwich lifted her chin with the point of his sword. "You pried the stone from the setting and replaced it with glass. Admit it!"

Cary retraced his steps with a groan of disgust, covered

Dulwich's face with one hand, and spurned him into the gravel. "If you ever come near my wife again, I shall tear off *both* your stones and feed them to my dog," he said crankily. "Come along, Abigail!"

"Your wife?" Dulwich sneered, scrambling to his feet. "She's your wife, is she? Well, if you don't mind giving a little consequence to one of my castoffs, that's your affair, I suppose. But I still want my diamond back."

Cary spun around. "*What* did you say?"

Dulwich laughed unpleasantly. "Didn't she tell you? We were once engaged, you know. Her father offered me quite a lot of money to take her, as a matter of fact. Against my better judgement, I allowed myself to be persuaded. After all, her mother was not too contemptible."

Cary's voice shook with fury. "Abigail, were you engaged to this loathsome tick?" She had never seen him so angry. "When I thought you were his sister," he spat, "that was bad enough. But this? Engaged? To *him*? What else haven't you told me?"

"I haven't got a sister," said Dulwich. "But if I *had*, she wouldn't be the freckle-faced halfwit brat of a Glaswegian whisky merchant, I can promise you that."

Without a word, Cary turned on his heel and strode away.

"Cary, please! Let me explain," Abigail begged, running after him.

"My diamond!" said Dulwich, starting after her. With a sharp cry of pain, he fell in the gravel, clutching his sandal-clad foot. "My ankle!"

Cary stalked out of the garden onto the wider path. From the slight elevation, he had a fine view of the bridge where his father-in-law was waiting with twenty thousand pounds' worth of diamonds. He skidded to a stop as he caught sight of a Cleopatra stepping onto the bridge, a golden serpent glinting on her brow.

Abigail bumped into him. "Cary, I tried to tell you," she whispered, pressing her face against his shoulder. He could feel her shivering. "I tried to tell you as soon as I learned that Paggles had got it wrong. But you wanted to marry me. You said it didn't matter."

"Didn't matter!"

"And it doesn't matter!" she went on quickly. "He never meant anything to me. But there was a time when I didn't think it mattered who I married. I only wanted to make my father happy. It was before I knew you."

Cary was not looking at her. "I have a question for you, Abigail," he said quietly.

"Yes, of course. Ask me anything."

"If you haven't been kidnaped," he said thoughtfully, "why is that woman collecting the ransom from your father?"

"What?" Abigail turned to look as her father handed over a velvet pouch. "No, Papa!" she yelled at the top of her voice, running as fast as she could towards the bridge and waving her arms. "It's a trick! I'm perfectly all right."

Red whirled around. "Abby?"

Cleopatra turned and ran straight into the arms of the Duke of Auckland.

Chapter 20

Red Ritchie was so overjoyed to see Abigail that he dropped the velvet pouch, spilling diamonds on the bridge. "You found her!" he cried, catching her in his arms as she ran to him.

Cary stooped to gather up the diamonds. Though by no means overjoyed by his father-in-law's identity, he conceded that the man's affection for Abigail did mitigate his execrable habit of sending overdue notices to gentlemen. "Your diamonds, sir."

Red ignored the diamonds. "Sir, I can't thank you enough! My God, Abby, you're soaked through," he fretted, hastily pulling off his bottle-green coat and placing it around his shivering daughter. "Did these ruffians try to drown you? What a good thing you could swim, sir!" he added, after observing that Cary was wet too. "I know you won't let me pay you, sir, but, indeed, I owe you much. Let me shake your hand."

"Gladly," Cary said, looking past him to where the Duke was having a devil of a time holding onto a hissing, spitting Cleopatra. "Abigail!"

His voice was harsh. As he handed her the pouch of

diamonds, she wondered if he would ever again speak to her in that warm, gentle voice that made her bones melt.

"Does that woman look familiar to you?"

Puzzled, Abigail turned to stare at Cleopatra. The heavy application of exotic cosmetics could not entirely conceal the familiar features. "Vera!" she exclaimed after a moment.

With her crown of serpents still glinting on her brow, Vera Nashe faced them defiantly. "Miss Ritchie," she said coolly. "Was there ever an heiress so aptly named?"

Abigail gasped at her impudence. "Did you know who I was the whole time?" she cried. "Did you *always* mean to kidnap me? I thought you were my friend."

"I didn't know who you were until I went through your trunks," replied she.

"How dare you go through my belongings?"

"How else was I to steal your lovely jewelry?" Vera asked sensibly.

"And my stockings! You lent me my own stockings! Vera, how could you?"

"I was tired of watching you stomp around in those dreary boots, my dear. And so was Mr. Wayborn." Her dark eyes twinkled with amusement. "He likes a light foot, doesn't he? A light foot and a light skirt, eh?"

"Abby, do you know this woman?" asked Red, his eyes wide with shock.

"I beg your pardon, Papa," said Abigail, flustered. "Mrs. Nashe, may I present my father, Mr. William Ritchie. Mrs. Nashe was with me when I was lately in Hertfordshire. She was employed as Mrs. Spurgeon's nurse."

"How do you do, sir?"

Lady Serena Calverstock pushed past the gentlemen to stand with Abigail. "But it's Mrs. Simpkins, surely," she said, clearly pleased to have something to add to the curious denouement on the bridge. "I recognize you from *She Stoops to Conquer* last year. I vow, I never saw a better Kate Hardcastle in all my life."

"Your ladyship is too kind," said the other woman, with a graceful curtsy.

"My dear, I mean it," Serena insisted. "We've tragedians enough, but your talent for comedy is very rare. When you have put this unpleasant business behind you, I hope you will return to the stage. I should so like to see you as Lady Teazle in *School for Scandal*."

"When she has put this business behind her," said Abigail, "she will be in Australia with her fellow convicts! I suppose Evans was your accomplice?" she went on angrily. "We did hear she had been caught redhanded with Mr. Wayborn's silver and my pearls."

"Evans? Good heavens!" Vera murmured. "Why, Miss Ritchie, poor Evans was as pure as they come. I *planted* the silver in her room, along with your pearls and a few worthless trinkets of Mrs. Spurgeon's. I knew she was going to blab to Mr. Leighton about me. She actually objected to my giving the old cow laudanum to keep her quiet."

This new revelation shocked Abigail even more than the previous. "Mrs. Spurgeon trusted you, Vera. How could you drug her?"

Vera arched a brow. "Don't tell me you missed her scintillating conversations! Anyway, what are you complaining about? It all worked out well for you." She chuckled. "I *had* thought of taking Mr. Wayborn for myself, you know. But he *would* know there were no cavalry at Ciudad Rodrigo. There went my dearly departed Lieutenant. Arthur? Was that his name?"

"You are not even a widow?" cried Abigail.

Vera looked archly at Cary. "I couldn't risk our becoming more intimately acquainted, Mr. Wayborn. I do hope you understand. Who knows how many lies you might have caught me in, with your superior knowledge of the rank-and-file? But I regretted ending our friendship almost before it had begun."

Abigail felt Cary's hand on her shoulder. "Look here, Nashe," he said grimly. "If Evans is not your accomplice in this vile plot to kidnap Abigail, then who is?"

"Don't look at me," exclaimed the Duke, to general surprise. "I only kidnaped her by accident. As a matter of fact, I'd like to see that ransom note."

"Here you are, Auckland," said Serena, extremely interested in this new development.

"Just as I thought," he snarled. "It's a complete forgery! *I* certainly didn't write it."

"Of course you didn't write it, sir!" said Abigail. "You did not intend to hold me for ransom when you kidnaped me."

"You kidnaped Abigail?" Cary barked, his hand tightening on her shoulder.

"Not personally," the Duke explained. "My man Bowditch did it. He was supposed to kidnap your sister."

"Oh, that's all right then!" said Cary, his eyes blazing.

Red was horrified. "Abby! Did the Duke of Auckland *kidnap* you?"

"It was more of an abduction, really," the Duke said haughtily. "Also, a case of mistaken identity. It was quite her own fault for making herself at home in Mr. Rourke's dressing room."

Abigail winced.

Red scowled at her. "What were you doing in Mr. Rourke's dressing room?"

Cary spoke up. "She was with me actually, sir. We were—We were—We were looking for Mrs. Spurgeon's bird," he finished just as a huge scarlet macaw flew onto the bridge.

"Yes, of course!" cried Abigail. "You *stole* Cato, and

gave him to Mr. Rourke, didn't you, Vera? *Mr. Rourke* is your accomplice! You must be old friends from the theater."

"Ha!" said the Duke. "I knew it!"

"Hullo," said Cary's acquaintance from the theater, coming through the crowd on the bridge. "Pardon me. Bloody bird seems to have gotten away from me." He stopped short as Vera held out her arm and Cato obediently flew to her, landing on her wrist.

"Yes, Rourke is my accomplice," Vera replied, clicking her tongue at Cato. "Since the Duke has cut him off without a penny, he's going to need to supplement his income as an actor. It's bloody expensive at the Albany, you know."

The Duke of Auckland panted with excitement. "Julie should be here. Wait until she hears of her favorite's guilt! She'll beg me to take her back." He rubbed his hands together. "If I could just find her," he murmured anxiously.

"I might have known he'd bungle it," Vera went on bitterly. "He's such a Lumpkin. All he had to do was find Miss Ritchie's carriage and drive off to Kensington with her in it."

Lady Serena tittered appreciatively. "Such a Lumpkin," she repeated. "Why, he was absolutely magnificent in the role of Tony Lumpkin! I remember, I was laughing so hard, I nearly fell out of my chair."

"Really?" said Budgie. "So did I."

"We need more comedy," said Serena firmly. "Did anyone else find it cringe-making tonight when the clown wished Cleopatra *all the joy of the worm*? Ugh! Mrs. Simpkins, if you promise to be good and do something amusing on stage in the very near future, I'm sure Miss Ritchie will be merciful. After all," she added, turning to Abigail, "you were not kidnaped—not by Mr. Rourke, at any rate—and your papa still has his diamonds."

"What about Evans?" Abigail protested. "What about Cary's miniatures?"

"Oh, all right," said Vera, stroking Cato's head. "You caught me fair and square, and I'm nothing if not a good sport. He can have them back. But, I beg you, do not send Evans back to Mrs. Spurgeon. If you have a heart at all, Miss Ritchie, you will offer her a position with you. It seems to me that you could use the services of a real ladies' maid. Paggles hardly fits the bill anymore, if she ever did."

"I say!" Budgie protested as someone pushed roughly past him.

"There you are!" said Lord Dulwich, limping onto the bridge. "We have not finished our conversation, madam. You still have my diamond."

"Please," said Vera, as Cary made a move. "Allow me. Hullo, Dully," she said, stepping forward. "Looking for this?"

Slowly, she turned the simple gold band on her finger until the large glittering stone could be seen. Abigail gasped at the unusual carnation-pink color. "*You* took the Rose de Mai!" she cried. "When you were a maid to Lady Inchmery!"

"Oh, I was never a maid to Lady Inchmery," Vera replied. "Nor was I a maid to her son, Lord Dulwich, though I do believe the poor dear fool really thought I *was*. I am, as your ladyship has so kindly noted, an accomplished *comedienne*. But no, I bade my maidenhood farewell long before I ever met his lordship. So I was no maid. I was Dully's mistress."

"Augh!" Abigail breathed.

Vera chuckled. "It wasn't so bad, Miss Ritchie. I gave his lordship lots of laudanum, too! He was rarely conscious in my presence, let alone . . . In return, I was pretty well set up."

"You bloody cow!" said Dulwich.

Vera paid him no attention. "You will laugh, Miss Ritchie, but I had my own house and carriage. I even left the stage for a while. Then, alas, it all went sideways. Dully got into debt and his papa took his allowance away. He was ashamed of himself, of course, but not so ashamed that he didn't take back my house, my carriage, and even my jewels."

"Lady Serena, I assure you, I don't know this vulgar person," Dulwich stammered.

No one regarded him in the least.

"What could the poor man do but marry an heiress?" Vera went on complacently. "He *did* promise me that once he'd married Miss Ritchie, he'd buy me this little house I had my eye on in Curzon Street. But in the meantime, it would never do if her papa found out he kept a mistress. Well, I love a good joke, so I did as he asked. I disappeared while he wooed the fair Miss Ritchie. I transformed my humble self into an impoverished war widow and took a lowly position as a nurse. Admit it, Mr. Wayborn, I took you in completely. Well, except for the cavalry! It was great fun. I have always had a talent for shedding tears." Her smiled faded and, in the next moment, real tears glittered in her lashes. "Still, I wasn't quite sure I *believed* Dully when he said he would always love me and take care of me," she said, brushing her crocodile tears away, "so I took his diamond for insurance."

"And the one his lordship gave Abby was glass," Red growled. "I knew I should have had that ring appraised immediately. Well, there's your thief, milord!"

"Thief, Mr. Ritchie?" Vera clucked her tongue. "Not at all, I assure you. The man gave it to me. He liked looking at it on my hand while I . . ." Her dark lashes skirted her high cheekbones. "But that is, perhaps, better left unsaid." She began laughing.

"You give that back to me, you lying jade!" cried Dulwich, flying towards her.

Still laughing, Vera slipped the Rose de Mai from her finger and gave it to the macaw, which swallowed it as if it had been a nut.

"No!" screamed the viscount as the bird flew away. "Come back here!"

Serena clapped her hands as Dulwich pursued the macaw, hobbling away on his injured ankle. "Oh, well done, Mrs. Simpkins! I've been trying to get rid of him all evening."

"Cato is such an immensely talented creature," Vera said wistfully. "We were going to make him swallow all your lovely diamonds, Mr. Ritchie, and then take him for a little holiday on the continent, and live like kings. Let me assure you, sir, that your daughter would never have been in any danger. Rourke was to have taken her in her own carriage back to your very comfortable home. When I got the diamonds, I was to have a friend of mine set off one or two of the fireworks early. That was the signal for Rourke to meet me at the Albany. Miss Ritchie would scarcely have been inconvenienced at all."

"How can you say so?" cried Abigail. "I should have been *there* instead of *here*."

"But you're not," the Duke pointed out. "You're *here* instead of *there*, thanks to me. There's no need to be vindictive, Annabel, or Smith, or whatever your name is."

"I daresay Dulwich will be vindictive enough for all of us," Cary said, looking at Vera. "He'll see you hanged for this, you know."

"I shouldn't think so, sir. I was pleased to discover a written apology from his lordship among Miss Ritchie's many treasures. As they say in Ireland, I'm sitting on the pig's back!"

"Abigail!" said Cary. "What on earth did you keep it for? You ought to have burned it!"

"You wrote your name and direction on the back," she explained. "I had to keep it."

"Monkey!" he said, pulling her into his arms.

"I'm glad you're not going to be hanged," said Budgie, offering Vera his arm. "I like you. Shall we all go up to the house?"

"Yes, let's," cried Serena, taking Budgie's other arm. "It's so amusing. Everybody's got snuffboxes just like Sir Horatio's. He's beside himself. He actually accused *Lady Jersey* of stealing it from under his pillow. He'll be eating grass for breakfast for the next ten years!"

The trio swept off the bridge, laughing.

Watching Cary Wayborn kiss his only child was too much for Red Ritchie. "Abigail! Come here at once! I am taking you home."

The Duke caught his arm before he could attack Cary. "It's all right," he said cheerfully. "He's Mr. Pigs-and-Chickens."

"He's Mr. what?"

"You know, man! Her husband." The Duke groaned. "Bloody hell! She did say it was a secret. She wanted to tell you, but she didn't have the courage. Now, don't worry," he went on, drawing Red off to one side. "I know you wanted a title, and all that, but they're not all that hard to come by, if you don't mind spending a little."

Red frowned. "How much? Mind, I want a peerage."

"Don't expect to get a dukedom or a marquisate," the Duke warned him. "But with me behind you, and your money up front, I don't think a barony is out of the question."

"My Abby, a baroness!" Red said eagerly. "You can have the diamonds, for starts, your grace, and any amount besides."

"Oh, no," the Duke said. "But if I could just get Julie's carriage back . . ."

"Done!"

* * *

At long last, Cary lifted his head. "Have they all gone?" Abigail asked hopefully.

"Your father's still here," he answered, looking over her shoulder. "Auckland is with him. I daresay I should probably stop kissing you for a while and go talk to him."

"Does he look very angry?"

"He looks bald," Cary replied.

"Julie really should be here by now," the Duke was saying fretfully as he consulted Red's watch. "I can't understand it, Ritchie. I've had servants searching the grounds for over an hour. She doesn't seem to be anywhere."

"Cary!" Abigail suddenly clutched Cary's arm and spoke in a hollow whisper. "What if Mr. Rourke *did* take my carriage, only *with your sister in it?*"

The Duke whirled around, scowling. "What did you say?"

"Sir," said Abigail. "I am *here* instead of *there*. What if Miss Wayborn is *there* instead of *here?*"

"What the devil is that banging?" Cary demanded for the fifth time as the Duke's carriage rolled to a stop on the quiet Kensington Road.

The Duke flung open the carriage door. It struck his servant in the back, then came back and hit the Duke as he jumped out. The giant hardly noticed. The banging noise stopped abruptly, but a nearby dog began barking hysterically.

Outside, Bowditch was struggling to keep a grip on a slippery young woman with butterscotch-colored hair. "Abigail!" Cary said angrily, as he climbed out. "I told you to stay at Carlton House with your father! You told me you would."

Abigail bit the hand covering her mouth. Cursing,

Bowditch released her. She flew straight at the Duke, but once she got to him she hardly knew what to do. "That is the *second* time you have kidnaped me, sir!" she cried, stamping her foot ineffectually. "If you *ever* stuff me under the seat again, I–I—" Her imagination failed her and she was forced to be honest. "I don't know what I'll do!"

"Good God, Smith!" said Cary. "Why didn't you make a noise or something?"

She turned to Cary in exasperation. "Didn't you hear me beating with my fists on the seat? I'm all over bruises! I could hear you talking."

"Was that you?" he asked ruefully. "Look here, you'd better wait in the carriage."

"We'll need her," the Duke protested, "if we're going to work a trade with Rourke."

"No one's working a trade," Cary snapped.

"Think, man! He don't want Julie. He wants *her.*"

"No, he doesn't, you ass! He wants the bloody diamonds."

The Duke's face fell. "Oh. Ritchie offered them to me, and like a fool, I declined. Took the carriage, instead. Do you think he'd take Julie's carriage for a ransom?"

"He's already taken her carriage," Cary pointed out.

"Dammit! How much have you got in your purse, man? I've got half-a-crown."

"I've got nothing. I paid my bill at Hatchard's today."

"What in hell's name did you do that for?" the Duke complained. "He's not likely to take half-a-crown."

"I had two florins and a guinea in my reticule," said Abigail. "But I left it at the theater."

"Bloody stupid of you," the Duke observed.

"I didn't know I was going to be kidnaped!"

"Never mind!" Cary snapped. "I've no intention of paying any ransom."

"Good God, man!" said the Duke, turning pale. "This is your sister we're talking about."

"Rourke's not getting anything but the boot of a Praetorian Guard up his Irish arse." Cary cursed violently under his breath. "I wish someone would silence that bloody dog! I can't think in all this racket."

"It's Angel," Abigail said. "Don't you know his voice? Someone's shut him up in the back garden. You know how he hates to be shut outside when there are people in the house."

The four of them crept towards the house. Candlelight gleamed from several of the downstairs windows. "That's the music room," Abigail explained as Angel continued to bark.

Cary stared at the mansion. It was huge, modern, and constructed of white marble in the Neoclassical style that was currently in vogue. "Where are the servants?"

"Paggles is at Tanglewood. Papa took the rest with him to Carlton House to help serve the drink. Anything for the Prince Regent, you know."

"And this is your house?"

"Yes."

"It's got a lot of French windows, Smith," he said severely. "I don't see why I can't put French windows in my Tudor monstrosity if you can put them in the Temple of bloody Apollo."

"Your Tudor monstrosity is authentic," she explained earnestly. "My temple is a fake."

He chuckled, which did not much please the Duke, who was desperately worried that his Juliet was even now succumbing to the Irishman's charms.

"Can we climb over the garden wall, do you think?" he demanded.

"There's a key hidden in a little hollow rock," she said. "I'll show you."

Cary instantly caught her arm. "No, you stay here."

"It's *my* house, Cary. I can always get in," she told him. "There's an oak tree in the garden that goes right up to my window. We can sneak downstairs and catch Mr. Rourke."

"Let's get on with it," growled the Duke. "The fireworks are going to go at any moment."

"Can you really see the fireworks from here?" Cary asked Abigail as they crawled forward through the rhododendrons dotting the lawn. "From Kensington, I mean?"

"Oh, yes, it's particularly nice from the roof."

As they neared the house, they could hear music coming from inside. Abigail recognized the "Moonlight Sonata." "That's Julie," said the Duke. His breathing sounded labored. "I'd know her phrasing anywhere. Hurry up, can't you?"

Abigail scampered past the windows, found the garden key in its hiding place, and admitted them into the garden. In the moonlight, the landscape appeared painted in stark black and white. The corgi rushed up to his master and mistress and greeted them with joyful whines. The music inside the house stopped abruptly. An ominous silence fell over Kensington.

"For God's sake, make it bark again," whispered the Duke.

"Flap your arms," Abigail instructed. "He'll bark at you."

The ducal fingers snapped twice. "Bowditch. Flap."

The ruse worked. The Duke's servant flapped, the dog barked, and Miss Wayborn continued to play Beethoven with her distinctive phrasing.

"There's the tree," whispered Abigail, pointing. "And there is my window."

"Well, up you go, Smith," said Cary, kneeling down and making a stirrup of his hands.

"Me?" she said quickly, shying away from his hands. "Can't you go?"

"It's your tree. You do it."

"She's your sister! Anyway, I can't. I don't have my . . ." She moved closer to him. "I left my drawers in Mr. Rourke's dressing room," she whispered in his ear.

"Ah," he said. "That *is* a problem. I never wear drawers—don't believe in 'em. And I left my breeches at Carlton House, just like it says in the song. Dammit, Smith, I left your pearls, too! You'll never see them again, I'm afraid."

Completely indifferent to the whereabouts of her pearls, Abigail glanced down his body. "You mean, there's nothing under your skirt?" she asked, fascinated. "All this time?"

"It's a tunic, not a skirt," he corrected her. "I wanted to be . . . authentic."

"Your grace?"

"Don't look at me," said the Duke of Auckland, creeping closer to the house. "I'm a senator. We'll just have to break one of these French windows."

"They're thirty pounds each!" Abigail protested.

It was a false economy, as it turned out. The Duke took a running start at the nearest French window, and might very well have broken it if Miss Wayborn had not been so good as to open it for her estranged fiancé. As a consequence of her kind act, the Duke plunged straight through and demolished a satin-covered French recamier worth fifty guineas.

"Julie!" he cried, jumping to his feet. "Julie, you're all right! You're safe now."

Juliet slapped his face. "You went to Carlton House in a silly costume without me?" she cried. "Do you know what I have endured this evening?"

"He kidnaped you, didn't he?" the Duke blazed. "Rourke kidnaped you. My poor darling. My angel! I'll kill him for this, you realize."

"Well, you *might* have killed him," she fumed,

stepping out into the garden. "If you'd gotten here a bit sooner."

The Duke followed her out. "You let him get away?"

"Why's your man flapping his arms in that ridiculous manner?" Juliet demanded to know.

"It's to make the dog bark," the Duke explained.

"Well, he can stop it at any time!" she shouted at him.

Bowditch ceased to flap. The corgi saw his advantage and attacked.

While Cary and Abigail were occupied in trying to coax Angel away from Bowditch, the Duke ventured to touch Miss Wayborn on her proud back. "Never mind if you let Rourke go, my darling. I shall hunt him down like the Irish dog he is."

"No, you won't," she snapped. "In just a moment, he's going to walk out of here."

"You mean he's still in the house?"

"Yes. He's going back to the Albany. And *you* are going to pay his bill."

"Am I indeed?" the Duke roared at her.

"Yes, that was the wager," she calmly replied.

"What wager?" he snarled.

"Oh, didn't I tell you? I would have done, if you'd been here rescuing me instead of frolicking at Carlton House. Did any of you even *care* that I'd been kidnaped? Cary? You're supposed to be my brother!"

Cary dragged Angel from the now prone Bowditch and handed the little corgi, still snarling, to Abigail, who, upon reflection, threw him into the house and closed the French window. He lunged against the lower panes, growling fiercely.

"Are you all right, Bowditch?" Abigail cried, dusting off the fellow who had twice stuffed her in a box under the driver's seat.

"I'm sorry, Julie," the Duke was crying under the oak tree. "I'm sorry for everything. I know now you were only trying to make me laugh by stealing Horatio's snuff-box. I'm sorry I was so beastly jealous. But *why* won't you let me kill him? Can it be that I have driven you into his arms? Tell me now if that is the case."

"Into his arms," Juliet hissed. "I should kick you for saying that. I told you we were just friends. This is completely your fault! He only did it for the money, because *you* cut off his funds. You can imagine his embarrassment when he realized he'd kidnaped the wrong woman."

"No, I can't," said the Duke. "It's unforgivable. Putting you in a filthy potato sack and stuffing you in the box under the driver's seat!"

"Potato sack, indeed," Juliet scoffed. "What an imagination you have! All he did was shove the driver off and take up the reins himself. Got clean away before the footmen knew what was what. He drives pretty well, too. I noticed nothing amiss until we stopped. Then he opened the carriage door, and things got pretty quiet. I could tell he was embarrassed, poor man, so I offered him a little wager. If you didn't come for me by midnight, I should let him go. And, of course, it's half past. So you see, it's your own fault you can't kill him."

"It's *her* fault," said the Duke, pointing at Abigail. "I tried to kidnap *you*, Julie, but Bowditch got *her* by mistake. The little beast hit me in the face with a red-hot poker!"

"Let me see," she said, peering at his face in the moonlight. "I thought *I* did that," she cried, taking out her handkerchief and dabbing at his face. "Oh, my poor Ginger! Did you really try to kidnap me? You're not just saying that?"

The Duke seemed to feel all at once that talk was superfluous. Instead, he grabbed Miss Wayborn and proceeded to kiss her. Juliet offered no resistance and rather a lot of help.

In the meantime, the corgi had worked his way up

through the house to Abigail's open window high above them and was barking continuously. "Excuse me," said a friendly voice from amongst the branches of the spreading oak. "Is it safe to come down now?"

"What are you doing up there, Mr. Rourke?" Juliet asked him.

"The dog seemed to want me to go," he replied. "Naturally, I jumped out of the window. I take it, you've squared things with his grace, Miss Wayborn?"

"Oh, yes. You may go," she assured him.

Mr. Rourke dropped down from the branches dressed as a Marc Antony, and he was not . . .

"Oh, Cary, he's not wearing any drawers," Abigail whispered, averting her eyes.

The actor was already kissing Miss Wayborn's hand.

"You may take his grace's carriage back to the Albany," she told him. "It's sitting in the middle of the road. Have as much champagne as you like. And I *do* look forward to having you at Auckland Palace in the summer for another go at *Twelfth Night*. One more thing," she added, pulling a ring off of her finger and giving it to him. "I want you to have this."

The Duke was appalled. "Julie, I forbid you to give Rourke my ruby! It's been in the family for a hundred years. How could you do such a thing?"

"It's not your ruby, darling," she replied. "I hope I know better than to give a ruby to an Irishman! It's an emerald, of course." She looked directly at Abigail, who had cried out rather sharply. "Yes! I fetched it from Mr. Grey's this afternoon, *Miss Ritchie*. Indeed, I'd rather give it to Mr. Rourke than see you wear it! I'm sure my brother will feel quite the same when he realizes who and what you truly are."

Abigail's mouth worked.

"You bitch!"

Abigail gasped. "Oh, God! I didn't mean to say that!"

"You didn't," said Cary, shaking his fist under Juliet's nose. "Now, you listen to me, you pest. You give that ring back to Abigail this instant, or I swear I'll feed you to my dog."

For a moment Juliet actually appeared cowed. Then her hard chin came up. "It's legally mine," she told her brother. "You gave it to her, and she gave it to me when she gave me the receipt. I have given it to Mr. Rourke. That's my final word."

Cary pulled out his wooden sword and whacked his sister on the bottom with it. Abigail thought she would burst with pride and happiness. In her opinion, there was no other bottom in England who deserved it more, not even Lord Dulwich's.

"Cary, you can't mean it!" Juliet cried, covering her rear with both hands. Tears coursed down her face. "Her father is in Trade! She's no one."

"She's my wife."

"What?" Juliet's lip quavered pitifully. "No, this can't be. You only just met her."

He turned away from her in disgust. Sword in hand, he faced Rourke. "You have something that belongs to my wife, sir."

Rourke laughed easily. "Besides her drawers, you mean?"

"You'll pay for that." Cary lunged forward, but to his consternation, his short wooden sword was blocked by metal.

"I too have a sword," said Rourke, easily deflecting the blow. "And, as you see, mine is made of metal, and I know how to use it."

"Stagecraft, actor," Cary sneered. "I've killed men in battle."

"Not with that bit of wood, you haven't," David Rourke replied laconically. His odd light eyes flashed in the moonlight. Suddenly, Abigail was very frightened.

"Cary, don't," she pleaded. "It doesn't matter."

"You should listen to your pretty wife," Rourke said, his smile flickering coldly. "I have also killed men in battle. I am not afraid of you."

"How *dare* you attack my brother," cried Juliet as the two men circled each other.

Rourke laughed as he and Cary crossed swords again. "*He* attacked *me*, but since I am Irish, and he is English, perhaps you think I should beg his pardon. Now, as I understand it," he went on pleasantly, as the fight continued, "you gave the emerald to your darling wife, but she, for reasons unknown to me, gave it to your charming sister, who in turn has given it to me. That makes it legally mine, does it not?"

"It belongs to my wife," said Cary, gritting his teeth, "by right of a higher law."

"A higher law? Oh, yes, you English do have a higher law, don't you? One for yourselves and another for everyone else."

At his next lunge, Cary's wooden sword broke in half. "What an unfortunate occurrence," Mr. Rourke remarked. "And now all that remains is the *coup de grace*." He flourished his sword menacingly.

"No!" screamed Abigail, darting in front of Cary as Rourke drove his blade home. The blow struck her full in the chest, knocking her back into Cary's arms. A red spray spurted from her breast as Rourke pulled back his arm.

"Another unfortunate occurrence," he observed coolly.

White with fear, Cary lowered Abigail to the ground. "Abby! Abby, can you hear me?"

She could hear, but she could not speak. Her chest hurt and she felt as though she couldn't breathe. She panted and choked.

"Abby, don't leave me," he whispered, rocking her in his arms.

Juliet's face was ashen as she clung to her Duke.

"Actually," said Abigail, feeling the front of her Roman stola. "I think I'm all right."

"No, you're not all right," Cary choked. "He's murdered you, the bastard."

"Really, I'm all right," Abigail insisted, trying to sit up.

"It's shock," the Duke theorized. "Remember when we overturned that time, Julie, and you were thrown clear of my curricle? You jumped up and down for a bit, yelling at me, before you realized you'd hurt your leg. Shock."

"Jesus, Mary, and Joseph," said the Irishman, considerably annoyed. Holding out his sword, he demonstrated to Cary how the blade retracted neatly into the hilt. "It's stagecraft, just like you said. I only wanted to put some manners on you, man. I didn't think there was any blood left in the reservoir. I thought I used it all in my death scene."

Cary's face was still white. "You bastard!"

The actor quirked a brow. "Now you wish I *had* killed her? Make up your mind. Here you are," Rourke said, tossing the emerald into Abigail's lap. "All you had to do was ask," he told Cary. "But you just couldn't, could you, being English and all? You had to threaten me."

Abigail snatched her ring and put it on.

"And I'll be drinking to your health this night, Mrs. Wayborn," he added, giving her a curious bow.

"Shall I stop him?" asked the Duke, as Rourke strolled towards the gate.

"No, let him go," said Cary. "He won the wager, after all." He helped Abigail to her feet. "You're sure you're all right?"

"Yes," she answered, using his handkerchief to wipe away some of the sweet-smelling stage blood. "It knocked the breath out of me, that's all."

He seized her hands. "Abby, you love me," he said fiercely.

She blinked at him. "You mean *you* love *me*," she corrected him gently.

"I meant what I said, woman! You love me," he snapped. "Are you in the habit of stepping in front of swords meant for other people? For God's sake, I thought you were going to die without saying the words. Why can't you just admit that you love me?"

"Of course I love you," she said impatiently. "I've always loved you, from the moment I saw you, I think."

He sucked in his breath. "You never said so. In fact, you've been rather hard on me."

"I'm sure I must have told you," she protested, trying to think. "Didn't I?"

"No. Not once. I have been in agony for weeks."

Abigail squirmed uncomfortably. "Well, you must have suspected. You're so conceited, I can't believe you would ever doubt it! And I married you, didn't I?"

"You weren't very eager, as I recall," he said. "I had to drag you to Little Straythorne. It was bloody humiliating. But I remember thinking: I love her enough for both of us."

"No," she said indignantly. "That is what *I* thought."

"And when we were at the theater," he went on, frowning. "All that rubbish about ours being a physical relationship. That cut me to the bone."

Her eyes widened. "I was talking about *you*. Cary, I've always loved you."

For a long moment they stood staring at each other.

"Well," said Juliet. "I think I've had enough fresh air for one night! I think I should like to go home, Ginger." She paused. "Mr. Rourke has taken the Duke's carriage. You don't mind if I take *my* carriage, do you, Miss Ritch—er—Mrs. Wayborn?"

"Please call me Abigail."

"Very well, Smith, I shall," said Juliet pertly. "I'm glad you weren't stabbed. No. No, that's not enough," she added firmly. "I was a perfect beast to you, and I know it. Tell you what I'll do. This summer, you shall come to Auckland and be Countess Olivia in our *Twelfth Night*. I'm Viola, and Cary's going to play the part of my brother, Sebastian. Aren't you, Cary?"

"Yes, I most definitely am," he said softly, taking his wife in his arms. His lips touched Abigail's and he found everything else disappeared.

"Well, Smith?" he said presently, when the others had gone. "Shall we go up to the roof and watch the fireworks or straight to your bedroom and make our own?"

"Cary," she protested. "We still haven't told my father we're married."

"We'll tell him tomorrow at breakfast," he answered, as high above their heads, the corgi jumped into the oak tree.

More Historical Romance From
Jo Ann Ferguson

Available Wherever Books Are Sold!

Visit our website at **www.kensingtonbooks.com**.